THE
BAR End of the
WORLD

TOM ABRAHAMS

THE BAR AT THE END OF THE WORLD
©2020 TOM ABRAHAMS

Aethon Books
PO Box 121515
Fort Worth TX, 76108
www.aethonbooks.com

Print and eBook formatting, and cover design by Steve Beaulieu.

Published by Aethon Books LLC.

Aethon Books is not responsible for websites (or their content) that are not owned by the publisher.

ALSO BY TOM ABRAHAMS

THE WATCHERS

BAR AT THE END OF THE WORLD

BAR AT THE EDGE OF THE SEA

BAR IN THE MIDDLE OF NOWHERE (FORTHCOMING)

THE SCOURGE

UNPREPARED

ADRIFT

GROUNDED

THE TRAVELER

HOME

CANYON

WALL

RISING

BATTLE

LEGACY

HERO

HARBOR

A DARK WORLD: THE COMPLETE SPACEMAN CHRONICLES

SPACEMAN

DESCENT

RETROGRADE

THE ALT APOCALYPSE SERIES

ASH

LIT

TORRENT

AFFLICTION

POLITICAL CONSPIRACIES

SEDITION

INTENTION

JACKSON QUICK ADVENTURES

ALLEGIANCE

ALLEGIANCE BURNED

HIDDEN ALLEGIANCE

STAND-ALONE WORKS

PILGRIMAGE: A POST-APOCALYPTIC ADVENTURE

EXTINCTION RED LINE (WITH NICHOLAS SANSBURY SMITH)

"Hell is empty and all the devils are here."

—William Shakespeare

CHAPTER ONE

Zeke Watson punched the accelerator. The motor of his 1970 Plymouth Superbird roared in response. The steel chassis vibrated around him as it was pushed to its limit, rattling his clenched teeth.

With one hand, Zeke held the Superbird in its lane. With the other, he clutched the sucking wound beneath his rib cage. His stomach felt turned inside out. It might have been. For all he knew, his hand was holding his guts in place.

The highway ahead was a black zipper joining two parts of a sunlight-bathed wasteland. But Zeke was absorbed by the fierce group of men behind him. They wore helmets and bandanas that covered their faces and heads. Some of them drove motorcycles; others rode in the backs and atop the cabs of large pickup trucks.

They're gaining.

Zeke stood on the pedal, lifting himself from the split driver's seat. He'd been meaning to get the upholstery fixed, but things kept getting in the way.

The vast wasteland zoomed past on either side. The only sign he was even moving was the disappearing dashes of the center line under his Plymouth and the occasional boulder dotting the barren landscape. He assumed he was in the Badlands. It was the nebulous region that surrounded the city. Maybe these were Badlanders giving chase, the outsiders who ruled the uncivilized Badlands.

Or are they part of the underworld? Government agents? Bounty hunters?

It didn't matter. What mattered was that they were right behind him.

A bolt of pain flared in his gut. Sweat stung his eyes as he squeezed them to fight it. His back, his neck, and his face were all coated in a blossoming sheen of perspiration.

He tightened his grasp on the wheel and urged his machine forward. The mob was closer. Closer. Closer.

One of the hunters had broken from the mob and drew near on a motorbike. It was a low-slung hog, the kind Zeke recognized from an old Peter Fonda movie or he'd seen parked outside a sports bar cleverly named with some double entendre celebrating women's anatomy.

The biker wore a black bandana wrapped across the lower half of his face and large reflective sunglasses. He was bald and clean-shaven on his dome. Despite the size of the bike, the man dwarfed it. It wasn't his size, though, that held Zeke's attention between brief glances at the blacktop ahead. It was the enormous .45 revolver he held in one hand. The weapon's steel barrel gleamed with sunlight.

Zeke thought he was the target. Then he realized, with his foot pressed to the floor, the beast was targeting his rear tire. Zeke made a split-second judgment.

He studied the rearview mirror, spotting the Horde only yards back. He tapped the brake hard enough to drop his speed, and at the same time he jerked the wheel to the left.

The Plymouth's tires smoked; the car shuddered. Zeke's

body resisted the sudden inertia. Its tires gripped the scalding highway, and he kept his hand on the wheel.

It was enough to clip the front wheel of the bike, knocking it off its path and the revolver from the behemoth's hand.

The man lost control of his bike, wobbled, and toppled into a pair of other bikers on the left edge of the Horde. The chain reaction took out a half dozen of them, two or three disappearing under the oversized tires of a jacked-up rig. Red spray punctuated the collisions, and Zeke turned his attention back to the road.

That was when he saw it.

Off to the left, maybe a mile or more ahead, its shape undulating like a mirage beyond the waves of heat lifting from the sour earth, was a lone building. Wisps of smoke rose from the form and dissipated into the cloudless sky above.

Zeke checked his speedometer. He was cruising at one hundred and five, the needle vibrating at the top end of the muscle car's push. That was good. Fuel wasn't, though.

E? How long have I been at E?

He flicked the gauge with his finger. It didn't move. Zeke slammed an open palm against the wheel. As he did, he caught a glimpse of the warbling image of the building again. Now he was close enough to see the muddy shapes of vehicles parked outside. There were people there.

A loud *pop* caught Zeke's attention, and he eyed his rearview mirror. A man standing atop one of the trucks' cabs pointed a rifle at him, smoke drifting from the muzzle. Another shot flashed and his rear window exploded. Glass flapped from the frame.

Zeke hunched forward, keeping his focus on the building ahead. If he could just get to it, maybe someone would help.

With the back window gone, the growl of the open road echoed through the cabin of his Plymouth. The wind whipped.

The devilishly dry heat and the odor of burned rubber mixed with exhaust was instantly suffocating.

He was still a few hundred yards away. The wasteland distorted distance and time.

Another *pop*, this one louder and more percussive than the last, reverberated in his torso above the jar of the Superbird. A sharp, burning sensation in his shoulder followed. His right arm went numb and dropped to his side.

Zeke's heart rate sped up. The sweat bloomed. His pulse thumped in his temples and his neck. With each successive throb, the burn in his shoulder swelled.

He winced in agony, held his breath, and steered the Plymouth with his left hand, his fingers white-knuckling the wheel. His muscle car straddled the center line. The boulders on the sides of the highway grew bigger and then disappeared behind him. Zeke's vision blurred for an instant, and he bit the inside of his cheek to focus himself.

I'm losing blood. I won't make it.

A large truck bumped him from behind. Then again, harder than before, and Zeke braced himself with his one good arm.

He looked ahead. The building was only fifty yards away, its parking lot closer than that. Zeke checked the shoulder ahead and saw no obstacles. No rocks, no cacti or decaying plant life, no animals. A straight shot.

The truck bumped him one last time, and Zeke swung the wheel to the right. The Plymouth squealed from the blacktop and onto the desert floor. The suspension resisted and gave in to the uneven terrain. It wasn't as flat as it appeared, but the parking lot and the building were straight ahead now.

Zeke bounced in his seat, the worn springs not much of a match for his movement and weight. His right arm hummed with electricity, the sensation returning. He glanced down and saw blood drenching the right side of his shirt. His vision blurred again. He felt woozy. He stared forward, resisting the urge to focus on his wounds.

The engine roared. The tires spit rocks that clanked and dinged against the undercarriage. Maybe he'd make it.

Zeke tasted the heat and the dust in his mouth. His head buzzed with wooziness. Then the Plymouth died.

Its engine faltered and coughed. The gauges flared and pinged to the left edge of the circular displays. The speedometer reflected the rapidly declining speed.

Zeke cursed again. This time the expletives flowed from his mouth like the blood spilling from the bullet wound on the back of his shoulder.

What little distance he'd gained on the Horde instantly evaporated. The Plymouth coasted, decelerating, not able to hold its edge. And when the front tires of the Plymouth bounded over the chipped concrete curb that separated the cracked asphalt parking lot from the desert wasteland that surrounded the property, Zeke shouldered open the door and rolled out of the car.

The Plymouth only stopped when it slammed into the back of an '85 Ford Bronco. Zeke didn't see the collision as he struggled to reach his feet, but the sound of two heavy vehicles colliding was unmistakable.

Without looking back, Zeke ran. He was out of breath, his legs jelly underneath him, and his right arm hung at his side. His stomach felt as if it was tearing more widely open with each dragging step toward the building.

Almost there.

Through the haze of onset-delirium that came with shock, Zeke saw the two-story structure was wood and limestone, a large covered porch wrapping three sides. A blue flag hung from a post at the front steps, flapping in the hot wind. At the flag's center was a six-pointed star, with wings on the tips, and from the top spike rose what looked like flames.

He staggered forward, his chest heaving, his legs weakening.

Behind him, the rumble of the trucks grew deafeningly loud. The fuzzy shapes of twin motorcycles zoomed toward him.

He was so close now. Only steps from the stoop.

Semiautomatic fire crackled behind him. A pair of shots zipped past him to his left. Two more didn't. He felt them, thick punches of searing heat drilled into his side, one at his armpit and the other above his hip. Zeke's body twisted and he stumbled forward. He wailed in agony and lost his balance.

Spinning in a macabre pirouette, Zeke landed on the bottom step of the porch. His head knocked against the thick pine with a thud, and the world fell silent.

The desert wind quietly rustled the flag above him. Was he dead? Was this the afterlife? A windswept wasteland replete with Hordes and a scalding sun beating down from on high?

Then he focused on the sound of someone panting. No. Some*thing* panting. An animal. Its breath was on his face, hot and dank. It sniffed him, snorting. A warm, thick tongue slathered his cheek with viscous slobber.

A dog.

A strong hand touched his good shoulder. The fingers gripped him and lifted him from the bottom steps to his knees and then to his feet. An arm wrapped around his failing body and pulled him onto the porch, and then a pair of them hoisted him onto a shoulder.

Only vaguely aware of his surroundings, and only able to see shadows and light beyond the porch and into the parking lot, Zeke heard and felt the booming voice that belonged to the man holding him.

The man carried him across the threshold, his bootheels *thunking* against the wooden planks of the porch. A pair of louvered doors swung back and forth, groaning on their hinges as Zeke's guardian dragged him inside.

There were other people inside. Zeke sensed them. He heard them. Their voices mixed with the sounds of glass clinking and music straining in the hot, still air. Dusty. Old. Worn. Yet, somehow, welcoming.

Zeke felt the inertia of his body swinging. His shoes slapped against the swinging doors creaking on their hinges. The man spoke to the gathered Horde outside. His baritone voice vibrated through his chest and into Zeke's. It was comforting, paternal, yet somewhere within its gravel was a stern, didactic tone dripping with unspoken threats.

"That'll be all, gentlemen," the man said. "You know the rules. Go back to whatever hellhole you crawled from and leave us be. My friend here has had enough."

CHAPTER TWO

H e's risen," said a voice that stirred Zeke from that ethereal place between sleep and consciousness. "It took long enough."

Zeke blinked away the blur of a dim yellow incandescent bulb. It came into focus, and he saw it hung above him at the center of a slow-rotating fan that rocked in its housing.

When he tried to move, pulsing jabs of pain lanced his gut, his right shoulder, and his left side. Then he remembered being shot. An overwhelming urgency, panic almost, replaced the pain. He needed to be somewhere. Someone was in danger.

"Take it easy," said the bearded, steely-eyed man standing over him. "Your body doesn't know what to do with itself."

Zeke sank back onto the thin feather pillow that wrapped the back of his head. He stared at the ceiling fan for a moment, catching the individual blades as they rotated around the single bulb.

"We've fixed you up for now," said the man. "Give yourself a minute or three and you can join us downstairs. You've all the time you need."

He patted Zeke on the thigh as a father would his son and

turned to leave. Zeke reached out and grazed the man's arm with his fingers.

"Hang on," Zeke said, not recognizing his own raspy voice. It sounded like sandpaper on balsa.

The man stuck his hands into his pockets. He wore a brown leather vest the color of a worn saddle. His white linen shirt was rolled up to the elbows and tucked into a pair of loose-fitting, dark, denim jeans at his trim waist. A large brass buckle adorned his belt.

The man was fit but aged. His strong hands bore the discoloration of age spots. His ice-blue eyes were framed with the deep crow's feet of a man who'd spent eons in the sun. His thick dark hair and wiry beard were streaked with white and shades of yellow. His tanned skin was leathered like his vest, giving him the appearance of someone who'd lived the life of a workingman. Who'd toiled and earned every cent through guile and grit.

"Thank you," said Zeke.

"Sure thing," said the man. The corners of his mouth twitched. "Anything else?"

"I'm Zeke," he said.

The man revealed pearly teeth, which shone especially white against his olive skin.

"I know," he said. "I'm Pedro."

"Where am I?"

"My place. You're in one of the upstairs rooms. People need places to stay while they figure things out. I help. Underneath us is my saloon. C'mon down when you're up to it. I'll buy you a drink."

Using his elbows, Zeke shrugged himself up in the bed. The pillow slid to his shoulders, but he propped himself up enough to see Pedro open the door and disappear around a corner. With the door open, the sounds of music and conversation drifted into his room.

It took him a half hour or more to get the courage to sit up straight. It was another fifteen minutes to put his feet on the floor and test his weight. The wood planks were smooth, slippery from dust. With one hand on the bed for balance, Zeke gingerly walked toward a full-length mirror on the wall next to the door. He didn't recognize himself.

His coloring was wrong. His eyes seemed off somehow. Even the way he held his shoulders was different. But it was him. Zeke recognized the scoundrel. The most prominent confirmation was the grisly scar across his chest, and the two missing fingernails on his right hand. He traced the keloid line on his chest with one of his fingers, remembering distinctly how he'd gotten it and who'd given it to him.

Wherever he presently stood, and he couldn't be certain within a thousand miles where that was, he deserved to be here alone and in pain. He'd earned it. A wave of guilt washed through him, and he chastised himself.

Where was the guilt before I did what I did? Why is it stronger now? Why is everything more acute, except for the pain?

He was in his boxers and nothing else but the dressing covering his wounds. He eyed the white gauze tinged with the seeping amorphous stains of yellow pus. From the unexplainable absence of pain, he'd forgotten how badly he'd been hurt from the rifle shot that punctured his shoulder. He could use the arm. It felt good, if not better than before.

The largest dressing was over his gut. He touched it, expecting a reflexive pain, but didn't feel it.

The wounds on his left side irritated him in the same way a bee sting lingered beneath the skin. The searing heat was gone. The sharp, radiating pain had vanished.

How long have I been asleep?

He remembered leaving the city, reaching its edges before encountering Marines at the gates. Then he drove in darkness before it dissolved into the bright, hazy light of midday.

There were disconnected snippets of memory. He sighed and tried not to dwell on the mysteries, knowing it would sap what little energy he had.

Zeke's hair was unkempt, greasy, and matted to one side. Stubble peppered his chin. Dark purple circles hung under his eyes. His lips were blue, as was the skin under his nails. But he was breathing deeply, and his legs felt stronger while he stood there.

As the pain dissipated, however, the thirst intensified. Incredible thirst. He opened his mouth wide and stuck out his pasty tongue. It looked gross, and he closed his mouth with a grunt.

Zeke studied the reflection of the space behind him. There was a wooden rocking chair, some clothes, not his, draped neatly over its back. On the floor was a pair of black hide boots, some socks, and a brown leather belt coiled and set atop the boots. Hanging from one corner of the chair was a brown felt shirt. Next to it, on the chair back, was a pair of jeans. On the seat cushion was a Stetson hat.

He dressed and adjusted the clothing on his renewed body. The clothing fit. The boots were as comfortable as any boot he'd ever worn. More than that. The clothes were clean. They were absent the stench of dried sweat or the grains of sand in every fold. They smelled almost otherworldly. Zeke searched his mind, trying to remember the last time he'd worn a clean shirt or pants or socks. He couldn't. He wasn't sure if that was because of the fog clouding his memory or if it was because he'd never worn truly clean clothes. Comfort was an alien concept to Zeke. Right now, in this place, in these clothes, everything was alien. He ran his fingers through his hair and put on the hat, trying to straighten it as best he could, and stepped from his room into the hallway.

He was on the second floor, which opened at its center to the saloon below. It reminded him of one of those ancient hotels he'd seen pictures of, with rooms located off a lofty atrium.

Zeke touched the hat on his head, running his thumb and forefinger along the front dip. He leaned into another step and moved to the wooden railing and gripped the oak beam, feeling its sturdy thickness rub against calluses at the base of his fingers, and leaned over to take in the scene below.

The place was a study in contrasts. Naked wooden floors were as worn as the railing under his grip. The walls were rough-hewn cedar. But the lighting was decidedly LED. It was bright and carried with it a bluish hue that washed over the large space like ice.

Equally as modern as the lighting was the glowing digital jukebox on the wall opposite the entrance and its swinging bar doors. Next to the jukebox hung an electronic dartboard. Zeke's attention drifted from the board to the spot on the floor a little less than eight feet away, where the dark floor was worn pale from players.

The centerpiece of the saloon was a massive, wall-to-wall oak bar. Its top was nicked and worn from countless years of use, as was its ornately decorated face. The thing looked old enough to predate the entire bar. Behind it was a mirrored wall, speckled with black at the corners. On both sides of the mirror were planks of wood that served as liquor shelves.

Liquor.

Pedro was behind the bar, a yellowed rag over his shoulder, an empty glass in his hand. He glanced up at Zeke and waved for him to come downstairs. He whipped the rag from his shoulder and stuffed it into the glass, twisting it along the inside.

The barstools were empty, but the tables that filled the rest of the space were decorated with a colorful mix of characters drawn straight out of a dime-store novel.

They were men and women as dusty as the building's

surfaces. They played cards, nursed highballs, shot glasses and mugs. They spoke in low tones. Some chuckled or outright laughed. Others had dour looks of resignation sewn into their leathery faces.

He lifted his eyes and slid his fingers along the railing. What was this place? He moved from the spot in front of his room toward the next. Boards creaked under his weight, and his boots *thunked* on the solid wood.

The door next to his was closed. But from within the room echoed laughter and the faint strains of music. *Is that jazz?* The soft, melancholy strains of a saxophone cried out. A woman giggled. A man said something in a low baritone, and she giggled again.

Zeke moved on to the next room. This door was open. Specks of dust danced in the shaft of bright light filtering in through the lone window inside.

He stepped to the threshold and, with a hand wrapped around the wide doorjamb, he peered into a room decorated like his own. It was tidy but had the stale odor of a neglected place. It seemed to Zeke nobody had slept in the bed in some time. The corners were tucked neatly underneath the thin mattress. A thin layer of dust, that which no longer spun in the air, coated the floor. No footprints.

He spun around and scanned the rest of the rooms on the second floor. All of them had matching doors, some open and some shut. Zeke decided it was time to head downstairs and join the fray.

He followed the railing to a staircase at the front corner of the building. One step at a time, he descended to the main floor. His boots thumped on the floorboards, betraying the silence with which he was trying to move. He needed to get back to his car, wherever it was, fill it up with gas, and find a way home. Time was running out. No matter the cost, no matter the obstacles, or Hordes, that confronted him, Zeke's conscience tugged at him.

Feeling everyone in the place watching him, he kept his gaze on Pedro and the bar. The conversations stopped and the place fell silent except for his boots against the floor. His cheeks flushed from the attention he was trying to ignore, and he tightened his fists at his sides. He slid onto one of the barstools. The conversations began anew. Zeke exhaled, unaware he'd been holding his breath. Despite the urge to get out of this place, whatever it was, he needed answers to more pressing questions.

Where am I? What is this place? How long have I been here?

"Morning," he said to Pedro.

"Evenin'," said the barkeep with a wry smile. "I see you found the clothes. They fit nice."

Zeke looked down at himself and nodded. "Thanks. I like the boots."

Pedro's grin widened. "I thought you might. Most comfortable you'll ever have. I've got a pair. Figure I'll be buried in them someday."

Zeke touched the brim of the Stetson atop his head. He tugged on it, adjusting it for effect as much as comfort. "The hat too," he said. "Thanks."

"You wear it well enough," said Pedro. "What can I get you?"

Zeke shrugged. "What do I owe you for the clothes? Seems I oughta settle up for these before I start drinking."

Pedro winked. "How about I just put it on your tab?" he said. "We run a balance for pretty much everyone you see in the place."

Zeke checked over one shoulder, then the other. He wondered which of the assembled didn't owe the barkeep money. He adjusted his weight on the barstool and leaned forward on his elbows, but he said nothing.

"How about a whiskey?" Pedro suggested. It was less of a question than a statement. "I've everything from Rebel Yell to Macallan. You tell me."

The barkeep moved to the top shelf left of the mirror, pushed aside the lone book sitting on it, and pulled from it a long-neck bottle filled with a honey-colored liquid. On its face was the number sixteen in large red numerals.

"I don't have time," said Zeke. "I did something that I...I need to get back. I appreciate your hospitality. But I really do—"

"You have time," said Pedro. "Relax. I promise you that whatever it is you find so urgent will still be waiting for you when we're done here."

Zeke started to get up from the seat, but the barkeep's gaze stopped him. It was like a tractor beam that held him against the bar.

He sighed. "Fine, but only one."

His eyes flitted across the bar, across the jewel-tone bottles and the thick bar glasses. Then he focused on the worn volume sitting on the end of its thick, tattered spine. The letters were in gold leaf against the black leather of the binding. He made out three letters: *E*, *O*, and *H*.

"What is this place?" asked Zeke. "Who are you?"

Pedro set the bottle on the bar in front of Zeke and pulled a large glass from behind and underneath the oak top. He set it next to the half-full bottle and pointed a thick finger at Zeke. "You want it on the rocks?" he asked, ignoring Zeke's questions.

Zeke's mouth went drier than it had been. His chest tightened. His stomach lurched. A bolt of fear shot through him like lightning and instantly consumed him. His expression must have given it away, because Pedro's face condensed with concern. He frowned.

"What?" Pedro asked, placing his hands flat on the bar. "Did I say something wrong?"

Zeke wasn't sure how to respond. Slowly, he glanced over one shoulder and then the other.

Nobody was looming. The patrons at their tables were preoccupied with their own games and conversations. A slender woman and a tall man forged from granite were throwing darts now. A heavyset bearded man with a feather-adorned gray bowler on his head leaned on the jukebox.

Zeke turned back to Pedro. He shook his head. "You asked me if I wanted ice."

"I did. If it's a problem, you can have it neat. It might even—"

"You're not with them, are you?" Zeke leaned heavier on his elbows, inching his face toward the barkeep. He checked over his shoulders again.

Pedro's wiry eyebrows arched in unison. He leaned in and mimicked Zeke's tremulous hush. "With whom?"

"The Tic."

"The Tic?" Pedro asked in a way that suggested he'd never heard of the black-market cartel, which Zeke found hard to believe.

Zeke leaned back with suspicion. Everybody knew about the Tic. They controlled the flow of all things water. They were the reason he was here, wherever *here* was. They were the reason he needed to go back.

Zeke leaned closer to the wide-eyed Pedro. "The Aquatic Collective," he said in a power whisper. "You know, the *Tic*."

Pedro's brows relaxed and he shrugged. "Never heard of 'em."

Zeke eyed the empty glass on the table. Then he glared at Pedro. He didn't know whether to believe the man or not. He wanted to believe him. He did. Truth might ground him, give him something to hold onto while he wobbled through this surreality.

"Then how do you have ice?" he asked.

Pedro picked up the bottle, which looked small in his hands, and uncapped it. He drew it to his nose and inhaled the aroma. "I have plastic trays. I fill them with water and stick them in a freezer. Amazing things happen when the water hits thirty-two degrees Fahrenheit, or zero centigrade, depending on your preference."

Pedro reached underneath the bar. His hand returned grasping two large square cubes of ice. He dropped them into the glass with a *clink* Zeke hadn't heard in ages.

The barkeep lowered the bottle to the rim of the glass and glugged the amber liquid atop the cubes. He slid the glass to Zeke once it was full, and some of the contents sloshed onto the bar.

"So, tell me more about this Tic Tac group of which you speak."

"*Tic*," said Zeke. He hadn't touched the drink. It was as if sipping from the glass would engage him in some Faustian pact. He put his hands flat on the bar, his weight resting on his elbows.

"Tick, then," said Pedro, "as in bloodsucker."

Zeke chuckled. "Yeah, I guess."

Pedro raised his finger in the air. "Oh, almost forgot."

He reached underneath the bar and pulled out a worn brown leather wallet. Its corners were threadbare, the hide having worn through, and it was molded to the oblong shape of its contents. He slapped it on the bar and pushed it toward Zeke.

Zeke reached for his wallet. "I'd forgotten about this."

He pushed himself to his feet to return it to his back pocket, but stopped short. He removed a crisp bill and held it out to Pedro.

The barkeep waved him off. "Oh no, your money's no good here, Zeke. Put it away and take a load off. I want to hear more about the ectoparasites that have you shaking in your new boots."

Zeke put the bill back into the wallet, folded the leather, and slid it into his back pocket. He hopped back onto the barstool and leaned forward, wrapping a hand around the glass that was now damp from condensation.

A cold drink. And free. None of this felt right. It was too good to be true. He should leave. His business was elsewhere.

But he was parched. So, against his better judgment, he lifted the glass and let the sweet liquid fill his mouth and run down his throat. He relished the aftertaste on his tongue and the electric buzz rushing to his head.

"Thank you," he said, toasting Pedro. "It's good."

Pedro bowed his head. "Glad you like it. I aim to please."

Zeke took a deep breath. He studied the barkeep.

Before he responded, the crackle of static stopped him. The noise gave way to the strains of a saxophone. The woodwind's tone danced through the space, filling it with warmth. Zeke spun on the stool to see the heavy bearded man in the bowler strolling back to an empty seat at the table nearest the jukebox. He absentmindedly flipped a coin back and forth amongst his fingers.

"That's Phil," said Pedro. "He's a regular. And he loves jazz."

To Zeke, hearing jazz was one of the anachronisms here. He took another, longer pull of the whiskey. His head buzzed again. The tension in his shoulders eased. His soreness loosened.

He regarded the glass, which was now empty aside from the rounded lumps of ice at its bottom. Before he said anything, Pedro was adding another three fingers' worth of whiskey.

"I really should go," Zeke said. "I'm wasting time. I told you, I've got somewhere to be, something to make right."

Zeke knew he should leave, but something held him here. There was a disconnect between his mind and body. It reminded him of the feeling he sometimes had when awaking from a bad dream. He'd try to move his body but couldn't. It felt like paralysis until he'd fully awake and get his wits about him.

Is this a dream? he wondered. Though, it felt both too real to be a dream and too surreal to be his life.

"Just enjoy it." The barkeep motioned to the drink.

Zeke couldn't deny such a luxury. He wrapped his hand around the cool glass and thumbed away some more condensation. His head was swimming. The high-proof alcohol, the readily available ice, and Pedro's ignorance served as opposing forces swirling against each other in his mind.

"You've never heard of the Tic?" Zeke asked again. "You're sure?"

Pedro pouted and shook his head. "Nope. Never."

None of this makes sense.

Anybody who had water, let alone ice, got it from one of two places. A saloon like this, in the middle of absolutely nowhere, holding sway over a marauding Horde, must be in league with the Tic. Unless...

Zeke looked up, an epiphany blooming. "You're with the Overseers?"

Pedro stared back at Zeke with the same lack of recognition as when he'd referenced the Tic. The barkeep tilted his head to one side. "Overseers? What is that?"

"The Overseers are the government," Zeke said. "Or the best we've got, that is. They ration water. They ration everything. The Tic became the Tic because the Overseers were too stingy, in their opinion."

Pedro took the rag from his shoulder and swiped a puddle

of moisture from the bar in front of Zeke, then slung it back across himself. He rubbed his chin, his fingers digging into his beard and making a scratching sound.

"I'm neither an Overseer nor a Tic," said Pedro. "Nor do I have relationships with either. I'm on my own here."

Zeke shifted in his seat and scanned the saloon once more. There were twenty or twenty-five people. None of them paid him any mind now. None except the woman approaching the bar.

How did I not notice her?

She slinked more than walked, and she did it in a way that told Zeke she knew how to handle herself. He swung back around to face Pedro. "Where is *here?*" he asked.

Before Pedro answered, the woman sidled up to the bar next to Zeke. The floral scent of her perfume overwhelmed his senses. The pleasantness of the perfume was in stark contrast to her appearance.

She'd been poured into her clothing. Tight black leather hid the parts of her she didn't want people to see, and boldly colorful body art covered the rest. Only her palms, face, and scalp were unpainted as far as Zeke could tell. The most prominent of the ink was on her hip, in the space between the waistline of her low-slung pants and the bottom of the short leather top. It was a flaming sword that ran diagonally toward her navel, encircled with a disc that looked like a simplistic, flat rendition of the sun.

Her head was shaved on the sides, but the auburn mane of hair that ran along the center of her head ran to the middle of her back. It was braided with a pink bow.

On one wrist was a collection of knotted string, like a friendship bracelet. On the other was a paracord bracelet with a metal point at the clasp.

Her eyes were stunningly green, glowing almost. Her light-colored lashes were long, her nose sharp. It was what Zeke had heard was once called a Roman nose. She wasn't beautiful, not in the classic sense. She was, however, intriguing. There was a story behind her appearance. Zeke was sure the tale was rich.

She was a study in contradiction every bit as much as the bar itself. Her voice was as sure as it was feminine. There was a raw, controlled power when she spoke.

"This is Pedro's Cantina," she said. "And I'll have what he's having."

Pedro withdrew another glass from underneath the bar as the woman adjusted herself on the stool. She brushed against Zeke, and he swore electricity sparked across his body.

He tried not to look at her. Instead, he stared into his glass. The ice shrank against the heat of its surroundings. So did Zeke.

"You want it on the rocks?" asked Pedro.

"Why not?" she said.

Pedro tipped the bottle to the new glass and filled it half-way. He paused, eyed the woman, who raised her eyebrows at him, and topped off the glass. Pedro's dog waddled over to her and rubbed his side against her leg like it was a cat. She made kissing sounds and stroked the dog's head until it had had enough attention and waddled back toward its master.

She lifted the glass. "Who's the new meat?"

Zeke knew she was talking about him, but he wasn't about to answer. He hadn't been this intimidated by a woman since, well, he didn't want to think about it. He tightened his grip on his glass and took a healthy swig. The ice bobbed, and he resisted the urge to suck it into his mouth and gnash it between his teeth.

"This is Zeke," said Pedro. "Zeke, this is my friend Uriel."

Uriel pivoted to face Zeke, but her gaze lingered on Pedro. She smirked and tipped her glass toward the barkeep. "So, we're friends, are we?"

"I've never met a stranger," said Pedro. He capped the

bottle, whipped the rag from his shoulder, wiped clean the rings left by the twin glasses, and stepped back to replace the bottle on the shelf.

Uriel turned her attention to Zeke. Her eyes moved down toward his boots and back up again, holding his gaze with an invisible tractor beam.

Zeke couldn't look away, even as his pulse quickened and heat flushed his cheeks. He was mesmerized by her.

She set the drink on the bar, punched her tongue into her cheek, and twirled the end of her ponytail. She kicked one of her heels up and down impatiently. "Zeke, huh?" she said. "Momma didn't love you?"

Zeke's brow furrowed with confusion. He swallowed hard.

Uriel laughed and slapped his thigh with her hand. He noticed the length of her nails. They were manicured to fine points and painted with the same shade of pink as the bow, diamond studs embedded in the thumbnails.

"Loosen up, *Zeke*." She said his name like the four-letter word it was. "I'm playing with you."

"Oh, okay. Got it." He secretly cursed himself. Who was this guy inhabiting his body? Why wasn't he the confident, bordering-on-cocky man he'd been? He was an alien unto himself.

Uriel gripped the top of her glass and moved it in circles without lifting it from the bar. It scraped rhythmically against the surface, the liquid swirling around inside, washing against the sides.

"Of all the joints, in all the towns, in all the world, he walks into mine," said Uriel, clearly paraphrasing a familiar quote. He couldn't place it but thought it was from a movie or a book.

"Are you a bad guy who's struggling with goodness or a good guy fighting off the bad?" she asked.

Before Zeke answered, Pedro did. "Aren't we all a little bit of both, Uriel?" he asked. "I think we are. Now, you've been monopolizing Zeke here. I've got some things to discuss with him. Why don't you go dance with Phil or play darts with Gabe?"

Uriel leered at Zeke, threw back the rest of the whiskey, and eyed her options. "Well," she said to Pedro, "Gabe's already claimed himself a woman this go-around, and Phil's not so light on his feet. I think I'll deal in a hand or three with Raf and Barach."

Zeke observed the table where he'd seen men playing cards. He didn't know who was who, but one of them had a large stack of chips. The others appeared frustrated, fidgety in their seats.

By the time he'd spun back to the bar, Uriel was on her feet. She straightened her top, tugging at the leather partially covering her breasts, and apparently caught Zeke lingering on her efforts.

She reached out with a long finger, touching the underside of his chin with her fingernail. A flirty twinkle sparkled in her eyes. "You're definitely bad," she said. "Def. In. It. Ly."

Zeke's mouth was dry again. He chuckled nervously.

Uriel let him off the hook with a wink and sauntered away from him. Zeke blew out a mouthful of air.

"Uriel is a piece of work," said Pedro, scanning his establishment, "as is everyone here." His gaze drifted back to Zeke and locked on him. His features darkened. "That includes you, Ezekiel Watson."

"How did you know——" Zeke started, then stopped, remembering the wallet in his back pocket. "My ID?"

Pedro nodded. "Why do *you* think you're here?"

Zeke studied his host, trying to understand the question beyond its face value. He cleared his throat. "Uh," he said the most obvious of all the possibilities, "because the Tic chased me here. You took me in. Helped me out."

Pedro's ice-blue eyes drilled into Zeke. They were suggesting, no, strongly denying, that Zeke's arrival was as coincidental as that. But Pedro didn't correct him. Instead, the intensity in his gaze relaxed.

"Why does the Tic want you?" he asked. "What did you do?"

Zeke lowered his head. "That's a long story," he mumbled. "And, Pedro, as thankful as I am to be here, I need to get going. People need me."

"I'm well aware of that," said Pedro. "Otherwise you wouldn't be here. But truth be told, son, we have all the time in the world."

Zeke paused, considering. "Suffice it to say, without getting into specifics, I've done some bad things. I abandoned people...well, a person...I shouldn't have left behind. She's in trouble. I have to get back to her."

"What did you do?" asked Pedro.

"A lot of things. Some of which couldn't be helped."

"Whom did you abandon?"

"My girl. Adaliah."

"Adaliah," repeated Pedro, the name sounding musical when he said it.

"Li for short."

Pedro asked, "What couldn't be helped?"

Zeke shrugged. "A lot of things."

"Like what?"

Zeke didn't want to answer, but something unseen compelled him to speak. He was in a trance, unable to resist the lull of Pedro's voice, smooth as the whiskey he'd been drinking. "Joining the Tic."

"What *could* be helped?" asked the barkeep.

Zeke's stomach turned. His head swam. Perspiration formed at his temples. The longer he was here, wherever *here* was, the more it felt...*wrong*. He wanted out of here. He had things to do, people to find. Nausea crept up his throat.

"Leaving her," he said.

"Adaliah," Pedro clarified.

"Yeah." Zeke sucked in a deep breath, the lingering floral scent of Uriel's perfume filling his nostrils. Adaliah was the one who'd tried to make him a better man. She was the one who'd accepted him for who, and what, he was. He'd dragged her down with him, a drowning man clinging to his rescuer until she too was pulled beneath the surface and unable to breathe.

Pedro's next question shook him from his reverie. The old man had leaned in so close now, his licorice-scented breath overwhelmed the perfume. His leather vest creaked against the bar as it stretched.

"So your quest is to retrieve her from the violent clutches of the Tic before they exact your punishment on her?" he asked, one eyebrow raised.

Zeke straightened his back, putting space between him and Pedro. "I guess. Yeah. I owe it to her."

"Would you like some help?"

Zeke studied Pedro's flat expression. The man wasn't joking. At least Zeke didn't think he was.

"Uh, okay?" he stammered. "But how do you—"

Pedro suddenly shifted his focus over Zeke's shoulder. Zeke turned and sensed the weight of a presence behind him. He spun to find Uriel was back, hands on her hips. Her finger was tapping the flaming sword tattoo. Her seemingly permanent smirk gave her the look of someone who knew things, secret things she shouldn't know but did.

She wasn't alone, however.

She stood amongst four of the other bar patrons, all of whom had snuck up on Zeke. There was Phil, Gabe, and two of the men from the card table, who Zeke assumed were Raf and Barach.

Phil stroked his beard. The bowler was pitched back on his

head, revealing a high forehead and a few locks of curly hair peeking out the sides.

Gabe had his muscular arms folded across his barrel chest. The veins that snaked under the surface of his forearms accentuated the strength of his artfully chiseled physique. On his neck was a scripted tattoo that read "Do Not Fear." Zeke wondered if he was trying to be ironic.

One of the remaining two, the one who'd had the pile of chips in front of him, held his shoulders back and his chin up. He had jet-black hair that ran in waves across his head. A sweep of bangs covered one of his eyes, almost disguising a long, thin scar that ran along one side of his face. Around his neck was something that looked like a stethoscope.

The other card player was smaller than the others. He was bald and clean shaven. In his hand was a torn piece of bread. He chewed on what Zeke imagined was the rest of it. Despite his stature, he stood closer to Zeke than the others and gave the distinct impression he was the leader of the group.

Zeke stood from the stool and backed into the bar. In his experience, a ragtag-looking group like this sneaking up on you always meant bad news.

"What is this?" he asked.

"These are the people who will help you," Pedro replied.

CHAPTER THREE

Adaliah Bancroft saw Zeke. He was at the far end of a long, brightly lit tunnel. Or was it a hallway? She couldn't be sure. The light, so bright it was blinding, made it difficult to sense her surroundings. But she knew Zeke was there. His arms were outstretched. He was trying to reach for her, pull her toward him. She couldn't move. She was stuck in place, her feet cemented to the floor beneath her.

"Zeke," she called, "can you see me? Can you see me?"

He yelled back to her, but his words were muddled and unintelligible. Why wasn't he coming to her? Why was he so far away?

Then water rushed in from the sides of the corridor's walls, like a dike spilling its charge. Roiling water, cold and impatient, flooded the space. It was above her ankles. She was shivering now. Zeke's image was fading. The water was at her chest. The light dimmed. Her body shivered in the cold. The water, metallic and sour, was at her mouth and rising above her nose. She was stuck to the floor, unable to swim or float. Panic swelled in her chest, pushing a wave of anxiety through her tired, aching body. Her knees weakened despite her inability to move. She was stuck.

Adaliah Bancroft gasped for air as she regained consciousness. She was on her back, tied to a bench. A sopping cloth that smelled like cooking grease covered her face. She felt no pain, but her body trembled uncontrollably.

A shadowy figure stood above her, a vague form against the diffused light that shone through the cloth over Adaliah's head. Then she felt weight press against her body, like the woman sat on her.

"Where is he, Li?" asked Brina. Her hot, stale breath filtered through the cloth. Her voice was gravelly and strained from years of chain-smoking. It was as masculine as it was feminine, and had Adaliah not known the woman, she'd have thought her a man. But she did know her. She knew the monstrous enforcer named Brina. Everybody knew her. Even those who'd never met her, never seen her vacant, reptilian gaze, knew the legend of the Tic's sadistic information extractor.

Li shook her head in denial. She tried moving her legs. They were bound. Her wrists were too. "I don't know," she coughed out. "I told you. I don't know."

"Where is he?" Brina asked again. "I will not stop until you tell me. This is personal for me, which makes it personal for you. Where is he?"

It was the only question she'd asked during the countless hours Li had been here, over and over again. Where was her boyfriend? Where was the man who'd betrayed the Tic and left her to fend for herself?

A confusing stew of sadness, worry, and anger swirled amongst her innumerable thoughts, emotions, and sensations. Part of her understood. He'd been caught. He had to leave. But couldn't he have told her his plans?

Maybe not. Maybe plausible deniability was her best

defense. He was thinking of her. But as she lay strapped to a bench, tortured for what she didn't know, there was no defense for what he'd done.

"I. Don't. Know," Li said defiantly, punching each word with as much force as she wished she could unleash on Brina. "He left me. The coward left me here. I don't know where he is. I don't know."

Brina removed the cloth from Li's face. She shook it free of the remnant water, sprinkling Li with it. Then she tossed the cloth aside and pulled up a chair. Its legs raked across concrete, screeching until Brina stopped and plopped her heft into the seat.

Li squinted against the light and blinked back the combination of tears and water that blurred her vision.

Brina put a hand on Li's midsection, and Li instinctively recoiled from the touch.

"I believe you," said Brina. "I believe you don't know where Ezekiel went. If you did, you'd have told me. My experience, which I assure you is extensive, tells me you aren't the kind to keep secrets against the threat of pain. You'd have spilled anything you knew by now."

The funny thing was that there wasn't any pain. In fact, if anything, the torture was painless. The repeated *threat* of drowning was worse than the drowning itself.

Li had survived all four of the attempts to extract information she didn't have. But her mind believed she might be dying. Every time she'd passed out, it was as if she was on her way elsewhere, to the place between life and death. That hadn't been the case though. She'd returned to this hell every time, wishing more and more that she *had* drowned.

She'd always known this was a possibility. The Tic was known for its brutality, even more than the Overseers. They met violent oppression with violent subterfuge. There was something brutal about using water for punishment. There was so little in the world now. It was such a precious commodity, the center of the legal and illegal economies. Yet, here was Brina using gallons to flush out the truth. It was a layered torture, Li understood. It was as much mental as physical. She'd seen it applied to others before. She'd stood and watched, never understanding its purpose.

Was it to extract information, snippets and clues, which gave power and wealth to the already powerful and wealthy? Or was it a sick game those charged with enforcing the Tic's underground kingdom enjoyed regardless of its efficacy? Regardless, Li was aware violence was part of the world now. It was a commodity like water, though more plentiful in its abundance and, in some ways for some people, more valuable.

Still, she never thought she'd experience it firsthand. At least not from Brina. Not this way.

Li was attached to one of the Tic's most valuable assets in Zeke. So when the masked, anonymous enforcers stormed her modest apartment before dawn, she'd thought they had the wrong place. She was sure, in fact.

In the haze between sleep and consciousness, she'd shot up in bed at the sound of banging at her front door. She'd felt beside her, expecting to feel the familiar warmth of Zeke's body. Instead, she'd gripped a handful of cool cotton sheet, and her heart had leapt into her throat.

"Zeke?" she'd called. No answer.

She'd planted her feet on the travertine floor, the cold seeping through its hard surface, and moved toward the bathroom. A chill had traveled up her spine as the pounding at the door amplified. Men yelled.

"Open up!" they'd demanded. "Open the damn door!"

The bathroom had been empty. The kitchen too. The cramped living room, stuffed with the trinkets of the life they'd tenuously built, had been as she'd left it the night before. Along one wall was a collection of books. They were ancient tomes from Homer, Shakespeare, and Goethe. Dog-eared copies of the *Farmer's Almanac* were wedged between rare books by men named Obama, Trump, and Kennedy. There was one by a woman named Clinton and another by one called Mata Hari. These were the possessions that had turned this house into a home.

"Zeke?" she'd called, her voice cracking with the realization he was gone. Ignoring the fisted pounding on the door, she'd scurried to the window and swept back the white sheer stained yellow with age.

Li had leaned in and pressed her forehead against the window, her breath fogging the glass. On the street below, the spot where Zeke kept his Plymouth was empty. The cracked asphalt and faded parking lines had stared back at her mockingly. He'd abandoned her. She'd cursed him and brought her hands to the glass, her fingers raking it as she stared at the empty parking space. She'd curled her fingers into fists, clenched her jaw, and marched back to the bedroom.

She'd opened the nightstand beside her bed, pulling the knob to reveal a biometric safe. She touched the sensor and then swiped her index finger across it. The safe's lid clinked open and the hydraulic hinge hissed.

Behind her, from the front of the apartment, a percussive bang had preceded the crack and splinter of the worn mahogany door. She'd reached into the safe, her hand shaking, and grabbed her 9mm handgun, slapped the adjacent full magazine into the trusty weapon, and had pulled the slide to chamber the first round when she'd heard the heavy tread of boots bounding into her home. She'd spun, her finger on the trigger and ready to fire, when she'd felt the prick and sting of a pronged sensor. Instantly, she lost control of her motor functions as her body convulsed from the electric charge coursing through her. Her hand had seized, causing her to fire a single errant shot into the ceiling.

The last thing she'd remembered was the sprinkling of plaster dust and the glower of masked men who'd leveled her with a stun gun. As she'd lain there, immobile other than the reactive twitching of her muscles, one of them had withdrawn a syringe. The bite of the needle stuck her arm, and then, despite fighting to stay conscious, her body sank onto the floor and she'd slid unwillingly into a drug-induced slumber.

Now she was here, wherever *here* was, bound to a board, naked, at the mercy of the merciless.

"We found a note," said Brina. A hint of her teeth revealed the lack of care she'd taken with them. They were brown in spots, black in others. Dental hygiene was among the things that had vanished with the lack of water.

Brina placed her hands onto her knees and rose from the chair. Her triceps flexed, her neck tensed, and she tilted it from side to side. It cracked and she walked away from Li, out of her field of view. Li heard her heavy footsteps on the floor, the shuffle of thick fabric between the woman's thighs.

Brina was large, but not overweight. She was an anomaly in a world where rising temperatures and lack of rain had wrought a slow-motion apocalypse called the Dearth. The farms went first, then the towns, then the cities. Eventually, the government fell. Now everything was rationed. Every drop of water was gold. People didn't grow like Brina. Not anymore.

Brina reappeared with a large blanket clutched in her mitts. She tossed it onto Li's body, and the warm, scratchy wool covered most of her body.

Brina watched her squirm for a moment but did nothing to help her. She lowered herself mechanically back into the chair. It scraped against the floor under her weight as she pulled it closer to the side of the plank to which Li was affixed.

"It was in the sheets," Brina said.

Li looked at Brina, incredulous.

"The note," Brina clarified. "It was in the sheets on your bed."

Li's mind raced. *A note? In our bed?*

The corners of Brina's mouth twitched. Her eyes flashed with the sick satisfaction of someone picking at another person's festering sore. The twitch spread into a broad grin.

"Would you like to know what he wrote?" Brina asked.

Li clenched her jaw and steeled herself. Beneath the blanket and against the binds, she balled her hands into fists. She curled her toes. She wouldn't give Brina the satisfaction of asking.

"I don't care," she said. "The bastard left me."

Brina ran her head up and down the length of Li's blanketed form, sniffing like a hound dog in a hunt. She clacked her teeth; the sound of them snapping echoed in the room. "I don't believe you," she said. "You're not a good liar, Adaliah. Not a good liar at all."

A knot thickened in Li's throat. Her chest tightened. Shivering, she swallowed past the knot before turning to face the ceiling.

In the distance, the metallic click of a lock preceded the slide of a heavy metal door scraping against concrete. The awful noise reverberated off the walls. Li strained to see what she could, but it was out of her field of view. The sound of footsteps, heavy boots, clacked against the floor. There was more than one person coming.

Brina stood from the chair and adjusted her clothing, the familiar black ensemble of the Tic's enforcers. Brina bowed her head, submitting only slightly to whoever was approaching.

"Sir," said Brina, stepping away without turning her back.

"What have you extracted?" came a low, booming voice that sent chills traveling along the gooseflesh of Li's skin. "What does she know?"

"Nothing," said Brina.

Li trembled. She couldn't see who it was that had entered the room, but after hearing him, she didn't need to. He was a man she'd met once before, when Zeke had gotten in trouble. The man had warned her boyfriend that mistakes were understandable as long as that was what they were and they never repeated themselves.

He'd frightened her then. He frightened her now. He was Graham. *His* legend, as Zeke had nervously revealed in the dark of their bedroom in a whisper, made Brina seem like Betty Crocker. Graham was a man who relished the prospect of mixing sour violence into a batter made of fear and misery.

He stepped into view, his shiny bald head reflecting the white circles of light from the bulbs above, and he bent over to pull Brina's chair underneath himself. He sat with a sigh, his wiry frame ramrod straight. He wore reflective sunglasses that showed Li a warped image of herself. On his hip, in a black leather sheath, was the long bone handle of a knife. She'd heard about the knife.

His neatly trimmed beard was salt and pepper, more the former than the latter. His dimples belied the evil within.

"We've met before," he said, crossing one thin leg over the other. "A year ago? In your apartment."

Li's focus danced between the oval lenses of his glasses, not sure where to focus her attention. Although she didn't want to look at him at all, she couldn't help herself.

"I remember thinking how beautiful you were then," he said, his voice like a V-8 purring. "Quite a figure, porcelain features, and naughty sprinkled in amongst your self-righteousness."

Bile crept up Li's throat. She winced against the sting as it sank back into her gut.

"I wondered what you saw in a punk like Ezekiel Watson," he said, waving his long fingers in front of him. "He was beneath you, I thought."

Graham adjusted the glasses, grasping the metallic frame between his fingers. "Or maybe you liked him beneath you."

Li's fists tightened, her fingernails digging into her palms. She wanted to leap at Graham, attack him, gouge out his eyes.

He tilted his head slightly and leaned forward in the chair. He was close enough to touch her.

He raised a hand, and Li flinched. That brought a genuine, leering smile to Graham's face. His dimples deepened beneath his cheekbones. He let his hand hover for a moment before pinching a corner of the wool blanket. He lifted it to peek underneath.

Graham stared at Li's naked body for several seconds before lowering the blanket back into place. He leaned back and whistled a catcall. "I was right about you," he said. "You are beautiful. A little thin for my taste, perhaps, but sumptuous."

Li's eyes burned with tears now. She couldn't stop them from coming. She couldn't keep her emotions at bay.

"Zeke's twice the man you are," she blurted without thinking. Then she added, "So is Brina."

As soon as she spat the words, she expected, braced for, an immediate and violent response from Graham. Instead, Brina stepped forward and backhanded her across the face.

Graham's eyebrows arched above the rounded frames. He chuckled and dismissively waved Brina back to her place.

"Oooh," he said, in a voice an octave higher than normal. "You're as feisty as I'd hoped. A real wild pony. I like that."

He uncrossed his legs and planted his boots flat on the concrete floor. His hands were on his knees, his fingers flitting up and down like a pianist. Without taking his attention off Li, he spoke to Brina.

"I don't think we've exhausted the possibilities just yet," he said. "I think there is gold to be mined." His tongue hung on the last word for emphasis.

Brina stepped forward, her hands flexing at her sides. Her expression was flat, absent emotion.

"If you insist, sir," she said, repeating the submissive bend she'd offered as Graham entered the room.

Graham stood. He was a tall man, whose body seemed even longer given his thin physique. He tugged at the cuffs of his shirt, pulling them lower on his wrists. "I do," he said and turned to leave. He took several steps toward the door, other unseen pairs of boots joining in the march, and stopped.

Li was looking at the ceiling again, considering what torture awaited her. She wasn't looking in Graham's direction, but couldn't have seen him if she were. He was too far from her field of view, yet he was close enough for her to hear his voice, for her to understand his parting message.

"He never loved you," the monster said as an aside. "That's what his note said. He wrote that he never loved you."

The metal door screeched open against the floor, the scraping sound deafening from its echo off the hard surfaces of the room. Straining against the wet leather binds that held her to the plank, Li screamed at Graham that he was a liar, that he was trying to get to her, to make her offer information she didn't have. Her wrists and ankles were raw. Her body shivered with cold. Her mind raced with fear.

The door shut with a clang. The lock clinked. The room was silent again. Li's pulse throbbed in her ears.

None of this was supposed to happen—not Zeke, not the Tic, not torture at the hands of this woman above her.

"He's lying," Li said to Brina. It was as much a question as it was a statement. "Graham is lying."

Brina pulled one hand from behind her back. In it she held a piece of paper ripped from an old notepad. The pale yellow paper was decorated with muted pink and blue flowers at its corners. Li recognized it as her own, from a drawer in her kitchen. But it wasn't the paper that sucked the air from her lungs.

It was the familiar scratch at its center that left her breathless. It was barely legible in its careless haste. It was, with no doubt, Zeke's handwriting.

"It wasn't real," it read. "Nothing about us ever was."

She read the eight words again. And again. And again. Did he know something? Was it a code? Or did he really mean what he'd written before leaving her alone and trapped?

Brina pulled the paper away, and Li's attention drifted to the woman's other meaty hand. In it was a pair of pliers.

CHAPTER FOUR

Commander William Guilfoyle splashed cold water across his face. The sound of the running faucet was musical, and the rush of the water from the decorative brass faucet into the deep porcelain sink reminded him of the time he'd stood behind a waterfall, cocooned inside a mossy grotto hidden from the rest of the world.

As he spun the faucet off and reached for a plush cotton towel, he wondered if waterfalls existed anywhere anymore. That was something he wanted to know. It was something he had to know.

He inhaled the herbal aroma of the towel and blotted the last of the moisture from his brow and neck, then dropped the towel onto the heated marble floor. He plodded barefoot across the expanse of the bathroom and onto the plush Berber carpet of his suite. The light changed once he'd crossed the threshold, from the artificially blue-white illumination of the bathroom to the warm, natural glow of the sunset beyond the seamless floor-to-ceiling glass panels that wrapped the expanse of the living quarters.

He dipped his hands into the deep pockets of his silk robe

and strode confidently to the overstuffed leather chair he affectionately and only half-jokingly called the command center.

"Theo," he called as he sank into the leather, the air whooshing from the thick cushion. "Theo, can you hear me?"

A well-groomed man in an impeccably tailored gray suit atop a white collared shirt and glossy black leather shoes appeared from another part of the large suite. He walked briskly and stopped at the foot of the command center. He tugged gently at the French cuffs of his shirt so that a hint of his lemniscate-design platinum cufflinks peeked from underneath the jacket. "Yes, Commander Guilfoyle, sir," said the pinch-eyed Theodore Pannopolis. "How might I serve you?"

Guilfoyle planted his elbows on the wide arms of the chair and ran his palms across the soft grain of the leather. It was more suede than saddle, and it tickled the tips of his fingers.

"Are there any waterfalls?" he asked musingly.

Theo blinked. His plucked brows angled toward one another. "I'm sorry?"

Guilfoyle waved his hand like a magician producing a coin from thin air. He looked up at Theo without raising his chin. "Waterfalls," he repeated. "Are there any left?"

"Where, sir?"

Guilfoyle huffed with frustration. "Anywhere. Do they exist, or are they extinct?"

"I'll find out, sir," said Theo. "Off the top of my head, I'd suggest there aren't many, if any. But I'd hate to give you incomplete information. Is there anything else? I was preparing your meal, but I am happy to—"

"How long have you been with me, Theo?" he asked.

"Excuse me, sir?"

"How long?" repeated the commander. "How many years have you worked for me?"

Theo folded his hands in front of him. Usually, his pensive look appeared well-rehearsed. He and Guilfoyle knew Theo had volumes of information easily accessible from his steel trap of a mind. Feigning to search his memory was something he did for his employer's benefit, so as not to make the commander feel inferior. This look was different though. Theo appeared genuinely stumped.

"I couldn't say, sir," he answered after opening and closing his mouth several times. "I know it's been years, but time tends to run together for me. All I can say is that it's been a pleasure and feels as though it was just yesterday you saw fit to entrust me with your person."

"Fantastic," Guilfoyle said, appeased. "I don't know what I would do without you, Theo. You're the best sounding board I've ever had. And your chicken tetrazzini is impeccable." The commander pinched his fingers together. "Impeccable," he repeated.

Theo adjusted the tie at his buttoned collar and offered a slight bow. "I'm flattered on both accounts, sir."

"What am I eating tonight?" asked the commander, changing the subject without addressing Theo's admission. "I hope it's not the engineered tilapia again. It's bland and unsatisfying, regardless of your skill."

Theo shook his head. "No, sir. I took note the last time I was remiss. Tonight, I've prepared a wonderful game hen with an organic vegetable and root medley. The herbs are fresh from the garden."

"And the wine?"

Theo held up his hand and copied the finger-pinching motion Guilfoyle had just performed. "A fabulous and earthy Pinot Noir. It has notes of cherry that complement the robust flavor of the hen."

"Great," said Guilfoyle. "As you were, then, Theo. I'd like to know about the waterfalls by the time I've finished the bottle."

"Of course," said Theo, and the man hustled from the

room with the same fastidious jaunt that had brought him to Commander Guilfoyle's side.

"Oh," said the commander. "Don't overcook the hen."

"Yes, sir," Theo called from the kitchen.

Guilfoyle turned his attention to the view beyond the glass in front of him. This was his favorite part of each day, the moments before the light slipped from the sky and the colors were their richest.

He was thirty stories above the city, or what was left of it. His was one of two skyscrapers functioning as intended. There was ample power without the threat of brownouts, and water, hot *and* cold, that seemed in endless supply. And the climate controls were as accurate as they had been when everything was in abundance.

His tower, the Torquemada, was residential. He lived in the penthouse atop the building. The entire floor was his. Other high-ranking Overseers lived in the levels beneath his. Some floors were divided; others were not.

The other tower, which stood fifteen stories tall, was for business. It was the central government headquarters for the Overseers and was known as the Fascio.

Where the residential building was glass and steel and gleamed against the sunlight, the governmental edifice was built of stone and mortar. It was adorned with avenging angels and gargoyles. There were centaurs and lions, two-headed dragons, and beckoning sirens.

An underground tunnel connected the two buildings, allowing for ease of movement and for protection from outside forces that might seek to harm the Overseers' position atop the hierarchy of this world.

As he did every night, Guilfoyle scanned the orange horizon, searching for the hints of purple that might reflect off distant clouds. Once he was satisfied, and the sun had reached the final stages of its descent, the commander would shuffle the short distance to the glass and take in the full scene of the kingdom below.

It was brown and gray. Dust hung in the air. Plumes of it rose like smoky wakes behind the engines of transport trucks, angular armored vehicles, and the occasional passenger car.

Aside from the two towers, the rest of the city was low slung. It was a mixture of single-story structures, the sporadic two-story bungalow, and open-air markets obvious by the connections of drab tarps and tents cloistered into blocks and irregular circular collections.

Near one collection of tents was a long line of people. It snaked for three city blocks, and from Commander Guilfoyle's vantage point three hundred feet above, those in the queue looked like ants awaiting an audience with their queen.

His eyes moved along the line and found another. It was at best a quarter mile north, and it was twice as long as the first, disappearing around a refueling station. That line was for water. He checked his watch. The sweeping second hand ticked silently in fractions of seconds as it moved around the gold face.

Yes. It was the water line. It was *that* time of day, on *that* day of the week, when rations were distributed. One gallon per person per week. No more than three per family. That was the rule. The lines were always long.

He shifted back to the shorter of the two lines. It wasn't water. It wasn't toilet paper. Toilet paper was tomorrow. Or maybe it was yesterday. But it wasn't today.

He squinted, trying in vain to gauge what treasure awaited the patient. He did notice, as he looked closely, members of the Overseers' Tactical Marine Force, TMF, patrolling up and down the line. He made out the vague but easily identifiable shapes of the M27 Automatic Infantry Rifles cradled across their chests. The barrels were aimed at the sky, stretching diagonally above the helmeted Marines' heads.

Flashes of bright light drew his attention back to the water line. Focusing on the source of the strobing pops of light, he saw there wasn't much of a line anymore. It had dissolved into a spreading mob of ants running away from what Guilfoyle realized were muzzle flashes. At least three of his Marines were engaged. He leaned closer to the glass, watching the miniature drama unfold below.

The flashes stopped, but not before a half-dozen bodies lay strewn on the ground. Guilfoyle sighed and watched the Marines drag them away. The line reformed, survivors shuffling forward to take the spots of those who'd left on foot or by bullet.

Guilfoyle nodded his approval. The people were conditioned, as he'd long predicted they would be, to mind their own business and move along. There were rabble-rousers who caused trouble in the lines or at the ration exchange centers. But in the scheme of things, they were little more than flies on a bull.

The vast majority of the citizenry understood they needed the Overseers to provide for them. Guilfoyle knew what his herd needed. He knew how to keep them alive amidst the aftermath of the Dearth. He knew how to keep them from tearing each other's throats out.

"Tough love is what's needed now," he'd said during his public broadcast address earlier in the day. "We cannot waver. We cannot stray."

He'd delivered the speech that morning on the steps of the Fascio, Marines flanking him on either side, his lieutenants seated behind him. An oak lectern was emblazoned with the Overseers' emblem of a carafe of water flanked by twin ax heads, projected atop the steps from bundles of birch rods tied together with red straps. Guilfoyle stood behind it, delivering his speech from memory.

Beyond the crowd, towering above them and standing

watch, was a monument to the original Overseers who'd built the protectorate a generation earlier.

"Our mission is clear—survival of the species by any means necessary," Guilfoyle said, pounding a fist on the lectern. "To have the means by which we survive, we must do what is necessary. We must think of the common good. We must put our neighbors above ourselves."

The sycophantic crowd roared its approval. Guilfoyle relished the applause.

"The victory of the many requires," he said when the crowd quieted, a finger raised to the heavens, "no, it demands, the sacrifice of the few."

It was then he'd announced the new allotments, reducing the lawful distribution of water and rations. That wasn't met with the same enthusiasm as his call for vague nationalism.

"Our enemies are stealing from us," he said. "They are stealing from *you*. They take our scant resources and sell them for profit. They enrich themselves at your expense."

Boos and calls for blood met his words. The jeers were intoxicating; they empowered him.

"Do not let these selfish parasites bleed us dry," he went on. "Do not buy their wares. Do not sell them your precious rations. Do not be complicit in the destruction of our state, our homeland."

He raised his outstretched arms, embracing all that lay before him to thunderous applause. And then he stepped aside as a quartet of Marines brought forth a thin man in shackles.

The prisoner was gaunt, his greasy hair matted to one side of his head, his skin almost gray. He blinked, squinting as if someone aimed a bright light at him. He was hunched in submission, his tattered clothing hanging on his frame, the frayed cuffs of his torn pants covering his feet as he shuffled to the steps.

The man struggled against the two Marines who held him by the biceps and under his arms.

"This man is a bootlegger." The words dripped from Guilfoyle's lips like acid.

The crowd hissed. Someone threw a rock that hit the man in the side.

Guilfoyle pointed at him accusingly. "He takes water from us and sells it for profit!" he shouted. "He is a thief and a traitor. He is a Tic."

The crowd cheered in agreement, chanting an insistence for the man's death.

"Kill him!" one yelled.

"Make him pay!" barked another.

Guilfoyle gestured for the crowd he'd whipped into a frenzy to calm itself, and waited for quiet.

"We cannot abide this," he said. "We have to send a message to that underground movement of enemies who would take from us what is so precious. They are stealing life. They are profiting from your thirst."

The bootlegger knew what was coming. It was the same thing that had happened to captured bootleggers for years, as long as anyone remembered. It was the same punishment.

A dark stain spread across the man's groin and leached across the dirty cotton of his pants. He looked down, color flashing across his face for a moment before the tears began to stream.

Guilfoyle gave the man a disapproving glare and jabbed his finger at the prisoner. "While we barely have enough water to drink or cook," he declared, "this man is hydrated enough to both cry and wet himself. It's further proof of his betrayal."

Guilfoyle stepped toward the man, wrinkling his nose at the strong uric odor, and put his hand on the criminal's shoulder. "May you find mercy in this world and the one that comes after," Guilfoyle said, the sarcasm pasted atop his blessing.

He nodded to the Marines. They tightened their grip as the bootlegger protested, trying to hold his ground. He cried out for forgiveness, for a second chance. He offered compliance and information about the Tic. The chants and jeers from the crowd drowned out his prayers for clemency.

They watched as the Marines affixed a harness to the man's torso, strapping it tightly across his chest and shoulders. They stood witness as one of the Marines cut a long gash across the man's midsection. Blood poured from the slice, and the man cried out in pain and grabbed at the wound. They listened as the other Marine cranked the winch. It had been attached to a chain that had been, in turn, connected to the harness.

As the man whimpered, sheets of sweat covering his pale body, the winch lifted him from his feet. He kicked, trying to keep himself grounded. It didn't work.

He hung from the front of the stone building. The chain, which ran through the gaping mouth of a gargoyle above the steps, pulled at the harness. It rode up into the man's armpits, jerking back his arms so he couldn't protect the wound.

His body stretched, tearing at the wound and eliciting more unearthly howls from the dying man. The chain twisted in its ascent, and as it unwound, the bootlegger's body spun with it. Blood drained from the wound, down his leg, off his bare foot, and dripped onto the stone plaza below.

Guilfoyle watched admiringly. His back to the crowd, which began dispersing, he admired the newest of the admonitions—from the dying man to the dead one hanging next to him, and the dead one next to her. Three was a good number.

"Commander, sir, your meal is ready."

Theo's words shook Guilfoyle from his memory. He glanced over his shoulder to see Theo standing at attention.

The manservant guided Guilfoyle from the salon to a large

dining area, a wide oval room surrounded by glass that protruded over the building, making the space float.

Theo referenced the neat place setting at the circular glass table to his right. Then he moved to slide out the chair and seat the commander. Guilfoyle sank into the armed chair and inched himself forward.

The bone china plate was gold-rimmed. The cooked hen steamed at its center along with a generous portion of carrots, long green beans, and red potatoes. Guilfoyle inhaled the aroma.

He reached out and plucked a long-stemmed glass from the table. It clinked against the china as he lifted it, swirling the blood-red wine inside. He tipped the glass and sipped. He held the liquid in his mouth for a moment, letting the tannins seep into his taste buds.

"Great," he said.

Theo's body relaxed. "Thank you, sir. I think you'll find the hen to your liking. It's cooked as you requested, tender and gamey."

Guilfoyle eyed the knife and fork beside the china plate and reached for them. But he stopped short, his fingers hovering for a moment before descending toward the bird.

"Sir," said Theo, "Iguazu in the former nation of Brazil, Victoria in Africa, and Niagara in the Northeastern Overseer Protectorate."

"What about them?"

"Those are the only significant waterfalls left in the world," answered Theo. "The rest have dried up either naturally or from manmade devices."

Guilfoyle gripped the top of the bird with his right hand. He tore at a leg with his left. He twisted it, the gristle popping and snapping until he freed it from the rest of the carcass.

With his hands he hungrily drew the leg to his mouth and

bit down, ripping at the flesh with his teeth. Pink juices leaked onto his chin as he chewed.

His mouth full of bird, Guilfoyle eyed Theo with an approving glance. A meaty grin spread across his face. "Superb," he said, juices collecting in the corners of his mouth. "Much better than the tilapia."

CHAPTER FIVE

Zeke squinted against the hot wind and lowered his Stetson. Sand sprayed his exposed skin and stung as it blasted him. It found its way into his ears and nostrils.

He stood in the parking lot next to Pedro's Cantina. His traveling partners were gearing up for the trip back to the city. They were a motley crew.

Uriel and Phil dug around in the bed of a Ford F-150. Raf and Barach loaded the trunk of a Chevy Impala. Gabe leaned against the Impala, speed loading ammo into the magazine for a large rifle. Sticking out of his waist was a wide knife handle, the blade hidden beneath his belt.

On the ground in front of the men there were various-sized bags and packs. Extending from one, Zeke saw the ends of matching black wooden sticks. From another, he noticed a spiked silver ball attached to a chain that disappeared into the satchel. They were strange-looking weapons that Zeke hadn't seen before.

Should I trust these people? Do I have a choice?

"Here," said Pedro. "Take this. It'll help."

The barkeep handed Zeke a black bandana. Like his new

clothes, this too was clean. Zeke folded the stiff cotton into a triangle, wrapped it around his face, and knotted it at the back of his head. He adjusted it over the bridge of his nose. He inhaled the floral aroma. It promised a place he'd never known, one lush with green and color.

"It'll keep you from getting sand boogers," said Pedro.

That made Zeke chuckle. It was the first time he remembered himself laughing in, well, he didn't know how long. It had been a while though. Real laughter was as scarce as water and just as life-sustaining these days.

Still, the grin faded from his face, and he dipped his head toward the gang assembling their gear. There was nothing funny about the task ahead.

"You never told me what this place is," said Zeke. "Don't I deserve to know?"

He still had trouble wrapping his head around what was happening let alone really knowing who these people were who were intent on helping him find and rescue the woman he'd abandoned. How were five people going to get past the Overseer Marines and into the city, let alone infiltrate the Tic?

"Deserve," Pedro said in a way that made it sound as though he'd never said it aloud before. He was testing it out, taking it for a spin. "Interesting choice of words."

"I didn't mean—"

Pedro raised a hand. "Of course you did. And you're right."

"That I deserve to know?"

Pedro shook his head. "That I haven't told you what this place is."

"This is a weird place you got here," Zeke said. "No offense. You saved my life and all, you gave me clothes and some great liquor, but I come from a place where people look out for themselves, damn their neighbor."

Pedro snickered.

"That didn't come out right," said Zeke. "I appreciate it. I do. And I don't know how I can ever repay you."

"I'll think of something," he said. "And remember, you do have a tab."

"They don't have to do this," Zeke said. "I can go on my own. It's my mess. I made it; I should clean it up."

Pedro raised an eyebrow. "That they don't *have to* is why they will."

What does that mean?

The two men stood there at the front porch for the next few moments. Zeke scanned the lot and beyond. It was hard to see much past the paved parking lot to the left of the main building. The sand and dust clouded the air like a brown fog or the haze from a wildfire.

Zeke adjusted his bandana. On the other side of the endless highway, obscured by the haze, still stood the Horde that had chased him to the cantina.

They were in a long line against the shoulder of the road, facing the bar. The men stood in the beds of their trucks, some straddling their bikes. All of them stared through their masks at Zeke.

"You don't have to worry about them," Pedro said, seeming to read Zeke's thoughts. "They can't touch you now. Not yet."

His dog padded from the bar, clopped down the steps, and joined them in the parking lot. It looked up at Pedro, its tongue hanging from its maw. It plopped onto its belly, impervious to the heat emanating from the asphalt.

"Why's that?" Zeke asked.

"It's the rules," said Pedro. "You made it here. You're under my protection now. And you will be until I say otherwise."

"So they're, what?" asked Zeke. "Waiting for you to say otherwise?"

"Something like that," Pedro said. "We have a healthy

respect for one another. I don't interfere with them beyond the property, and they don't mess with me and mine."

Zeke sighed, smelling the stale aroma of alcohol from his own breath. It was like every time he got one question answered, five more popped up.

Uriel drew his attention from the awaiting Horde and the overwhelming sensation that things were not what they appeared to be. She stepped to him, an inch inside his personal space, and beamed.

"Look at you," she said, "all bandit-like with your little handkerchief. So cute."

Pedro shifted his weight, his hand pulling up on the buckle at his waist, and yanked up his pants. "You have everything you need?" he asked her. "Weapons, maps, extra fuel?"

"We do," she said, her eyes flitting from Zeke to Pedro. "And Zeke's car is all fixed up. The glass in the back isn't tinted like it was before, but it was the best we could do. It's fueled up too."

"The Superbird?" Zeke asked. "It's…fixed?"

"Yep," Uriel said. "Gabe's good with cars. Yours is around back."

She dug into a concealed hip pocket of her leather pants, wrestled free a lump of fur attached to a set of keys, and tossed them at Zeke's chest.

He caught them and then held the rabbit's foot in his fist, rubbing it with his thumb. "Thank you."

Uriel motioned to the keys. "About that," she said. "The rabbit's foot? So douchey."

Zeke frowned. "It was my dad's," he said. "Only good thing he ever gave me."

Uriel's features softened, and it appeared as though she was about to apologize. Then she shrugged. "Then your dad's a douche too."

She spun on her heels and started toward the F-150, stopping ten yards into her saunter. "You coming?" she asked. "We don't have eternity to get this done."

Zeke offered his hand to Pedro. "Thank you."

Pedro took Zeke's hand in both of his. His large muscular grip dwarfed Zeke's, swallowing it whole, and the man shook up and down. "Good luck," he said. Then he reached behind his back and withdrew a large revolver. He spun it skillfully so that the grip was facing Zeke. "Take this."

Zeke glanced at the weapon. "I can't. You've done enough."

Pedro pushed the butt into Zeke's chest. "Take it. You'll need it. It's six shots. It kicks hard and carries a punch a lot stronger than you're used to feeling."

Zeke took the gun. It was heavy, heavier than any weapon he'd ever held. True, he wasn't a marksman with lots of gun-toting experience, but he knew enough to understand this weapon was unique. And it was old. Really old. It wasn't something he'd seen in real life before.

The steel was cold in his hands and the six-shooter felt foreign. He'd seen people who gripped firearms as though the machines were extensions of themselves. He wasn't one. Though Zeke had grown up in the underworld of his city and had lived most of his life as a relative outlaw, running ill-gotten water for the Tic, he wasn't much for weapons. As he'd proven repeatedly, he was a runner, not a fighter. Everyone he knew could attest to that now, especially Li. Most of all Li. More than anyone, Li.

"Use it wisely," counseled Pedro. "I'll catch you on the flip side."

"Thanks," said Zeke. "I'll try."

Zeke glanced across the road at the patient Horde and crossed the lot toward his awaiting band of misfits. He studied the sky as he approached, his boots crunching on the thin drift of sand and grit that coated the lot.

The sun's bright yellow hue was a smudge beyond the haze. It was late in the afternoon, yet the daylight felt like noon. The wind whipped around Zeke, swirling sand into his face. He tilted his head down, lowering his hat.

"Phil and Gabe will take the truck," said Uriel as he reached the team. "Raf and Barach will share the Impala."

Zeke's attention darted amongst the brooding trio and landed on Uriel. "What about you?"

Uriel ran a hand along the mane of red hair atop her head. "I drew the short straw," she said, a mischievous twinkle in her green eyes. "I ride shotgun with you."

CHAPTER SIX

Zeke cranked the ignition, and the purr of his Superbird's V-8 engine comforted him. He reached over to put on the aftermarket seatbelt he'd had installed, more of a racing harness than a typical belt.

The RPM dial tipped to the right, marking the press of the pedal. He grinned and looked over at Uriel already strapped into her seat.

"Do you put a quarter in this thing to make it shake?" she asked. "I mean, seriously, my brains are gonna scramble."

Zeke shifted the car into first and slid his fingers across the wheel. He sped up and the car responded, punching forward and sinking them into their seats.

"That's what you get for drawing the short straw," he said.

A wash of familiar comfort spread throughout his tensed body. There was something about being behind the wheel of his Superbird. This was where he was most comfortable in the world. *This* was his weapon, the extension of himself. He'd spent so much time at its controls, the Plymouth was a living, breathing thing. He spoke to it; it listened. He asked it questions; it contemplated answers. He told it secrets; it kept them.

Zeke spun the wheel and peeled around the bar. The truck and Impala awaited him at the shoulder of the highway. Across from him sat the Horde. Zeke reached the lot and downshifted. He held his foot on the brake and motioned toward the Horde with his chin.

"They can't chase us?" he asked.

Uriel shook her head. "Not this time. It's against the rules."

Zeke shifted into the next gear and slammed his foot on the gas. The car shot forward. The tires grabbed and then slipped as he drifted onto the highway before jetting forward. He and his new crew zipped past the Horde, still worried they'd give chase. They didn't.

The engine roared its approval as he pushed into fourth gear, and responded with a jerk. Zeke relished the sensation of acceleration shoving him back into his seat.

He checked the rearview to spot the truck keeping pace with him. He couldn't see the Impala, but he assumed it was behind the truck. He noticed the front of the truck was outfitted with a large chrome frame. It was a cattle catcher.

Uriel sat with her knees pulled up to her chest, her feet on the dashboard. She hadn't asked permission, but Zeke would not scold her for it. She already thought he was a douche. No need to add to that perception by being a territorial gearhead, given her willingness to help him rescue Li.

"Why are you helping me?" he asked.

Uriel stared out the window, through the thin varnish of dust coating the glass, and spoke without turning to face him. Her response, which Zeke half-expected to be fueled by sarcasm, was seemingly genuine.

"Because that's what good people do," she said. "They help others in need."

"I'm not a good person," he said.

Uriel turned to face him. Her expression was flat, unaffected by what he'd admitted. "So? None of us are. What does that have to do with anything?"

The incongruity of her response struck him as odd. On one hand, she was telling him good people selflessly helped others; on the other, she was admitting her own failings.

"So are you good or bad?" he asked.

She shrugged and looked back out the window. "A little bit of both. One more than the other."

She didn't elaborate. Her mood was markedly subdued once they'd hit the road and reached cruising speed. When he'd climbed behind the wheel, he'd expected a nonstop barrage of innuendo, double entendre, and teasing insults.

"You okay?" he asked.

"Yeah," she said. "Just never been a fan of this part."

The speedometer swept to the right, reaching ninety-five miles per hour.

"What part?"

"The approach," Uriel said. "I want to get there, dig in, and do what needs to be done. I don't have a lot of patience, if you haven't noticed."

She spun in her seat to face him. Her heels were on the dash.

Zeke's attention bounced between the road ahead and the woman next to him. There *was* something intoxicating about her. She was at once judgmental and accepting. Her style was a mix of individuality and trite conformity. And then there was the perfume. Zeke tried to focus on the conversation, on the implications of what she'd just revealed.

He pushed his thoughts about her to the back of his mind, shoving them to the overstuffed part of his brain that held off the unanswered and unasked questions he'd hoarded since falling onto Pedro's front stoop.

"You've done this before?" he asked.

"Yep. A few times," she answered.

"You've gone to rescue the girlfriend of a bad guy from other worse guys?" he asked.

Uriel slid her feet from the dash and sat upright. She tightened the end of her ponytail and draped it over her left shoulder. "That's specific."

Zeke tipped his hat back on his head. "You know what I mean."

"I've tried to help people before," she said. "I never gave much consideration to whether they were good or bad. One, that's a sliding scale. And two, it's subjective."

"Morality's subjective?"

"Is that all that makes someone good or bad? Even if it is, who's to say what's good and what's not? It's all perspective."

Zeke shook his head. "I get it. You're avoiding the question though."

"What's the question?"

Zeke checked his rearview mirror. The Ford flashed its headlights.

"What does he want?" Zeke asked.

"Who?"

"Phil. He's flashing his lights at me."

Uriel undid the harness and craned her neck to look out the back window. Then she sank back into her position, sliding low into the seat. "He wants you to get over and let him lead."

"Why?"

"Do you know where you're going?"

"Yeah," said Zeke in a tone that feigned offense. "The city."

Uriel put her feet back on the dash and crossed her legs at her ankles. She wasn't wearing her harness. "Do you know how to get there?"

Zeke thought about it. He didn't know where he was. Even if he knew where he was going, he didn't know how to get there.

"That's what I thought," said Uriel. "Might want to let him lead."

Zeke took his foot off the gas and eased to the right lane, the tires humming along the smooth asphalt. Up ahead, the distance warbled from the heat; the low hills danced and shimmied.

The truck's loud engine roared as the jacked-up rig rumbled past him. The Impala kept its distance and maintained its course along the center of the highway. Once the truck had eased into its spot, Zeke sped up and moved to the center.

He glanced at Uriel. She was nibbling on a fingernail.

"How many times have you done this?" he asked, picking the conversation back up.

"Like I said, a few."

"Why?" Zeke asked, his attention on the back of the F-150 and the impressive chrome frame on its nose. "I mean, none of this makes sense. I show up. I'm a total stranger. I've got baggage. I'm badly hurt. You guys fix me up, give me water, and then offer to help no questions asked?"

"And?"

Zeke slapped the steering wheel. He gritted his teeth, clenching his jaw. There was being coy and then there was being evasive.

"Aaannd," he said, his frustration evident, "that's weird. It's just weird. None of this makes sense. I tried to get Pedro to answer my questions. He wouldn't. If I had a choice, I'm not sure I would trust you, any of you. But I don't have a choice. Choosers can't be beggars."

"You've got that backwards, Socrates," she said. "It's beggars can't be choosers."

Zeke considered that. "Huh," he said. "That makes a lot more sense."

"It's an old saying," she said. "You're young."

"See," he said, "it's things like that. Little things that put more questions into my head. Nothing feels right about this. Nothing. Give me something, Uriel. Anything."

Nothing. Something. Anything.

Uriel sighed, although perhaps it was a huff. She uncrossed her legs and sat up, using her balled fists to push her torso higher in the seat. Unharnessed, she leaned toward Zeke and put her hand on his right thigh.

She was staring at him, the emerald green of her irises hypnotizing him with their rich color. He looked back toward the road ahead and the rear of the truck leading them on a path toward the city.

"Here's the thing," she said. "All of us owe Pedro. He helped us when we needed it. So we stick around and help others. We *try* to help others. Some are beyond help. We try though. It's just what we do. You should be thankful more than skeptical."

"I am thankful," Zeke said.

"What's that saying? Don't look a gift horse in the mouth?"

Zeke considered her point. She was right. He was better to take the help and not ask questions about it. It wasn't often in his life that people had been on his side without there being something in it for them.

"I can't pay you," he said. "Not yet anyhow. I don't have any money."

"We don't expect any. That's not how we roll."

She tugged at the harness and pulled it back over her shoulders. She buckled the straps and eased herself more comfortably into the seat. They rode in silence for what felt like twenty or even thirty minutes. She continued picking at her fingernails, nibbling at them. What she'd said kept resonating in his mind, replaying like a recording.

Don't look a gift horse in the mouth.

Behind him, the sun was beginning to set. It had sunk from

its zenith and was slipping beneath the outcropping of jagged peaks beyond the end of the infinite highway he'd already traveled. He'd lost track of time. It had been a long day. Or had it been longer than that?

This didn't look like the vast Badlands he knew. It had a network of roads, highways remaining between the eastern and western protectorates. They all ran perpendicular to each other. Some were north and south; others traveled east to west. It was a relic network of highways that predated the protectorates and the fall of the United States, to a time when natural farming ruled the central North American economies.

Because the roads, despite being in the middle of the Badlands, were so well-known, they were dangerous.

There were Badlanders, savages who lay in wait all along the routes to ambush and steal the Tic shipments. Also, the protectorate's Tactical Marine Force from eastern protectorates would try to control access to some of the highways. They would send large contingents of Marines to set up checkpoints in the Badlands. The Badlanders would sometimes challenge them, but given that the Badlanders lived and worked in small nomadic tribes, the Marines most often had them outgunned and outmanned.

The far western protectorate, beyond the mountain range, was a supplier of metals. Iron, gypsum, marble, and titanium were valuable commodities the eastern and southern protectorates needed and didn't have. The western protectorate needed water. Without snowmelt, and there was little of it now, those city-states in and west of the mountains had no reliable supply. The Tic supplemented the "official allotment" with its own lucrative black-market trade.

Zeke had made the run countless times in large trucks. It didn't make sense to carry small volumes of anything in his Superbird such a long distance west and east.

This place didn't look like any of it. The topography was similar, but different.

He glanced at Uriel; her head bobbed gently against the headrest. She looked sweeter when she was asleep. There was still an edge, though. Sleep couldn't dull that, not with the red mane, the tattoos, and the leather.

Don't look a gift horse in the mouth.

As the bright light outside the car diffused into orange and yellow with the setting sun and the distant hills ahead of him came into focus, the proverb Uriel had so expertly proffered was replaced with another one with which Zeke was acutely familiar.

"If it seems too good to be true," he muttered to himself, "it probably is."

CHAPTER SEVEN

Li couldn't keep from shivering. Her teeth chattered, her hands trembled, and her fingers were bloodied and throbbed with the sharp, unmistakable sting of trauma. She was crouched in the corner of a dark cell, alone and afraid. But she was determined not to die here and not to give the Tic what it wanted. There was only so much life they could suck from her before she'd bite back. She'd reached that point.

In the darkness of the room, she couldn't see her wounded hands. She couldn't see the tray of food they'd left for her two days ago. Or was it three? There was no way of knowing how long she'd been in this room.

Her only company, save the occasional delivery of dry cereal and her thoughts, was the skittering of rodents across the floor on the opposite side of the space. She sank deeper into the corner and pulled her knees tight against her chest.

Li was nude. They had neither clothed nor bathed her. The stubble on her legs was rough on her fingertips as she rubbed them, trying to focus on a sensation other than the throbbing pain that came from her missing fingernails. Three of them were gone, plied from their beds.

She leaned her head back against the wall, inhaled, and gagged. The mélange of odors that clung to her unwashed body reeked. They were nauseating. She held her breath then inhaled, trying to avoid the whiff of stank that coated her bare flesh.

She was exhausted but could not sleep, and she knew dehydration was taking its toll on her psyche. Her mind would drift in and out of reality, swinging from the present to the past and back again.

In front of her, floating in the darkness, was the note Brina had shared with her before using the pliers. It was the note Zeke had left in their bed before he'd disappeared.

It wasn't real. Nothing about us ever was.

Ever?

He'd loved her. He'd told her that countless times. She'd believed him. Maybe she was the fool.

They were together for over two years. They'd built something together. He'd shown her his world, as filthy as it was, and shared with her the rush of adrenaline that came from clandestine work.

He was a master at his trade. And while she'd judged him for it, she came to admire him for how good he was at doing what he did. It was an aphrodisiac, watching a man like Zeke exude the confidence it took to outrun the law with such aplomb. It sent chills up and down her spine just thinking about it.

The dark cell in which she now rotted was a world away from the place where she'd met Zeke, from the place where they'd first connected. Though, as she thought about it, perhaps they weren't that far apart at all, despite the passage of time between now and then.

———

She'd scored a job at a speakeasy on the city's outskirts a few years back. It was underground, built in the cellar of what was once a butcher shop. The place now exchanged vouchers for engineered fish and modified grain. In the back, behind the storeroom, was a door that led to the secret bar where the Tic's top generals would meet and make deals to move their wares.

Through a friend of a friend, the speakeasy's owner hired her. His name was Semion Mogilevich. He looked nice enough, but she knew he was as tough as nails. He had to be to run an illegal Tic-infused bar. There was something about him, the way he carried himself, that gave off the impression he was more important than he wanted people to believe he was. Or maybe it was the opposite. It could be that he *wanted* people to think he was more important than he was. Either way, he was hiding something. Li saw the layers in people. It was part of who she was. With Mogilevich, there were a lot of layers.

He'd given her an elevator stare when he hired her. She was used to it in the unjust patriarchy that was the post-Dearth world. She'd smiled back at him, her bright red lips spreading into a broad grin that revealed her near-perfect teeth.

He'd hired her with a wink and told her the job was easy if she followed the rules. If she didn't, the job was likely a dead end. He'd said it in a way that told her he meant the more literal version of the expression.

"There are three things you gotta do," he'd told her during her first shift, his accent slick with northeastern grease. "Look good, fill orders, and keep quiet."

"Not a problem," she said to him. "I'll do all three."

"You got the first one," he said wryly. "The second one is straightforward. That third one, though…"

"Yes?"

"That third one's the toughest," he warned. "You're gonna hear things, sweetie. Some of 'em you will not understand.

Some of 'em you might. Either way, best to forget everything. It's like them three monkeys, you know?"

"Monkeys?"

Mogilevich covered his eyes, then his ears, then his mouth. He looked at her. When she shrugged, he huffed out the answer. "See no evil, hear no evil, speak no evil," he said. "Sheesh. Sure don't gotta worry about you understanding anything. Just look pretty, doll. Let the rest take care of itself."

Li had pretended not to be offended. He slapped her on her backside and told her to get to work.

The speakeasy was little more than a bunch of tables in a dimly lit basement. At one end of the room was a bar. Behind it was a long table that held a menagerie of cheap liquor. There was a pair of battered stainless-steel kegs sitting on one end of the bar.

Mogilevich worked the bar along with another man named Markus. The two of them took and filled the liquor orders from Li and another waitress named Rose. Li and Rose filled the beers themselves.

The pay, what there was of it, was lousy. The place stank of stale beer and cigarettes. The concrete floor was sticky, the lighting was poor, and the ambience was decidedly crummy. All of it was worth it, though, when a thin young man with a boyish face, kind eyes, and blond hair sat down at a table by himself on her third day of work.

"Hi," he said to her when she eased up to take his order. "How are you?"

He was the first person who'd asked her how she was doing. Other men had complimented her appearance, some of them graphically, but not Zeke.

"Good," she answered. "You?"

He shrugged. "Okay. Thirsty."

In her experience, most men in this type of place would

have taken the opportunity to answer her with some pickup line. He hadn't.

"What can I get you, then?" she asked.

"Beer."

"You got it."

She sauntered away and glanced at him over her shoulder when she reached the keg. He wasn't looking at her. He wasn't giving her that elevator stare like all the others. He was deep in thought, pinching his nose and leaning on his elbows.

She tilted a mostly clean mug under the tap and filled it with what passed for beer. Anything water-based, which was nearly everything, was rationed and controlled by the Overseers. The Tic circumvented that control. They ran a parallel service, even if the quality of what they ran wasn't always the finest or purest.

The Tic was loved as much as it was feared amongst the regular people constricted by inequality and oppression. It gave them things the legitimate, and totalitarian, government would not. And in that, the Tic had its power.

She carried the beer back to the table and set it in front of the young man. It sloshed a little and shook him from whatever had held his concentration.

"Sorry about that," she said, tugging a bar rag from her waist and swiping up the foamy puddle. "My apologies."

He peered up at her. "No problem. Thanks for the drink."

"You look serious," she said. "Most guys come in here ready for a party."

He took a swig of the beer and wiped the foam from his mouth. "I guess I'm not most guys."

She extended her hand. "I'm Adaliah. My friends call me Li."

He studied her and put the mug on the table before shaking her hand. Electricity sparked between them. She hadn't expected that. Her heart beat against her chest.

"Does that make me a friend?" he asked. "I'm Zeke."

"Zeke," she said with as flirty a smile as she could muster, "I guess it does."

Their eyes locked long enough for the electricity to spark again. Then his drifted past her at the same moment she felt the grip of a heavy hand on her shoulder.

"Rule three," said Mogilevich. "First warning."

She lowered her chin. "I'm sorry," she said to her boss. "My bad."

"It's not a problem," said Zeke. He pushed his chair back from the table and stood, his balled fists on the table.

Mogilevich stepped to the side of Li and closer to Zeke, staring up at the taller man. From his hip pocket, he withdrew a three-inch blade set into a four-inch handle. He touched a button, unlocking the blade. It clicked and opened.

He brought the knife up toward Zeke's face and turned it over, the dim bulbs of light reflecting off its Damascus steel. "If I say it's a problem, Zeke," he exaggerated the vowels in Zeke's name, "then it's a problem."

Zeke, surprisingly fast, grabbed the bar owner by the wrist with one hand and used the other to free him of the blade. He flipped it around in his palm and slid the blade back into the handle.

Zeke smirked at Li before tightening his expression and eyeing Mogilevich. He took a step toward the proprietor. "Look," he said to Mogilevich, planting a finger in the middle of the man's chest, "I've had a rough day. I think you know without guys like me, guys like you wouldn't have a place like this. So, I'm going to ask you, as politely as I can, to let this woman talk. I'll even pay you double for the beer."

Mogilevich hesitated. Zeke wasn't a big guy by any stretch, but Li had a gut feeling he could take Mogilevich in a fight. Still, there was something about the way Mogilevich responded that told them he was allowing Zeke to win the battle, if not the war.

Mogilevich nodded. "All right," he said, avoiding making eye contact with Li, "this once. I'm good with it."

Zeke put his hands on Mogilevich's shoulders and patted them. He smiled again. Li liked it. It was another unexpected treat.

"Thanks, Mogilevich," he said. "I appreciate it. And I hope that when I leave, you don't treat our friend poorly because of my insistent behavior."

"Of course not, Zeke. It's all good here." Mogilevich offered his hand. Zeke handed over the knife. Mogilevich took it and filtered his way through the growing crowd and back behind the bar.

"You shouldn't have done that," said Li.

"He shouldn't have talked to you that way," said Zeke. "He's your boss. He's not an Overseer."

"I should get back to work," she lamented. "To be honest, I'm not so sure who he is. Some people treat him like he's a king."

Zeke chuckled. "He runs a bar. Yeah, sure, he's connected. But c'mon. He runs a bar."

"I get the feeling it requires a lot of power to run a bar," said Li. "I know that sounds funny, but in my experience, the people you least expect to be at the top of the pyramid are the ones who are, and those who flaunt their power have little."

"The old religion and money saying."

"What's that?" asked Li.

"It was an old saying," said Zeke. "I read it in a book once. It was something about religion and money. The more people profess to have of both, the less they have of either."

"You read books?"

"Sometimes. You?"

"I have a collection." Li lowered her voice to above a whisper. "Some of them aren't legal."

"So we're rebels, then," said Zeke.

Li's cheeks flushed. "Something like that."

"I'll hang out until your shift is over if that's okay," offered Zeke. "Make sure you get home safely."

"I'd like that."

———

Now, years later, Li sat waiting. A scratching sound caught her attention and brought her back to the present. She looked up, narrowing her gaze to better focus in the dark.

The vague outline of a rodent sat a few feet from her. It bobbed up and down and then scurried away. The room was bathed in silence again.

It wasn't real. Nothing about us ever was.

Did Zeke know what he'd done to her? Did he understand the torture she'd endured? He had to know they'd come for her, didn't he?

That he'd abandoned her for this, to protect himself, was incongruous with everything she thought she knew about him. He'd always put her first. He'd protected her even when she didn't need it.

Anger welled in her gut. The man who'd beguiled her was off running free. He'd escaped. He'd left her here. That thought repeated in her mind over and over. She'd never planned on loving him the way she did, but his innate goodness, cloaked in his outwardly roguish nature, had charmed her. She loved him. He loved her. Or so she'd thought.

He'd left her. And nothing was real. The anger bloomed into a seething desire for revenge. The thought of his boyish charm, of his arms wrapped around her as he promised her a life better than the one they lived, nauseated her.

As she remained there, stewing, eventually the anger ebbed and hope swelled. She needed something to hold onto. To help her push through. Foolish as it was.

Zeke will come back. He wouldn't leave me here.

If she could survive this, she would hold him again. He would hold her. The Zeke she knew was loyal to a fault. Yet he'd left her alone and vulnerable. It was a difficult thing to reconcile what she believed to be true and what was. After all, she'd tricked him, hadn't she? She'd lied to him. He believed she was something, someone she was not. It was her job to lie. She was good at it. Too good.

There was a fine line between love and hate. While she'd never anticipated loving him, she hadn't, until now, considered the possibility of hating him. But she had and she did. The emotions teetered back and forth. She wanted to hate him, for her love of him to unravel. But a single thread held that love in place. It was confusing and overwhelming. That made her hate him even more.

The ripe odor of her own stench overwhelmed her senses, and the throbbing pain of her wounds focused her raw emotions into a razor point. She stared into the darkness, seeing only a clear image of his face. She wanted to scream.

CHAPTER EIGHT

Commander Guilfoyle stood on the steps of the Fascio, staring up at the three bodies hanging there as a warning to those who might try to undermine his authority in the city. His hands were behind his back, his chin high, as he stood when inspecting his Marines before sending them off to fight the infidels or patrol the city's perimeter.

The dead man to the left, the slender one, was in the worst shape. Even though he'd been there the fewest number of days, the birds had gotten to him. There must have been something tasty about the frayed flesh at his midsection. He looked like what farmers had once called scarecrows, back when there was such a thing as farmers.

A black crow sat atop the corpse's hanging head. It checked the sky for competition and flapped its broad wings before returning to its task of picking at his scalp.

Guilfoyle didn't know the man's name or his story. He only knew what his Marines had told him. The dead man had been among the greasy criminals known as bootleggers. They hustled goods, mostly water, for the Aquatic Collective. The Tic.

The funny thing about the Tic was that it was the worst kept secret in the city. Really, it was a scourge across the entire protectorate of what used to be the continental United States. From the northeastern provinces to the far west, the Tic had developed into a shadow government running parallel to the true power of the Overseers.

Although the Tic did its dirty work in plain sight, it was smart enough about its business to avoid direct confrontation with the Overseers' outward authority. Occasional payments to some of the more powerful Overseers didn't hurt either. They were smart, they were politically astute, and they were brutal.

While Guilfoyle would like nothing better than to stamp out the Tic, he understood the water cartel's reach was far too vast to entirely undo all at once. Truth be told, they were two sides of the same coin. Both used fear and violence to consolidate their power, their wealth, and their control. Whether or not he liked to admit it, he held an uneasy respect for the faceless nouveau cosa nostra.

As long as the Overseers had their thumb on the vast majority of surviving people after the old world ended, Guilfoyle's superiors were content to pick away at the Tic-like scabs. Eventually, they might weaken them enough to destroy them. Of much bigger concern to Guilfoyle and his superiors were the whispered rumors of a growing resistance amongst the regular people.

Those were the ones who were most dangerous. If the rumors were true, they posed a far bigger threat to the existing hierarchy than the Tic, which needed the Overseers to survive. The resistance wouldn't be interested in bribery or oppressive violence to achieve its goals. They would be less predictable. And despite the primal desire for power, Guilfoyle understood that freedom and self-determination were far greater motivators than anything else.

Guilfoyle pushed the worrisome thought of an unproven

rumor from his mind and relished the sight above him. As long as he reminded his citizenry of his power, trapping rats and hoisting them up for display, all was well.

He whistled at the bird, which stopped its business and cocked its head at him. In that moment of distraction, a larger bird swooped in and claimed dominance. It took the perch atop the bootlegger's scalp, shooing away the smaller bird with a squawk and peck.

Guilfoyle commended the larger fowl. It did what was necessary. It took what it wanted. It did not apologize for its position in the order of things.

He marched the final distance from the steps to the grand entrance of the Fascio. A pair of Marines met him at the large metal doors and swung them open, standing at attention as he passed them without acknowledgment. He crossed the threshold, and a wave of cool air met him in the large ornate lobby.

Two more Marines stood at the base of a large marble staircase in the space's center. They looked forward, unmoved by their approaching commander. They saluted only when he passed them on his way up the stairs, his boots clacking on the polished stone. He moved to the right of the wide steps and used the polished brass handrail to guide himself.

When he reached the top, Theo awaited him. The aide bowed his head. "Commander," he said, "they're waiting for you."

"As they should," said Guilfoyle, turning left and marching the first steps along a wide corridor that led to the executive wing of the tower.

"I took the liberty of pouring your coffee, sir," said Theo, following at the same brisk pace as his charge. "It should be at the perfect temperature by the time we arrive."

"Excellent," said Guilfoyle. He strode with purpose along the hallway until he reached its end. Then he stood, awaiting Theo.

"Let me get that for you, sir," said the assistant, rushing ahead to grab the brass knob and twist.

Theo shouldered open the door and stood back so the commander might enter the space first. This was the council room. Guilfoyle's top lieutenants all sat quietly in their seats. At the head of a long glass table sat a single cup and saucer. From the cup, fingers of steam rose and twisted until they evaporated into the cool air in the cabinet room. Theo stood at the back of the room, watching and listening silently.

The man was good at watching, at disappearing into the fabric of a room. He somehow found the imbalance in any space and corrected it with his presence. He had a sixth sense about him.

It was amazing to Guilfoyle how skilled Theo was at so many things. Theo brought a balance to the business of governance. He was the one who always read the room, knew exactly what to say and do. Guilfoyle knew his servant to be a powerful man whose gentility belied his strength. There were moments where the commander even thought he could see an ethereal glow surround Theo, a halo of energy.

Guilfoyle thought the man could have been one of his lieutenants. He'd even spoken of it once as he sipped on a faux Beaujolais. He'd savored the sweetness on his tongue and then toasted the servant.

"I'm not interested in power," Theo had said. "I'm interested in serving those who wield it."

Guilfoyle hadn't quite understood the man. How could anyone align themselves with those in power without he himself seeking it in some way. Everyone wants power. Good or evil, benevolent or narcissistic, everyone wants to hold sway. It's human nature, Guilfoyle was convinced.

But he hadn't argued with Theo. He'd let the man stand there in his tailored gray suit, his starched white collar, his sparkling cufflinks, and pretend to be happy as a facilitator.

He'd toasted the servant and congratulated him on the choice of wine.

"I didn't know the Saône River still existed," Guilfoyle had said of the winding waterway that ran along the Beaujolais vineyards and provided the grapes with their supple and fruity flavors.

"It doesn't," Theo had said. "This is a skilled imitation."

"The balance is perfect." Guilfoyle had toasted again.

Theo had said nothing. He'd smiled, his pinched eyes almost disappearing beneath his plucked brows.

Presently, Guilfoyle lowered his coffee cup to the table and spun it so that its handle was perpendicular to him and aimed at Catherine. He ran his tongue across his teeth and placed his hands flat on the glass. It seemed all six of the lieutenants were holding their collective breath.

"Good morning," the commander said to the assembled. "We've a cool front today. I took advantage of it and walked the street this morning."

Guilfoyle sat in the high-back wooden chair at the head of the long conference table. While all the others sat in ergonomic ceramic chairs set on casters, Guilfoyle's seat was an ornately cut oak armchair with blood-red velvet on the seat, along the back, and on the wide arms. It was more of a throne than a chair.

There were six lieutenants at the table, three on each side of the thick glass slab that served as the centerpiece of their meetings. The one to his right was Catherine.

She wore a pinstriped black pantsuit, white shirt, and silver tie. The tie was knotted in a double Windsor. Her white hair was pulled tight into a bun and gave her face a permanently surprised expression. She scowled at the commander.

"That was a stupid thing to do, William," she said. "We've had an increasing number of riotous events. The tunnel is there for a reason."

The other five lowered their chins, looking at their laps. It was obvious none of them wanted to make eye contact with the commander or Catherine. Theo, who stood at the commander's shoulder and behind his throne, stared out the large wall-sized window that overlooked the brown city. Dust hung in the air and clung to the glass's exterior, exaggerating the depth of the monochromatic cast.

Catherine's eyes widened and darted around the room. She settled on Theo. "What? I'm only saying what everyone else is thinking. The Tic is up to something. We can't be too careful."

Guilfoyle, who still hadn't acknowledged her, picked up his coffee and blew the steam from it. He took a sip. "The temperature is perfect, Theo. Well done, as always."

"Thank you, Commander," Theo said. "I hope it's balanced for everyone in the room."

"Catherine," Guilfoyle said, eyeing her without turning his head, "I have always appreciated your candor. Where others feign loyalty, you are true. Where others seek to appease, you seek to advise. I appreciate you."

Catherine's stretched face forced a smile. She dipped her head.

"If what you say about the rioting is indeed true," he added, "I am best to take all precautions. I'll be sure to return home via the tunnel."

He took another long sip of the coffee. It was deliciously bitter. This was the blend from Ethiopia, or whatever that far-flung place was called this week. War-torn as it was, exporting coffee was a feat. It was worth it, whatever the price. He let the aftertaste sit on his tongue, leaching into his cheeks.

Catherine, his most trusted advisor, always sat to his right. Next to her was Frederick. Gustav sat at the end. On the other side of the table, Archibald sat to the commander's immediate left, Joseph in the middle, and Louis opposite Gustav.

"Shall we begin the business of the day?" asked Guilfoyle.

"Catherine, you begin, since you seem to have some intelligence regarding the unfortunate escalation of mayhem on our streets."

Catherine straightened her back. She was, as the top lieutenant, Guilfoyle's link to the other five. She handled the day-to-day operation of the city-state. While Guilfoyle made the decisions, Catherine provided the basis.

"Yes, Commander," she said. "I'll begin with the disorder at our distribution facilities. It appears as though the disruptions are coordinated."

"How so?" asked Guilfoyle.

"The timing. We reviewed video surveillance of the disruptions at seven different watering stations. On all the clips, it's clear the time stamp is the same."

"Is this your work, Frederick?" asked Guilfoyle.

Frederick was in charge of the vast surveillance network, which comprised signal and human intelligence. He had spies everywhere.

"My people," he answered, his focus flitting between Catherine and Guilfoyle. "They discovered the consistency in timing. Overlays of the video also revealed similar types of disruptions. At the same time, two men shove each other, complaining the other stole a place in line. The dialogue is similar. The actions are identical."

"Let me see it," said Guilfoyle.

Frederick tapped a device on his wrist. It was known simply as a Com. A holographic, three-dimensional image appeared, hovering above the center of the table. A queue of men and women stood in front of a watering station. The line stretched beyond the length of the display, which was clear enough that Guilfoyle saw the smudges of grime on the men's faces as they turned to confront one another.

"Hey," said one, shoving the other's shoulder. *"You can't cut in line. All these people have been waiting their turns."*

The one in front squared his body and clenched his fists. His neck tensed and his jaw tightened. He was larger than the antagonist. *"Not so,"* he said. *"In fact, I've been here the whole time and I haven't seen you. You're the one cutting in line."*

He shoved back; then the two men shouted as they grappled with each other. Neither of them threw punches. Within thirty seconds, TMF guards were on the men and separating them. One of them took the butt of an M27 to the nose. He collapsed to his knees and grabbed at his face, blood leaking through his cupped hands. The men were pulled from the line. When they were gone, the others in the queue promptly filled the gap. In another thirty seconds it was as though nothing had happened, save the splatter of blood droplets on the ground.

"Here's another one," said Frederick. He tapped his wrist, and the holographic image changed. "We believe an uprising is imminent, Commander. It could happen at any moment. This is not a hyperbole."

Two men stood in another watering station line. Again, they argued over who had cheated their way into the queue. They were separated and subdued within thirty seconds.

Frederick shared two more examples of similar activity before Guilfoyle told him he'd seen enough. Frederick tapped his wrist, and the holograph disappeared.

"They fight," said Guilfoyle, "they're removed from the line; they get nothing from it. What's the purpose? Archibald?"

Guilfoyle motioned to the lieutenant in charge of the TMF, the Tactical Marine Force. Archibald was the top military strategist in the city-state, the protectorate's general.

He wore the scars of many battles on his hardened face. His gray hair was cut high and tight, razor shaved above his ears on his bronzed face. Deep crevices ran parallel across his broad forehead. His jawline was pronounced, muscular even, and his large nose bore the irregular curves of having been broken at least once.

Although his knuckles were swollen, bearing the hints of arthritis, the man was spry. His attitude belied his apparent age and mileage. His voice was soft, measured, and self-assured.

"It's a classic maneuver, Commander," he said, his fingers laced together in front of him on the table. His thick eyebrows, wiry and unkempt, danced as he spoke. They appeared independent of everything else on his face.

"They're testing our response," said Archibald. "They're probing. This is a precursor to something bigger. Maybe the Tic is trying to take control of legitimate supply routes? Maybe the Badlanders are seeking to infiltrate. There's always a threat to our security, sir. It never ends. What this particular game might be, we don't know."

Guilfoyle picked up the no longer steaming cup of coffee and drew it to his mouth. He sipped from the cup twice and returned it to the table.

"Probing," he said, testing the word, seeing how it fit. "Probing. A precursory probe."

"Yes, sir," said Archibald. "We're confident in that assessment. It is absolutely no coincidence that multiple altercations, of a similar nature, occurred simultaneously and with no obvious purpose. They never harmed each other despite the animosity displayed. Their only injuries were at the capable hands of our Marines. The men lost their water rations for the day. They're tagged in the system. The only possible gain here is to learn how we'd respond."

"I'm not so sure I buy that assessment," said Louis. He was the lieutenant in charge of water rationing. He controlled the flow to the protectorates' watering stations and was one of two logisticians on Guilfoyle's council. Joseph was the other.

Frederick bristled, his jaw set, his eyebrows melding into one.

"Why is that?" asked Guilfoyle.

"We have skirmishes like this all the time," Louis said. "As

I'm certain Catherine, Frederick, and the good Lieutenant Archibald can attest, this thing is nothing new. Archibald just now said there are always threats."

Louis waved his hand. The man, younger than the others on the council by two decades, had a head covered in thick curly black hair. He was stout, more flabby than firm, liked to hear himself talk, and was the son of Guilfoyle's older sister. When his mother had died, she'd bequeathed him the seat on the council, and Guilfoyle hadn't objected.

"Yes," continued Louis, "there is the matter of the timing. I'll grant it's suspicious. That's as far as I'm willing to go, however. To suggest there is some organized movement testing our defenses is laughable."

Louis chuckled and adjusted the tight-fitting shirt he wore atop his girth. The weighty purple fabric stretched at his arms and across his chest.

Archibald eyed the others at the table, avoiding Louis, and sniffed.

"Your thoughts?" Guilfoyle prompted, sensing the TMF leader's desire to respond.

"Sir," said Archibald, "with whatever respect is due Lieutenant Louis, I disagree with him. There are always threats to power. However feeble they may be, we must remain vigilant. Vigilant against the enemy who commits its treason out in the open, flaunts it with our tacit approval."

"The Tic," said Catherine.

"Yes," said Archibald, pointing a gnarled finger at the window across from him and behind the three lieutenants facing him. "As such, what's laughable is that we might sit here and deny there are forces out there not actively trying to undo what we've so painstakingly built and maintained."

"You think this is the Tic?" asked Catherine. "This wouldn't fit their style, would it? As you said, they prefer to hide in plain sight."

There was no response. The room fell quiet.

Then Gustav spoke up. "Then who is it?"

The lieutenant had remained quiet until then. He was in charge of infrastructure and engineering. He'd designed the Fascio and the Torquemada towers. He'd overseen the reconstruction of the city's thoroughfares, sewer system, and electric grid. He was a small man with no hair and thick black-rimmed glasses. Although he typically only spoke when addressed, Guilfoyle knew the man's mind was a machine that never shut off. He was always observing, calculating, and solving for "x."

All attention turned to Gustav. He shrugged and pushed his glasses up his thin nose.

Guilfoyle smiled at the engineer. "Excellent question," he said. "If, in fact, there is a coordinated effort to test our defenses, and it's not the Tic, then who is it?"

"We don't know," Archibald said after clearing his throat. "But Frederick and I need more resources."

The room erupted into a chaos of conversation. The other five lieutenants dove into their own theories, agreeing with or refuting the one posited by the TMF's chief. They pounded their fists and gesticulated wildly. All of them fought for Guilfoyle's attention and for the floor.

Guilfoyle allowed the volume to rise for close to a minute then raised his hands, showing his palms to the assembled. One at a time they appeared to see the signal and quieted. All except for Louis, who was didactic in his assertion that the military and surveillance arm of the Overseer government was paranoid. They sought to consolidate power for themselves by inventing a threat to which they must respond with additional resources and attention.

Guilfoyle motioned to Archibald. "Why do you need more resources?"

"Frederick has a spy," Archibald said. "That spy is missing."

"Missing?" Louis sneered.

Frederick cleared his throat. "Yes," he said. "We don't know where she is at the moment."

"She?" asked Louis. "The spy is a *woman*?"

Catherine leaned into the table, her eyes blazing. "Why is that a problem?"

Louis rolled his eyes. "It's not, except that she's missing. They don't know where she is."

Guilfoyle slammed his fist onto the table. It appeared to startle all his lieutenants. His cup rattled and almost tipped.

"Enough of the bickering," he said. "We are on the same team. We are one. Act like it."

Louis tucked his double chin and apologized to his uncle. Had he been able to genuflect in his seat, it seemed he would have done that. Catherine said nothing. The others pulled nervously at their collars.

"Continue," Guilfoyle addressed Frederick.

"Our asset is loyal," said Frederick. "She has been in the system since childhood. We have had her undercover, with the Tic, for some time now."

"Frederick assures me she has provided invaluable information up to this point," said Archibald. He nodded when he spoke, evidently hoping this would accentuate their confidence in the spy. Even if she wasn't technically a TMF asset, Archibald and Frederick were often joined at the hip strategically. Guilfoyle knew this about him. He wasn't, however, sure of their confidence.

He considered they were saying it aloud to convince themselves as much as the rest of the council. Guilfoyle said nothing, though. He let them continue uninterrupted.

"We've searched her home," said Archibald. "She shared the place with a Tic bootlegger."

Louis laughed. It was a condescending laugh that bordered on a cackle. "A bootlegger?" he asked. "All of these years undercover and the best you could do was attach her to a bootlegger?"

Guilfoyle shot Louis a narrow gaze that told his nephew to be quiet. "It's irrelevant," he said to the room. "What matters is why she has disappeared."

"We think they made her," said Frederick. "The bootlegger made a run for it the night before she vanished. As Archibald said, we searched her place. There was evidence of a struggle. We don't think she went willingly."

"Could it be staged?" asked Catherine. "Did she turn? Did she leave with the bootlegger?"

Frederick shook his head. "No," he said. "That is to say, no, she didn't leave with him. My troops have no reports or sightings. Frederick's surveillance corroborates that assessment."

"But she might have turned?" asked Gustav. "How long was she undercover?"

Archibald and Frederick nodded at each other after a brief pause. Frederick lowered his eyes and stared at the table. He sucked in a deep breath and exhaled.

"It's possible," Frederick said, lifting his eyes. "We don't know. She's been under a while. We can say she's been providing valuable intelligence as recently as a week ago. So we don't think she's flipped. But there's no telling, honestly."

"And you're suggesting that if she did turn," said Guilfoyle, "we need to be concerned about what else might happen. What the Tic will know about how we operate?"

"Or that they somehow retaliate," said Archibald. "The spying was a violation of our, well, unspoken agreement to let the other operate without interference."

Archibald shot Frederick a glare that told Guilfoyle they weren't necessarily of the same mind on this. There was a division.

"And we worry this might not only affect our protectorate,

but the others," said Frederick. "Maybe the Badlanders get involved. They're always looking for a fight."

Archibald pulled back his uniform sleeve and pressed the device on his wrist. He tapped it and then swiped until a new three-dimensional hologram appeared above the center of the glass table. This image was not video, however. It was a map.

Archibald began. "This gives reference for all the thirteen protectorates, or city-states, that exist in—"

"We know what it is," Louis snarked.

Guilfoyle shot Louis a look that shut him up. He sank back against his ergonomic seat with a huff. The man was a child, Guilfoyle knew. He had no choice though; the man-child was blood.

"Separating all the existing protectorates are the Badlands," Archibald went on. "You'll see the areas where we believe Badlanders have large encampments."

"You mean the unwashed?" Louis asked.

"I mean Badlanders," Archibald said. "The ungoverned tribes who roam the Badlands."

"The unwashed," Louis repeated.

"Let him speak," said Catherine.

"Yes, please," Frederick chimed in. "Let the man finish, Louis."

Louis folded his stubby arms across his flabby chest, the purple fabric stretching and bunching in unflattering places.

Archibald tapped his Com, and clusters of colors highlighted circles in various spots within what he'd identified as the Badlands.

"We know the Badlanders stay to themselves," he said. "They prey on those who threaten their vague territory by encroaching on their lands. They attack without question. But..."

Archibald manipulated the image to show clusters of color surrounding some of the other, smaller protectorates on the map. "We have seen instances, as modeled here," he said, "of the Badlanders creating barriers around some of our more moderately sized brethren. We have intelligence that tells us they were working with someone. I'll ask Frederick to relay that information."

Now Frederick was the one at center stage. The head of surveillance leaned forward on the table with his elbows.

"Our communication with other protectorates is, at best, spotty," Frederick began. "As you all know, our relationships with them are shaky. Up and down. So our intelligence about what happened in these instances you see modeled before you does include some guesswork."

"Then what good is it?" asked Louis, his mouth curled into a frown.

Frederick glanced at Louis but ignored his question. "Our guesswork is based on years of experience with such things. I've had my best people working on this. Archibald has as well. Our reconnaissance teams are among the best."

"We know this to be true," said Guilfoyle. "I have every confidence in you."

"We've seen the Badlanders providing passage for the Tic in ways they haven't before," said Frederick. "They're not as aggressive as they've been. And we've seen this around several of the protectorates."

"It could be the Tic is paying them," said Archibald. "That is a real possibility. It may mean nothing more."

"A bribe," said Catherine.

"Sort of," said Frederick. "Maybe. We don't know. This may be a red herring. But we do think it's cause for greater resources. We need more men, more weaponry, more vehicles. Even if all of this is nothing, it can't hurt. Remember, the Badlanders are anarchists who refused to join the safety of the protectorates when the Dearth took hold. They're nomadic tribes who can move anywhere at any time."

Guilfoyle shifted in his seat, the wood creaking at its joints, and looked past the lieutenants to his right to the view beyond the dust-caked window.

This protectorate was all he'd ever known. He'd risen to power, grabbed it from those who didn't deserve it, and held steady the city-state's course toward a more productive future. The people had enough food. They had enough water. There was no gluttony among the citizenry, there was equanimity. His was an egalitarian state wherein all were equal. Some were more equal than others, as the great psychic philosopher Orwell had once written. But that was the way of the world. His world.

He blinked from his momentary reverie and directed his attention to Frederick. Before he could say anything, Catherine spoke.

"How much more?" she asked. As the right hand, she controlled the purse strings. She knew the budget, its constraints, and where it could be stretched.

"Double," Frederick said without hesitating.

"Same," said Archibald. "At least until we have a firm grasp on how all of these facets fit together."

Louis pushed his chair back from the table. Its rollers squeaked on the marble floor, and he stood. He tugged at the tail of his purple shirt, pulling it beneath the cinched waist-band of his pants. Then he leaned onto the table with his fists. He banged on the glass with each sentence, punctuating his obvious lack of patience for the topic.

"We've known for years the Badlanders have aided and abetted the Tic. This is not news. It's not intelligence. It's two lieutenants in league with one another to broaden their own power and consolidate valuable resources in their direction."

He leveled his gaze across the table at Frederick, held it, then aimed his stare at Archibald to his right. Chairs creaked in the uncomfortable silence. A strong gust of wind pushed at the large window.

Red-faced, Louis straightened and wiped the front of his blouse. He exhaled loudly, and his tight expression eased. He lowered himself back to his chair. The red diffused to pink. "I think I've said my piece."

"I think you have," said Guilfoyle. "And I appreciate your passion, your conviction on this matter. I also appreciate the potential threat from this undercurrent of disobedience, be it random, organized, or both."

Guilfoyle thought his nephew might vomit right there at the table. He'd seen Louis puke before. The man wasn't known for his self-control. He was a glutton and a drunk. However, there was a brilliant man underneath the clear self-loathing. His mother had taught him well, and his masterful control over water, the Overseers' most valuable commodity, mitigated his petulance. There was a method to his madness Guilfoyle did not question.

He was honestly surprised that Louis was as good a lieutenant as he'd become. Guilfoyle knew his sister had never much cared for him. She didn't want to be a mother in the first place. The protectorate was her child first and foremost. Louis was an afterthought.

Guilfoyle raised a hand in anticipation of Louis's response. "Now, Louis, before you go off all half-cocked again, understand that this is exploratory in nature," he said. "It's a temporary expenditure."

Catherine nodded. "Temporary," she said. "I can assure you it will not affect the administration of any other lieutenant's responsibilities."

Louis reddened again, but he held his tongue.

Guilfoyle let his nephew seethe. There was no harm in that. For all the bluster and commotion Louis might employ to prove a point, none of it meant anything.

Guilfoyle was the one who flew above it all and saw the big picture from high above everyone else. He was the one who sheltered the protectorate underneath his broad wings. He was the one in control of what did or did not happen. His nephew knew that. His council knew it. And anyone who dared challenge him would find out the hard way just how tight a grip he held.

CHAPTER NINE

Arms of dust rose like brown smoke to the left of the highway ahead. The dust moved, expanded, like it was pouring from a locomotive. Zeke tightened his grip on the wheel. It was the first sign of life he'd seen in the hours they'd been caravanning across the broad expanse of lifeless terrain.

"See that?" he asked Uriel. "Somebody's coming."

She sat up in her seat, thumbing the harness from her shoulders. She looked through the windshield, past the truck in front, and toward the plumes of dust. "Badlanders," she said. "We must have reached the Badlands. This will get nasty. Those sons of futher muckers don't play. They shoot first and never ask questions."

Zeke stole a sideways glance at her. He hadn't heard the last half of her reply. "Reached the Badlands? I thought that's where we were."

"That is where we are," she said. "We're in the Badlands. If we're going to get to the city, we need to get past these pains in my expertly sculpted ass."

"Seriously," said Zeke. "Where *were* we?"

Zeke only left the city on his bootlegging runs. There were

prescribed routes. He ran them again and again. So much of what lie beyond the city's walls was foreign to him.

Uriel ran her hands along the sides of her head and then checked her ponytail. She pulled down the visor in front of her and checked the clipped, aftermarket mirror. She puckered her lips, stretched her eyes wide. Was she…primping?

"When?" she asked.

"Before we were here," said Zeke, exhaling with frustration. "Before we were in the Badlands, where was that?"

She flipped up the visor, unbuckled her harness, and cranked down her window. She said something to him, but the blowing wind drowned out her voice, swirling dust into the cabin. Her pompadour of hair waved wildly atop her head, and the ponytail whipped over her shoulder.

She stretched her body and pushed her torso through the open window, craning around the front of the car to get a better look at the coming storm. Zeke caught a glimpse of the flaming sword and sun tattoo rising from her hip.

She sank back into her seat and then leaned into Zeke, using his shoulder to maneuver her head and arms to the back seat. She rummaged around, unzipping and zipping, grunting, and hauling herself back into the front passenger seat. She returned holding a large black rifle. She pulled out the curving magazine, checked it, and slapped it back into the bottom of the weapon.

"What are you doing?" Zeke asked above the roar of the wind, his attention mostly on the road.

"Don't slow down," she answered. "Maintain your speed."

He pulled the bandana up over his nose and mouth to keep out the thickening dust cloud that had filled the Superbird's interior. A Badlander vehicle approached through the dust. Armed people filled its bed. More vehicles filled in behind the truck, obscured by the endless dust. They were all headed straight for one another.

Zeke held the distance behind Phil's F-150. He was sweating now, his breath hot underneath the black cotton covering half his face. He blinked past the dust and powered the Superbird forward, as he had so many times before.

Another truck turned onto the highway and sped toward them. There were at least four of them now. Zeke guessed they were less than two miles away and closing. At this speed, they'd meet in less than a minute.

Uriel aimed the rifle out the window, her hair whipping into her face. "When I tell you," she said, straining to talk above the wind and road noise, "pull to the right and then move even with Phil and Gabe."

"I'll be off the road," Zeke said.

"I know what I'm asking, just do it."

Zeke eyed the rabbit's foot swinging from the ignition and nodded. He could do it.

"When Phil stops," she said, "you stop."

Zeke leaned forward, his body pressed against the harness, and stepped on the gas to keep pace with Phil.

They were close enough now to the approaching Badlander caravan, but he couldn't make them out. There was too much dust, too much noise, too much everything to focus on anything other than the impending command from Uriel and the control of his car.

He did know these weren't the same people, or things, who had chased him to Pedro's Cantina at the start of this journey. They didn't look the same. They didn't move with the same grave intensity.

Uriel leaned out the window again, wrapping one of the harness straps around a leg, and looked back to Zeke, yelling something at him. He couldn't hear her. It wasn't necessary.

He accelerated, pressing the gas. The Superbird responded instantly, jolting forward with a roar as Zeke eased the wheel to the right. The beast jolted, bouncing, as it exited the blacktop for the dirt.

The rear tires drifted and Zeke steered into the skid then straightened the wheel. The F-150 was ahead and to his left now. He applied more pressure to the accelerator. The sensation of acceleration forced him back into his seat. The Superbird effortlessly surged forward. Its engine hummed, sending a low vibration through the car's body that Zeke felt in his own.

The car was even with the truck now. Zeke held his speed. His heart raced, the adrenaline coursing through him like jolts of electricity. His hat bounced on his head, nearly flying off.

Uriel was perched on the window, her legs and feet inside the car, the upper half of her body outside. She had the rifle pressed to her shoulder. Her eye lowered to its scope.

From the corner of Zeke's eye, he saw a muzzle flash. Another. Then a third.

Uriel slid back into the car. The harness tangled around her.

The second she dropped into her seat, a flash of movement caught Zeke's attention from the driver's side mirror.

He held his attention there, watching a Badlander truck tumbling over itself, rotating in the air. Bodies flew from the bed, some of them crushed, blood exploding from them like popped zits. A second vehicle skidded sideways, a blown tire flopping against the blacktop before it too tumbled over itself.

Zeke winced.

"Keep going," Uriel said, waving him on with her right hand. "Speed up."

The car surged again, acknowledging the push. He cleared the F-150 and saw Gabe in the passenger's seat, holding a rifle similar to Uriel's.

"What now?" Zeke asked.

He felt the pop of rocks and low brush under the tires. The suspension responded, but the ride had become increasingly rough. His jaw chattering, he adjusted his grip on the steering wheel.

Uriel braced herself. Her right elbow was on the bottom of the window opening, her hand gripping the outside of the top of the door. The rifle was in her lap. Her left hand held it in place. Her body bounced with the car's momentum.

"Stay on the dirt," she said. "Punch it, Zeke. Show me what you got."

Zeke planted his bootheel and pressed the pedal to the floor. The RPM gauge slammed to the right, and the Superbird zipped. The ride roughened on the uneven terrain. Zeke was sure he would break a tooth.

To his left zoomed the caravan of Badlanders. Three, four, five trucks in various states of repair rumbled in the opposite direction.

"Let the guys handle them," said Uriel. "We have bigger fish to fry."

He didn't know what she meant. Straight ahead was a clear road, a clean shot to the city as far as he could tell. Then he saw it.

Through the haze of dust that obscured the road ahead like a brown fog was a roadblock. Two jacked-up, oversized SUVs were parked perpendicular to the road. One blocked each lane. He couldn't see if there were people there from so far.

"Go around them," Uriel directed.

Zeke scanned the road ahead. It didn't seem like much of a roadblock if he drove around it. That wouldn't make sense.

As he drew closer, he saw the roadblock was staged on a bridge. If he didn't make his way back onto the road and fast, he'd bury the car in a ten-foot-wide dry gulch. It stretched as far as he saw in either direction. There was no going around it.

He looked to the SUVs again. There was nobody standing outside them or perched on the roofs, ready to take aim with high-powered weapons. He saw only one lone driver in each vehicle, sitting behind the wheels.

He checked his mirrors. A smile crept onto his face.

Without saying anything to Uriel, Zeke jerked the wheel to the left, his body straining against the right side of the harness. Uriel hurled a string of guttural curses at him as she braced herself against the space between the door and her seat. Her leg was still tangled in the harness.

The car leapt onto the blacktop. It bounced as the rear suspension compressed and expanded. Zeke leaned right, turning the wheel into the drift to straighten the car. Then he punched the gas.

Rubber squealed, then bit the road. They were roughly one hundred and fifty yards from the blockade and closing.

"What are you doing?" Uriel asked.

"Trust me," said Zeke. "Strap in."

Seventy-five yards.

While Uriel fumbled with the harness and untangled her leg from it, Zeke drilled his gaze onto the driver of the Badlander SUV to the right. The man was staring back.

Uriel snapped her harness in place. "You're going to slam into him. There's no—"

Zeke checked his mirrors. "I said trust me."

Thirty yards.

Zeke grinned maniacally. He stepped on the gas, leaned into the wheel. He was headed straight for the center of the SUV on the right.

The driver cranked the SUV into gear and lurched forward, but there wasn't enough time to avoid a collision.

Twenty feet from impact, Zeke took his foot off the gas and downshifted. The Superbird jerked, throwing them forward against their harnesses, and the engine whined as the RPMs slowed to match the lower gear. A blur zipped past them on their left and straight into the would-be roadblock.

Phil's F-150, with its reinforced cattle catcher stretched across its grille, exploded past the center line and into the idling SUVs. The deafening sound of metal on metal crashed above the rumble of the Superbird's engine. The SUVs gave way. The one on the right spun off the road and tumbled down into the dry bed.

Zeke accelerated and shifted, his car regaining momentum as they blew past the remains of the SUVs.

"I peed a little," said Uriel. "I hate you."

Zeke chuckled and shifted into fourth gear. They'd cleared the roadblock, but there were several Badlander vehicles chasing them. Raf and Barach's Impala was behind him now, the F-150 twenty yards ahead.

"You're funny," he said.

In his rearview, Zeke saw a flash of orange light. One of the SUVs was in flames, thick black pillows of smoke pouring from the burning vehicle. Its previous occupant fled.

Uriel punched his shoulder, refocusing him. He winced and grabbed his arm.

"I'm not kidding," she said. "I seriously wet my pants."

"I'm sorry," Zeke apologized. "There are napkins in the glove box."

"Napkins?" She snorted. "Really?"

Zeke shrugged and checked his mirrors. He reached up with one hand to adjust the brim of his hat and realized it wasn't on his head.

"It's in the back," Uriel said. "I should have sat on it."

They were fast approaching the jagged, scarred face of a sheer wall of rock that stretched into the sky as the face of a large bluff. Cut into the wall was a wide tunnel that swallowed the highway in its black mouth.

"The city's on the other side of the tunnel," said Uriel. She shifted around in her seat, tugging at her crotch. "Stay with Phil."

Zeke glanced at her and arched an eyebrow. "You really pissed yourself?"

Uriel glared at him. The scowl on her face, the one that told him another punch was building in her fist, answered his question.

Behind him, a pair of Jeeps pulled alongside the Impala, sandwiching it between them. Then one of the Jeeps zipped ahead and jerked right, putting itself between the Impala and the tunnel; at the same time a third vehicle took its place on the Impala's driver's side.

Zeke's car was close to the tunnel now. In a few seconds, they'd dip into the darkness underneath the granite bluff and be that much closer to the city.

In the rearview, the Jeep shrank in size, slipping farther behind. It was slowing down to trap the Impala.

Ahead, the F-150 vanished into the tunnel so that only its taillights were visible. And then they weren't.

Zeke downshifted, applied the emergency brake, and swung the wheel. The car spun, its tires squealing against the highway. White smoke spilled from the wheels, and the smell of burning rubber filled the cabin.

"What the—?" Uriel braced herself against the doorframe.

Zeke straightened the wheel and the tires caught. He engaged the clutch and sped up. He sped back toward the Impala and the Badlanders chasing it.

"Not a good idea," said Uriel, catching on to Zeke's plan. "They can take care of themselves."

The Jeep stopped. Armed Badlanders draped in black exited the vehicle, taking aim at the Impala and forcing it to turn back into the path of the other vehicle. "I'm telling you," said Uriel, "don't do this. Raf and Barach know what they're doing. They've done this sort of thing before. Trust them. Trust *me*."

Zeke gulped against the sting of bile in his throat. "There's no way they'll escape all of them. It's suicide. Both of them will die."

Zeke's vision blurred from the gloss of welling tears. He wiped his brow with the back of his sleeve. The car engine rumbled around him. He felt it in his chest.

Uriel punched him again in the shoulder. She hit the same spot, knuckle on bone, and the bruise refreshed its ache.

"Focus," she said.

Zeke rubbed the soreness in his arm and stared at Uriel. He studied the sour look on her face, not understanding what she meant. He gestured towards the disaster.

"But they—"

"Turn around," she said. "Let's go before the Badlanders lose interest in them and circle back to catch us."

Zeke bit his lip, drew a long breath, then finally threw the car into reverse. He spun the wheel and shifted into gear. He accelerated toward the tunnel again.

It's their choice, he told himself. *This is on them.*

The echoing rattle of gunfire behind them caused his stomach to roil. He shifted, eased off the clutch, and the car lurched into another gear. The engine rumbled. His throat seized and he coughed.

"You have a lot to learn," Uriel remarked.

She seemed unfazed, sitting back in her seat, settling her shoulders between the bolsters that cocooned her body. She really was tough to read. No emotion played on her face. It was as if their lives, or their deaths, didn't matter. He'd seen enough death in his time as a bootlegger and beyond the city walls to maintain his composure, but he'd never seen anyone so hard in the face of who he thought were her friends dying.

The tunnel grew larger as they approached, and he turned on the headlights when they crossed the threshold. Uriel's window was down. The sound of the engine reverberated off the rock walls that arched in a canopy over the highway. The air in the cabin chilled. The V-shaped spray of the headlights revealed little beyond their reach. It was as if they'd sped into oblivion.

"How long is the tunnel?" he asked above the mechanical whoosh of wind and engine noise.

"I don't know. Never measured it."

Zeke gripped the wheel tighter. He focused on the yellow beams of light illuminating the Superbird's path, and rubbed his sore arm. She sure could punch.

"You don't ever answer my questions. You either respond with a question of your own or you deflect," he said. "Come to think of it, none of you do. What the hell was I thinking going with you all?"

Really, what was I thinking? He'd seen people play both sides before, and he didn't know them. In his world, there was no shortage of cheats and liars. Everyone was out for number one. A world with limited resources did that. An oppressive government did that. A black market run by the modern version of the mob did that.

Uriel rolled up her window, cranking it one heavy revolution at a time. The mechanism creaked like it needed grease.

"Maybe it's not my answers that are the problem," she said. "Maybe you don't ask the right questions."

Zeke felt the road vibrate through his body. It was a comforting sensation, the rumble that shook him. It was like white noise at bedtime or the warmth of bathwater.

"Tell me about Pedro," he said. "Who is he? How'd you all meet him? I want to know his story."

"How about you tell me yours?" she countered. "Then I'll tell you ours."

Zeke sighed. Another deflection. He drove for a few seconds without responding. The darkness was like a blanket around them. There was no light beyond the headlamps in front of them and, behind them, only the faint red glow of the taillights.

"How about we swap stories?" he suggested. "I'll tell you something about myself; then you tell me something about all of you."

"All of us?"

"Yeah," said Zeke. "Pedro, you, Raf, Barach, Phil, Gabe."

Uriel sat in her cocoon for a moment without answering. The warbling rumble of the racing tires on the highway filled the silence.

"All right," she said, a hint of resignation in her voice. "You start. But it'd better be good. None of this 'my mama didn't love me' sappy crap, got it?"

"Okay," said Zeke. "But she didn't."

Uriel groaned. He could imagine her eye roll in the dark. "Of course not."

"It's true. I mean, sorta. She probably loved me in her own way, but she was never around. Neither was my dad. I don't remember him at all. She used to call him the sperm donor."

"Poor Zekie," she said.

His muscles tensed and he tightened his grip on the steering wheel.

Zeke wasn't one to open up, thinking it a sign of weakness. While Uriel's derision was cause enough for him to end the game right then and there, he wanted to know about the people who were sacrificing themselves for his, or someone else's, benefit. He had to understand why. So he let the tsunami of anger wash over him, taking several deep breaths.

"I don't want your pity," he said. "I'm just telling you who I am and where I came from. To understand how I ended up in this endless tunnel, in the dark, with you and the putrid stink of your piss staining the seat of my car, I have to start at the beginning. But if you don't want to hear it—"

"No," she said, cutting him off. "I do. Sorry. Go ahead."

"Your turn," he said.

"I never lived in the city," said Uriel.

Zeke glanced at her. He could make out her figure in the dark. The faint glow from the dashboard was lost in the black of her clothing and the deep colors of her tattooed skin.

"Which city?" asked Zeke, assuming this was her first revelation.

"Any of them. Your turn."

"The first person who gave me any attention was a bootlegger for the Tic," he said. "I was a lookout."

"That's how you got involved?"

"That was the start of it. I was a lookout for a few years. The bootlegger taught me how to drive. Then he gave me a car."

She reached out and rubbed the dashboard. "This one?"

"Yes. Your turn."

"I showed up on Pedro's doorstep like you did. He took me in, and I've been there ever since."

"How long ago was that?" asked Zeke.

"Don't remember. It feels like a lifetime ago. I don't even think I'm the same person now that I was back then."

"How so?"

She ran her hand across her pompadour. Zeke could only see the outline of movements. He couldn't tell her brow was furrowed, her eyes glossy. But when she spoke, her shaky voice gave away the rush of emotion she was trying to deny.

"I was," she said. "I was less of an ass back then. I'll leave it at that."

Zeke chuckled, trying to lighten the weight of the conversation. He stole a glance at her. "Less? Wow. I can only imagine."

"Ha ha," she said. "Your turn."

"I never planned on being a bad guy. It just happened."

"Nobody ever plans on it," Uriel said, sounding as though she spoke from experience.

"I mean to say, I didn't feel like I fit in. I wasn't running goods because I was against the Overseers or because I liked the money."

"But you liked the money?"

"Yeah," he admitted. "I liked the money. But I did it because the Tic accepted me. They treated me like family. They gave me purpose. So what was I going to do? Turn my back on the only people who ever invested in me? Nope."

"Then how did you end up here on their most wanted list?"

"Nope, your turn," he said. "Who were you running from when you ended up at the bar at the end of the world?"

"That's funny," she said without laughing. "I'd never thought of Pedro's like that, but it's a dead-on description."

"Thanks. Who were you running from?"

"Myself. My life wasn't good. I had trouble coping."

"Sorry."

"What for?" she asked. "You had nothing to do with it."

"That's not what I meant."

"Your turn."

"I'm giving you more than you're giving me," he said.

"Fine," she said. "I was a dealer."

"Of what?"

"Drugs. Mid-level. All synthetics."

"Oh, okay."

Uriel took off the harness and leaned toward the window. "That's judgey."

"No, it's not."

"Sounds like it."

"Sounds like you're putting your own issues on me," said Zeke. "I am...I *was* a bootlegger for a violent cartel that takes advantage of people's needs for the most important resource on our planet after the rivers dried up. Who am I to judge anyone?"

"You're not."

"Which is why I'm not judging."

"Yeah, well…your turn," she grumbled.

An involuntary shudder ran along his spine. He realized he was cold. His fingers were icy. He reached for the heater and cranked it on.

His stomach tightened. There was an elephant in the car they hadn't addressed properly.

"Tell me about Raf," he said.

"He's a healer. Superb at first aid. He's the one who fixed you up. Anybody shows up at Pedro's in bad shape, Raf is the one to handle it."

"*Was* the one," corrected Zeke. "There's no way he and Barach are getting out of that. No way."

"I prefer to be an optimist," she said. "We don't know what happened back there. They could have made it."

"If you think that, we should have gone back like I tried to."

"We couldn't go back," she said, leaving no room for debate. "We have to keep moving. Your mission is the important thing here."

Zeke slammed his hand on the wheel. "You're acting like two men I thought were your friends didn't just sacrifice themselves for us back there. What's wrong with you?"

"Nothing is wrong with me, Zeke," she said. "Like I said, I prefer to think that when I walk into the cantina again, both of them will be there waiting for me."

Zeke didn't know what to say to that. He couldn't keep arguing with her. It wouldn't do any good. She was obviously hardened to violence in a way he couldn't conceive, despite his own rough upbringing.

After letting the silence between them grow comfortable, he swallowed hard and glanced at her. He shrugged when he spoke. "Where'd he come from?"

"Who?"

"Raf."

"Same as anybody, I guess."

"Where's that?"

"Elsewhere."

"He had a scar on his face," he said. "How'd he get it?"

"Helping someone. A mission like this. Crossed the divide and into the tunnel. Came out the other side and tried to right wrongs. I don't know which time. There are too many to count."

"The divide?" he asked. "What's the divide?"

"It is what it is," Uriel replied. "It's the space between where we came from and where we're headed."

"You mean the Badlands," he said.

His hands were getting sweaty now. He reached over and turned down the heat, leaving it on but dampening the force of the air.

Uriel shook her head. "I mean the divide. It's not the Badlands. It's not anywhere. It's nowhere."

Zeke sighed, exasperated. "You should have been an Overseer."

"Why's that?"

"You're awesome at doublespeak. You say stuff without saying anything."

"Your turn," she said.

Zeke wanted to explode. He wanted to tell her he'd had it with the vague responses and nonanswers, but he reasoned, in that same moment of frustration, that there would be no point to it. The answers would come eventually, and fighting with his only ally wouldn't serve him well.

If there was one thing Zeke had always managed to do well other than drive, and until the point he screwed himself with the Tic, it was knowing when he should fight a battle and when he should let it march by without raising arms.

"Tell me about Pedro," he said. "*Then* it's my turn."

"He's Pedro. He runs a bar and boardinghouse. He provides shelter from the storm."

"Okay," he said, "but who is he? What is he?"

"Pedro is the guardian at the gate," she said. "He watches over all of us, over everyone who wanders into his place. He keeps the peace. He pours the drinks. He answers the questions and…"

"He didn't answer my questions," said Zeke.

She shrugged. "Like I said, it could be that you keep asking the wrong questions. Or the questions you ask don't have answers. At least not yet."

"See," said Zeke, "that's the vague sort of crap that makes me not trust any of you."

"That sounds like a you problem," she said. "Like you're putting your issues on me."

He didn't have anything to say to that. The car was warm now. He lowered the heat.

"Your turn," she said. "How did you end up on the Tic's bad side?"

"A woman," Zeke said.

"*The* woman? The one you later abandoned and are now hoping to find and rescue against all odds with the help of strangers?"

"That one," he said.

"So what happened?"

"Long story."

"We've got time."

Zeke shook his head. "No, we don't," he said and pointed beyond the dash. "We're at the end of the tunnel."

The speck of white light grew larger until it was the shape of the tunnel's walls and curved ceiling. It was virtually blinding by the time the tunnel spit the Plymouth from its mouth and the car zoomed ahead on the stretch of highway that led straight toward the shapes of a distant skyline. Two large buildings stood above the rest. They were framed against a low-hanging orange sun that appeared enormous against the edges of the horizon.

"Are we heading west now?" he asked. "Or east? I'm all off about the time. I don't know whether it's sunrise or sunset."

"Beats me," Uriel said. "I haven't thought about time in...a long time. The days bleed together, you know?"

"I guess."

His heartbeat pounded against his chest, his breathing shallow now. He was sweating and his neck was damp. So was his forehead. He turned off the heat.

Up ahead in the distance was his city. In that city was the woman he loved. So were the people who wanted him dead. He was anxious and apprehensive at the same time. It was a nervous, adrenaline-fueled excitement he felt at the start of every water run. He knew there was risk and there was reward out there. He hoped one was worth the other.

Uriel pointed to the side of the road. Up ahead was the F-150, parked and idling. Its brake lights were on and its tailpipe vibrated, coughing wisps of exhaust.

"Pull over," she directed.

Zeke slowed the Plymouth, downshifted, and eased along-side the truck. Phil sat behind the wheel. Gabe leaned forward in the passenger's seat, and Uriel cranked down her window.

Phil pinched the bridge of his nose.

"You saw what happened?" asked Uriel.

Phil scratched his beard, raking his fingers through the wiry tangle of hair. Then he adjusted his gray bowler hat, took it from his head, and lowered his chin.

"Yes," said Phil, his voice shaky. "I saw. I'll be buying the next round for them when I see them again."

Zeke studied Phil, then Uriel. It was like they shared a mutual denial of their friends' likely fate. Maybe it was a coping mechanism, learned from living in the Badlands, where loss was rampant. They pushed it from their conscious minds so they could focus on the mission. Only later would they deal with what happened. That had to be it. It was too weird otherwise.

"Puts us at a disadvantage," said Phil.

"It does," said Uriel. "What's the plan now?"

Gabe leaned over and spoke over the low rumble of the idling engines. "We know there are guards at the gates."

"TMF," said Zeke. "I know their posts. I've got ways around them."

"TMF?" Phil asked.

"Tactical Marine Force."

"You know where they're holding your woman?" asked Phil.

"*The* woman," Uriel corrected, a finger pointed at Phil. "Not his woman."

Phil smirked and winked at Uriel. "The woman. You know where to find her?"

"I think so," said Zeke. "The Tic has two places where they like to interrogate traitors or the occasional hostage."

"So we're dealing with two entities here," clarified Gabe. The veins in his neck strained against his skin. His ironlike jaw was mechanical in its formation of words.

"Yes," said Zeke. "The Overseers, which controls the TMF, and the Tic."

He realized they didn't know who, or what, it was they were up against. How could they not know? In what world, under what rock, had they been living?

Gabe motioned toward the road ahead. "All right. Lead the way, hero. You know where we're going."

Uriel offered the men a sarcastic salute and rolled up her window.

"Sheesh," she said, grunting as she cranked up the glass. "I'm gonna get arms like Gabe if I have to keep doing this."

"Strap in," Zeke told her and he put the car into gear.

———

The car hit its cruising speed, and within minutes, Zeke was in familiar territory. He checked his side view and saw the F-150 right behind him. In the distance beyond was the flat plain of barren land to which he'd become accustomed when smuggling water between protectorates or to drop-off points in the Badlands. The bluff, which must have been more of a mountain range given the length of the tunnel, was gone. There was only the low-lying dusty scape that stretched as far as he saw, speckled with the silvery outcroppings of dead trees, which stood as testaments to what was lost.

Zeke pushed the oddity from his mind, compartmentalizing it as he had so many of the irregularities he'd cataloged since arriving at Pedro's Cantina. He didn't have time to contemplate what all of it meant or might mean. He had to reach Li.

He momentarily took his eyes off the road and reached back to find his hat. He gripped the crown, his fingers grabbing the dents on either side, and set the Stetson on his head. He adjusted the brim with one hand, shifting it up and down a couple of times until it felt right, and put his hand back on the wheel.

He pressed the toe of his boot and the Plymouth zipped forward.

"You all good?" he asked Uriel, who squeezed her armrest.

"Yep," she said. She picked up the rifle from the floorboard and set it in her lap. "All good."

He eyed the weapon. "Where'd you get that?"

"Pedro."

117

"They look a lot like the guns the TMF uses," he said. "M27s, I think."

She shrugged. "All I know is they shoot bullets."

"You won't need it. Not yet."

He sank back into his seat. A half mile ahead was a large iron gate. A wall stretched in both directions on either side of it. Beyond the gate and the wall was the city.

The sun beamed in Zeke's eyes. He couldn't make out whether the TMF guards were at their posts. He assumed they were. He hit his turn signal, waited a beat, and then veered off the road. He checked his mirror and saw the F-150 following him onto the flat, dry terrain. The shocks absorbed most of the ruddy, packed clay underneath the tires, but the ride was rougher than it had been on the highway.

"Won't they see our dust cloud?" Uriel asked. "It's not like we waited for the cover of night."

"They see us," said Zeke.

"Isn't that a problem?"

The Plymouth hit a rut and bounced. Zeke corrected course, easily handling the Superbird as it dusted across the expanse, now running parallel to the gates.

"Not a problem," he said. "They expect to see Tics out here, Badlanders. They're watching, but they won't do anything."

The car hit another bump. The engine whined. Zeke and Uriel lifted out of their seats. The harnesses kept them from hitting their heads on the roof of the muscle car. They dropped back down when the tires hit the dirt with a crunch. The suspension sagged and expanded.

"There's a Tic tunnel up here about a mile or so," Zeke said. "We should be able to access that no problem. It'll take us under the walls and put us in the city."

"You're okay using a Tic tunnel?" she said. "Aren't they hunting you?"

"Nobody guards it. You have to know where it is. And it's only accessed when there are water runs. Those happen at night. Whether it's sunrise or sunset, doesn't matter as long as there's daylight. Plus the Tic pays off the TMF guards. They won't care what we do."

They bounded along to the spring of the suspension and growl of the engine without speaking. Zeke was focused on the task at hand. His eyes danced across the car's gauges and then scanned the expanse ahead. There was nothing in their path.

Until there was.

A large TMF troop transport emerged from the city gates, a plume of brown smoke trailing it. It was the kind of vehicle that carried four or six Marines. It was unmistakable even at a distance. Its blocky, straight-angled exterior and its beige camouflage paint gave it away.

"He's trying to cut us off," Zeke said under his breath. He cursed and pounded his fist onto the wheel. "The Tic must have tipped them off. Or maybe those Badlanders. They knew we were coming."

Uriel picked up the rifle. "I thought you said—"

"I know what I said," Zeke snapped. "We'll beat him there."

"So I guess the TMF knows where your secret little tunnel is?" she said as she loosened the straps at her shoulder one at a time. "And the payoff didn't work?"

Ignoring her, Zeke checked the RPMs. He didn't like the feel of the boot on the gas. He was used to his cheap, thread-bare sneakers. He could feel the road in those.

Still, the Superbird responded and the speedometer inched to the right. Ninety-seven, ninety-eight, ninety-nine, one hundred miles per hour.

"C'mon, baby," he coaxed the Plymouth. "C'mon."

He was a good mile from the tunnel access. He checked to the right. The TMF transport burned a trail across the terrain.

The large earth-moving tires raced across the desert without resistance.

"We're not going to make it," said Uriel. "How far do we have to go?"

Zeke checked his rearview. The F-150 was falling behind. He looked right. Now there were two TMF carriers. The second hadn't been visible in the dust trail of the first, and now took a different angle, going for the truck.

"Far," he said.

Uriel checked the rifle's magazine and slapped it back into place. Then she leaned over and cranked down the window.

Zeke pulled the handkerchief over his nose and mouth with one hand while steering with the other. He lowered the brim of his hat and squinted. Swirls of dust swam through the cabin.

"This is not good," she said. "Not good at all."

Uriel leveled the rifle and lowered her eye to the scope, using the door ledge to balance the barrel. The uneven terrain hammered it up and down.

"Can you keep steady?" she asked.

"I'm trying." Zeke held the wheel tight, feeling it respond to his touch and the earth underneath the car. He focused on the path ahead. They were getting close.

Up ahead were many clusters of dead trees. The gray trunks reached skyward, their branches extended and praying for rain that never came.

The area represented what Zeke was told had once been a swamp. It wasn't anything now other than a petrified, wooden testament to the barren wasteland the world had become thanks to the Dearth.

Zeke identified the cluster that hid the tunnel's entry and aimed for it. To his right, he saw the first armored transport. It blazed to intercept them before they could dip underground and escape.

His speedometer read one hundred seven. The engine was

maxed. He couldn't push it any harder or he'd risk blowing the engine. It roared and grumbled against the dirt.

"Hold your course," said Uriel. "Hold it. Hold it."

A percussive series of pops pierced the air. The rifle snapped back. Flashes of light strobed from its muzzle.

"Damn it," said Uriel. "I missed."

She lowered her head again, shifting the barrel of the rifle to the right. She was twisted in her harness, half-facing the open window.

Another series of loud pops cut through the air. Tendrils of smoke drifted from the rifle's muzzle back into the Superbird's front seat and danced with the dust twirling inside the cabin.

"Got it!" Uriel said excitedly.

Zeke checked and saw the transport's rear driver's side tire smoking. She'd punctured its thick, rubbery shell with an impossibly accurate shot. But the transport kept moving undeterred.

"They've got twin tires on the rear axle," said Zeke.

Uriel glared back at him. "You could have told me that," she spat.

"I didn't know you were aiming for the tires."

The car hit a divot, sank with a loud, bone-jarring thud, and then bounced into the air. Uriel lost her handle on the M27. It hit the top of the open window frame before falling through and skittering across the dead terrain.

Uriel cursed, using words Zeke didn't know women ever said. In the rearview mirror, he saw the rifle disappear in the wake of brown dust spraying from the back of the Plymouth.

Ahead, Zeke and the lead transport were on a collision course, aiming for the same spot. He didn't see any way to avoid it.

"What do we do now?" he asked.

Uriel checked the side-view mirror and then the transport. She punched the dashboard and cursed again. Her face was crimson. A thick purple vein strained underneath her skin, resembling part of a tattoo.

"Let me drive," she said.

"What?"

"Let me drive," she repeated.

"I can't."

"Well, either you let me drive, or you multitask."

"You're making no sense."

"I don't have a gun, Zeke. And it's not like mine was doing the trick anyhow."

Zeke tensed as they hit another rut. He felt it in his neck and shoulders and back. "So?"

"You have that revolver Pedro gave you?"

"It's under the seat."

"Can you drive and shoot at the same time?" she asked.

"Huh?"

"Don't be a moron. Stop answering my questions with questions. That's what I do. It's lame when you do it. Can. You. Drive. And. Shoot. At. The. Same. Time?"

"I guess. I don't know how accurate I can be though."

"You don't have to be accurate, as long as you can point the thing and pull the trigger."

They were closing in on the transport and the tunnel. There wasn't much time left, and it was obvious he wouldn't beat them.

"Why don't you do it?" Zeke reached between his legs, trying hard to keep his head up, and fished the weighty six-shooter from underneath the seat. He held it in his left hand. It was cold. He reached across his body to hand Uriel the weapon. She waved him off and inched her body into the space between the door and the seat bolster.

"No, Pedro gave that to you," she said. "I'm not allowed to use it."

"Why not?" he said.

"No more questions," she said, exasperated. "Fire at them, dude!"

There were fifty yards at most from the transport, close enough now that through the open passenger window, Zeke saw the driver's attention shifting between his own path and Zeke's.

Two armed Marines in the back had their M27s pointed at the Superbird.

Uriel leaned back and covered her ears. "Fire!" she yelled. "Do it now. Now!"

Zeke switched hands, the wheel in his left, the gun in his right. He lifted it, struggling against its unseemly weight. He leveled it, taking aim at the driver. He was yards away from the tunnel's entrance. The transport was closer still.

"Do it!"

Zeke shifted his aim toward the engine compartment at the front of the transport and put his finger on the cool trigger.

"Do it!"

He applied pressure and fired. Zeke expected the solid crack of a six-shooter; the spring throwing the hammer forward and into the primer, the primer exploding and igniting the propellant, forcing the bullet along the barrel. That wasn't what happened.

Instead of the *crack*, the weapon emitted a low, vibrating tone that sounded like a warbling hum. The weapon kicked up, its barrel lifting and Zeke's grip jerking back toward him. His bicep tightened. His forearm tensed.

The *whoomp* of the gun sent a shock wave into the ether. The air outside the Plymouth bent and warped like water around a tossed stone. Wave upon wave shot outward, expanding as they moved concentrically toward their target.

The Plymouth reacted as the laws of physics would dictate. It shot sideways, pulling Zeke toward Uriel and crushing her into the space at the door. Then the trunk drifted, spinning the front of the car to the left.

Despite the immediate vertigo, Zeke saw the effect of his shot. The waves of energy slammed into the transport, knocking it sideways and carrying it in its field until the truck slapped into a pair of thick tree trunks. Its windows were shattered. Its driver's side looked like a tin can crushed in a drinker's hand. All the men inside appeared unconscious.

Zeke managed to slam on the brakes of the Plymouth. The car shuddered before the engine hammered to a stall. They came to a stop twenty feet from the tunnel's entrance.

"What was that?" Zeke asked, breathless. His body trembled. His healing shoulder ached.

He held the weapon in hand, mesmerized by its cold steel. The cylinder glowed electric blue for several seconds before fading back to the stainless, reflective surface common to less effective revolvers.

Uriel uncupped her ears and blinked. She stretched her mouth wide, trying to pop her ears. "What?"

Zeke held up the revolver. "What is this?"

Before she could answer, the rumble of approaching vehicles caught Zeke's attention. He sat up and saw the second transport. It was closing in on them and about to intercept the F-150.

Without hesitating, or understanding what it was he was doing, Zeke unfastened his harness and opened his door. He shouldered his way out of the Superbird and stepped onto the dry ground. He rested his elbows over the roof of the car. The heat from the dark metal seeped through his shirt, burning his skin. He ignored it and gripped the weapon tightly, this time ready for the kick.

Zeke took aim at the other transport. Without urging from Uriel, he braced himself, clenched his jaw, and pulled the trigger.

The *whoomp* vibrated through his hands and the weapon kicked. He was ready for it this time.

Translucent waves of air pulsed outward, growing in size until they hit the front of the transport. They stopped the truck in its tracks, shoving it backward two feet before upending it. Its rear flipped forward and its nose pointed into the dirt. Then it crashed onto its side.

Zeke, despite his preparation, was no match for the equal and opposite force of the weapon. He was blasted backward into his car's door, crashing into its frame and falling to the ground in a heap.

Disoriented, he lay on the ground for a moment, not remembering how he'd gotten there. He was on his side, his back to the car, the grit of dirt pressed into his cheek. The smell of earth and sand filled his nostrils. From underneath the open door, he saw the thick, stubborn trunks of the trees to his left. They were gray with veins of brown and tan, like someone had peeled their skins.

And he saw the entrance to the tunnel, marked by a pair of stumps hardened into cylindrical boulders cemented into the ground. His head pulsed at the temples. He was staring at the petrified stumps when he heard the shuffling of dirt underfoot, and a pair of boots moved into frame, dominating his field of view.

"You okay?"

He tried to speak, but it came out as a muffled groan.

"You don't sound okay," Uriel said.

He leaned back against the frame of the car, the open door between them, and looked up at her. She had her hands on her hips.

Zeke cleared his throat. "I'm okay," he said, and realized the weapon was still in his right hand. He'd somehow kept hold.

"Good. Let's get going, then."

Zeke blinked the fog from his brain and picked up his hat. He set it on his head and stood. Behind him, the F-150 grumbled. He pivoted, resting against the roof of the Superbird, and saw Phil behind the wheel.

He and Gabe offered twin thumbs-up and nods of approval.

Zeke offered a wave with the gun in his hand. The smiles vanished from their faces and they shook their heads in unison. Both were fixated on the gun.

Zeke lowered it to his side and waved an apology with his free hand. Uriel had walked back around to the passenger's side. She stood at the open door.

"Nice shots," she said, leaning over the hood. "I guess you can multitask. Good to know."

Zeke slid back into the driver's seat, fitting in between the bolsters. He put the gun underneath the seat where he'd kept it for much of their road trip. Uriel climbed back into her seat. They sat there for a moment before she shrugged.

"What is it?" she asked.

"What is that thing?" he asked her. "Where did it come from?"

"Pedro. And it's a pulse gun. Or more accurately, a modified pulsed energy weapon."

"That's fictional stuff," said Zeke. "Like Jules Verne or Gene Roddenberry. That's not real."

"Two things," she said, holding up two fingers. "It's real. You saw it. Twice. And I don't know who Julie Verne or Jeannie Raspberry are."

"They wrote science fiction before Earth, well...died. You've never heard of them?"

She shook her head. "Nope. Don't know who those women are."

"They're men."

"Even less interested. We can talk comic books later. We have a tunnel to traverse before those dudes wake up."

He looked past her at the pair of crushed transport vehicles beyond her open window. The driver in the first transport was moving.

"They're alive?" he asked. A smile broadened across his face. He needed to get to Li, but he was a smuggler, not a killer. It hurt and he touched his jaw. He must have hit it when the ray gun knocked him backward.

"Yep," she said, "and it won't be long before they're angrier than red ants. Let's go."

Zeke started the car. It resisted for a second; then the engine turned over with a comforting rumble. He put it into gear and maneuvered to the hole in the ground that led into the single-lane, unlit tunnel, which would lead them smack-dab into the heart of the city.

CHAPTER TEN

Brina walked past the Torquemada, her arms full of the day's rations. She'd stood in line for a good four hours between the two queues. She was an enforcer with the Tic and had access to whatever she wanted, but appearances were important. Her mentor had taught her that all those years ago. He was gone now, but his lessons survived.

The streets were busy. Word had gotten out that engineered wheat flour was available, but in short supply. It was a commodity almost as rare as water, though not as valuable, as it wasn't life-giving. Still, a baked treat just couldn't be passed up. Life was hard enough.

Brina had scored a half bag of the flour. Along with her jug of water and a pound of the chemically produced enviro-pork, she'd be stocked for a good long while. She liked the sensation of feeling jealous eyes on her as she moved through and amongst the throngs of hungry, thirsty people. Some of them had water, some had the engineered pig, and a couple had the flour. Very few had all three.

She passed the Fascio government building. She shifted the weight of her wares in her bulky arms and gazed upon the rotting corpses hanging above the wide stone steps leading up to the grand entrance. It was hard to make out who the people had been. She tried to imagine what their appearances had been before the birds and heat had gotten to them.

Her eyes studied them until she was satisfied she knew them all. They'd been part of the Tic, but they'd gotten sloppy. They'd earned what they'd gotten. If the Overseers hadn't ended them, the job might have fallen to her, which would have meant less time for baking. She adjusted her packages and started her march again.

Crowds and the winding station queues that snaked into the streets slowed her trek back to the compound. She did make a point of slowing her march as she passed the stations. She listened to the Marines posted at each one, hoping for gossip, actionable intelligence, something that might give her superiors an advantage or opening.

There was always much to be gained by listening to the Marine guards. Few people understood this better than Brina. Water was like platinum to the protectorates. That was undisputed. But information was virtually priceless.

Her mentor, the man who'd saved her from a life of starvation and vagrancy, had taught her that too. Thinking about him, she clenched her jaw. Her teeth ground together as she worked through the swell of anger rushing through her body. She focused on the task ahead and reminded herself of the lessons he'd imparted.

Like water, information flowed in all directions. It surged, forged its own path, and shook things loose from their foundations. Brina twisted her way past the last of the watering stations and landed in a narrow alley, which fed to a back street offering the only entrance to the compound where she plied her violent trade.

She set her wares on the ground in front of her and pulled a set of special keys from her waist pocket, then slid one into the hole at the center of the door. She twisted it until it clicked, and turned the large patina brass knob, pushing inward. The door swung loudly on its hinges. They needed oil they would not get.

Brina stooped, picked up her belongings, and stepped into the cool darkness of the compound. She shut the door behind her with a swing of her hip. It groaned and clanked shut. She deftly twisted the deadbolt and headed for the kitchen.

She spent the next hour and a half preparing a meal. She cleaned up, wiping the blade of an heirloom knife given to her by her old master, and returned it to her pocket. She put a glass of water and a plate on a metal tray, draped a plain cotton frock over her shoulder, and carried them through the labyrinth of corridors that made up the Tic compound.

Incandescent light bulbs hung from the ceiling along the corridors. They were spaced apart enough for one cast to catch the next, giving the illusion of constant light as one traversed the narrow passageways.

At the end of the maze, Brina found a padlocked door. A glassless window filled with heavy gauge wire mesh sat lower than eye level for her.

She leaned over and then jerked back from the opening and winced. Her face turned sour at the stench seeping from the cell. She sucked in a cleaner breath and held it. Through the dark, she made out the small shape curled into the corner of the cell.

"Adaliah," she said, almost whispering, "are you hungry?"

The woman in the corner shifted. Brina could hear her raspy breathing.

"I have food for you," Brina said. "An enviro-pork biscuit. It's salted. And there's a glass of water. Both are preferable to the dry cereal, yes?"

Li coughed. It was a dry, hacking cough that spread goose-flesh across Brina's arms.

"I also have a dress for you," she said. "You've been without anything to keep you warm, and it's cold here. There's no denying that. How are your wounds?"

Li moved from the corner. She stayed low to the ground, crawling across the floor. She stopped short of the dim cast of boxed light that leaked through the opening.

"Water?" she asked. Her voice was so raspy now, Brina barely recognized it. "Food? Real food?"

Brina lifted the tray to the opening. "Yes. Would you like it?"

"Yes," said Li.

Brina squatted and set the tray on the floor. She slid back a metal bar at the base of the door and opened a pass-through large enough for the tray and its contents, then bundled up the frock and shoved it through. She closed the pass-through and locked the bar.

Li crawled to the tray and grabbed the biscuit. She shoveled it into her mouth and chewed. Crumbs of hard biscuit and flecks of artificial pork spilled from her dry, cracked lips.

"Don't eat it too fast," Brina warned, peering through the opening. "You're bound to get an upset stomach."

This was her good cop to the bad one she'd played days earlier. Her effort to peel back the layers of a ripened fruit. This wasn't kindness. It was calculated ruthlessness.

Li plucked the glass of water and guzzled half as she chewed the biscuit. She slurped and chomped, licking the dampened biscuit paste from the roof of her mouth. She worked it into a clump and chewed it again.

"I know where Ezekiel is," Brina said.

Li stopped chewing, her mouth open. The half-empty glass of water shook in her trembling grip. She lifted her chin, one eye twitching, and met Brina's gaze.

The corners of Brina's mouth curled upward. It wasn't a smile. It was a gloat.

"I know he's here in the city," she said.

The expression on Li's face shifted and morphed. She wiped her mouth with the back of her arm, taking a shaky sip of the water.

Li stood, her body much thinner than when the Tic had taken her from her home. Her ribs pressed against her skin like a wet greyhound's. Dried blood, brown and blotchy, covered her hands and wrists. She wobbled for an instant and steadied herself to step forward and over the tray of food.

She brushed her bangs from her forehead. "How do you know?"

"Overseers," Brina said. "I hear things. See things."

"They told you?"

"Indirectly," said Brina, "in so many words."

Li took another step, her pale skin stretching across her ribs as she moved. Her chest fluttered from her beating heart. "Where is he? Can I see him?"

"I'm not an Overseer," Brina said. "I'm not a Marine or a government worker. But you know that."

Li lowered her chin and looked at the floor. Her fingers balled into fists at her sides.

"You should get dressed," said Brina. "You're liable to catch a cold."

The tension eased from Li's body and she nodded. She bent over to grab the balled-up frock and lost her balance. She collapsed to one knee, then fell onto her side, rattling the tray and the glass.

Brina watched quietly. Li struggled with the dress, unable to unwind it. She tried finding the bottom of it, the armholes, the place for her head. She couldn't. Brina decided the girl was either too weak or too jumbled in her head to figure it out.

The matron glanced over her shoulder at the dimly lit corridor and then reached into her waist pocket. She fished out the key ring and found a rusted metal skeleton key that appeared to be the right size for the lock on the cell door.

"I can't watch anymore," said Brina. "Let me help you."

Brina slid the key into the lock and turned. It didn't budge. She tried another and then a third until the mechanism clicked and she was able to slide open the door. She heaved it to her left with all her strength, grunting. It scraped along metal tracks in the floor and ceiling and recessed into the wall to Brina's left.

A wave of vile odors washed over Brina as she finished opening the door, a mix of smells that reminded her of childbirth. She covered her face in her elbow sleeve for a moment and stepped into the cell.

Normal precautions would have dictated Li be bound and that an armed guard was present, but Brina thought this girl too weak to be a threat. She was covered in filth, was basically a living skeleton, and couldn't even figure out how to untangle a simple dress.

Brina sucked in a breath from the crook of her arm and knelt to help Li with her clothing. The girl inched backward, recoiling in fear.

"I will not hurt you, dear," she said, half-truthful. "I've done what I can do. I'm helping you now. That's what you need."

Brina was squatting, her heels flat on the floor. She picked up the dress and shook it like wet laundry about to hang on a line. Then she ran her hands through the sleeves, turning them right side out.

"Here you go," she said. "Dip your head."

Li eyed her warily for a moment and then did as she was told. She lowered her head and Brina slid the bunched dress over her head.

"Now," said Brina, "one arm at a time. Start with that one."

Li slid her left arm through one hole. Her hand popped out from the bottom of the fabric.

"Now your other one," Brina prompted.

Li slid her right arm through the other hole, twisting her body. Brina held the fabric firm, stretching it to aid the girl, when Li's hand popped through the end of the arm and grabbed the glass of water from the tray.

In a swift motion, she slammed the glass against the side of Brina's head. It shattered against bone and flesh. Bright stars filled Brina's vision. She fell back, dazed and bloodied. Shards of glass protruded from her temple and above her ear.

The dress hiked around her waist, Li jumped on her like a spider monkey. She blindly drummed Brina's face and neck and chest with her tightly balled fists.

Aside from the woozy grunts and moans from Brina as she was pounded into unconsciousness, and the thuds of Li's connecting blows, there was no sound in the cell or the corridor beyond. Nobody coming to help her.

CHAPTER ELEVEN

L i straddled Brina and kicked the woman in the gut with her heel. She pulled the dress down, pressing it flat against her stomach to lessen the wrinkles, and bent over to take Brina by the wrists.

She dragged the woman across the floor, dropping her in the dark corner next to the dead carcasses of three rats whose necks were broken. Li kicked her again. She searched her tormenter's pockets and found a set of keys. She took them and moved toward the open door.

On her way out, she grabbed the rest of the biscuit, picked it clean of glass, and shoved it into her cheek, letting the salty flavor of the fake pig soak into her gums as she exited the cell, closed the heavy door, and locked it.

It wouldn't be long before the woman was conscious again, calling for help. Li needed to find her way out of the dank labyrinth and fast.

Despite her wounds and her weak, malnourished muscles, she moved swiftly from hall to hall. Adrenaline powered her toward freedom. Freedom, she knew, was relative in the protectorate. But anything was better than this.

She turned left and left then right. Everything looked the same. The walls, the floors, the single incandescent bulbs that hung from the ceiling all ran together.

She'd been navigating her way through the maze for ten minutes and was convinced she was retracing her steps when she heard a man's voice. Its baritone carried across the solid surfaces of the compound. Li stopped moving. The man was close enough she could make out his breaths between words, but he was far enough away she couldn't understand what he was saying or to whom he was speaking. She pressed herself flat against a wall in that narrow space where the lights from the bulbs didn't meet.

Hiding there, she clenched the keys in her hand. She picked the longest and widest of the keys and set it beneath and between the knuckles of her right hand's index and middle fingers.

She inched along the wall closer to the voice. She turned another corner and saw a fan of yellow light stretching from an open door only twenty feet ahead of her on the right. He was in there.

One hand sliding against the cool wall, she moved toward the light. The man was clearly talking to someone on a Com device.

In a lithe movement, unencumbered by the loose-fitting frock, she edged her way to the door, squatted, and peeked into the room, into the light.

The man had his back to her, leaning against a table, headphones covering his ears. He held a transceiver in his right hand. A rifle lay on the desk behind him.

Li didn't know his role within the Tic. She didn't recognize him, at least not from behind. His broad, rounded shoulders and thick neck told her the man was an enforcer of some type. The Tic was full of men like that. She'd learned as much from her time with Zeke. She'd also learned the Tic's reach was far greater than anyone outside the organization could know.

Li crept into the room. She checked behind her in the hall. It was quiet. Nobody was coming. The man with the headphones laughed. He leaned back, his free hand flat on the table and his elbow locked. He held the radio in the other.

She crouched behind the opposite side of the table and listened. She waited for him to end the call so whoever he was talking to wouldn't be alarmed. When he said goodbye and stopped the transmission, he turned. That was when she pounced.

Li leapt up onto the table and lunged forward. She grabbed at him, latching onto his torso. She wrapped her legs around him and yanked his head to her chest.

The man staggered back from the momentum and dropped the radio. It clattered to the hard floor. He crashed into the wall and wobbled to one side. The headset twisted on the sides of his face. He groped at her, trying to free himself from her strong hold. She squeezed her thighs at his ribs and forced the air from his lungs.

With one hand she grabbed a handful of his hair, pulling on it. He grunted and tried pulling away. She slammed the other fist into the side of his neck. She pulled back and jammed her fist again. And again.

The key protruding from between her fingers punctured his skin and widened the jagged hole with each successive punch. The man cried out in pain. His voice muffled, he cursed and groaned. He reached for his neck and found her wrist, wrapping a hand around it.

She managed another jab before he stopped her. And it was too late. He lost his balance and fell. Li landed on top of him. One leg was trapped beneath his weight, but she wriggled free. As he lay on the floor, clutching his leaking neck and writhing in pain, she crawled to the radio.

She picked it up. It still worked. Li adjusted the frequency, finding the one she'd been trained to memorize. She took a beat to gather her breath and watched the enforcer slide into unconsciousness. She stood, crossed the room, and shut the door, locking it.

She leaned against it and drew the radio to her mouth. She slid down the door, resting on her heels, and settled herself as calmly as her fading adrenaline would allow. Exhaustion then threatened to overtake her. Her body ached. Her muscles throbbed with acid. Her vision spun.

She was dehydrated, she was weak, but she was the operative into which they'd molded her. This, she reminded herself, was why she'd trained, why she'd studied, why she'd given up years of her life. Everything was in motion now. She pressed the transmit key on the secure sub-channel and kept her voice low.

"Overseer base, this is 29," she said. "Do you copy?"

The reply was immediate. *"29, copy. What is your CP?"*

She repeated the code phrase, the one that defined the meaning of her name, Adaliah.

"Overseer base," she said, her fingers trembling as they held the transmission key, "this is one who draws water, poverty, cloud, death."

There was a pause. *"29, copy. We've activated your retrieval chip. Prepare for extraction."*

She looked at the inside of her wrist. A dim red light smaller than the hole in the enforcer's neck began to strobe. She exhaled, not realizing she'd been holding her breath.

"Overseer base, copy that," she said. "Awaiting extraction."

She dropped the radio to the floor and touched the flashing light in her wrist. Her time spying on the Tic, on behalf of the government, was finally over.

CHAPTER TWELVE

Archibald, the Overseer lieutenant in charge of the Tactical Marine Force, stood with his hands behind his back. His right hand held his left wrist, rubbing his swollen thumb back and forth. The sour look on his face was a mixture of disappointment and disgust. The relief he'd felt as he learned that his missing spy hadn't flipped on them evaporated with new information that made him want to punch something or someone.

His puffy left hand flexed and relaxed, flexed and relaxed. He said nothing as the Marine in front of him, hat in hand, explained the failure to stop and detain the two vehicles, which had escaped and destroyed two of their transports.

Frederick stood next to him with his arms folded across his chest. He too was silent.

The three of them were in Archibald's expansive Fascio office. It was sparsely decorated, save the tapestries that hung on the walls and the large blood-red rug that covered much of the honed, travertine floor. They stood on the rug, at the center of the room. Dust danced in the rays of sunlight that filtered through the shuttered windows.

The Marine wiped his brow with his sleeve and winced from touching the purple and yellow bruising across his forehead. He stared at Archibald's chest, not daring to look the lieutenant in the eyes.

"As I said," the Marine told him in as certain a tone as he could muster, "we had them, sir. We had them dead to rights. Out of nowhere, this—"

"You've already told me," boomed Archibald, breaking from his usual calm. He stopped rubbing his thumb across his hand. He held his hands out in front of his face and wiggled his fingers like he was sprinkling imaginary fairy dust. "Some magical weapon stopped you in your tracks. It crushed our armored transports and injured the entire TMF teams inside them."

The Marine glanced at his feet, squeezing his hat in his hands.

"They've slipped into the city, then?" Archibald pressed.

The Marine lifted his head. "Yes, sir. Through one of the Tic tunnels."

"These were Tic vehicles?"

"Yes," said the Marine. "Both ran on internal combustion engines, we're pretty certain. Telltale Tic."

"Yet the Tic tipped us off to these infiltrators?" asked Archibald, shifting his attention to Frederick. "Do I understand that correctly?"

Frederick nodded. "Partially. There was back-channel chatter that suggested we look for a 1970s Plymouth Superbird. There was no mention of the accompanying pickup truck."

Archibald stepped from the rug and onto the travertine. His footsteps echoed as he moved to his desk. He sat on the edge of it and picked up a glass full of melting ice.

He rubbed his thumb across the condensation and drank the melt, clanging the cubes around in the glass. Then he shook one into his mouth and sucked on it.

With it in his cheek, he spoke to Frederick. "Intelligence like that isn't unusual though." He motioned to his colleague with the glass. "The Tic tips us off all the time. They sacrifice one of their own here or there in exchange for occasional leniency."

"True," Frederick agreed. "They'll fall on the sword now and then; sacrifice the one for the good of the whole, so to speak."

"But we've never seen this *magic* weapon before," said Archibald.

The Marine stared at the rug, shifting his weight in his boots.

Frederick shook his head. He unfolded his arms and stuffed them into his pockets. He followed a swirl of dust moving across a shaft of light in front of his face. "Do you think it was a setup? Maybe they used us?"

"It's possible," said Frederick. "We should know soon."

"How so?"

"One of our operatives is coming in," said Frederick. "A woman we've had with the Tic for a while now. She was deeply embedded in their operations. She's been feeding back valuable intel for months now."

"Who is she?"

"Adaliah Bancroft," Frederick said. "She's a smart one. We recruited her into our ranks, trained her, set her loose."

"Is she the source of the information about the... Plymouth?" asked Archibald. "Was she the one who tipped us?"

Frederick shook his head. "No, she wasn't. I don't know the source of that information."

"Then how will she help us?"

"She'll know if the Tic developed that weapon," said Archibald. "She was intimately involved in their bootlegging operation. If there is some new technology the Tic is using or testing, she likely would have heard rumblings."

"Remind me again how long Adaliah was embedded?" asked Archibald.

"Years."

A smile spread across Archibald's face, deepening the already canyonesque crow's feet at his temples. His irregular nose shifted, accentuating its misshapen appearance. He set down the glass and ran his damp hand across the top of his crew cut.

"You're a sly one, Frederick," he said. "That's why I like you. That's why we work so well together."

"Thank you," said Frederick. "I try. I have to admit though, when she disappeared, my faith was shaken."

Archibald nodded, stood from his desk, and walked around it to the simple wooden chair on the opposite side. He pulled out the chair by its lattice back and sank into it, dragging himself toward the desk by grasping its edge with his hands. He waved the back of his hand at the Marine.

"You're dismissed," he said. "Go get those injuries looked at."

The Marine saluted his lieutenant. He spun on his bootheel, then marched from the room, shutting the large door behind him.

Frederick motioned toward the door. "That was a slip."

Archibald sighed. "Yeah," he admitted. "Truth be told, it wouldn't be the worst thing if rumors of a turncoat spy circulated among the ranks. It'll climb back up to the other lieutenants and only helps to validate our position."

Frederick shrugged. "Maybe. Or we look like we can't control our own assets."

Archibald leaned back, the simple hinges on the chair creaking under his weight. He put his feet up on the desk, crossing his legs at the ankles.

"We need to find these people with these new hi-tech weapons, detain them, and question them," he said. "If they're merely sacrificial Tics, so be it. But I have a feeling there's something bigger at play."

"Why do you say that?" Frederick asked.

"It's just a feeling."

"Tell me more."

Archibald rubbed his chin. "We've been talking about the possibility of a mutiny within our ranks for so long, I'm wondering if maybe the threat is from the outside."

"Outside?" asked Frederick. "How? You mean the Badlanders?"

Archibald shook his head and stared at the floor. He wasn't sure what he meant or how to explain it. It was a gut feeling that something was off. The balance of things had shifted.

"I don't know," he said. "I have a sense that whatever is happening here isn't coming from our own people. There's an outside force working to destabilize us. I can't put a finger on it."

"You're overthinking this," said Frederick. "You're being paranoid. Even for a man whose job is to be paranoid, you're going overboard here. There's no real evidence of anything happening outside the protectorate. Nothing at all."

Archibald grunted. In the ensuing silence, Frederick scanned the large red and black tapestry hanging behind his friend. It was adorned with scenes of horses and eagles. There were angels and, on one patch, a rotting corpse.

Archibald noticed Frederick's attention had shifted, and glanced over his shoulder at the faded images. "You look at those every time you're in here," he said. "You like them?"

"They haunt me," said Frederick. "It's like they judge me."

"Now who's paranoid?" asked Archibald. "Which, by the way, is your job, not mine. You're the one in charge of spies, the master of paranoia."

"First of all," said Frederick, "it's not paranoia if they're really after you. And that's not what I mean," said Frederick. "What I mean is that they speak of a time long ago and one yet to come."

Archibald raised an eyebrow. "That's not at all cryptic for a man who lives under cloak and with dagger."

"They're biblical, right?" asked Frederick. "The horsemen, the eagle…they represent the end of days."

"Yes," Archibald replied, studying Frederick's face. "It's a graphic representation from the New Testament."

Frederick's focus danced across the images. He appeared deep in thought.

"It's called the *Apocalypse Tapestry*," said Archibald. "French. Created for Louis I in the fourteenth century. Amazing that it still exists. Almost as amazing as all those twentieth-century motorcars the Tic keeps running. You'd have thought they'd be rust buckets by now, as I would suspect most wall hangings of that era were long ago burned or tunneled through by moths."

"Louis, huh?"

"The Duke of Anjou."

"Funny you'd have these here," said Frederick, "given they're from a man named Louis."

"Meaning?"

"Our own nemesis seems to be a lieutenant by the same name," said Frederick.

"I'd never thought about that before," said Archibald. "I guess that's how little energy I give to that sycophant."

"He has the commander's ear," said Frederick. "We have to spend energy on him. He's diametrically opposed to us. He's fighting us."

"He's not winning," said Archibald. "We've got our backing. But you're right in that he's got the commander listening to him."

"The tunnels only have so many openings into the city. We've got eyes and ears working for us."

There was a knock at the door.

"Yes?" asked Archibald.

The door creaked open. A young, frail woman stood there. She saluted and asked for permission to enter.

Frederick waved her into the room. "Take a seat."

She crossed the room, her shoulders back and her stride surprisingly confident given her waiflike appearance. She nodded at the men and stopped several feet from them. She stood at attention.

"Thank you, sir," she said. "I'll stand. I've been off my feet for a while."

Frederick motioned to her and said to Archibald, "This is Adaliah."

Archibald studied her. Her hair was pulled back into a ponytail. Her skin was pale, alabaster save for the yellowing at the edges of bruises on her cheeks, neck, and arm.

There was something about her, however, that mesmerized the lieutenant. An intensity of spirit. A defiance in her stance. Like she'd seen things, done things most couldn't or wouldn't.

"Adaliah," Archibald said, "I have questions for you, as does Lieutenant Frederick. May I call you Adaliah? Or would you prefer something more formal?"

"Li," she said.

"Pardon me?"

"Call me Li. Nobody calls me Adaliah anymore."

"Li it is," Archibald said, nodding. "Are you sure you'd rather stand? We have much to learn from you."

She bristled and pulled back her shoulders. She looked straight ahead, avoiding his stare.

"I'm fine. Thank you, sir."

"Let's get to brass tacks," said Frederick, leaning forward at his desk. "We know where your mark is. The bootlegger Ezekiel Watson?"

She winced at the mention of his name. "Yes," she said. "He's in the city, correct?"

Archibald eyed her for a moment, uncertain she knew the current circumstances or the exact whereabouts of the man she'd been assigned to find, seduce, and use. Frederick nodded at him, urging him to answer her.

"Yes," said Archibald. "He's here. What do you know about that?"

"Only that after he disappeared, the Tic told me they'd recovered a note," she said. "It was his handwriting. He wrote that what me and him had together wasn't real."

She brought a hand from behind her back to dab the sheen from the corners of her eyes. Archibald saw the gruesome wounds to her fingers. Her nails were gone.

"Why did he leave?" asked Frederick.

"Long story," Li said.

"We have time," said Frederick. "Why don't you take that seat?"

He motioned to the armchairs opposite Archibald. Finally, she sat. Her knees bumped the desk and she scooted back in the seat.

"He left, I'm pretty sure, because of a man named Mogilevich," she said. "He ran the club where I worked."

"The off-grid Tic club?" said Frederick.

"Yes. Mogilevich was my boss there. He hired me."

"Go on," Archibald urged.

She told the story of the handsy employer who'd gone too far several times. Archibald decided the details of Mogilevich's indiscretions, the unwanted advances, and the bar itself were too specific to be falsified. The stale smell of cigarettes and the foul odor of beer, the scum on the floor and the dim light that hid the faces of the patrons—the filth of the place rang true.

Even for a spy, some things were too difficult to make up out of thin air. Her left hand trembled as she detailed the day that ended his inappropriate behavior. She balled it into a fist on the armrest, apparently aware of the quiver. Archibald saw all of this. He took mental notes.

She described the man as oily. He was average in every way and wore eyeglasses. She said appearances were deceiving. The glasses gave him a studious appearance, made him look vulnerable. According to her, he wasn't.

"There was a woman named Rose," Li said. "She worked the club like me. I'd made it clear to Mogilevich I wasn't interested in him. I wanted to follow the rules, get paid, and go home to my boyfriend. He knew that."

"What were the rules?" asked Archibald.

"Look good, fill orders, keep quiet. See no evil, hear no evil, and speak no evil."

Archibald nodded. A smile flickered and disappeared. "Mizaru, Kikazaru, and Iwazaru," he said.

"The three mystic apes," Frederick said. "I didn't take the Tic for being Japanese scholars."

"I don't think they are," said Li. "I think they have rules, that's it. There's nothing mystic about it."

"Perhaps," said Archibald. "Though I'm one who believes there's a little bit of mysticism in everything. There are things beyond our control that bind us, lead us down our paths whether we choose them or not."

"Continue, Li," said Frederick. "Tell us what happened."

"Mogilevich stopped messing with me after a while. He was never too aggressive, I think because I let him know the deal. Rose didn't. She never laid down any boundaries."

"Boundaries?" asked Frederick.

Li rubbed her palms on the arms of the chair. Perspiration bloomed and evaporated. "Don't get me wrong, I'm not blaming her. He's the—was—the creep. I'm just saying she didn't tell him no. And he kept pushing it further and further. Then he got rough."

"With Rose," said Archibald.

"Yeah."

"What does that have to do with Ezekiel?" asked Archibald.

Li looked past Archibald toward the tapestries on the wall behind him. He knew she wasn't looking at them though, not the way Frederick had. She was somewhere else now. She was in the Tic bar.

"It was the end of the night," she said, her body tense. "We were cleaning up. The bartender, Markus, cut out early. So it was Mogilevich, Rose, and me. I went to the ladies' room. When I came back, he had her pinned down on a table, holding a knife to her throat. She was crying. I grabbed a bottle from the bar and hit him with it. Then it got worse."

"What kind?" asked Archibald.

Li blinked and refocused her attention on him, drawing it from the tapestries. Her brow pinched with confusion. "Of what?" she asked of the non sequitur.

"What kind of liquor was in the bottle?" he clarified. "The bottle you used to hit him."

"Whiskey."

"What brand?"

"Old Crow."

Archibald nodded. He was satisfied with the specificity and haste of her answer. "Go ahead with the story. You hit him with the Old Crow…"

"Yeah," Li went on. "That got him off her, but it made him angry. He turned on me. He told me I had no idea what I was doing, how powerful he was, and how he would use that power to make me miserable. We got into it. I struggled with him. He pinned me against the wall. He had the knife on me and said he would cut out my tongue."

She paused for a moment, her mouth half-open. "I kicked him a couple of times. We were struggling. I held him off, but I was getting tired. The knife was so close to my face. My training could only help me so much."

"Then what?" asked Frederick.

"Rose screamed at the same time Mogilevich's eyes went wide," she said. "His face froze like that. His grip tightened. Then he let go of me and fell to the floor. Zeke stood behind him. His hands were bloody. His face was twisted in this weird way. It was like he was mad and scared all at once."

"He killed Mogilevich?" asked Frederick.

"With the broken neck of the Old Crow bottle," she said. "He'd never killed anyone before. He started to panic."

"Panic how?"

"He knew, we all knew, that we couldn't hide Mogilevich's death for long," she said. "Everybody in the Tic knew him. We had to figure out what to do."

"So he tried to run," said Frederick.

She shook her head. "Not at first. We took care of the body. We acted like nothing happened. I showed up to work. Zeke did his runs. We were good for two weeks."

Li licked her lips. Thin pink lines of blood bloomed along several of the cracks.

"But Markus asked questions," she said. "And Rose, poor Rose, couldn't keep her mouth shut. When they came for her, we knew we'd be next. We talked about leaving together. Zeke wanted to get in the car and drive. He knew people in other protectorates who could help us. They were Tic suppliers who wouldn't rat us out. We could get far enough away that maybe we could escape them."

"But that didn't happen," said Archibald.

Li shook her head. Tears welled in her glossy eyes.

"No," she said softly.

"Because he knew who you are," said Archibald in a tone

that suggested he knew the facts. "He knew you worked for us."

"He didn't," she said firmly. "I told him I couldn't go. I couldn't leave and live a life on the run. He tried to get me to change my mind. I wouldn't. And then he was gone."

There was something tender in the way she spoke about him, a lilt in her voice. The tension in her face softened. Archibald recognized the signs. She'd fallen for the mark. She was in love with him. He wasn't the spymaster Frederick was. He didn't have to be. Her feelings for Ezekiel were as plain as day.

This meant he couldn't be sure of the reliability of whatever she said regarding the bootlegger. Still, she had come back. She didn't run off with the man. If she had tried, she wouldn't have gotten far. Archibald was certain of that.

"So you don't think he found you out?" asked Frederick. He stood next to her with his hands tucked underneath his pits.

She shook her head and sniffed. "No," she said, regaining her composure. "I don't believe so."

"Then what did he mean in his note?" said Archibald, a harsh edge to his voice. "That's decidedly on the nose for someone in the dark."

"I'm not sure," Li said.

"It's also strange, don't you think," said Archibald, his volume increasing as he spoke, "that in the minutes or hours after he left you alone, with a note decrying the truth of your relationship, the Tic appears at your door and takes you? They interrogate you, waterboard you. They take your fingernails, strip you naked and humiliate you, imprison you. Is there more?"

"No, sir."

"Do you understand my skepticism here?"

"Yes, sir."

Archibald leaned back, exhaling. The chair creaked. He

brought his hands to his face, matching his fingers to one another and tapping them together in a triangle at his nose.

"Waterboarding," he said wistfully. "Brilliant if you think about it. Such a precious commodity, yet they'll use it as a tool of frivolity. It speaks to their defiance of the law, don't you think? To their disdain of our society, our protectorate, and what we provide for the people."

"I don't have an opinion about it," said Li. "But I wonder where this is going, and I'm not sure I understand the line of questioning. You know what happened."

Archibald stood from his desk. He walked around it, his fingers trailing on the solid surface, and positioned himself in front of her. She seemed even smaller this close, like a twig. It was surprising to him she'd survived the Tic's treatment at all, let alone arranged extraction.

"There's something about you," he said. He motioned to Frederick. "I trust my friend Frederick. I believe in his judgment. But I don't trust you."

The words dripped like acid, seeming to sting her as he spoke them. She flinched. Her steady, confident gaze faltered. It was the second time he'd noticed it.

Frederick took a step forward, uncrossing his arms. He held up a hand toward his equal. Maybe he sensed the same thing Archibald did. That no matter how much the woman might deny it, she was connected to the bootlegger. If her allegiance to the Overseers, to the protectorate, was wavering, Archibald believed Frederick knew better than to push too hard. At least not now.

"Archibald," Frederick said, "I don't like this. Adaliah has served us well. She's regularly reported Tic activity. We've learned more about their inner workings since she went under than in all the previous years combined. There's nothing not to trust."

Archibald locked his gaze on her. His expression flattened.

"I'm not so sure about that. Regardless of the intelligence she's offered, the Tic functions with impunity."

"I'll prove it to you," Li said. "I'll prove my loyalty to the protectorate and to Commander Guilfoyle."

Frederick took another step forward. He waved her off. "That's unnecessary, Ada—"

"What do you propose?" Archibald cut in.

Frederick interjected again, "Archibald, I—"

The head of the TMF raised his hand. "Let her speak, please."

"She's my asset," said Frederick.

"Then tell her to speak."

Frederick said nothing.

"I can give you Graham," Li said.

"Graham?" Frederick asked. "The head of their intelligence?"

"He's their top enforcer. He knows everything there is to know about the Tic, about you…"

The last two words hung in the dry air between them. They seemed to echo, to repeat themselves with an increasing volume in Archibald's head.

About you. About you. About YOU.

Archibald was close enough to Li to smell the soap she'd used to wash herself. He chuckled. It was a throaty chuckle, the kind meant to tell others he didn't find them funny.

"I'll bite," he said. "How will you do that? We've been trying to take him into custody for years. Neither Frederick nor I have come close. We don't even know what he looks like. How could *you* bring us *him*?"

"I know how they work," she said. "After I got out of their hellhole, they'll be back to find out how. Graham will be there. He could be there now."

"You want to go back to the place where they held you?" asked Frederick. "Now?"

"Give me a team," she said. "We'll go back. We'll take him alive."

"I don't think so," said Frederick. "Not a good idea."

"How many men?" asked Archibald.

Now the tables were turned. Archibald was on her side and Frederick was the one resisting.

"Five? Six? Ten? Whatever you can spare," Li said.

Archibald studied her, then looked up at Frederick. "We were planning a follow-up raid, regardless. We know there's intelligence to gather there."

"We should have done it when we rescued her," said Frederick. "Now we could be stepping into a hornet's nest. We could start a war with the Tic. We don't need that. We should wait."

Archibald stood. He put his hands behind his back and strolled around his desk, his back to the others. He looked at the tapestries, appreciating their colors. They were mostly blue, red, and what had once been white. The silk threads were woven with shades of orange, green, gold, and silver.

"You know," he said, facing the wall, "there were originally ninety scenes in the tapestries. Ninety. It took decades of man-hours to create them."

He tilted his head back to scan the top portion of the twenty-foot-high hangings. He sighed and motioned to them with a wave of his hand. "All these centuries later, they have survived. They have withstood shifts in economy, and environment, and power. They have survived because those before me had the foresight to do what was necessary to save them from destruction. Even as their own empires fell, and they reached their own apocalyptic ends, this masterpiece lived and was reborn into a new home."

He turned on his heels to face Frederick and Li. He touched the sides of his irregular nose with his thumb and forefinger. He ran them up and down the bridge, recalling the moments that had disfigured him and left him hardened.

"I will not be one of those who meet his own end because I did not act," he said, leveling his attention on Frederick. "Commander Guilfoyle has put the TMF in my control. I can use the Marines as I see fit. And I see fit to send them with your little spy. Let her prove herself, Frederick. If she's who you believe her to be, then we've nothing to fear."

CHAPTER THIRTEEN

*Z*eke emerged from the tunnel. His boots crunched on the coarse dirt in the back alley. He'd stepped from the darkness of that tunnel and into the light of day countless times. This was different.

It was early morning, and the sun was rising, warming his cheeks. The bustle of the day had yet to begin.

His apartment building stood one hundred yards away. It looked familiar and foreign to him all at once. He motioned to his comrades, and they all began the march along a dusty street toward the building. This was once a warehouse district. So, unlike much of the city, which had crumbled during the early days of the protectorate before being rebuilt, this part remained what it had been before the planet's water dried up.

The corners of the brick buildings, mostly two and three stories, were chipped or missing pieces. The roofs were patchwork, most of the windows shattered, the curtains blowing in and out.

On the second floor of the building closest to Zeke's, a wrinkled man sat in the window, one leg dangling along the facade. His heel scraped along the brick as he kicked his foot repeatedly like a pendulum. Tendrils of smoke drifted from the cigarette in his hand. Zeke recognized the man as his neighbor, but with his new duds and the handkerchief pulled over half of his face, he was certain the man couldn't know who he was.

Uriel waved at the onlooker. He lifted the cigarette, took a long pull, and it glowed red at the end. He exhaled through his nose, and streams of smoke plumed away from him.

He was like a human gargoyle, sitting watch over those who came close. His eyes, dark and hidden beneath thick, heavy lids, followed them as they passed. He flicked the butt with his thumb, and a shower of ash drifted from his perch.

Zeke stopped in front of his apartment building. He stood in the faded parking space where he'd long kept his Plymouth. His gaze moved to the building itself. The red brick was washed out and covered with dust. Unlike the other buildings, his had glass in the windows.

He motioned with his chin. "Second floor. Up the stairs and to the right."

"You think she's in there?" asked Uriel.

He stared at the windows of what used to be his apartment. The glass was black. It was dark inside the home. No lights. Nothing to give him any sense that Li was there, that the Tic hadn't taken her. Still, he had to check.

Zeke shook his head. "No. But it's the best place to start."

Gabe nudged Zeke with his shoulder. "We gonna face any resistance in there?"

"What do you mean?" asked Zeke.

"The Tic. Maybe they're guarding the place?"

"Not if they think I'm dead," Zeke responded.

"We need to be ready," said Gabe.

He slung his rifle across his back and pulled his black rattan sticks free of the pouch he carried on his side. He clacked them together then spun them in his hands, twirling them among his fingers.

Uriel pulled free the magazine in her M27 and shoved a fresh one into place. Phil removed a weapon from his bag that Zeke didn't recognize.

It was a cylindrical spiked ball attached to a handle by a foot-long chain. The spiked ball looked like hammered steel. The chain was a different metal. The handle was wooden with carved finger grips.

"Where did you get that?" asked Zeke.

"This ole thing?" Phil said. "Pedro gave it to me."

"What is it?"

"It's a flail," said Phil. "But it's not your average medieval weapon. It's got a little more punch."

"Same with your sticks?" Zeke asked Gabe. He'd first seen them when they were packing up to leave Pedro's Cantina.

"They're called Escrimas," said Gabe. He touched the handle of the blade at his waist. "And yes. Same with the knife. Gifts from Pedro, they do special things. These are good for close combat, tight quarters. We don't need to be shooting off automatic rounds inside an apartment building."

Uriel scowled and mocked him by affecting his voice. "We don't need to be shooting off automatic rounds."

Zeke addressed Uriel. "What did you get?"

She shrugged. "I didn't need anything. I'm a woman. I'm special as is."

Zeke smirked. He drew his revolver and adjusted his grip. "Let's go."

He climbed the concrete stairs to a narrow landing at the front door. He turned the handle, pushed with his shoulder, and shoved. The door opened, its hinges responding with high-pitched creaks; then it banged against a doorstop. It rattled but stayed open enough for Zeke to lead his team into the dimly lit and narrow entry vestibule on the first floor.

The walls were yellow-tinged plaster veined with foundation cracks. The ceiling, also plaster, was low. It made the entry feel even smaller than it was. Recessed floodlights cast artificial light into the space, illuminating it enough to offer a dingy hue across the room. The floors were wood planks bearing the scratches and dents of wear and were absent finish or gloss.

He nodded at the trio and moved to the stairs.

Uriel was behind him, carrying her M27 at the ready with the muzzle pointed down. Gabe was next, sticks in hand. Phil brought up the rear, holding the flail's handle in one hand and the spiked ball in the other. The chain was taut between them.

Zeke started up the second flight. One step at a time, he moved closer to his floor, to the last place he'd seen Li.

He reached the second floor and crossed the narrow hallway to his door. Room 22. The numbers painted on the door were black and faded. He checked over his shoulder at his team. They were huddled behind him. Gabe stood watch, checking down the stairs. Phil looked toward the window at the end of the hall thirty feet away.

"You okay?" asked Uriel, perhaps sensing Zeke's apprehension.

"Yeah," he said.

He wiped his palms on his pants and reached for the knob. The brass fixture with a dent along its side was cold against his palm. He twisted it to the right. His heart thumped faster, harder in his chest. His mouth was drier than normal. He inhaled through his nose, the dry air suffocating, then pushed the door inward. As he opened it, the door swung oddly on its broken hinges. The door was splintered at its side and threatened to pull away from the jamb altogether. He stepped past it and over the shards of mahogany that littered the floor near the entrance.

The familiar smell of home washed over him as he stepped into the apartment. It was a mix of dust and scented candle wax. The furniture was as he'd left it, but Li's and his trinkets were tipped over, out of place, broken. One of the sheers on the window that overlooked the street below was torn, and books were strewn across the floor.

He picked up a thick hardcover by Homer and set it back on the shelf next to a collection of essays by Jonathan Swift. He ran his fingers along the spine of a title he'd never read called *Animal Farm*. Li had urged him to read it. It was among her favorites, as it was among the books forbidden in the protectorate.

They were her books. How had she gotten them? A wave of regret washed through him. He'd never asked her about them even though they were contraband. Maybe he'd never asked because he wasn't one to judge people's proclivities. After all, Zeke himself was a bootlegger who'd spent his life flouting the law.

He moved past the pile, stepping over a thin leaflet titled *A Modest Proposal*, and maneuvered his way to the bedroom.

The nightstand was open, as was the biometric safe. The 9mm handgun Li had kept for protection was gone. There was a sprinkling of plaster on the floor beside the bed. The sheets were wrinkled, the comforter a heap on one side of the mattress.

Zeke knelt, set his revolver on the nightstand, and leaned forward onto the bed. He gripped the sheets with his hands, balling the cotton into his fists and burying his face in them. He inhaled deeply, and he smelled her. Memories of her flooded his mind, a slideshow of their life together flitted from one scene to the next. Her eyes, her smile, her fingers running through her hair. He could feel her hands on him and his on her, their bodies connected, their hot breath on each other.

Uriel's hand touched his back, and he flinched. She retreated and apologized for startling him.

Zeke lifted his head. "It's fine," he said. "Don't worry about it."

"She's not here," said Gabe. "But it's obvious there was a

struggle. They took her." Gabe stood at the window next to the torn curtain, his attention on the street below.

"There's no blood," Phil said. "That's a good sign."

"Little victories, right?" said Zeke. He stood and brushed off his pants. He tugged on his buckle, tucked in his shirt, and retrieved the revolver from the nightstand.

"Where to next?" asked Uriel. "Where could she be?"

"There are a few places," said Zeke. "I know the most likely. It's close to the government buildings."

"The two tall ones we saw when we were driving in from the Badlands?" asked Phil.

"Yeah," said Zeke. "We can walk from here."

"Not sure about that," said Gabe. He was looking out the window. "Looks like we've got company."

"Seriously?" asked Uriel. She moved to the window. Phil joined her.

Zeke approached them and saw what they did. The human gargoyle had ratted them out. He was in the middle of the street, cigarette in hand, pointing up at them. Alongside him were a half-dozen men Zeke recognized. He cursed under his breath.

"You know them?" asked Gabe.

"Yeah," said Zeke. "They're Tic enforcers. There's a good chance they're the same ones who took Li."

Gabe stepped away from the window, and he and Phil exchanged knowing looks. Both readied their weapons.

"There's no going around them," said Phil. "Looks like we're gonna have to go through them."

Uriel returned to the bedroom, slid the M27 under the bedframe, and marched back into the confines of the living area. She grabbed an elbow and pulled it toward her, stretching her triceps. She repeated the motion with her other arm and twisted her neck from side to side. Then she hopped on the balls of her feet.

"What are you doing?" asked Zeke.

"Getting ready," she said. "Not enough space for gunfire. It's gonna get dirty, Zeke."

Zeke glanced out the window just as the last of the men disappeared from view. They were in the building now. He could hear their footsteps booming up the staircase.

Phil moved to one side of the open door. Gabe positioned himself on the other. They braced themselves.

Uriel stood next to Zeke and eyed his revolver. "Might want to take aim, big boy," she said. "You'll get one shot and then it's gonna be chaos."

Zeke lifted the revolver, stepped closer to the door to better direct the pulse, and braced himself.

The first man appeared in the doorway. A second was beside him. They were armed. It didn't matter.

Zeke applied pressure to the trigger. The gun kicked and a blast of energy shot forward. The displacement of air filled the room with the *whoomp* of a low pulse, and Zeke was lifted and thrown back until he hit a wall separating the living area from the kitchen. The back of his head slapped against the plaster, and a burst of white light filled his vision. Air surged from his lungs, and he slumped to the floor, gasping for breath.

He rolled onto his knees, holding the cold and glowing revolver. His world swimming, he struggled to his feet. What he saw happening in front of him didn't seem real.

Gabe was engaged with two of the Tics, fighting each one with a stick. The men were no match for his speed and skill. The weapons were an extension of him. They spun and twirled in his hands, and as the weapons hit the men, they glowed blue and emitted an electric shock. The men twitched and shuddered, their eyes wide with fear and shock, their faces contorted with pain. Gabe was unfazed by their failed counterattacks. He didn't even appear winded. He advanced on the men, attacking with a fluid intensity that seemed dispassionate.

Equally as skilled, Phil measured the weight of the flail in his hand, stalking his opponent. When the man made a move to raise his gun, Phil struck. With a flick of his powerful wrist and a whip of the grip, the flail swung back and then shot forward.

It struck the target in the shoulder, eliciting a squeal of pain. The man fired an errant shot before he dropped his gun and retreated a step. But Phil was on him again. He whipped the flail across his body, the chain unspooled, and the spiked ball hit its mark again. It slapped into the side of the man's face, cracking against his jaw, glowing a familiar blue when it connected. The man shuddered and jerked as he fell to the side and slumped to the floor unconscious.

Phil and Gabe turned to help Uriel. She didn't need it. She was on the floor, her legs wrapped tightly around the neck of her opponent. The man's red face was shifting to purple. His nostrils flared. He choked for air. But his movements only worsened his predicament.

Then Zeke noticed something odd about Uriel. The grit of her teeth and the strain of her muscles was frightening enough. But it was her tattoos that caught his attention.

They glowed the same shade of electric blue as the flail, the sticks, and his revolver. The color pulsed, making the tattoos appear three-dimensional and lifting from her skin to take their own form.

The man caught in her constrictive vise struggled for a moment more. Spittle sprayed from his lips. Then his muscles relaxed, and he slumped against her. She gave one last flexing squeeze and released him. Rolling onto her side, the blue glow dimmed with each successive pulse. Then it was gone, and the ink that decorated her skin returned to normal.

The room was silent save Zeke's own wheezing breaths. He bent over at his waist, hands on his knees, and worked to slow his heart rate. His temples throbbed.

"I think we need to move on," said Phil. He adjusted his hat, tucking a curl under the hatband. "There's nothing here. We're sitting ducks if we stay."

"I wouldn't say you're sitting anything," said Zeke, gawking at the bodies. "You're killing machines."

"You say the sweetest things," said Uriel. She adjusted her top and tugged on her ponytail. "Such a gentleman."

He raised the revolver and waggled it back and forth. "What's with the glow?" he asked and motioned to the others. "My gun, your flail, your sticks, and...your...body? I mean, your tattoos. They freaking lit up like one of those sea creatures you read about in books."

"You read?" asked Uriel. "Zeke is a gentleman *and* a scholar. I'm so impressed."

Zeke scowled. "Seriously. What do they call it? Bioluminous?"

"Something like that," said Gabe. "We can explain this stuff later. For now, understand that we need to finish what we came here to do. Let's find your woman and—"

"*The* woman," said Uriel. "Not *his*. You know I don't like that possessive crap. Plus, I wouldn't say she's his anything anyway. He left her here in this dump by herself."

Zeke stepped toward Uriel and jabbed a finger at her. "Hey, this isn't a dump. It's my...it *was* my home. And I had my reasons for leaving her."

"You tell yourself whatever helps you sleep at night," said Uriel.

"Stop it," said Phil. "We're here to help him, not chastise or counsel. You know our roles, Uriel. Stick to them."

She rolled her eyes. "Fine."

Gabe motioned for them to leave the apartment. He led them all back into the hall and told Zeke to lead them back into the street. They needed to go to wherever he thought Li might be, assuming she was alive.

Zeke pushed past them and descended the stairs. He knew he'd never be back. This was the last time he'd ever step foot in the place where he'd made a home with the only woman he'd ever loved.

"There are only a few places she could be," Zeke said over his shoulder as he reached the landing and turned back toward the first floor. "The Tic has dark sites the Overseers don't know about."

"Dark sites?" asked Phil.

They stepped from the building and into the light. Zeke squinted at the bright outdoors. He lowered the brim of his Stetson.

"Yeah," he said. His boots crunched on the gravelly sand that coated the street. "There are plenty of Tic-owned or controlled businesses in the protectorate—all the protectorates. The Overseers know about them. They don't do anything about them. Not really. But the Tic also has hidden places they don't want the Overseers knowing about."

"Sounds sophisticated," said Phil.

"Beyond," said Zeke. "The Tic has tentacles everywhere."

"And you screwed them over," said Phil. It was a statement and not a question.

"Pretty much," said Zeke.

All of them were outside now. They marched together, side by side. To their left stood the gargoyle man who'd tipped off the Tic. He leaned against an open doorway now, pinching a cigarette between his fingers. Streams of smoke plumed from his nostrils. He stared at them.

They'd passed him and reached the end of Zeke's street when Uriel handed Zeke her M27 and peeled away from the group. Phil and Gabe kept walking, ignoring her. Zeke stopped.

She moved toward the gargoyle, her hips swaying seductively. She stepped with a swagger born from immeasurable confidence, which struck Zeke as funny.

He admired Uriel, found her sarcasm endearing and biting, and he was impressed with her obvious physical skill. But he thought it all a little much. It was hiding something. It was an armor, a protection that masked an overwhelming insecurity.

Zeke squared his shoulders and put his hand on his weapon, touching it through the fabric of his untucked shirt. He readied himself to support her should she need it.

The gargoyle was unfazed by her approach. He took another drag, drawing in his cheeks and sucking on the cigarette like it was life-giving. He held the smoke in his lungs before blowing it out in a wide puff that swirled around Uriel as she stepped to him and stopped.

A breeze blew past Zeke, fluttering the brim of his hat and kicking up dust that drifted across his face. Uriel was speaking to the gargoyle, but Zeke couldn't hear her. The man watched her with disinterest. His eyes wouldn't meet hers, and instead they assessed the accouterment that attracted more attention. He lowered his arm to his side and flicked the ash onto her boot. Uriel lowered her head. Her fists tightened. Her shoulders squared. Her stance widened almost imperceptibly.

The man rubbed his chin. Before he could say a word, Uriel reeled back her arm and punched him across the jaw. The other side of his face slapped against the doorjamb, and he slumped to the ground. The cigarette was in his hand. His teeth were scattered onto the ground in front of him. His jaw was displaced and hung awkwardly as he lay there unconscious.

All of this happened in a split second. Uriel's fists clenched as she stared down at him. She said something, then turned and tugged on her top.

She sauntered back to Zeke. She reached him and extended her hand for her M27, which Zeke didn't dare not hand back.

"What did he say to draw that reaction?" he asked.

Uriel motioned toward Phil and Gabe, who were well ahead of them now and not slowing their pace. The two of them began walking double-time to catch up.

"It wasn't so much what he said," answered Uriel. "It was the ash on my boot that sent me over the edge."

"The ash?"

"Yeah," she said, giving him side-eye as she hustled. "Nobody messes with my boots. I was gonna give him a pass too."

Zeke picked up his pace to stay even with her. They were jogging more than walking now. She carried the M27 in front of her in the manner of a skilled Marine in training.

"I told him I didn't appreciate him being a rat," she said. "I told him that if he said anything to anyone else, I'd come back and personally make it so he'd be sucking on cancer sticks through a hole in his throat."

"He didn't like that, I'm assuming," said Zeke.

"Apparently not," she said. "He ignored my warning and instead chose to be disrespectful. So I gave him a stronger warning than initially intended."

Zeke noticed she was running with ease. She wasn't breathing heavy or even seeming to exert herself. It was like she was superhuman. She'd knocked a grown man out with a single punch despite her slight stature. She'd squeezed a man to death with her thighs. She was deadly accurate with a rifle.

All of his new companions were deadly. All of them seemed otherworldly.

They caught up with Phil and Gabe at a three-way intersection and stopped. People were gathering at a ration station nearby. The line was twenty people deep even though the station hadn't opened and no Overseers or TMF had shown up yet.

"What are you?" he asked his companions, looking to each

of them. "Where did you come from? What is it you want here?"

"All good questions," said Phil. He pulled back his hat and wiped his brow with a swipe of his shirtsleeve. "All good questions."

"It won't be long now," said Gabe. "Not long now."

Zeke scanned their expressions. None of them gave away anything.

"I don't understand," he said. "Those aren't answers. None of you ever answer my questions."

"That's because you'll answer them yourself when the time comes," said Uriel. "And as Gabe just said, it won't be long now."

CHAPTER FOURTEEN

H ow's the tenderloin?" asked Guilfoyle. "I hope it's to your liking."

He sat across his table from his nephew, Louis Donne. The question was unnecessary since Louis had devoured the engineered beef. He had the last cube at the end of his fork, which he was dragging across the juices that puddled on the china dish in front of him.

The portly lieutenant nodded dutifully and squirreled a bite into one cheek. "Yes, thank you, Commander. It's delicious. What's the marinade?"

Guilfoyle cut a bean into two pieces and stabbed at one with his fork. He shook his head. "I don't know." He called toward the kitchen, "Theo, come here, please."

Theo appeared. His gray suit hung perfectly on his thin frame. His black shoes were polished to a high gloss, and his hair was impeccably coiffed. The glossy sheen of his engineered silk necktie was knotted perfectly in a double Windsor.

"Yes, sir?" He stood at attention, his shoulders back, his chin lifted high. "What do you need, Commander?"

The commander took a sip of wine and let the cabernet sit

in his mouth for a moment. He stabbed another bean; then he gestured to the blood-red marinade on his own plate. "The au jus," he said. "What's the flavoring?"

Theo frowned. "Is something wrong, sir?"

Guilfoyle shoveled the bean into his maw and jabbed the empty fork at his nephew across the table. "No, Louis here asked about it. It's delicious."

Theo's tight expression eased. "Ah, very good. I'm pleased you like it. The tenderloin is seasoned with a wonderful combination of rosemary, thyme, minced garlic, nutmeg, some allspice, a pinch of salt, and dried tarragon."

"It's fantastic," said Louis. "My compliments."

Theo bowed in appreciation. "Is there anything else, sir? I'm preparing a palate-cleansing sorbet, if that's acceptable."

"Wonderful," said Commander Guilfoyle, dismissing Theo with a wave.

He took another healthy sip of the wine; then he dabbed the corners of his mouth with a cloth napkin and pushed himself back from the table. He stared out the window. It was morning, early in the day for a heavy meal. The ration lines had formed on the streets below even though none of them had opened for business.

"I'm happy you joined me for this unusual breakfast," he said to Louis. "Given that neither of us slept last night and we skipped dinner to cope with emerging threats, I thought this might be a nice treat."

"It truly is," said Louis. He was using a chunk of heavy, dark bread to sop up the juice on his plate. "Thank you for the invitation."

"It didn't hurt that Theo had already prepared the meal," added Guilfoyle, continuing without acknowledging what Louis had said. "And I didn't want his work to go to waste. He's so loyal."

Louis chomped on the soggy bread, sucking on the heavy flavor of the juice.

"Loyalty is an important trait in someone," said Guilfoyle. He looked through his nephew more than he looked at him. "It's rare too. That's what makes it so valuable. Don't you agree?"

"Yes," said Louis. "That's my concern about some of your lieutenants. I'm uncertain they're loyal to the protectorate as much as they are to their own interests."

"You think so?"

"Yes," said Louis. He swiped a napkin across his face and balled it up. "They seem to have each other's backs. They work as a team, independently from the rest of us."

"I'm not sure of that," said Guilfoyle. "I believe there may be some insurrection afoot. While I don't know if the Tic or the Badlanders have anything to do with it, I sense something is gnawing away at us, at our government."

"Why are you so certain of that?" asked Louis. "There's no hard evidence. There's only the loose affiliation of separate attacks on other protectorates."

"Did your mother ever explain to you how we came to power?"

Louis considered the question for a moment. Guilfoyle saw the gears turning in his mind. "Of course she did," he said. "But I always appreciate your perspective, Uncle."

Guilfoyle sighed. He stood and crossed the short distance to the window, stuffed his hands into his pockets, and surveyed the city. A transport lumbered along one of the streets near the Fascio next door. An old Dodge Charger rumbled along a parallel street on the other side of a monument to their forefathers. It was likely a bold Tic bootlegger thumbing his nose at authority. Dust waked behind the Dodge as it picked up speed.

"I was a child when it happened," Guilfoyle said. "The population explosion of the late twentieth and early twenty-first century, coupled with the Dearth and aging infrastructure, made for a perfect storm. It happened fast. It took most by surprise, all around the world."

Guilfoyle glanced at his nephew. Louis was seemingly entranced and hanging on every word. He knew this was symptomatic of his nephew's sycophancy and that Louis was likely bored. It didn't matter to him. He liked talking.

"There were groups, however, who knew better," said Guilfoyle. "Organizations that knew the end was coming. Once the water runs out, you see, and the food becomes scarce, people riot. They destroy their own communities. They plunder. They kill. Survival is a funny thing. When it's threatened, humanity wanes. It's a fact. And when it's threatened en masse, the masses reject civilized behavior."

Theo entered with two small bowls of pale yellow sorbet. He hurriedly delivered the palate cleansers to their places on the table and disappeared back into the kitchen.

"Have you ever watched fire ants struggle to survive in a flood?" Guilfoyle continued. He corrected himself. "Of course not. What am I thinking? There's no flooding. Suffice it to say that when their lives are threatened, the ants will cling to whatever they find to survive. They'll bite, they'll cluster, they'll climb all over each other. Whatever it takes is what they'll do. Humans are no different."

Louis picked up his spoon and dipped it into the sorbet. He scooped some onto the silver and into his mouth. His cheeks puckered from the sour citric taste.

"Knowing this about human nature, and foreseeing what was inevitable," said Guilfoyle, standing at the window, "we prepared. I say we, although it was our forefathers. Your mother and I were children, but we saw it happening. We listened to the adults' conversations, saw the huddled meetings in living rooms, and overheard the hushed video chats over encrypted lines.

"We had hundreds of people, professionals in all areas, who understood what was happening. They joined forces. There were scientists, military leaders, titans of industry, agricultural barons, and even skilled politicians."

Guilfoyle took in a deep breath and moved from the window. He went back to his chair and sat, leaned over the bowl of melting sorbet, and spooned a small portion onto his tongue. He winced. "Tart," he said and then took another taste. "Delicious but tart."

Louis scooped the last of the sorbet from his dish. The silver scraped against the china.

"They stockpiled supplies," continued Guilfoyle, shifting back to the story of the protectorate's genesis. "They hid large caches of weapons before the second amendment was repealed."

"Second amendment to what?" Louis asked.

"The Constitution of the United States. It was the document that governed the nation. This was only seventy years ago, Louis. It was a facsimile of the Magna Carta. You've heard of that, haven't you?"

"Yes," said Louis. His cheeks reddened with embarrassment or frustration, or both. "And I've heard of the Constitution."

"There were twenty-seven amendments," said Guilfoyle. "The first ten comprised the Bill of Rights. As the thirsty country began to deteriorate into chaos, many of those rights were abridged. The first, second, and fourth amendments were the first to go. That only made things worse.

"Local and state governments dissolved; law enforcement disintegrated. It was anarchy. For years, there was steady decay. The already fragile infrastructure worsened. Small communities evaporated. Large cities imploded. The only constant was the supply of oil and gas. The government made certain they kept control of that. It was the main source of revenue. They sent the military to protect the pipelines and refineries. They spread themselves thin. We bided our time."

"Until what?" asked Louis.

Theo reemerged with twin cups and saucers. The china rattled against itself as he glided across the room to deliver the drinks.

"Coffee," he said, placing the first on the table in front of the commander. "Already made as you like it, sir, with engineered lactic-free milk and two lumps of synthetic sugar."

"Black, please," said Louis. "I like mine black."

"Yes," said Theo, delivering the coffee to Louis. "Black. If memory serves, you enjoy a splash of rum?"

Theo winked. Louis nodded in reply and thanked the servant for his hospitality and good memory.

"It's my job," said Theo. He cleared the plates and scurried, arms full, back to the kitchen.

"The coffee is made from filtered spring water," said Guilfoyle. "It's the only way to have it."

He picked up the saucer with one hand and gripped the cup with his other. He blew the steam from the hot, saddle-colored liquid and gingerly sipped it. He nodded at his nephew, giving the cue he too should take a drink. Louis obliged.

Guilfoyle took a second sip and lowered the saucer to the table. He ran his hand along the white linen cloth and brushed crumbs to the floor. Leaning forward, he laced his fingers together and eyed his nephew.

"You asked what spurred us into action," he said. "Mind you, I was a young teen by this time, so I had a better handle of the machinations. I wasn't privy to everything, but I knew enough. I saw what was happening. When the time was right, when the government was weak and the people were begging for authority and for protection from the riotous and untenable conditions, the protectorates were born.

"They were spread across the continent," he said with a

sweep of his hands before clasping them together again, "and each protectorate had its own authority. The provisions were divided equally, as were the experts in each of the necessary arenas. All protectorates came under the Overseers' authority simultaneously."

"They were military coups?" asked Louis. "You had help from what was then the United States military?"

"Yes," said Guilfoyle, "and members of congress. Had it not been for their help from the inside, we'd never have been able to destabilize the already-weakened federal government to the point of disbanding it."

"Then the protectorates became independent city-states?" said Louis. He sipped from his coffee, having let it cool.

"Correct, and the people welcomed it. They wanted the structure. They wanted someone in charge who would ferret out the malcontents and provide fairly for the obedient citizenry."

"*Obedient* being the operative word," said Louis.

"Yes," said Guilfoyle. "Left to their own devices, people fail. They need firm leadership. They need authority dictating what they need and what they don't. Even if they're unaware of this need, it exists. Throughout history, we've seen that when people are free to determine their own futures, without the sage wisdom of firm leadership, they fail. The more liberal or accepting societies become, the less focused they are on their own preservation. They need strict enforcement of a basic codification."

Louis took a healthy sip of the coffee.

"But it's also this need for regimented control, like the control we Overseers exert for the sake of the people, that has some dissatisfied," said Guilfoyle. "These are the people who want power for themselves for the sake of it. They think they can do it better, govern better, provide better, and lead better.

They are wrong, of course, and deep down they know it. History teaches us this."

"If people had governed themselves, we'd have never fallen into this predicament," Louis said.

Guilfoyle, about to take another sip of his coffee, stopped. He held the cup at his chin and then lowered it to the table. He placed it onto the saucer, spun it such that the cup handle was to his right, and then moved it aside.

"What," he whispered, but with a hint of derision, "*predicament* is that, Lieutenant Louis?"

Louis's expression flattened. His eyes skittered across the room, searching for help he would not find. "Predicament?" he repeated, drawing out each syllable as if it were stuck on the roof of his mouth.

"You said if people had governed themselves, they wouldn't be in this *predicament*. I asked, to what *predicament* are you referring?"

"I don't think—"

"You used the word *predicament*," said Guilfoyle. "It's an odd choice with a specific meaning."

Guilfoyle pushed back his chair and stood. He picked up a fork, dragging the tines across the tablecloth as he ambled toward his nephew at the opposite end of the table. "I think—no, I *know*—people are like hogs in slop. They're happy in the mud. They snort, they roll around, they consume, they defecate, they procreate. They are smart enough to understand their surroundings yet not intelligent enough to find a way out of the mire. Hogs are fat and complacent. Although they might seek something better, might want something better, they do nothing about it. Ultimately, they are content in the mud."

He stopped in front of Louis and raised the fork. He pointed it at his nephew, noticing the sheen of sweat beading on his forehead.

"I'll ask you this, Lieutenant," said Guilfoyle, flicking the end of the fork up and down as he spoke. "Why don't hogs walk on their own two feet? Why don't they set limits on themselves? Why don't they have a set of laws that is simple and firm and short enough to paint on the side of the barn?"

Louis's expression tightened with confusion.

"I'll tell you why," said Guilfoyle, not waiting for a response. "They don't do these things because ultimately they know they can't hack it. Regardless of what they try, they'll fail. What they need is an overseer. They need someone who will open the pen in the morning and lock them in at night. They need someone to fill the tins with feed and water them."

Guilfoyle stabbed the fork into the table with such force it stood up straight and pinched the cloth into folds. Louis jumped in his seat, blinking back droplets of sweat. White flecks of dried spit stuck to the corners of his open mouth. Everything he'd said was building to this moment, to this revelation.

"They need someone with the guts and guile to care for them through harvest and Dearth. This is the truth of our world!" Guilfoyle bellowed. "All of us are human. All of us are people who want to survive, and eat, and screw, and sleep, and believe sustenance will always be at the end of a line. But some of us, few of us, will stand on our hind hooves and unlock the gate ourselves. Few of us will leave behind the slop for the farmhouse and do what it takes, whatever it takes, to ensure the piggies stay happy enough not to mess up what we've built for them with such care!"

Guilfoyle stood, face reddened, jaw set, until his scowl eased into a smile. He stood up straight and plucked the fork from the table.

"I-I meant the p-predicament of responsibility," Louis stammered. "If people had governed themselves, they wouldn't need us as much as they do. It's a heavy burden for us, for you."

Guilfoyle studied his nephew for a long moment. "I'm sorry," he said, his tone different from what it had been seconds earlier. "Forgive me, Louis. I'm so passionate about caring for our citizenry, for providing a stable society the way we have now for over three generations, that sometimes I overreact."

Louis was holding his breath, or at least it appeared that way. Sweat stained his shirt now and his face was pallid.

"Understand that I always want what's best for our protectorate. I always want what's best for our citizenry," Guilfoyle said. "I allow the Tic to exist because it gives some the sense they have control even though they don't. That false power keeps them at bay. It keeps them happy in the mud, thinking they have escaped the pen. Those with real power can see this."

He was conducting now as he spoke. His fork moved in waves to stress his every point.

"But the power we have, that heavy task of real, unadulterated power, comes with it stressors that those in false thrones don't suffer. Some of those stressors are easily seen, identified, and rooted out. Some of them are more insidious."

Guilfoyle turned and stared out the window. He ran a hand across the top of his head and then scratched his neck. "Few can empathize with the burden we carry, Louis," he said without looking at his nephew. "Few know to keep the peace. War is sometimes necessary, however inconsequential that war might be. What's the saying about an omelet?"

The commander's glare shifted to Louis's girth, which hung at his waist and made it impossible for the young man to sit with his legs together. He kept his gaze there for a moment, awaiting an answer. Louis took a napkin from the table and swept it across his brow. Guilfoyle slinked back toward his seat as Theo emerged carrying two bowls of ice cream topped with whipped cream. A bright red cherry adorned the crown of each dollop.

"Ahh," said Guilfoyle, returning to his seat. "Dessert. Just in time. This looks wonderful. Thank you, Theo."

Guilfoyle sat and poked the fork into the stemless, sugared cherry on top. He popped it into his mouth and bit down into the fruit's center. Bright red juice leached between his teeth and threatened to dribble onto his chin before the commander slurped and swallowed.

CHAPTER FIFTEEN

Brina didn't recognize herself. The swelling on her face and the dried blood that crusted her lips and the edges of her nostrils made her look monstrous. Her trembling hand moved toward her plum of a purple eye and stopped short of touching it. Breathing hurt. The relentless throb of her pulse at her temples made her vision waver.

As she sat on the bed looking at herself in the mirror, a lean figure appeared behind her. He stood at the edge of the shadows in her dimly lit room.

The sight of the man startled her. She spun around and a bolt of pain shot through her midsection and she winced. Her muscles tensed against the wave of lingering pain that rolled through her body.

The man stepped closer, seemingly unaffected by her discomfort. He wore reflective sunglasses that hid any hint of expression on his face. His salt-and-pepper beard hugged his angular jawline. His bald head and wiry frame spoke of a man in peak physical condition. Her eyes fell to the bone-handled knife at his hip. He'd told her stories about that knife, about its origin, about its connection to the rise and fall of empires. She thought it hyperbole.

Graham was a man for whom everything was about effect, about inflicting fear and doubt. As much as he'd taught her, she'd never fully trusted him. He liked to read books and, in her experience, people who read books couldn't be trusted.

His deep voice cut through the room. The sound of it aggravated Brina's headache.

"How are you?" he asked. "I came to make sure you're healing up. I need you on your feet."

"I'll be fine," she said. "Nothing stitches and nano-injections can't help."

The swelling in her jaw slurred her words together as she worked to enunciate, making her own voice sound alien.

Graham nodded. Clearly, he understood her despite the damage done to her face. He tilted his head to one side and then the other, popping his neck. He took another step toward her, more into the light now. His hand fell to the knife, his fingers sliding up and down the bone handle.

"You screwed up, and not just a little bit, Brina. This is royal. This is epic. This is—"

"I get it, Graham," she said, spitting out the words with a venom that surprised even her. "I'm aware of what happened."

He stepped next to the bed, a mattress set atop simple plywood and cinderblocks. He folded his arms across his chest, tucking his hands underneath his biceps to make the muscles appear larger than they were. "Do you though?" he asked.

Graham inched close to her. He stood next to the bed and dipped his chin to look at her over the top of the sunglasses.

"Yes," she hissed.

"Why did you let her leave?" he asked in a way that suggested to Brina it wasn't a question.

She glanced past him and noticed there were two other

men, enforcers, standing at the door to the room. Neither of them spoke. They stared straight ahead, like marble sentries.

This wasn't a wellness check. It was an interrogation.

"I didn't let her leave," she said. "She jumped me. I didn't expect it. I'll admit I let my guard down, but—"

"But nothing," interrupted Graham. "Three of our men died because of your lowered guard. One here in the compound and two who tried to stop her once she'd found her way to the surface. A team of TMF Marines rescued her."

"I'll take care of it," said Brina. "I always take care of it."

Graham laughed, a belly laugh that shook his body. He turned to the enforcers at the door.

"Take care of it?" he said. "Take *care* of it? Not only did you fail to learn anything about the whereabouts of our misguided youth, Ezekiel Watson, until after he was dead," chided Graham, "you let his girlfriend get the better of you and leave here with the help of the Overseers. Now they know about this location. They'll be back. What are you going to do to take care of it?"

Brina's head was pulsing with pain. The tension in her rigid body amplified the sharp discomfort that radiated through her wounded body. She couldn't defend herself. There was nothing that could mitigate the damage she'd done. Still, she found her anger welling. She didn't need the tongue-lashing, the admonishment from a man whom, for so long, she'd served without error.

In her experience, leaders shared successes and owned failures. Graham was her superior. He was in charge. She was following orders. His orders. He should take responsibility too.

Brina nodded at him. "I failed," she said, gritting through the pain and the desire to punch him in the gut. "I didn't bring you Ezekiel, I didn't collect actionable intelligence from Adaliah, three of our friends are dead, and our compound cover is blown. All of this is true."

Graham pushed his glasses up on his nose. He had to know there was a *but* coming.

"But I'm not the only one responsible," she said. "You know as well as I do that you gave Ezekiel to the Overseers. You wanted him to pay for Mogilevich's death, and you didn't care who did it. You doubled the odds by engaging your people in the TMF."

Graham bristled. His dimples disappeared.

"Holding Adaliah here after she'd failed to give us anything was reckless," Brina said. "You were thinking with your junk, Graham, not your head. We should have killed her on day one. We knew what she was. We had our suspicions."

His jaw tightened.

"We kill people who can't help us," she said. "It's always been that way. The Overseers do it; we do it. It's the way of the world. You kept Adaliah naked in a cell for…"

Her sentence trailed off. She didn't need to finish it.

Graham stood silently, watching her from behind the shade of his glasses. Her warped twin reflections stared back her.

"I think we know this debacle is as much your fault as mine," she said, the venom lacing every word. "Everybody has to answer to somebody. Who do you answer to, Graham? What would he say about what happened here? What has he already said?"

Graham's posture shifted. His shoulders sank. His chin dropped. His fingers flexed and balled into fists at his sides. He cleared his throat again and removed his sunglasses. "You know I can kill you right here," he said. "Snap your neck, put a bullet in your brain, strangle you with my bare hands."

He made a sweeping motion with his hand holding the sunglasses. Light flecked off the reflective lenses. "Any of it, I could do with impunity. Nobody but my men would know what happened. We'd pin it on our good friend Adaliah Bancroft."

He put the glasses back on, stretching his face to adjust

them on his nose. He snapped his fingers. "Like *that* you'd be another cautionary tale. Your life would be an annotation to the rich history and future of the Aquatic Collective. I could do that."

Brina didn't flinch. She did nothing other than stare back at him, expressionless. She knew she held the real power here. He could off her, sure, but to what benefit?

She knew she was more valuable to him alive than she was dead. And they knew it was likely the Overseers would send back their TMF to scour the facility for whatever they could find. They would have to work together.

When she didn't respond, he smiled again. This one was fake. They were all fake, but this one reeked of condescension and anger boiling beneath the surface.

"What do you propose I do, Brina?" he asked, his tone far less aggressive.

She pushed from the bed and lowered herself onto her feet. She wavered and balanced herself with her fingertips on the bed. Her equilibrium took a moment to right itself, and then she stood flat on the floor.

Brina wasn't as tall, but her imposing physique made her appear large. Even injured, battered, bruised, and dizzy, she was a warrior, and Graham knew it. "You're not going to kill me," she said. "I know that."

Her words slurred as the blood rushed to her legs. She felt cemented in place. It grounded her.

"Instead, you and I will ready this bunker for an attack," she said. "We know it's coming. The TMF won't be able to resist. That arrogant SOB Archibald won't be able to help himself. He'll send Marines here. He might even send little Adaliah as a guide. There's no doubt she's working for them. She played Zeke. She played us."

Graham raised an eyebrow. "And?"

"Now we play her. I told you when you first came in here

wagging your junk and acting all superior, I can fix it. We can fix it. Those superiors of yours will sing your praises when we decimate a TMF force, take their weapons, gather intelligence, and use them as bargaining tools."

Graham stared at her from behind his glasses for a moment and then clasped his hands behind his back. He paced the room, his head down. He was clearly mulling over his options, what few there were.

"I like it," said Graham. "Let's get to work. We don't know how long we have to make this happen, and we'll need reinforcements."

"I've already got an idea," she said. "And they won't see it coming."

CHAPTER SIXTEEN

Zeke stood near a collection of low-slung buildings, some of them ramshackle at best, which cast short, slim shadows across the dirt. Together, the buildings shielded the group from the main crowds gathering in the market exchange for this part of the city.

In the back alley, where they stood at the rear of the shacks, the few people milling about on their stoops or readying the carts weren't paying any attention to the oddly dressed Zeke and his three companions. These people were used to looking the other way, Zeke had explained, but the alley gave them only temporary refuge. They'd have to step clear of its safety to reach their destination, wherever that ultimately was.

"Pull up your bandana," suggested Phil. He was standing in front of Zeke to one side. His bowler was low on his head. His rifle, identical to Uriel's, rested on his shoulder. "You don't want people knowing who you are."

Zeke hadn't realized it had slipped beneath his chin. He raised the leading edge of the bandana over his mouth and nose. The loose knot at the cloth's back pressed into his neck. He looked from side to side again. When he was satisfied nobody was interested in his appearance, he settled his gaze on his companions.

Uriel held her M27. She stood with her feet shoulder width apart and stretched her neck from side to side. She noticed him watching her and blew him a kiss. Then she scowled. "We have other things to worry about, darling. And aren't we here to rescue *your* woman?" The emphasis on the possessive word was dipped in sarcasm.

Phil and Gabe glanced at each other and then at Zeke. Their wry grins matched. Neither of them said anything. Though Gabe, who had his pair of black rattan Escrima sticks in one hand, chuckled and winked at Zeke. The curved steel handle of a knife and its bolster stuck out of his waist at his belly.

Zeke rolled his eyes. "We don't have long," he said. "If they knew we were coming, they know we're here. There are only four exits from the tunnel. I'm kind of surprised reinforcements aren't already here. And we haven't seen anything from the Overseers yet. They're not on the ball."

Gabe motioned with the sticks past the closest of the one-story shacks. "They are."

Zeke followed Gabe's line of sight and saw he was right. A TMF transport parked, smaller than the ones in the Badlands. Three armed Marines stood in front. One of the men was pointing directions.

"They're splitting up," said Phil. "How do you want to handle this? Together?"

"I say we split up too," said Uriel. "I'll take the big one in the middle. He's beefy. I like beefy."

"You're depraved," said Gabe.

Uriel batted her eyes. "Deprived," she countered. "Or maybe a little of both."

"Where do we need to meet up?" asked Phil.

"There are only a few places they could be holding Li,"

said Zeke. "The first is close. It's on the other side of the market near the government buildings. Maybe a mile from here? There's an old monument there. A dude on a horse."

"Okay," said Phil. "We split up. Each of us takes a Marine. Zeke, you head straight for the monument. We'll meet you there."

Uriel agreed. Gabe nodded.

"Let's do this quietly and discreetly," said Phil. "The less obvious we are, the easier the rest of this will be."

Zeke regarded the heavy weapon in his hand, the mystery revolver. "All right then," he said under his breath.

He moved between the closest two buildings, sticking to one of its rough-hewn walls. He inched to where it opened into the market. The transport was straight ahead.

Zeke surveyed the crowd. It was larger than it had been minutes earlier. The market featured tents and tables full of things worthless to anyone but the people selling them. Odd bolts, pieces of rusted machinery, ragged swatches of brocade fabric, and random masonry decorated the stalls, as they were. Their sellers pleaded with passersby, lowering their prices with each step the prospective marks would take farther from them.

An odor of cooked meat wafted past Zeke, and he spotted fingers of smoke rising from atop a trash can covered with a piece of sheet metal. A man poked at the chunks of flesh cooking atop the hot plate. It was rat. And the smell, at first appetizing, now stewed into something that turned his stomach.

He lifted his shirt and tucked the revolver into his waistband. He thought it easier to blend in with the masses without clutching a large steel weapon. He took his first step into the open, not seeing any of the Marines. He merged into the first pool of foot traffic when a flash of motion to his left caught his attention.

Others saw it too, and the swirling tide of humanity began

to shift and move in that direction. Something loud, a clacking sound, was drawing their attention. Zeke checked straight ahead. With the distraction, he could have easily moved closer to his destination. He took two large steps toward the cluster of tents and tables in front of him, leaned into a jog, and glanced back at the tightening circle of people to his left.

He cursed, touched the revolver's grip under his shirt to make sure it was there, and moved with the ebbing tide of bazaar-goers turned carnival audience. Beyond the crowd, he saw Gabe's profile and the tops of the weapons. He was clapping them together and using them in some offensive maneuver.

He swung them like an artist performing a ritual dance. The crowd moved closer and then backed away with his wide, arching movements. They throbbed in and out, oohing and ahhing.

Zeke craned his neck to see more of what was happening but couldn't. He glanced back in time to see Uriel climbing into the cab of the TMF transport. A Marine was a few steps behind her, his weapon raised.

She slammed the door shut. The Marine took a series of shots that peppered the side of the transport, sparks flecking off the armored plating. The crowd behind him screamed at the sound of gunfire. The men and women were scattering now, some on the ground crawling with their heads in their hands, others running.

Zeke saw what had held their attention until the gunfire. Gabe had beaten a Marine to his knees. An M27 lay harmlessly on the ground. Each time the injured Marine made a move for it, Gabe enlisted a series of twirling motions that struck the trapped Marine and kept him from reaching his weapon. With each strike, a flash of blue light strobed from the ends of the sticks. The Marine jerked, seizing, and his body spasmed as if jolted with electric voltage.

Another rapid burst of gunfire drew Zeke's attention back to Uriel. She now had the transport in gear and was backing it up. The Marine firing upon his own vehicle was helpless to stop her as she mowed down a row of tables.

Zeke reached for his revolver. He gripped it in his right hand and lifted it toward the Marine. He put his finger on the trigger, steadied himself, and brought up his other hand to better hold the weapon of mass destruction. He took aim.

Before he applied pressure, he realized that if he shot at the Marine attacking the transport, his blast would also hit Uriel. He couldn't focus the energy blast enough unless he got closer.

Zeke spun back toward Gabe and lifted the weapon. Again, he hesitated and reconsidered. At this distance, he'd hit everyone in the crowd and likely blast Gabe along with them. As incredible as his revolver was, he didn't fully understand what it was, and he couldn't use it indiscriminately. He tucked the revolver back into his waist.

Caught between these two scenes, with no option to truly help either of his companions, Zeke knew he'd made a mistake not to run for it when he'd had the chance. Now there was no waiting, no hesitation. He sprinted in the monument's direction, which he couldn't see from the market.

He weaved past crying and ducking market-goers, rushing into the maze of flea market stands. He knocked over tables and kicked loose the taut lines supporting tarps and tents. He tripped twice, but kept his balance. Behind him, the chaos intensified.

The transport's engine revved. A loud crash and the earsplitting sound of metal grinding on metal carried through the morning air. Zeke picked up his knees and ran. He was past the market now and closer to the paved roads that connected at the monument.

To his right, a queue of people awaiting a government handout watched him bolt by. His boots rubbed against his heels; the revolver jostled at his waist. His breath, reflected back at his face underneath the cover of the bandana, was hot and sour.

Gunfire rattled in the distance, echoing. It made it hard for Zeke to know how many shots were fired, how many weapons were involved. He darted past a woman holding a child in her arms, when a black-clad figure stepped in front of him and yelled at him to stop.

Zeke ignored the command until he saw the M27 leveled at his chest. He raised his hands above his head and skidded to a stop ten feet from the Marine.

"Figured you'd be coming this way," said the Marine. "It's the only way to the city center."

The Marine took another step and tilted his head. At that distance, Zeke figured there was no way the man would need the magnifying lens. All he had to do was squeeze the trigger and it would hit Zeke dead center in the chest.

Dead center.

"Remove the mask," said the Marine. He planted a foot in the dirt and leaned forward at his shoulders. "Take off the hat."

Zeke kept his arms above his head. He was breathing heavily, his chest heaving. He said nothing.

The Marine jerked the rifle as he snapped, "Do it."

Zeke, with his palms open, lowered his arms. Slowly, he drew his hand to the bandana covering his nose and mouth.

"Faster," said the Marine. He scanned the area around him, keeping the rifle aimed at Zeke.

Pops of gunfire snapped in the distance. The Marine glanced past Zeke, then fixed on him again.

Zeke pinched the fabric at the bridge of his nose at the moment two shots pierced the air at close range. He was sure the impatient Marine had shot him. His body twitched. He took his hand from the bandana and, with the fingers of both hands spread, felt his torso. He swiped at his chest. Nothing.

But the Marine's body tensed, jerked, then slumped to the ground. He slapped against the packed dirt with a sickening thud. Blood oozed from underneath him, spreading out across the earth.

"You okay?" came Phil's voice from behind him.

Zeke was trembling from what he thought was a near-death experience. He nodded and thanked Phil as the big man stepped next to him.

Phil slung his rifle over his shoulder and tipped his bowler. A black smudge from his thumb stained the front of the hat. "Sorry about that," he said. "That was my guy. He got away from me for a minute."

"No problem," said Zeke.

Phil put a hand on Zeke's shoulder. "Let's keep moving. We've got a lot to do and even more ground to cover."

Zeke eyed Phil and glanced over his shoulder between them. He didn't see Uriel or Gabe. He didn't hear any gunfire. There was no rumble from a rogue transport.

"What about them?" he asked. "We can't leave them."

"They're fine," said Phil. "They'll meet us. Now c'mon."

The big man grinned through his beard and motioned with his head toward the statue in the distance. He patted Zeke on the back, hard, and gripped the flail, holding it diagonally across his body.

Zeke touched the revolver at his waist, checking to make sure it was there. Phil took two big steps.

"All right," Zeke said. "I'm coming."

They moved from the vacant dirt lots to the crowded streets. Nobody gave them a second look despite their appearance and Phil's large weapon.

The people were too consumed with their own lives, their faces sullen, dragging their feet from one line to another, carrying empty sacks. Zeke knew why the Tic was so successful. The Tic gave people hope. They helped them get the things they needed, offering a belief that not everyone was subject to the iron fist of the Overseers.

Still, he wished he'd never been a part of the syndicate. He wished he'd been strong enough to survive without the help of criminals, to drag Li with him when he'd left. He wished a lot of things.

———

They reached the monument close to the government towers and found Uriel and Gabe already there, impatiently waiting for them. Uriel's body language told Zeke she was agitated at how long it had taken them. But as they got closer, he understood her uneasy stance wasn't from agitation. It was from discomfort. She was pacing because she was anxious. Something had happened.

Phil didn't appear to notice their unease. He stepped up to them and slapped Gabe on the shoulder. "You beat us here. Good for you."

Neither of them spoke. Neither of them would even look up from the ground.

"What is it?" asked Zeke. "Did you find her? Is Li okay?"

Uriel exhaled, puffing out her cheeks. She shook her head.

Zeke's heartbeat fluttered. His chest tightened and he felt light-headed. He stepped closer, invading Uriel's space. "What's wrong?" he asked quietly. "What happened to Li?"

"It's not Li," Gabe said. "That's not who we found."

Zeke didn't understand. His mind raced. Who else was there to find?

He scanned the muted crowds of people and spotted Overseer guards at the steps of the Fascio, who didn't seem to notice them.

"Tell me," he said, his voice trembling. "What is it?"

He tried to imagine who else he'd failed. What person had fallen into his sphere of crime and death? There was nobody. It was only Li.

His mind flipped through a catalog of people.

Rose? They wouldn't know her. Mogilevich? Why would they care? Was this about Raf? Barach?

What possibly could have happened in the short span of time between their emergence from the tunnel and this moment? What was it that had them so spooked, so speechless?

He turned in circles, searching for something, anything. He was shaking now.

Then he saw it. And Zeke's world turned upside down.

He gasped. He stood frozen. Somebody touched his shoulder. Somebody else put an arm around his waist, trying to comfort him. But he only vaguely processed it. He was too focused on the bodies hanging from the Fascio.

He took a step forward, closer to the trio of corpses that now looked like scarecrows more than humans. His bandana was cold and damp against his cheeks. He realized tears were draining from his eyes. He couldn't speak. He couldn't understand what it was he was seeing. Yet he fully understood it. It all made sense now, and the gaps in his memory flooded with what he'd forgotten. For the first time since he'd found himself behind the wheel of his Superbird, trying to escape the Horde, he remembered the end of his natural life.

The visions snapped through his mind like someone turning the pages of a picture book with increasing speed. The world spinning around him teetered and darkened from view as those memories consumed him…

———

He was in his apartment. He sat at a table in the dark. The pen in his hand scratched against the paper in front of him. He folded it, rose from his seat, and navigated the blackness into the bedroom.

Li was sleeping, her breathing soft but audible. It was the same pattern to which he'd found himself falling asleep as he tried to match it with his own respiration. She was on her side, her knees curled, and her hands tucked between them. One foot stuck out from beneath the covers and teetered on the mattress. Behind her, on his pillow, he set the note. He picked it up, drew a deep breath, then set it down again. He adjusted it, centering it on the pillow.

He left the apartment and whispered a goodbye. A knot swelled in his throat, making it hard to swallow. He wasn't sure he breathed at all on the walk to his car. Then he sped away, lights off, cutting through the darkness and edging toward the Tic smuggling tunnel.

The streets were empty. The gravel crunched under his tires. His window was down, the air dry and cold. The sky was inky and cloudless, freckled with points of light from distant stars. The moon was a sliver, waning and almost gone. Its vague outline was gray against the night sky.

He turned on the wipers to swipe away the dust coating the windshield. It did little but move it around.

He was at the entrance to the tunnel. His path was clear. And then it wasn't.

Bright lights flicked on in unison, blinding him. Men shouted above the low rumble of his idling Plymouth. The barrels of M27s pointed at him.

He was on the ground, knees in his back and shackles on his wrists. He was punched, kicked. He was imprisoned and questioned. He kept quiet. He slept, he dreamt, he regretted, he prayed.

Then he was on the Fascio steps. Four Marines led him

there. The commander was shouting to an assembly of hungry, bloodthirsty rubberneckers.

The sun was blinding. Zeke winced. His back ached and his clothes hung on him like rags.

"This man," the commander said, "is a bootlegger."

The crowd hissed. A rock punched him in the side. He felt it in his ribs. He bit the inside of his cheek to squelch the pain.

The commander pointed at him. "He takes water from us and sells it for profit!" he shouted. "He is a thief and a traitor. He is a Tic!"

The rubberneckers screamed, "Kill him! Make him pay!"

Zeke's heart pounded. He knew what was coming. The crowd cheered. They chanted. They fell quiet.

"We cannot tolerate this," said the commander. "We have to send a message to that underground movement of enemies who would take from us what is so precious. They are stealing life. They are profiting from your thirst."

A wave of fear, of knowing what was next, washed through him. His body trembled and warmth spread across his groin. Then it was cold. Tears blurred his vision.

The commander taunted him. "While we barely have enough water to drink or cook," he declared, "this man is hydrated enough to cry and wet himself. It's further proof of his betrayal."

The commander stepped to him, his face sour. He squeezed Zeke's shoulder and offered judgment disguised as mercy.

The Marines tightened their grip on him. He asked for forgiveness. He wanted a second chance. He promised to tell them what he knew.

They fixed a harness to him, tightening the straps at his shoulders and chest.

Then pain. Searing pain. A long gash at his midsection burned. Someone screamed. It was ear piercing and he wanted it to stop. But the cries wouldn't stop. Then he realized he was the one screaming, crying out in agony.

A mechanical sound droned somewhere close. The harness pressed against him and he was weightless. He was lifted off the ground. He kicked, he sweated, and he bled.

The wound widened as his body gave in to gravity. His flesh ripped and tore. The harness rode up his body, trapping his arms.

He spun as the chain that held him twisted and then unwound again. He grew weak. The world around him grew darker…

———

Presently, he was back in front of those bodies. *He* was a rubbernecker now, taking delight in a public execution. He was staring at his own remains.

"I'm dead," he said. He looked at his hands, touched his chest. He blinked. His brow twitched and he turned toward his companions. "I'm dead."

They stood quietly watching him.

He pointed at himself and then at them, waggling his finger amongst them. "If I'm dead, then what are all of you?"

Uriel looked up. She was as serious as he'd ever seen her. Her expression was flat, her brow furrowed with genuine concern. "We're the Watchers."

Zeke studied each of them and glanced back at his corpse. His hands were picked clean of any flesh.

"The Watchers?" he asked.

Phil took off his hat and wiped his sweaty forehead, the curls of his matted hair, with the back of his arm. "Ever heard of Enoch?"

"We don't have time for this," said Gabe. "Not right now."

Phil raised a hand toward Gabe. "Give us a second," he

breathed. "Our friend here is in shock. We have time for the basics."

Gabe looked toward the Fascio and then beyond the statue back toward the market and the distant queues of citizens.

"The basic basics," said Gabe. "We need to find Li and get out of here."

Zeke shook his head. "Enoch, Watchers, the overwhelming evidence I'm freaking dead? What the hell is going on?"

Zeke fell to his knees.

I'm going to be sick.

His stomach churned and all he wanted to do was vomit, but nothing ever came out. So many of his questions had answers now. But those answers begat more questions. He couldn't process this. It was too much.

His body trembled. His eyes couldn't focus. He was at once cold and hot. He wanted to scream and cry and laugh.

Is any of this real? Is it heaven? Is it hell? Is it somewhere in between? Am I physically experiencing any of this, or is it some manifestation of my dead soul, an ethereal projection?

Phil knelt before him, rubbing his back.

"Enoch was a man," said Phil. "He was a good man who traveled the world and saw good and evil. He was a religious guy. He saw things that were of this world and things that weren't. There was a book written about him. Some people think he didn't exist. Some think his life was allegorical. The book got some things right. It got others wrong. It——"

Uriel rolled her eyes. She interrupted Phil by putting a flat hand in front of his face. She stepped closer to Zeke. "Enough with the history lesson. We can do that later. Bottom line? We're angels. Sort of."

Still trembling, only half present, Zeke lifted his head and tried to focus. The world was spinning. All he could manage was a single, one-syllable word.

"Angels?"

"Yes," said Phil.

"We need to wrap this up," said Gabe. "They're gonna see us here."

"So you're dead too?" asked Zeke. "But people can see you. Can they see me? Of course they can see me. They can see me?"

"That's three questions," said Uriel. She counted off the answers with her fingers. "First one? Sort of. Not really, but yes. Second, yes. Third, yes."

"Are all of the Watchers in…at…with Pedro? Are they all part of your team?"

Phil shook his head. "Unfortunately, no. Every once in a while, a Watcher goes on a mission and doesn't come back. They disappear and so do their weapons."

Uriel flexed. "Especially if their weapon is their body."

Zeke rolled his eyes at her, then asked Phil, "Where do they go?"

"They stay wherever Pedro sent them," answered Phil. "Maybe they get tired of the grind. Maybe they find a cause to which they connect."

"That's allowed?" asked Zeke.

"No," said Uriel. "They're rogue. They're breaking the rules."

"Pedro can't stop them?"

"Sheesh," said Gabe. "We're going to be here for eternity if we keep answering questions. Enough."

"Pedro doesn't venture outside his territory," said Uriel. "He stays put. The only way a Watcher goes back is when he's 'killed'. And if a rogue Watcher chooses the right situation, that's unlikely to happen. The longer he stays rogue, the more powerful he becomes, the more influence he has over the imbalance of good and evil. Typically, it's going to take another Watcher to find them and bring them back."

"Or send them back," said Phil.

"What about the weapons?" asked Zeke. "What happens to them?"

Phil shrugged. "They become the stuff of legend. Usually."

"Usually?"

Gabe tensed. "We really should go."

Phil held up a hand, stalling Gabe. "You've heard of the Bajiaoshan, the giant fan that creates whirlwinds?"

"No," said Zeke.

"The Pasha? It's a lasso."

"No."

"What about the Kalevanmiekka?" Phil asked. "It's the Finnish sword."

"Nope."

"Sheesh," said Uriel. "You've been living under a rock. What about all those books in your apartment?"

"They weren't for me," said Zeke, unable to restrain the harsh edge to his tone.

"All of those things are Watchers' weapons," said Paul. "They find their way into the mythology of every culture. But they're very real."

All of this was too much to digest. Gabe was right; Zeke didn't need all of this thrown at him right now—Watchers, rogue Watchers, books, mythical weapons, Enoch, the undead. But he did have one last question.

"So what is all of this about?" asked Zeke, taking a step back from the trio. "Why are we here? What does any of this have to do with angels? And Li…and the Badlands and… everything? Who is Pedro?"

"That's a bunch of questions," said Uriel. "As for Pedro, that's complicated. But the bottom line is it's all about redemption, Zeke."

"Redemption?"

"We have got to go," said Gabe. "There are three Marines

headed from that watering queue. They're coming this way. This could get messy."

Zeke glanced at his body again. Countless more questions ran through his mind, and he wanted answers to all of them.

Something in his gut had told him the world was off-balance from the moment he'd seen the Horde in his rearview mirror giving chase. His wounds had been too severe. He'd known it. And when he'd awaken in the cantina with those grave injuries all but healed, he'd known it. When there was ice in the glasses and nobody knew who the Tic was or who the Overseers were, he'd known it.

Yet he'd also believed, deep within the recesses of his consciousness, his soul hadn't found a resting place. Racing. Searching. Aching redemption. And he'd never once considered the possibility he was dead. The truth was there all along and he didn't see it. Uriel was right when she'd told him he was asking the wrong questions.

Seeing his body here, dangling at the end of a chain, crystallized all of that buried supposition. He was dead. The Overseers had killed him. The Tic had likely tipped them off.

Yet here he was, his heart beating, his body sweating, his adrenaline pumping. He was back in that same place where his natural life had ended. These angels had brought him here for redemption. They were giving him a chance to right his wrongs. A strange sense of comfort washed over him in the fraction of a second it took for him to process all of these things, this new understanding of the world around him and how he fit in. This was the proverbial second chance.

He stepped forward, between the Watchers and the trio of Marines marching toward them with their weapons drawn. Each of them had an M27 pulled tight to his shoulder. They were shouting commands.

In a swift series of seamless, skillful moves born of someone with far more practice than he, Zeke drew his revolver from his waist, raised it, leveled it, braced himself, and pulled the trigger.

A blast of energy pulsed from the weapon with a *whoomp*, expanding outward. The ground vibrated, warbling the air. Its barrel lifting upward, the weapon kicked in his hand, but his aim was true, at least as true as it needed to be.

The trio of Marines was lifted off the ground and spun awkwardly up and backward. They rose, tumbling head over feet, their limbs flailing, until they fell. Their weapons clattered and snapped. Clouds of dust rose into the air, marking the spots where their now twisted bodies had landed.

Incredibly, Zeke stood his ground against the recoil. He looked at his feet to see thin skid marks leading forward from his boots in the dirt that coated the pavement. He'd slid back six inches, no more, and had kept his balance.

He looked back at the Watchers, all of whom had large grins plastered on their faces. Uriel winked and blew him a kiss.

"Now that you know you're dead," she said, "the rules are different."

"That is to say," added Phil, "there aren't any rules."

Zeke looked at the gun. It glowed blue as it had before. "I've got two shots left."

"Best not waste 'em," said Uriel. "Let's go. You lead the way."

"I've got more questions," said Zeke.

"They'll be plenty of time to get them answered later," said Gabe.

"Right," said Zeke. "Redemption." After the blue glow disappeared from his weapon, Zeke tucked it back into his waist.

"There is one thing you should know before we head to the Tic hideout though," said Phil.

"Yeah?"

"Since you're already dead, you can't die."

"What happens, then?"

The three Watchers exchanged glances and Uriel answered, "If your physical form gets offed, you go back to Pedro's."

"That's it? It's like a game? You *lose* and you go back to the start?"

"Not exactly. Once you get offed, you can't come back here."

Zeke tilted his head to one side.

"This is your one shot to set things right," Uriel explained. "You don't do it now, you won't ever get to do it again."

CHAPTER SEVENTEEN

L i tightened the belt around her waist and sighed. She wore the gear of a TMF Marine, down to the boots and the tactical belt. She looked like part of the monolith, the expansive collective of well-trained peacekeepers who were as adept at ending life as they were sustaining it.

Frederick and Archibald insisted that if she were to accompany a team of TMF Marines back to the underground compound in which the Tic had tortured her and held her hostage, she would have to blend. Although she'd agreed, she was glad there was no mirror in the room. Li didn't want to see herself as a Marine. That was too much. She was never one for uniforms, never one to broadcast who she truly was, which was why being a spy fit her so perfectly.

Li was in a room on the third floor of the Fascio. Frederick had led her there himself. The third floor was full of offices and bureaucratic niceties. This room, it appeared, was for small meetings, containing a conference table and six chairs. A large monitor decorated one wall, split into a multi-display of security cameras on the perimeter of the building. On the opposite wall was a cherrywood sideboard topped by a bowl filled with engineered or genetically modified fruit. There was a cluster of bananas, a pair of bright red apples, and an orange. Next to it was a silver tray with four leaded glasses atop it. Adjacent to the sideboard sat a large keg of water, a tap at the front.

Li moved across the room to the keg. She noticed the water was vibrating from a low hum at this end of the room. She carefully approached the keg, reverent in her movements, and placed her palm on the side of the barrel-shaped glass container. She spread her fingers apart on the glass, sensing the vibration and feeling the hum.

The keg was cold, the glass wet with condensation. This was refrigerated water. No doubt about it.

Despite working in a Tic bar, living with a bootlegger, being a spy for the highest levels of Overseer government, among other things, Li couldn't remember the last time she'd had a sip of cold water. Room temperature, sure. Even hot water wasn't as much of a delicacy. But cold water was something altogether different.

She reluctantly pulled her hand from the glass and eyed the tumblers on the sideboard. She rubbed her wet thumb and fingers together. Her eyes danced between the tap on the front of the glass keg, the shimmering surface of the water inside, and the empty glasses inviting her to partake of the rare treat.

Li leaned over and picked up a glass. It was heavy in her hand. She drew it to the tap. With her other hand, she gripped the tab atop the tap's nozzle and was about to turn it open when a knock at the door startled her.

Spinning in time to see the door opening, a portly man dressed in fine clothes a size too small entered the space. A knowing smile spread across his cherubic features when his gaze fell to her hand on the unopened tap.

"Oh, don't mind me," he said. "Please, fill your glass."

She appraised his appearance. He was wearing purple, and

upon closer inspection, the clothes were more like two sizes too small. It was as if he'd put them on and then inflated himself to the popping point. His hands looked soft and swollen, his face clean shaven, assuming he shaved. There was a cynical quality about him despite the youthful glow of his skin.

He waddled a few steps closer to her, shutting the door behind him. He motioned with his hands for her to pour the glass. "You're not in trouble," he said. "You've earned a glass of cool refreshment, don't you think? Of anyone in the protectorate, I'm the one to tell you it's okay to drink."

Then she knew who he was. He was Louis Donne, the man in charge of water for the city-state. He'd risen to his position through nepotism and wasn't well-liked. Commander Guilfoyle protected him, though she wasn't quite sure how they were related.

He'd come to power after Li went undercover in the Tic, so she'd never gotten a firsthand assessment of the man. Everything she'd learned about the Overseers during her time undercover was second, third, or fifth hand, all rumor and conjecture. But everybody knew who Louis was, if not by appearance then by reputation.

"You're Louis," she said, removing her hand from the tap. She held the glass. The air in the room suddenly felt lacking. She tried sucking in a deep, calming breath. His presence made her deeply uncomfortable.

"And you're Adaliah Bancroft," said the lieutenant. A low belch escaped his mouth as he spoke. Cheeks vibrating with the baritone of the burp, his face flushed. He pulled a closed fist to his mouth. "I apologize. I had a large breakfast," he explained. "More of a fine dinner, actually. I'm not sure it's agreeing with me so early in the day."

Li gulped. What was he doing here? What did he want?

A waft of foul air that smelled like a cross between stale coffee and lemons hit her nose and she winced. Louis must have noticed the sour look on her face. The rose color of his cheeks shaded darker.

"Get yourself some water and take a seat," he ordered.

"I'm okay," she said, moving to return the glass to its tray.

His expression tightened. "That's not a request, Adaliah. Pour me a glass too, would you?"

Louis gripped the back of a chair and rolled it out from under the table. He shuffled his feet, plopped into the seat, and used his heels to scoot himself forward until his belly touched the table. Elbows thunking onto the table, he drummed on its laminate surface with his palms, playing pretend drums. At the far end of the room, security images flickered on the wall-mounted monitor.

Li turned from him without acknowledging the command. She squeezed the tap and turned. Water splashed into her glass, which grew cold in her hand. When the tumbler was full, she turned off the tap and delivered the glass to the lieutenant.

"Thank you." Louis raised the glass in a toast and then gulped like an infant with a sippy-cup. The man appeared enraptured with the drink, as though in the moment there was nothing else in this world, or any other, that could draw his attention from the invaluable commodity.

When he'd finished the glass and set it back onto the table, he drummed his palms again. Li poured herself half a glass and found a seat as far from the lieutenant as she could.

Louis stopped drumming. He spread his fingers wide on the table like a child about to trace them. "Adaliah Bancroft," he said, testing the sound of her name. "You're thinner than I expected. I've heard tales of your beguiling beauty, the soft angles of your face."

Where is he going with this? she thought.

"I know about this Tic raid," he went on. "I know Frederick and Archibald are hoping you can give them their smoking gun, so to speak. So when I say you're the face that launched a thousand ships, it's not hyperbole," he said.

A condescending smile, the kind she'd seen before on powerful men, spread across his face.

"That's correct," said Li. "But it's more specific than just *Greek*. You're referring to Helen of Troy. It was her beauty, and her kidnapping, that started the war between Sparta and Troy. She was the daughter of Zeus and Leda. And her legend is just that, it's mythology."

Louis nodded. He lifted his index finger and wagged it at her. "You're the reader," he said. "I know this about you. Old books, right? The kind of stories not acceptable to the protectorate, yes?"

Li shrugged. Her half-empty glass of water was untouched. How did he know about her books?

"Tales of intrigue," said the lieutenant, "subversive allegories, stories of military heroism. There's even one on your shelf about a famous woman spy."

"You could say famous spy," said Li. "There's no need to add the qualifier to it."

Where had he gotten his information? She noticed the wall display flip from one set of images to another.

"You're right," he said, lowering his head in deference for a moment. "But I only use the qualifier because you're a woman spy."

"Where is this going, Lieutenant?" she asked. "What do you want? Why are you here? I have somewhere to be."

The lieutenant pushed back from the table and rubbed his hands on his pants so fast Li wondered if he might spark a fire.

"Yes," he said. "I'm aware. You're going back from whence you came, to the Tic torture chamber. Somehow you convinced the twin conspirators, Frederick and Archibald, that returning there with valuable resources was a good idea." He waved a hand. "You've got time. The team is prepping for your mission."

"Conspirators?"

"The two of them are always working to consolidate power," he said, sighing. "But that's an unrelated story and I need not digress. Back to your questions. Ask them again."

"Why are you here? What do you want? And how do you know about the mission?"

Louis stared at her before answering. It was long enough that Li shifted uncomfortably in her chair and took a sip of the water. It was cool in her mouth, not cold, having sat at room temperature for several minutes now.

"That's three questions," Louis said. "I'll take them in order. Is that acceptable?"

Li nodded. Setting the glass down, she gave him her full attention. It was unlikely that he'd answer her questions honestly. More than what he said, she wanted to study his body language.

"This is a meet and greet," he began. "I've heard so much about you, Adaliah. Your reputation precedes you. That the protectorate Overseers are content to let you keep contraband in your apartment says something about the esteem with which they hold you and your value. I had to meet you."

There were always signs someone was lying. Tells. The most important of which, comparing current to typical behavior, wasn't relevant here. Li didn't know him and had nothing with which to compare his tone of voice, his nonverbal cues, and his tics.

She could say he hadn't changed his demeanor since entering the room. What he'd just told her was consistent with how he'd behaved during the entirety of their encounter. He hadn't tightened his body, pulled his legs underneath him, or hidden his hands. The man had appeared relaxed the entire time, save his embarrassment after belching.

"Go ahead," Li said.

"I'm here because I wanted to see for myself," said Louis. "No offense, but you're not the intoxicating ingenue some would have me believe. I like my women a little…thicker. To each his own."

Li wasn't offended. This man's opinion was as irrelevant as a non-protectorate-sanctioned gardener. To think people used to plant their own food and harvest it. That seemed so insane. What seed was this man planting?

"To question three now," he said, running his hand across his mouth. "I don't want anything other than to satisfy my curiosity." Louis shifted in his seat, drawing his legs together. The fabric bunched and pulled against his thighs. "You realize that the first two questions are different ways of asking the same thing?" he asked, his voice pitching higher. "I'd have thought you cleverer than that."

Studying him, she knew the answer to that question was a lie. The lieutenant was hiding something. What was it?

The lieutenant gripped the top of the glass with his fingers and lifted it. Tilting it on an angle, he tapped its bottom corner on the laminate.

"What about question three?" she pressed. "How do you know about the mission? Did Frederick tell you about it?"

The lieutenant let go of the glass and shifted in his seat. Opening his mouth to speak, he paused, closed it, and opened it again. The man was thinking about his response. There was no doubt he was being deceptive at best, and outright lying at worst. Either way, Li eagerly awaited his response, repressing a smile that came from having figured him out. This wasn't a simple meet and greet.

"I…I have sources," he said. "Suffice it to say I am not on the best terms with my brother lieutenants. And so, I don't always trust what they trust. They trust you. It doesn't automatically instill the same instinct within me."

Li's brow furrowed. She said nothing.

He pushed farther back from the table and used his chair's arms to lift his considerable heft to his feet. Lieutenant Louis Donne bowed, genuflecting before her.

"It was a pleasure," he said. "I'm so glad I took the time to come meet you, to gauge for myself the allure of your…of you. I'm sure we'll be seeing more of one another, Adaliah."

Louis lumbered toward the door, opened it wide, slid past it, and left it ajar. Li reached for her glass and emptied the water into her mouth. The hum of the cooler filled the silence in the space.

Had he come to learn about her? Or had he visited her so she could learn something about him? She was considering these questions when something on the wall-mounted display opposite her caught her attention. Li rolled the chair back and stood, walking past the open door toward the monitor. There were four color images on the screen, each of which took up a quarter of the display. They alternated every few seconds, giving the observer different views of the Fascio's exterior. She'd not seen this before. When she'd arrived, they'd brought her to the building through an access tunnel and, for security reasons, hadn't allowed her outside yet.

The images cycled from one to the next. It took several minutes before the one that had drawn her attention reappeared. When it did, her knees weakened. A thick stream of acid rose in her throat and her stomach roiled. Tears blurred her vision and a wave of dizziness forced her to place a hand on the wall to steady herself.

On the image in the upper left corner of the monitor, in full color and in sharp focus, were three bodies hanging from chains at the entrance to the Fascio. The body on the left was unmistakable. Despite the gore, the exposed bone, and the blood, she recognized the person whose soul had once occupied the flesh that hung there purpled, swollen, and rigid.

Li didn't want to believe it. She took her free hand, the one not keeping her from collapsing in a blubbering heap on the floor, and gently touched the display.

Her fingers distorted the image, pressing into the soft display, as she reconciled in that moment the truth of what Brina had told her. Her chin quivered, and she used her black shirtsleeve to wipe the sheen of tears from her eyes.

As much as she'd wanted to kill Zeke for having left her to fend for herself, as much as she'd convinced herself she hated him as she rotted in her rat-infested cell, as much as he was a coward and a weak-minded petty criminal, he was a man she'd once loved. He'd been a mark, a target, but he became more than that. She loved him. That emotion, which she'd suppressed as she struggled to survive in the Tic's dungeon, bubbled to the surface.

She loved him.

She was in love with him.

Now he was dead.

The full-color digital representation of his body made it unmistakable. He was a partial corpse rotting in the sun, which, in the arid heat of the city-state, was a long process.

Li clenched her jaw. She steeled herself, slowing her accelerated heartbeat as her masters had taught her to do so many years ago.

The torture hadn't broken her. The imprisonment hadn't killed her resolve. And this new development—the death of a targeted liaison with whom she never should have shared any emotional connection—would not stop her. It couldn't. She'd come too far, survived too much, for *this,* of all things, to break her.

Yet there Zeke was, dead. The man she'd foolishly allowed herself to love, killed by the very people she'd dedicated her life to...

CHAPTER EIGHTEEN

The Watchers scowled at Zeke.

He raised his hands in surrender. "I'm doing my best," he said through the fabric of his bandana and beneath the din of the crowd surrounding them on all sides. "Remember, I found out I'm dead. You could give me a break."

"We could," said Uriel, "but we'd rather your failure irritate us."

They sat in the bar where Zeke had murdered Mogilevich. It was midday, but the place was busy. A new waitress hustled from table to table while Markus worked the bar. He'd glanced at them twice but didn't appear to take further notice, being preoccupied with the string of drink orders. They were at a table in the back corner of the room so they could observe the comings and goings of everyone in the place. They'd entered the lion's den with much of the pride already hunting them. This was dangerous.

Uriel threw back a shot of engineered Cocuy and slammed the glass onto the table. Gabe nursed a beer. Phil lit a cigarillo and puffed it to life. Smoke hung in the air around his large head. He took a drag and blew the smoke out through his nose and tucked a lighter back into his pocket, letting the cigarillo hang as he spoke from the corner of his mouth.

"How many more places to check?" he asked. "This was number four."

"One more," said Zeke. "She has to be there. It's an underground compound."

"Connected to the tunnels?" asked Uriel. She raised her hand to get the waitress's attention. She pointed to her shot glass.

Zeke shook his head. "No. It's separate from everything. They store weapons there, coordinate shipments, extract information."

Gabe raised an eyebrow. "Extract information?"

Zeke rubbed his thumb along his ruined fingertips. "Torture. If they think someone has betrayed them, they find out, and they…"

Letting the sentence trail off, he shrugged. There wasn't a point in delving into the details of what the Tic did in that place. Truth be told, he didn't want to consider the possibilities of what had happened, or was happening, to Li.

The waitress arrived at the table. She wiped her hands on the filthy apron at her waist. "Another shot?"

"Two, please," Uriel said. "Same stuff and fill it to the rim."

The waitress pointed a finger at Gabe. "You good with the beer?"

Gabe picked up the mug and toasted her. "I'm good," he said, with a flirtatious lilt to his tone.

"Anyone else?" she asked. She eyed Zeke, and she squinted. "What's with the scarf?"

"It's a bandana," interjected Uriel. "It's his thing. He's trying to make it happen."

The waitress's eyebrows twitched with confusion. "Make it happen?"

"You know," said Uriel, trying to explain with her hands, "make it a *thing*. Like a fashion statement. He's on the leading edge of a trend."

"A trend?" the waitress said suspiciously.

Uriel put her hand on her chest, speaking as if Zeke weren't sitting right next to her. Leaning in, she lowered her voice. "Personally, I think it's douchey. Nobody's gonna wear a bandana over half their face all the time. It's hot, it's uncomfortable, and it smacks of someone who tries too hard."

The waitress appeared to scrutinize the four strangers at the table. Then she settled on Uriel. "I haven't seen you in here before. Are you making a run from another protectorate?"

Zeke spoke up before Uriel could answer. "Isn't it your job to bring us drinks and not ask questions?" he said firmly. "If I remember from the last time I was in here, Mogilevich had rules about talking to customers and whatnot. Right?"

The waitress nodded sheepishly. "I'll get the Cocuy." She hurried off toward the bar.

"Douchey?" Zeke grumped to Uriel. "Really? Aren't you supposedly an angel? Not a demon?"

"Yeah," said Gabe. "With her it's debatable."

"We should go," said Zeke. "We shouldn't be wasting time here now that we know Li isn't here. Every minute we waste—"

Phil held up a hand to stop him, took another drag of the thin, sweet-smelling cigarillo, and blew the smoke out in twin streams from his nostrils. He tapped the ashes into a black plastic tray at the center of the table and pointed at Zeke with the ashy end of the butt. "We'll head out in a minute, as soon as Uriel throws back her shots. If we hustle out of here, we'll draw attention to ourselves. Better to act natural."

Zeke scanned the bar. He didn't notice Markus staring at him as the waitress whispered into his ear.

"Can people see you?" Zeke wondered aloud to the

Watchers sitting with him in the corner of the dank watering hole. "I mean, I know they can see you. I guess, *how* can people see you? How can they see me? We're dead."

"You want me to take this?" asked Gabe, checking with Uriel and Phil.

They nodded their consent. Gabe took a sip of his beer and planted the mug with a heavy *thunk* that spilled the foamy, pale liquid over the rim and sloshed it onto the table. "We're all dead, but we're not dead. We're in that middle ground between life and death. We can walk amongst mortals, act as them, mingle with them."

"Be intimate with them," Uriel cut in. "And let me say, there is nothing like doing it with a Watcher. It's heavenly. Or so I'm frequently told."

"That's the perfect segue," said Gabe. "We're not in heaven; we're not in hell. We're—"

"In purgatory," said Zeke. "Seeking redemption. Trying to earn our wings?"

"More or less," said Gabe. "It's a little more complicated than that. Phil?"

Phil flicked the back of the butt with his thumb and then smashed it into the ashtray. "There's good and evil everywhere. Not just here, not just now. It's always existed. It's the balance of things. To know good, you must know evil. To know light, you must know darkness."

"To everything there is a season?" Zeke surmised.

"Not really," said Phil. "And it's not right. There's not a purpose for *everything*. Some things just happen. Anyhow, as I was saying—"

"Sorry I interrupted," Zeke apologized.

"As you do it again," Uriel chastised with a smirk.

"As I was saying," repeated Phil, "we have a job as Watchers. We seek out where there are imbalances. When there's too much of something, our job is to tip the scales back to an even balance."

Zeke blinked. "Wait, you're saying that sometimes you fight on the side of good, and sometimes you fight for more evil?"

"That's an oversimplification of it," said Gabe.

"But yes," said Uriel.

"This is a place with too much wickedness," said Phil. "So we're here to help with the recalibration."

"Is that why you're allowed to kill people?" asked Zeke. "I mean, that would seem to be an immediate disqualifier for an angel, or whatever we are."

"It's part of the balance," said Gabe. "We're empowered to do whatever we need to in the course of restoring stability between the good and the not so good."

Zeke's eyes widened. "And you're helping me because you think I'm good?"

"No," said Gabe flatly. "You're the cog that got this gear spinning. That's it."

"That's not entirely it," corrected Phil. "Redemption does have a role to play, but, like we've said multiple times. It's compl—"

A pair of loud blasts punctured the air, like the sound of two metal sheets clanging together. Screams and the clattering of people scattering or grabbing their weapons followed. Mouth agape, the color draining from his face, Phil's chin dropped as he reached for the back of his head with a trembling hand.

Zeke saw the blood leaking from the corners of Phil's mouth in the instant before the big man sank in his chair, wavered, and dropped face-first onto the table. His nose smashed onto the hard wood with a sickening crack. The bowler hat flipped off his head and rolled onto the floor.

Behind Phil, moving forward with purpose and a raised

rifle, was Markus. His body jerked from the recoil as he sent another volley of shots toward the Watchers.

Zeke dove to the floor, as did Uriel. Gabe took a shot in the shoulder, but freed one of his fighting sticks as he spun and rolled onto the floor.

He sprang to his feet and whipped the stick at Markus. But the barkeep was fast on the trigger. His M27 unloaded another trio of shots, which hit Gabe's center mass. Still, somehow, the warrior struck Markus with the weapon. It glowed blue as its energy pulsed and sent a shock wave through Markus's body.

The barkeep spasmed and dropped his rifle. He cried out in pain and dropped to one knee. Other Tics were scrambling to gather their wits and their weapons.

Uriel was on her feet now and engaged in hand-to-hand combat with a pair of them. Her body glowed as she kicked and spun at her opponents. They were no match for her.

All of this had unfolded within seconds. Zeke returned to his feet and tried to help Phil, but it was too late. A pair of spaced holes had bored through the back of the big man's neck. Zeke's hand came away wet and painted with his friend's blood.

They might not be alive, but it was impossible to know from the carnage in front of him. Bullets whizzed past Zeke's head and splintered the wall behind him. He ducked and knocked over a chair.

It was chaos. He reached for his revolver, but stopped short. He couldn't fire at Markus with Gabe in the fight or at the men engaged with Uriel. It was too risky. So he reached behind him and grabbed Uriel's M27.

He knew she'd reloaded it with a fresh magazine and that it was ready to fire. He aimed at the struggling Markus, who was working to get to his feet, and applied pressure to the trigger.

The rifle barked, repeatedly recoiling against his shoulder. Keeping the trigger depressed, a quintet of shots kicked from the barrel and rocketed into Markus. His body jerked with each of the impacts in a macabre dance, and the bartender collapsed to the floor.

Zeke caught a man taking aim at Uriel with his own handgun. He was shielded behind an overturned table. Zeke shouted a warning to her, swung the barrel toward the Tic, and pulled the trigger. A short burst of rounds shot from the automatic rifle, peppering the face of the overturned table until the horizontal line tracing the impact of 5.56-millimeter rounds found the target's face and erased it.

Zeke whirled toward the door in time to see three Tics trying to leave. They weren't armed as far as he could tell. It didn't matter. He leveled the rifle and pulled the trigger. It pounded against his shoulder and jackhammered rounds into the trio.

One slammed against the wall and slid to the floor, leaving a bloody Rorschach on the painted plaster. The other two fell into each other, tackling one another to the ground.

Zeke released the trigger, uncertain how much of the fifty-round magazine he'd emptied. Hands tingling, his body vibrated from the aftershock of the heavy fire, and he spun to see the waitress crouched against the bar, curled into a ball, her hands over her ears.

He shifted to see Uriel slam her palm into the chest of an outmatched Tic. His body shot backward and he crashed to the floor several feet from where he'd stood an instant before. The blue glow pulsed on Uriel's skin, strobing and weakening with what Zeke imagined was each of her successive heartbeats.

Nobody else moved in the bar other than him and Uriel. She glanced at him before darting to Gabe. The Watcher lay on his back, holding a stick in the tight grip of his left hand. Somehow, he still breathed, but it was labored and audible. The only other sound was the whimpering waitress at the bar.

Zeke crossed the room and aimed the rifle at the woman. Adrenaline coursed through his body. His rapid pulse thumped in his ears, the rush of blood deafening.

It didn't matter to him that the Watchers couldn't truly die, that they were already somewhere between life and death. It was irrelevant that Phil, and likely Gabe, were rejoining Barach and Raf, who'd undoubtedly been caught by Badlanders. What mattered was that the Tic had tried to kill them in cold blood.

"Get up," he snapped at the waitress.

Behind him, Uriel was offering solace to Gabe as he clung to whatever his existence was. Uriel, the tough, sarcastic, strutting double entendre, was crying. He could hear it in her voice as she reminded Gabe that everything would be fine, that this was temporary, and the eternal awaited him.

The waitress stood shakily. Her legs quaked. She appeared as though she might vomit right there. Then she did, retching chunks of indistinguishable rations onto the floor, on her shoes, on her shirt, and the already nasty apron that clung to her waist.

Zeke lowered his bandana, finding no use in hiding his identity now. He raised the rifle's aim to her forehead. She gagged again. Her cheeks ballooned and bile leaked from the corners of her mouth. Mascara-stained tears streaked her face. Bright red lipstick was smudged at her chin.

"Don't kill me," she pleaded. "Please don't kill me."

Zeke stood there silently watching the blubbering mess of a woman in front of him. The tsunami of anger that had crashed through him subsided as his adrenaline waned. Sympathy replaced wrath.

"I'm not going to kill you," he said, his voice barbed with hints of aggression. "Clean off your face."

The waitress lowered her shaking hands and bent at her waist. Clutching the bottom edges of the apron, she pulled it up to her face and cleaned off the remnants of her makeup and vomit.

When she finished, Zeke lowered the weapon but kept the muzzle aimed at her. The woman looked upon his face, then covered her mouth. Her eyes were swollen from the tears that welled there and threatened to spill down her cheeks.

"You're the dead man," she said through her fingers, her head shaking with disbelief. "Markus said you killed Mogilevich, and the Overseers killed you."

Zeke knew from his experience delivering illicit goods to bad people that the less he said, the more likely it was the other person would talk. People were uncomfortable with empty silence. They'd say anything to fill it, especially in tense situations.

"I saw your body," she said, her voice warbling with emotion. "It hung there next to Rose's. You know Rose?"

Rose's final moments flooded his memory. She'd been the one to tell the Tic he killed Mogilevich. After he'd saved her from the lecherous misogynist, the Tic's enforcers leaned on her. Graham, the head of the expansive enforcement team under Tic control, knew they could break her. Sometimes Zeke wondered if all the Tic ever did was seek retribution on those it perceived as having wronged the cartel. It was as much a part of Tic culture as was trafficking in water and other hard-to-find things.

After the Tic used her and extracted what she knew under threat of violence, or violence itself, it had turned her over to the Overseers for hanging. Murder was illegal in the protectorate. The Tic didn't need the Overseers' TMF breathing down its neck over the death of a bar owner. They'd readily sacrifice their own to keep the bought-and-paid-for peace that existed between the government and its black-market purveyor.

Rose had confessed to Zeke as they awaited their hangings; she'd told the Tic what they wanted to know and asked his forgiveness. Zeke told her he understood. He didn't blame her. If they'd done to her what he'd seen done to others, and had experienced himself, he couldn't blame her.

He learned from his time with the Tic that the threat of violence was often more coercive than the violence itself. Seeing the instruments of pain in a torturer's hands was worse than absorbing their bite.

Now he stood in front of this new waitress, Rose's replacement. He held his gaze and his breath and waited for her to keep talking.

"I know you knew Rose," she said. "You had to know her. She was there when you killed Mogilevich. People talk about it. They talk about seeing your bodies hanging next to one another in front of the Fascio."

Uriel cursed, drawing the woman's attention over Zeke's shoulder. The M27 was heavy in his hands now, straining the muscles in his neck and shoulders. Adrenaline was like a sugar rush. The burst of energy was powerful, but when it faded, it left him weaker than he'd been before.

"Why shouldn't I kill you?" he asked the waitress. "You started this mess by saying something to Markus."

Her eyes shifted back to his. "You said you weren't going to kill me. I don't understand. Is this real? How are you here?"

"What did you tell Markus?"

"I said I thought you were the man who killed Mogilevich," she said. "I said I didn't recognize the people at your table. None of them looked like Tic."

Uriel stood behind him now. The waitress's focus darted between them.

"You okay?" Zeke asked his companion without unlocking his stare on the waitress.

"I'll be fine," Uriel said. She didn't sound fine.

Those three words were a stew that conveyed a mixture of

things Zeke hadn't thought possible in such a brief declaration. In them, he heard anger, resignation, sadness, vengeance.

"She wants to know how I'm here," he said. "If this is real."

Uriel chuckled. The guttural, spine-chilling sound echoed through the bar. Then, without warning, and from her position on the floor, she jumped into the air and lunged toward the waitress. Her body glowed, the tattoos coming to life in a bluish hue that appeared ethereal. Her right leg shot forward, straight in front of her. Uriel's boot landed on the waitress's chin, forcing it to her chest. The waitress jerked backward, her body hitting the wall with an electric spasm.

The after-echo of Uriel's chuckle hadn't finished before she was back on two feet and the waitress lay unconscious on the floor. Zeke didn't know what had happened until it was over. He lowered the M27.

"Did you kill her?" he asked, incredulous.

"No, but when she wakes up, she won't question whether this was real. It'll feel real with every heartbeat."

Zeke hung his head. "I'm sorry about Phil and Gabe," he said. "It's my fault."

"It's not your fault. This is what we do. This is all we do."

"Still, I can't repay the debt. Whether or not it's my fault."

The strain of the day was clear. Her tattoos weren't glowing anymore. "Maybe not," Uriel said, "but can you do me a favor before we go find that girlfriend of yours?"

Zeke adjusted the Stetson, moving the front of the brim up and down to find the comfortable resting spot on his forehead. "What? Anything."

"Leave a tip for the waitress," said Uriel. "Twenty percent for the service and another five for the trouble."

CHAPTER NINETEEN

Brina was on one knee, looking out the window of a building across the street from the entrance to the Tic's hidden compound in a crappy part of the city the Overseers neglected more than most.

It was late afternoon. The sun dipped behind the taller buildings in the city, casting long shadows across the streets and onto the crumbling facades that lined them. The nearest watering queue was two blocks away. This street was devoid of life, but the various structures that surrounded the entrance to the underground lair teemed with Tic enforcers and their assigned muscle.

They were at the end of the street. The entrance, hidden from those who wouldn't know to look for it, was inside what appeared to be a four-foot, square power transformer. In reality, it was a pale green shell for the transformer and, when unlocked, provided access to a set of stairs that led to the compound.

The transformer box was between a pair of three-story apartment buildings, which were in poor condition, even by the standards of the city-state. The buildings had housed no one for years. Instead, they served as surveillance posts and drop points for the Tic, their informants, and the Overseer elite on the Tic's payroll.

Brina knew that should Li return with an army, they'd expect to find armed guards in those two buildings. They might even attack those buildings first before attempting entry into the compound.

She had stationed no one in those buildings, but had laced them with explosive charges set to detonate on command. Brina had placed her assets farther up the street and on adjacent, parallel streets.

That way, when the TMF converged on the compound entrance, the armed legion at her disposal would surround the intruders, ambushing them before they could do any real damage.

The plan wasn't only Brina's. She hadn't studied warfare or counterinsurgency, as had her superior, Graham. When she suggested trapping the coming army, he'd helped her flesh out the details.

They'd worked fast to mobilize the needed cadre of armed personnel. Now they had three dozen men and women positioned and ready to strike.

Brina's eyes were still swollen thanks to Li, and it was hard to breathe through her nose. Her mouth stayed open to offer the requisite air to keep her conscious. The backs of her arms and her chest ached from the bruising she'd sustained. Remnants of a headache flared with every beat of her heart. Blood pumped through her arteries, to her organs, into her veins. It was as though she could feel it coursing through her as she knelt before the window.

She was far enough back from the dingy panes of glass that darkness hid her from anyone who might happen along the street. Such was the case, she imagined, with everyone awaiting the coming storm.

Brina was hungry and, more than that, thirsty. Reaching for the canteen at her side, she licked her swollen lips, feeling the bulge of a wound with her tongue. Her fingers worked the cap, unscrewing it. The water was warm. It had the aftertaste of its metal container, but it quenched her thirst enough to help her refocus.

This wasn't how Brina imagined her life: an enforcer whose sole purpose was to glean information through violence. There was a dichotomy in her line of work. There was power. There was subservience.

Brina was like most of the Tic, recruited into the cartel from the fringes of society. The Tic preyed on those who had nothing to lose. Its membership was heavy with people who didn't know their parents or siblings, who stood off to the sides of ration queues, hoping for morsels or drops of charity.

Someone of authority within the gang had seen her begging. She was thirteen or fourteen, but looked older. Her size and strength gave her the appearance of a woman in her early twenties.

The gang member, thinking she was an adult, took her to Mogilevich to work as a waitress. That was always the entry-level job for a woman new to the Tic. Sometimes it was the only job.

Brina confided her age to Mogilevich. She told him she was orphaned and didn't even know who her parents had been. For as long as her memory served, she'd lived on the streets.

Mogilevich took her in, gave her a place to stay, and taught her to hide her emotions and to take out her frustrations on those who didn't serve her best interests. He trained her as a bouncer. Her size was obvious to anyone who saw her, but her raw strength was surprising to anyone who tested it.

For years, Brina learned the intricacies of the Tic under the tutelage of Mogilevich. The man was more than a bartender or the owner of a Tic dive. He was the Tic's most powerful man in the protectorate. That was why he got away with as much as he did without repercussions.

Few people under his command knew Mogilevich was at the top of the food chain. That was how the Tic worked; who somebody was and what authority they held was on a need-to-know basis. A bootlegger like Ezekiel Watson only knew who his immediate superiors were. Should he ever fall into the wrong hands, that kept him from revealing too much information about the organization's structure.

Typically, Brina wouldn't have been in a position to know how powerful Mogilevich was. She knew only because she'd lived with him, learned from him, and in her own weird way, loved him as a father.

She was seventeen when Mogilevich introduced her to Graham. He told the head of the Tic's enforcement team she had outgrown her job at the bar and that she was destined for something more important.

"Treat her like your own," Mogilevich had said at the first meeting. "Teach her everything you know."

Graham did exactly that. He taught her about surveillance, interrogation, persuasion. Brina absorbed it like a sponge. More than anything, she wanted to please Mogilevich, to make him proud of her. She was a natural at dissociating emotion from her job and performing the task at hand dispassionately and expertly.

"You enjoy this," Graham had said to her during a gory interrogation of a low-level Tic supplier who'd conspired to steal from the cartel. It was the first time he'd let her lead what he liked to call "fact-finding missions."

"If I didn't know better," he said, "I'd think you were smiling."

Brina *was* smiling and couldn't hide it. Graham's observation made the hint of it broaden across her face. It stayed there, the muscles in her face tiring even as she broke the subject of his will. It wasn't so much that she was happy with inducing terror or inflicting pain. Her joy came from being good at something, from having an unrivaled skill.

Coming from the dregs of the city-state, a nobody from nowhere, she never dreamed of a job that wielded such influence. By the time she was twenty, she was Graham's top enforcer. Better than the men. Her patience propelled her to superstardom amongst the growing force of Tic muscle.

People whispered as she passed them. Their eyes followed her. They knew her. They feared her. She owed it all to Mogilevich.

Then Ezekiel Watson took Mogilevich from her. So what if Mogilevich thrust himself upon women? They owed him. Acquiescing to his whims was the least they could do for the security he provided. Brina had, many times. It was her duty.

Now, she'd never touch him again. If Brina were capable of feeling loss, it was what might have consumed her. Instead, anger boiled inside her as she hid in the shadow beyond the window.

Ezekiel had paid his penance for what he'd done, and so had Rose. If it weren't for Graham wanting Adaliah alive, she'd be dead too.

She was about to be. The woman would pay for what she'd done.

Brina checked the magazine in her M27 for a third time. It was fully loaded, as was the magazine she kept in a vest pocket. She touched the pocket and ran her fingers along the silhouette of the curved magazine. She touched the other pocket, feeling for the hand-forged Damascus steel knife that once belonged to Mogilevich. She'd found it on the floor of his bar after he disappeared.

It was the perfect instrument for revenge.

CHAPTER TWENTY

L i stepped from the transport, her new boots crunching against the layer of grit on the main artery leading to the part of the city under Tic control. The truck idled loudly, its heavy engine rumbling such that she felt it in her chest as she moved past the hood to survey the path ahead.

These neighborhoods, which had served as her home turf for the years she spent undercover, were enemy territory now. The air hung thick, dry as it was, with the tense anticipation of what Li knew would be a bloody incursion.

A TMF Marine named Davis walked up behind her. He was clad in all black, his tactical helmet strapped onto his head.

"Ma'am," he said, "I know Lieutenant Archibald has given you authority on this mission, but may I make a suggestion?"

Li nodded at the Marine, and he pulled a palm-sized tablet from the Velcro pocket on his chest. He tapped it with a haptic-enabled glove, held it up to his eye, and the screen glowed to life. He stepped even with Li and held out his Com to show her a real-time map of the area that lay ahead of them.

"We're here," he said. "This spot is our position. It's noted by the green dot."

"I see it," said Li.

The Marine swiped his finger downward and then touched it with his thumb and forefinger, spreading them apart to zoom in on the display's graphic image. There was a red dot at the center of the screen. "This is our target location. Note the series of buildings on either side. They're multistory in some cases and essentially form a wall along this stretch of the approach. I call it a valley."

"Okay," said Li. "Your point? Davis, is it?"

"Stephen Davis, ma'am," said the Marine. "My point is that I'm concerned about what looks like a chokepoint. We could be walking into an ambush. They have the high ground, essentially, if they put snipers atop those structures."

"Okay," she said. "Though it's not like there's only one way in and one way out. We've got multiple access points. Here. Here. And here."

"You're correct. That doesn't change their inherent advantage as we begin the approach march. The Tic knows this part of the city better than we do. There is a good possibility that spotters have already identified us and alerted anyone who is bent on protecting the target asset."

"That's based on the assumption they know we're coming," Li countered. "You patrol the city. For all any of these people know, you're on patrol and nothing more. It's a leap to assume they not only expect us, but they've had time to plan some sort of ambush."

"With all due respect," said Davis, "my job is to assume the enemy knows everything. Only then can we anticipate and counter with what they don't expect. Either way, we have to be prepared for the enemy to engage here and here."

Davis pointed to two intersections that fed into what he'd effectively identified as a valley leading to their target destination. When he touched the points on the real-time graphic map, yellow dots appeared on the display to mark the locations.

Li put her hands on her hips and scanned the road ahead of them. The Marine knew better than she did. A spy had a certain set of enviable skills, but battle planning wasn't one.

"When we came to rescue you, ma'am, we drove straight up the gut," he said. "No waiting, no planning, just a cut-and-dry rescue. We had four men. We were in and out."

Li studied the display and folded her arms across her chest and glanced up at Davis.

"They weren't expecting us," he said, "so we weren't at risk of an ambush. It would have been a straight-up urban firefight. We deal with that all the time. This is different."

"So what do you suggest?" she asked.

"We have twelve men," said Davis, "and you, ma'am. That's stealth. It's agile, and good for a quick insertion, assessment, acquisition, and departure. It's not ideal for a street fight with an unidentified number of combatants. We don't have actionable intelligence on the ground. We don't know the force size, assuming there is one."

"Assuming," said Li.

"Yes, ma'am. Like I said, we have to prepare for the worst-case scenario."

"*Again*, Davis," Li said, a hint of frustration creeping into her voice, "what do you suggest?"

The Marine looked over his shoulder, appearing to take stock of their assets. "We have three tactical assault transports. I think we split up here. Identify your truck as Alpha. Mine is Bravo. The one in the rear is Charlie. I'll take my men here."

Davis pointed to a position one block from the valley. He pinched the screen with the haptic-enabled fingertips of his glove, and the map widened. It revealed the area around the target point and gave Li a clear, overhead perspective of the valley.

The Marine was right. This was dangerous. Each block held four buildings, or what was left of them. Not only did they give the enemy the potential high ground, but ample strategic angles from between and among the quartet of multistory structures between intersections. She counted twelve structures along the valley: eight that stretched along the length of it leading up to the target, and four on both sides of the compound's access point.

"From this position, with my team in front, we can identify potential hostiles and either engage or hold our position," he said. "Your team should move here."

He tapped the screen. A yellow dot appeared on the opposite side of the valley two blocks from the entrance to the compound.

"At that point, we should be able to identify whether there's an immediate threat. That's when we send Transport Charlie in one of two directions. Either that team drives straight up the gut of the valley, or it sits at the mouth and waits for us to converge."

The dot representing Transport Charlie was on the same street as Davis' team, but was on the northern side of where the valley intersected it. Davis' team, Bravo, was on the southern side. Together, the three teams formed a positional triangle.

His finger traced the two possible routes for Transport Charlie. It could go around the back side of a block of four buildings and re-enter the valley just north of the target, or it could go south, turn east into the valley, and proceed up the gut.

"That's a lot of ifs," said Li with a sigh. "A lot of moving parts."

"All fluid machines have a lot of moving parts, ma'am," he said.

At first glance, Davis appeared kind. He had boyish looks,

smooth, light-brown skin, and a toothy grin. His eyes, though, were dark and hardened from whatever they had absorbed during his time as a Marine. Theirs was not an easy existence.

On the surface, the TMF Marines were peacekeepers who made sure the queues for water, paper, or food didn't get unruly. They were armored security at the most visible spots in the protectorate.

Clad in all black, the force was unmistakable against the brown and tan hues that dominated the city-state. They stood out, and not just because of their distinct appearance or the ubiquitous M27 rifles they carried with purpose.

The men and women of the TMF Marines represented the power of the Overseers. They were everywhere, all-knowing, and they had the autonomy to act first and seek permission or forgiveness later.

On one hand, the Marines were there to keep law-abiding citizens safe. They maintained order and assisted those in need. On the other, they were no better than the Tic enforcers, who might use their authority to ruthlessly intimidate or physically assault anyone they thought had crossed an imaginary, often fuzzy, line.

The Overseers and their armed Marines used information as power. They used it to invoke fear. There was an imbalance of information in the protectorates. The Overseers knew where the water came from. They knew how the agro-engineering labs functioned. They knew what lay beyond the walls of their own city-states.

The reason the Tic was successful was because it too had information others didn't have. It leveraged that information, that power, to its advantage.

As much as water appeared the basis of the protectorate's, and the Tic's, economy, it was centered on the exchange and withholding of information. If the citizenry had as much information as the Overseers, if there was a balance, Commander

Guilfoyle and his lieutenants would lose their control. These Marines would lose their power.

All of this swirled around in Li's mind before she looked at Davis. It didn't matter what kind of Marine he was—if he used his power to threaten and coerce or to help people—as long as he facilitated the aim.

"Let's do it," she said. "The longer we stand here, the less chance there is they're not ready for us."

"Yes, ma'am," said Davis. He hustled toward Transport Charlie and communicated with the Marine in the front passenger seat. A minute later, he was in his own vehicle and they were moving.

Li explained the plan to her driver and told him where they needed to be. He put the truck into gear without questioning their mission.

The two men in the rear compartment worked on their rifles. One of them checked the scope attachment while another replaced one magazine with another. The one with the optic hummed a tune that sounded familiar to Li, but she couldn't place it.

The rumble of the transport's slow roll shook Li's body. She steadied herself by pressing her hands against the dash in front of her, taking in the ramshackle collection of structures on both sides of the street on which they drove. They inched toward their destination, moving so she might have been able to run faster than they traveled.

"Heads on a swivel," said the driver, a Marine with the last name George. He lowered the windows. The humming Marine heaved his M27 to the sill and planted the barrel on it. The other one in the rear compartment did the same.

"Bring it," said the humming Marine.

"Good to go," said the other. "Loaded, locked, and eyes on the prize."

Li rolled her eyes. Sure, these guys were battle-hardened,

but their machismo was over the top. All they'd ever really faced was a pathetic, hungry populace who barely knew what the world was before the droughts.

George swung the wheel to the right. The transport turned, its wheels crunching the debris on the dirt road. The driver accelerated out of the turn.

"Turn left up here," said Li. "Then make another left at the next block."

The driver nodded and the truck jerked as he shifted gears. Li noticed a man standing on a corner, hands in his pockets. He avoided making eye contact with her as the transport rumbled past him.

When they passed him fully, she eyed the large side-view mirror at the front edge of her door. The man jogged away with purpose. He rounded a corner a block behind them.

He was definitely a spotter. Davis was right. The Tic were expecting them.

"Give me your Com," Li said to George.

Without questioning her, George reached into his chest pocket and removed the electronic device identical to the one Davis had used. Li was familiar with it and its multiple functions, but they hadn't issued her a new one since her return. Things had moved fast.

"It's unlocked?" she asked.

"Yes." He made the second left, swinging south toward the valley.

Inertia from the turn shifted Li in her seat. She adjusted herself and touched the display on the Com with her haptic-enabled gloves. A short pulse rippled through her finger, and she tapped an application that allowed her to communicate with the other transports.

"Bravo, this is Alpha," she said. "We're nearing our position."

"Good copy, Alpha," replied Davis. His voice was clear above

the audible noise of his transport. *"We're in position, south of the valley. We're all clear. Charlie, what's your position?"*

"This is Charlie. We're north of the valley, one block from our position. All clear."

"This is Alpha. We're not clear," said Li. She was vaguely aware of the stare George was directing at her. He'd apparently not noticed the spotter. "They know we're en route."

"Good copy, Alpha," said Davis.

"Good copy, Alpha," said the lead for Transport Charlie. *"We'll move to alternate position and report."*

"This is Bravo," said Davis. *"Once in position, report your status. We'll reevaluate."*

"Good copy," said Charlie.

Li hesitated. "Good...copy," she said, mimicking the radio lingo. The road running east and west in front of them was what Davis had identified as the valley.

"Stop here," she said, referencing a two-story, roofless structure that looked more like a rusting cage than the frame of a building. "Davis said this is a good spot for some surveillance before we proceed."

George steered to the right and eased the transport to the side of the road, then jumped the curb to park the truck. The ruins would give them complete cover from whatever awaited them in the valley.

He shut off the ignition and the truck coughed before going silent. They sat there for a long moment, listening to their surroundings.

A warm, subtle breeze drifted through the open cab, carrying with it the familiar sour odor from this part of the city. It smelled to Li like rotting flesh. That was probably what it was. The ground was too hard for proper burial here. If people didn't burn the dead, they carried them to abandoned buildings and left them there for whatever surviving rodents might find them.

Li thought about the rats in her cell. Their skittering and incessant squeaking noises had almost driven her crazy. Then one night she'd caught one. She'd held it by the tail, pinched between her fingers. She'd watched it kick at the air and paw for some purchase it wouldn't find.

She'd stared at it in the dark and talked to it. She'd told it what she had planned. She'd confided in the mammal who she was and what she'd done to survive.

It had struggled, not willing to give up and not understanding what was coming. Watching the rat, Li had thought people were sometimes like rodents. They scurried along searching for food and water, but ultimately their fate lay in the hands of something more powerful, something with information they couldn't possibly know.

Smell was the strongest memory. It surpassed the other senses in catapulting Li back to those experiences she'd just as soon forget. The odor of death, pungent and unmistakable in its sour mixture of gasses and rot, was everywhere here. It was among the most familiar of all scents, Li knew. From her youngest days, she couldn't escape it.

Presently, she sucked in a deep gulp of fetid air that made her want to gag, and then she held her breath. She unlatched the heavy transport door, shoved it open, and exited the transport. She needed to focus on the here and now and not on the past. Now was what mattered.

Her team, Alpha, was in position. They were ready to round the corner and be the bait. Two of the three Marines were at the corner already. The third hustled across the north-south street to the opposite corner to get a different perspective of the valley.

Li checked both positions and decided to join the lone Marine, who by now was on one knee, eye to his rifle's sights. He was pressed up against the west-facing, crumbling stone wall at the intersection of the street on which her transport was parked. The long stretching valley ran east and west.

As she began her soft-shoe to the other side of the street, a flash of light caught her attention to the north of her. She stopped and swung around, M27 in her hands, leveled waist high. She didn't see the source of the bright flicker. It was there, though. Li was sure she hadn't imagined it, and was exposed here in the street's middle.

A quick scan told her there was no safe place to hide if, in fact, something was there, stalking her team. Li raised the rifle to her shoulder and moved north. She tightened her grip on the rifle, her finger just off the trigger. Blood surged through her veins, and the beat of her heart was so fast against her chest it almost hurt.

It was quiet. Other than the clatter of her men behind her and the sound of her boots on the road, there was nothing to distract her from listening for the source of the flicker. She was closing in on the next intersection when she noticed it again. This time she saw its source.

Li lowered her weapon and took off running at a dead sprint. Within a second, she'd reached the intersection and rounded the corner to the left. She stopped and raised her weapon again.

"Stop!" she shouted. "Or I'll empty this into your back."

The man twenty yards from her stopped. He raised his arms above his head without her having to tell him anything.

"Keep 'em raised," said Li. Drawing closer to the man, she ordered him to his knees and then flat onto the asphalt. She recognized him. In his left hand was a radio transceiver, the same kind of radio she'd used to signal the TMF before she'd escaped the compound. This man was a Tic.

"I know you," she said. "You were on the street back there. We passed you."

The man kept his chin on the hard surface and faced

forward. Li kicked at his legs to spread them farther apart and jabbed at the small of his back with the barrel of her rifle.

"Who are you?" she asked. "I know you're a Tic. But who are you?"

The man remained silent. Li pressed the heel of her boot into the man's calf, applying pressure with her weight.

"Staaahhp," he groaned, his painful cry echoing off the buildings.

"Answer me, then," Li said.

Turning his head toward Li, he released the radio and pushed it away. It skidded, raking across the rough asphalt a couple of feet. "I'm a scout," he said through gritted teeth.

She leaned into her bootheel, pressing into his leg. He groaned. "Are you armed?" she asked. "Keep your hands flat on the ground."

He shook his head. His fingers fanned out on the asphalt. Tears drained from his left eye, which was against the dirt.

"Who are you scouting for?" she asked.

"The Tic," he said, spittle flying from his mouth.

She dug in harder with her heel. His leg twisted awkwardly, and he squealed.

"I know you're working for the Tic," she hissed and checked over her shoulder for the Marines. She didn't have much time. "What is your job?"

The man sobbed from the pain. Snot clung to his nostrils.

Li eyed the radio feet from him. "Who's on the other end of that thing?"

He whimpered and sounded on the edge of hyperventilating.

"Who!" Li barked.

He caught his breath long enough to answer her. "Brina," he said. "The enforcer. Brina's on the other end."

"Where is she?"

"Near the compound," he said. "They know you're coming."

It wasn't surprising the Tic was expecting them. That Marine, Davis, was right. Whatever upper hand Brina thought she had was gone now.

CHAPTER TWENTY-ONE

Zeke's boots were giving him blisters. It didn't matter that until now they'd been the most comfortable things he'd ever worn on his feet. They'd somehow rubbed his heels raw. With every step, he acutely knew of the inside of the boot rubbing upward against his skin.

Wincing and cursing, he squatted awkwardly to adjust his socks. As he fished around inside the boot with his fingers, Uriel exhaled loudly enough for Pedro to hear her back at the cantina.

"Again with the boot?" she asked. "If I'd wanted to work with a child, I would have had one. Every time you complain about them, I want to throat punch you."

It wasn't twilight yet, but the day was long and there wasn't a lot of time left before sunset. Uriel ran a hand along the sides of her shaved head and adjusted the knot at the end of her ponytail. One hip jutted out as she stood between Zeke and a single-story strip of businesses that weren't open.

"What's today?" she asked.

Zeke finished picking at the socks and stood to test the adjustments. It was better. Not much better, but the sting wasn't as acute. "How should I know? What day it is, what month it is, I couldn't tell you. It's like it was wiped from my mind."

"Maybe it was," said Uriel. "Dying has different effects on different people."

Zeke took two steps toward the corner of the long building and peered around the corner. A family walked hand-in-hand along the center of the street. A mother and father, with two young boys who were barefoot. The clothes they all wore were threadbare.

Zeke noticed the father had an empty-looking pack on his back. The mother carried a large shoulder bag at her side under her arm. It too appeared empty. They were likely headed to the nearest watering or ration station.

A wave of guilt washed over him. His blisters were nothing compared to what that family, and so many like them, faced daily.

He stared at the bare, dirty heels of the boy holding his father's hand. It reminded him of his childhood and the abject poverty, the loneliness, and the constant pang of hunger that ate at his gut. The sensation of hunger and thirst was so omnipresent that it became part of the white noise of his life. Without its absence, he became unaware of its presence. Would these children turn to crime to pull themselves, kicking and screaming, from the mire of the protectorate? Was that the best future they could hope to have? Would they die with regret as he had? His mind drifted back to Uriel's assertion that death affected everyone differently.

He snuck back behind the building and told Uriel it was clear. Only a harmless family stood between them and the next block closer to the Tic compound where he hoped to find Li.

Using the wall to push himself to his feet, he stood and stretched his back. The fabric of his waistband pulled taut against the revolver at his midsection, and he touched it, remembering he had two shots left. Zeke moved around the corner of the building. Uriel followed and eased alongside him, the M27 in both hands, her heavy steps matching his as they marched forward.

Uriel tightened her grip on her weapon when the family fifty yards ahead of them stopped and the father turned around. The man whispered to his wife before tugging on her hand. They quickened their pace, the smaller of the two boys struggling to keep up. The father glanced over his shoulder as they widened the distance between themselves and Uriel and Zeke.

"Can't blame them," said Uriel. "I'd run too if I saw us coming."

Uriel raised her rifle, pulling its butt to her shoulder. The muzzle was aimed at the street, but her finger was on the trigger guard now, and she scanned one side of the street to the other. The rumble of a heavy truck droned in the distance.

A TMF transport roared across the intersection ahead of them, almost mowing down the family of four. The father jerked to a stop, tightly holding onto his child and wife. Arms pulling taut, one of the children stumbled to the ground.

Uriel planted her feet and raised the weapon. She tracked the slow-rolling armored vehicle with her scope. Her finger moved to the trigger.

Zeke started to reach for his revolver, but with the family in the way, he pulled back. He was beginning to dislike the limitations of his weapon thanks to its overpowered nature.

The transport kept moving through the intersection, headed elsewhere. Uriel removed her finger from the trigger and lowered the rifle. The father up ahead held the child who'd fallen. His son's face was cradled in his shoulder and neck, and they crossed the intersection in a hurry. The transport's rumble faded as it moved farther from the street, the boy's muffled cry filling the void.

"I've got to get another weapon," said Zeke, patting his untucked shirt where the grip strained the fabric. "This thing, as great as it is, has way too much potential for collateral damage."

Uriel pouted, the corners of her mouth turning downward in an exaggerated display of pity and annoyance. "I'm gonna say the gun's not your problem," she said, motioning with her head to keep moving.

Uriel relished being a critic. Zeke was sure of that. A dozen pithy retorts fluttered through his mind. None of them made the cut.

"Oh yeah?" was all he managed, then cursed himself for not having the guts to tell her what he thought. Even in death, Uriel was intimidating.

Uriel didn't acknowledge him, marching faster up ahead. When they reached the intersection, she turned left, following the path of the transport. Until now, Zeke had led the way. He was about to question her about the turn, but she spoke first.

"You think you're focused on the mission?" she said. "You think because your head didn't explode when you saw your dead body hanging from the building, you're doing a good job of managing things?"

Raising the rifle again, Uriel aimed at the dark storefronts and broken windows that lined the sides of this new path. Her attention on these potential targets, she continued her diatribe.

"Everybody freaks a little bit when they figure it out. Some get to that point earlier in the process than you did. I've seen newbies understand they were dead when they were running from the Horde. I've seen them straight up confront Pedro about it when he offers the first drink. Others take longer. They're either thick or in denial, pinching themselves or willing themselves awake. They'll make many irrefutable arguments about how they couldn't be dead. This couldn't be purgatory. It was too familiar to the world they knew."

A clattering noise drew her attention to the right and she whirled around. An emaciated cat hurdled through an open window and sauntered onto the uneven sidewalk to the right. It was the first cat Zeke had seen in months, maybe years. Cats and dogs weren't long for the protectorate. Every part of them was too valuable: their hides, their bones, their meat.

He'd never eaten either of them himself, but his mind drifted to the young boys he'd seen with their parents minutes earlier. What had they eaten to survive?

"You're doing it now," said Uriel, shaking him from the distraction. "Your head's in other places. It's not here, where it needs to be. All those other people I mentioned, the quick ones and the slow ones, regardless of how long it took them to understand their predicament and accept their possible fate, the vast majority find their focus because of what's at stake."

"I'm focused," said Zeke. "I'm present right now."

"Then stop with the questions," said Uriel. "I'm the first to wax philosophical when confronted with the wonders of existence…"

She said the last sentence in a way that made it clear she wasn't the first to wax anything when it came to the wonders of everything. Zeke didn't interrupt or show in any way he found her hyperbole unnecessary.

"…but I know the time and place for that stuff," she finished her thought. "This is neither the time nor the place."

Uriel leered at him.

"Got it," said Zeke. He did. He'd always been a man who thought three and four steps ahead. It was how he'd avoided getting caught as a bootlegger.

Every bellwether moment in his life had infinite possibilities, many of which he'd consider each time a new one presented itself. The lone exception to the behavior that had served him so well was his rash murder of Mogilevich. He hadn't processed the ripple effect of that decision, hadn't thought about the various life paths it might forge.

When he'd angrily shoved the broken liquor bottle into that leech with enough adrenaline-fueled force to bury its jagged edges deep into his body, severing blood vessels that essentially exsanguinated the man on the floor of his own bar, he'd been in the moment.

That was what Uriel was asking of him now. It was what he needed to do. He needed to be in the moment.

Zeke reached to his waist and drew the enchanted revolver. Its heft was comforting now. The weight of the weapon wasn't intimidating. She was right, the gun wasn't the problem. He was in his own head and he needed to get out.

He pictured Li in his mind. She was all that mattered now. Getting her to safety, freeing her from whatever the Tic had done, was his sole purpose. This was where he proved his mettle, where he earned his redemption and a shot at somewhere better than this forsaken wasteland oasis.

They reached the next block, rounding a corner to follow the audible rumble of a TMF transport, when Zeke stopped them. He held a finger up to his lips. Uriel stood virtually motionless, the rifle pressed against her shoulder.

After a moment, Zeke whispered, "You hear that?"

"Yeah." Uriel looked up, scanning the deepening blue sky. There wasn't a cloud above them or in sight. The sun was dipping. It was low enough it cast shadows from the taller structures and dead trees that stretched the length of this new east-west street in both directions.

"I think there's more than one transport," Zeke whispered.

The rumble was growing louder again. That was only possible if there was more than one.

Uriel nodded her agreement. "You're right. I don't think they're here for us though. If they were, they wouldn't have driven past us before. I know that driver saw me with the M27 leveled at his face. He didn't react."

"Yeah," said Zeke, his voice above a whisper now, "that's not the TMF's MO. They harass everyone for everything. If that driver saw you and he didn't have somewhere else to be, we'd be roadkill right now."

"Dude," said Uriel, "you *are* roadkill. Or whatever the hanging-from-a-building-while-varmints-chew-on-you equivalent is."

Zeke suppressed a chuckle. "You said varmint. Never make fun of me for anything ever again."

Uriel beamed. "So, you have spunk. C'mon, varmint, let's go rustle up transports."

The two of them hadn't moved twenty yards east when the sound of automatic gunfire thumped through the air. Zeke couldn't tell where the gunfire emanated from or where it was targeting. But the cracking echoes, displacing the air like shards of summer lightning, told him they weren't in any immediate danger. He crouched and followed Uriel, who bolted to one of the single-story brick buildings on one side of the road. It was in better condition than most, with an overhang, and offered relative obscurity from any threats.

Focus on the moment, he reminded himself.

The gunfire was incessant. It sounded like war.

Uriel counted aloud. A sharp divot creased her brow.

"That's at least a dozen weapons. Most are M27s. I can't tell what the others are, but there's a lot of them."

She looked at Zeke like she was searching for something.

Does she want guidance? Affirmation? Reassurance?

Zeke didn't know. He was aware that, for a split second, Uriel was freaked out. Whatever was happening was on a big scale. It was violent. And even if she couldn't die, he understood that human nature, or the nature of sentient beings, was to survive. Fight or flight. It was instinctive.

"Whatever is going on," she said, "it has to have something to do with why we're here. The timing isn't a coincidence."

Zeke balled his free hand into a fist and playfully punched her in the shoulder. Then he held up his weapon at eye level between them. "I've got two shots left. What are we waiting for? We'd better find out what's happening firsthand."

The worry on Uriel's face dissolved into a smile. The divot relaxed. She nodded toward the direction of the reverberating gunfire. "Ladies first," she said, but stood still.

Zeke waited for her to move before understanding what she'd meant. He smirked and moved past her toward the battle.

CHAPTER TWENTY-TWO

Brina heard them coming before she saw them. The TMF transports might have been a preferred mode of mobility for the Marines, but they weren't stealthy. The rumble of their engines and the low vibration of their hulking armored hulls gave her, and the awaiting Tics, plenty of time to steady themselves and take aim.

Then the thundering approach, which was growing louder, abruptly ceased. There was quiet again. A radio at her hip squawked. She twisted the volume lower and unclipped the radio, bringing it to her ear. A half dozen of the others had matching radios, all dialed into the same frequency.

"*This is position four. I hear 'em,*" said one of the men. "*I don't see 'em yet. Over.*"

"*Copy that, four,*" replied another. "*This is two. I hear 'em. From the sound of it, there are at least two transports out there. Over.*"

"*This is five,*" said a third. "*We copy that. We have eyes on one. It's three blocks east of us. It's sitting there. Not moving. Over.*"

"*Copy that, five,*" a voice chimed. "*This is position two. We see the same transport. Engine running. Stationary. Over.*"

Brina knew most of the teams by sight. Naming the

enforcers who Graham had told to volunteer, however, was another matter. Matching the voices to their faces was near impossible. So all the chatter might as well have been strangers. Then a familiar voice, and its accompanying name, called out over the radio.

"Brina, this is Graham. What's going on out there? Over."

Brina moved the radio to her mouth and pressed the transmit key. "Copy, Graham," she said. "Approaching vehicles stopped. Over."

"Say again?" Graham asked. *"Over."*

She needed to be careful about what she said, not wanting too much information being broadcast should the Marines compromise one of the other positions.

"Approaching vehicles stopped," she repeated. "Over."

"What does that mean?"

"Wait. Out," she replied, telling him she didn't have the answer but she would try to get it to him. Until then, she was finished talking to him.

"Copy that," said Graham. *"Out."*

Brina pushed a series of buttons on the radio transceiver's face and switched communication channels. On a new frequency, unknown to the other Tics and Graham, she issued one more message over the radio, this time to her spotter. "Scout, this is Brina. What do you see? Over."

Before the Tic troops had deployed to their positions, she'd privately communicated with one man she wanted to serve as a lookout. She wanted him farther away from the action in a location that might give her a heads-up to the TMF's arrival.

The young enforcer had already communicated with her once, when he'd seen a transport roll by him minutes earlier. There was a familiar-looking woman in the front passenger seat of a TMF transport. He told her he'd thought he'd seen the woman in a Tic bar.

Brina thanked him for the intel and asked him to move

closer to the street they'd readied for their ambush. The described woman could have been Li, but he couldn't be sure yet. He was to alert her to any other findings. Brina knew there must be more than a single transport on its way.

He hadn't provided any additional information since. She tried again.

"Scout," she called, "this is Brina. What do you see? Do you copy? Over."

The radio crackled for a split second before a short high-pitched tone showed someone was about to transmit. Brina lowered the volume and held the transceiver up to her ear to listen. The voice wasn't the scout's. It wasn't even male.

"I copy, Brina," said a woman on the other end. *"I'm coming for you."*

A chill ran down Brina's spine. She wasn't scared of many things. Her mentor and his proxy, Graham, had made certain her fears were compartmentalized in the deep recesses of her being. She was to access them only when they could provide fuel for her tasks.

This was not that kind of fright. It was a sensation, completely unfamiliar to Brina, which came with being hunted.

Sliding her fingers to the transmit key, she pulled the radio to her mouth.

"Who is this?" she said, staying as low as possible. "Scout? Is this you? Over."

Brina let go of the transmit key. The muscled enforcer, not used to finding herself cowering from anything, shifted her body and moved the radio to the side of her head. The response was instantaneous. It was clear and the voice was devoid of emotion.

"You know who this is," said the woman.

An image of a drenched, broken Adaliah Bancroft materialized in her mind. Those were the exact same words Brina had said to Adaliah when the Tic bar whore was strapped to a board and she was trying to extract information for her.

How had she lost so much leverage?

A burst of gunfire jolted Brina away from the window, followed by a percussive blast that knocked her onto her behind. A spray of plaster rained down on her head. The radio shot from her hand and flew across the room, hitting a plaster wall, shattering into several pieces.

Dazed, and deafened by the volleys of return fire on all sides of her, Brina crawled back toward the window.

How had the ambush not worked?

Brina clenched her jaw. There was no way that Adaliah and a small band of TMF Marines could get past the number of Tics she'd placed along the corridor of buildings that led to the compound. And then there was the compound. What awaited the Marines in there, if they got that far, would be more than a little surprising.

Brina tucked her arms underneath and rolled to the other end of the large window. There she reached out and found her own rifle. She wasn't used to the protectorate's ubiquitous automatic weapon, but given that the Tic trafficked them, she'd handled the rifle before and knew how to fire it.

She got to her feet and moved along the wall toward the door that would lead her downstairs and out to the street. Being hunted didn't agree with her. The chill that had run along her spine and tingled the ends of the hairs on her neck and arms had metastasized into an acidic nausea that crept from her gut and into her throat. The only way to keep it at bay was to go on the offensive. That was what her dear Semion Mogilevich would have wanted her to do.

When she moved into the hallway, the sounds of the gunfight dampened for the moment, and she could hear Mogilevich talking to her. His gruff voice was a source of comfort. It helped her focus.

"Remember the rules about fear," he'd said once. He was a man of rules. *"Number one: Fear is a weakness exposed. It is a weed evident of deeper roots. Cut weakness at its roots and you'll know no fear."*

It was a silly metaphor now that she considered it, sweat dripping into her eyes, the rush of adrenaline surging through her body.

The rifle's grip was comfortable in her right hand, and she grazed the bottom of the trigger guard with her finger. Rubbing it nervously, she moved her left hand to a better position underneath the barrel and drew the stock to her shoulder. She pressed it there, remembering that if she fired without holding it tightly against her body, the recoil would slam the butt into her arm or chest. The weapon could fire thirty-six rounds per minute, depending on the temperature outside. It could do serious damage if handled improperly.

The sounds of the battle, an earsplitting combination of gunfire and men shouting, amplified as Brina neared the exit of the building. The door was open, and outside she saw the orange-purple sky. It was dusk. They'd be fighting in the dark soon.

Two men rushed past the doorway, hurrying east along the street. A third, with red hair and pale skin, stopped near the opening, shouldered his rifle, leaned into the scope, and fired. The weapon rattled in his hands, the gas-powered rifle spitting a burst of smoke-emitting rounds from its sixteen-and-a-half-inch barrel. The enforcer lifted his head, glanced over his shoulder, and bolted forward.

Brina reached the opening and stepped outside, swinging her rifle and her body to the left. The percussive snap of automatic fire was deafening now. She'd entered the chaos of urban war.

Sticking close to the building, she advanced east toward the enemy. Ahead of her, against the building, was a trio of men.

Two of them returned fire. One stood, one kneeled, and the third was facedown on the street, his legs splayed awkwardly at the curb, the rifle under his body. His left hand twitched. Nothing else moved. Brina noticed his red hair before she saw the growing pool of blood leaching from his head onto the asphalt. She forged ahead. In the street, twenty yards from her, two more men were down. One of them was moaning and trying to drag himself to safety. The other was motionless.

She reached the two enforcers in front of her and called out to them. She dropped to one knee.

"How many are there?" she asked.

Neither man answered her. They were engaged with the enemy. The one on his feet stepped away from the building and into the street. He whirled to his left and ripped a short burst from his rifle before moving back to the relative cover of the building.

"How many are there?" she repeated. Her pulse thumped in her ears. Another wave of nausea surged and ebbed.

The kneeling enforcer fired a volley of rounds and popped the magazine from underneath the rifle. As he pulled a full mag from a chest pocket, he shot Brina a look of confusion. Slapping the fresh ammunition into the weapon, he called back to her, "What are you doing here? Get inside, *ma'am.*"

Brina prickled at the order. First, he wasn't one to give her orders. She had authority over all these men, the ones fighting and the ones dying or dead on the asphalt. Second, she didn't like the implication that because she was a woman she shouldn't be out in the open. The way he said "ma'am" made her want to jam the barrel into his mouth and hold the trigger.

"I'm not going anywhere," she said, glaring at him. "How many are there?"

"We don't know. The——"

His head snapped to the left, and the right side of his face disappeared behind a spray of blood. The man slumped to the ground, his weapon clattering onto the street.

Brina's body tensed and the adrenaline that had almost frozen her into inaction surged through her. Dropping to the ground, she shoved the body forward and used it to balance her rifle. Lying prone, she took aim at a TMF Marine firing from behind a row of empty concrete planters. The planters were taking the brunt of the incoming fire, and they wouldn't hold much longer. That Marine was pinned. Brina eyed the scope and put her finger on the trigger. Applying steady pressure, she fired. The weapon kicked against her. A spray of rounds shot from the barrel and toward the pinned Marine. They drilled the planters; clouds of concrete plumed in the air, creating a dust cloud that obscured the target.

Brina swept either side of the dissipating gray haze and to the right saw a better target. She wasn't sure at first glance, but the more she watched the potential target move along the edge of a building, she grew confident she knew who it was.

She settled into a new position and readjusted the rifle. The body shifted underneath the weight, but Brina made do and touched the trigger. She had a woman in her sights.

CHAPTER TWENTY-THREE

Li's team had waited until Bravo and Charlie were in position. With the Tic's radio in hand, they'd known where the enforcers were positioned. They'd converged at once, hitting the front edge of what was intended to be an ambush before they entered the valley.

There were only twelve against an unknown number of enforcers. However, with automatic weapons and the bouncing sounds of gunfire, Li figured they appeared to be a much bigger force than they were.

It had begun well. They'd knocked out the first positions on the first and second floors of the buildings at the eastern edge of the valley, and the twin snipers stationed on high ground at its effective entrance.

Then it quickly descended into chaos, and Li couldn't tell any longer whether they had the upper hand. She'd trained in mock street fights before and had studied small-arms tactics. None of it prepared her for the mind-melting reality.

The volume of the gunfire was deafening. The speed with which the environment around her changed was disorienting. The cries of the injured and dying made her want to plug her ears and curl into the fetal position in a safe corner somewhere far away from this mayhem.

Li reminded herself this was part of the end goal. It had to happen, and she had to suck it up. With the rifle in her hands, and Bravo team advancing west, she crossed the street without engaging any hostiles. Now she was flat against a building, hidden in the shadows under a canopy. To her left, a cloud of gray bloomed larger from the incoming M27 fire.

Davis was pinned behind the cloud and a pair of battered concrete planters. The Marine was on his stomach, his head down. There was too much incoming fire for him to do anything but lie there under what little cover he had. Li considered whether he was expendable. Checking over her shoulder, she saw two Marines who hadn't made it. They were dead in the street. That meant there were ten. Davis was critical, at least for now.

Li inched from the cover of the canopy and into the fading light of dusk. Her weapon drawn, she moved toward the street to offer cover fire. Much of it was from the second story of a building across the street and west of her position. There was also a pair of threats on the ground. One of them looked like he was using a body to balance his weapon.

Glancing back to Davis, Li caught his eye for a moment and nodded. He returned the acknowledgment and Li pivoted back to open fire. She wasn't fast enough.

A spray of rounds zipped to her right, two of them nicking her. One bullet hit the outside of her thigh and the other at her hip. Li dove to her left and rolled behind a heavy metal barrel used for trash.

Another volley of shots pinged off and into the metal barrel. Now she was pinned and unable to identify the source of the fire. The pain swelled in her side and at her thigh. She checked the wounds and saw her black pants were soaked with glistening dark fluid, with tears at the edges of the fabric.

Li was certain they were flesh wounds and she'd escaped serious injury, but she was bleeding, and the stinging wounds were already throbbing.

Another round of adrenaline surged through her and she refocused. Whoever had her pinned would reload eventually. A volley of a half dozen shots peppered the barrel in front of her and the abandoned storefront behind her.

After a fourth round of automatic fire and a brief pause, Li took her chances. Staying low, she peered around the barrel. The Tic using the body for leverage was struggling to reload the weapon. This was her chance.

Li shot to her feet, leaning on her uninjured left leg, and leveled her weapon at the shooters on the second floor. Three of them were visible through the open windows.

Through the scope she targeted the first and pulled the trigger on her M27, sending a burst of rounds into him. He slumped against the window ledge. She shifted her aim to the right and fired again. A trio of bullets drilled into another, and he dropped from sight as she sent another stream of 5.56x45mm bullets into the third target. It was a longer pull and the spate of deadly projectiles riddled the man's body, forcing him to convulse before sinking from view.

The impressive, and lucky, feat had taken seconds, and now she lowered her aim to the two Tics on the ground. The one who'd hit her twice was taking aim. The two of them locked eyes and, sensing she was too exposed, Li ducked behind the barrels.

As a torrent of shots rattled the barrel right in front of her, Li snuck a look toward the concrete planters. Stephen Davis wasn't there anymore. Had he been hit before she could free him?

She scoured the streets as best she could from cover to find him. And then she did. He'd crossed the street to her side and was twenty feet behind her, unloading a flood of bullets, smoke rising from the muzzle of his weapon as he laid down cover fire for a trio of Marines advancing west.

The two Tics on the ground were surrounded now, but the advancing Marines weren't concerned with them. They'd moved twenty yards beyond to attack another high-ground position and were entering a building. A second trio was already on the roof on the north side of the street, taking potshots at retreating Tics.

Li waited for another lull in the incoming fire and rose from behind her cover, weapon already in position. As soon as she'd cleared the top of the barrel, she applied even and constant pressure to the trigger. Her aim was off, and she missed her target, but she hit the man closer to the building. A cluster of shots peppered his side and slapped him against the wall before he stumbled and fell hard to the concrete.

Before his body had stopped falling, Li found her aim. Brazenly approaching the body-leveraging Tic shooter head-on, she unleashed a burst of fire, hitting the man in the shoulder and hand.

He screeched with a high-pitched cry that sounded feminine and dropped his weapon. Li marched toward the man, ignoring the pain in her leg and side. Stephen Davis met her at the wounded Tic's position to cover her. A pair of Marines hustled past them, taking new positions closer to the compound's entrance. The battle was inching its way west.

Ears ringing, and not understanding the words coming from the wounded, squirming Tic's mouth, Li crouched beside him. Li's jaw dropped. Her gut tightened.

This wasn't a man. It was Brina. *Brina.* The sadistic, water-boarding, nail-prying Brina.

Li's nostrils flared with swelling rage. It was a rage she thought she'd abated by beating the living daylights out of the torturer inside the compound's cell. But instead, it was back and more consuming than before.

"Do you know her?" asked Davis, glancing at her before returning his attention to their surroundings. His voice cut through the ringing in Li's ears.

Brina's body trembled. Rocking in pain, she held her mangled hand at the wrist, gripping it with white knuckles straining against her virtually translucent skin. Li recognized the woman was already descending into shock.

"I know her," she said, standing up and straddling Brina's twitching body, "and she knows me."

Li pointed her rifle at Brina's face. The enforcer, once a confident extractor of information, appeared more like a frightened little girl now. Raising her good hand and the chunk of gore that served as her other one to cover her face, she begged for mercy.

"Please," she warbled. "Don't. Please, Ada—"

"Don't say my name," Li hissed, pushing the barrel of the rifle into Brina's wounded shoulder.

The enforcer wailed in pain and rolled onto her side. The cries softened to whimpers as she pled for her life. It was an unexpected weakness, as Li saw it. Why would she give Li the satisfaction?

"C'mon," said Davis. "We don't have time for this. We need to get to the compound. Our guys can't do this on their own. They need our help."

Davis touched Li's shoulder, and she shot him a glare that had him pull back his hand as if she were about to bite it off. His brow furrowed with concern. His eyes flitted ahead toward his teams engaged west of their position. He looked at Li and shook his head with disappointment.

"Give me a second," she said. "One second."

Davis took a step toward the center of the street. "Fine," he said, raising his weapon and pointing it west. "One second."

With her boots planted on either side of the blubbering

Brina, Li squatted over her. Brina was on her back, tears running down her temples, mixing with the beads of sweat.

Li grabbed the woman's face with her hand and shook it as she spoke. Her voice was a growl. "Where's Graham? Where is he?"

Brina, the woman who'd begged for her life seconds earlier, was defiant. Was it the realization that nothing she did or said would spare her life? Had the pain drained her will to fight? It didn't matter.

The enforcer started laughing. She opened her eyes, reddened and swollen, reinforcing the husky cackle, and glared at Li.

Li stood and stepped over Brina's legs. Aiming the rifle at one knee, she flipped the selector switch to semiautomatic and pulled the trigger. A single shot cracked, and Brina howled from the explosion of pain.

While she squirmed, Li pressed the barrel of her rifle against the side of Brina's good knee.

"Where is Graham?" Li asked, seething.

Brina just continued to cackle. All sense of reason seemed to abandon her features. Li pulled the trigger again, leaving Brina's legs a tangled mess of gore. Li stood there reloading her weapon while the enforcer bled out. Still, the woman laughed.

"Let's go, Davis," she said, picking up Brina's weapon and slinging it over her left shoulder.

She and Davis headed toward the west, and she never looked back at her torturer. The eight Marines had already advanced another block, their handiwork littering the streets.

"That was brutal," said Davis, pulling his rifle to his shoulder and beginning his march forward.

"Yeah," Li agreed.

"You could have put her out of her misery. It would have been the humane thing to do."

Li glared at him. "I could have."

They moved west, crisscrossing the street to check for remaining hostiles. They didn't find any. The eight men who'd preceded them were thorough.

"Who's Graham?" asked Davis.

Li checked a dead Tic body with her boot. Pain shot up her wounded leg and caused her to wince.

"You don't know Graham?" she said, jaw clenched. "I thought everybody in the TMF knew Graham."

"Above my pay grade."

"He's the head of the Tic enforcers," she said. "He's the meanest son of a—"

An exchange of gunfire interrupted her, and the two scrambled toward a building. Finding a spot inside an open doorway, they stopped for a moment before advancing toward the rear pair of Marines, who were fifty yards from them.

"Sitrep?" Davis asked, putting his hand on the shoulder of one of the Marines. "Where are we, Marine?"

One of them motioned toward the small rectangular structure a block ahead. It was the target—the entrance to the compound. "Sir, two members of Charlie team are down—Eddins and Perkins. We're the last two. Bravo and Alpha are up ahead. Alpha is about to breach the target. Bravo is providing cover. They're awaiting your signal."

The radio crackled on Li's hip. She'd forgotten it was there thanks to the sting of her bullet wound. She plucked it from the clip and held it up, lowering the volume.

A hollow-sounding voice cut through the remnant static. *"Brina, I think they've gotten through the ambush. None of the positions are reporting. Brina, do you copy? Over."*

Davis eyed the radio. "Answer him. He'll think it's that woman."

Li held the radio close to her mouth. In the distance, a trio of Marines moved closer to the entrance to the compound.

Three more held positions twenty yards back, rifles ready. Pressing the transmit key, she affected her best Brina imperson- ation, lowering her voice and speaking. "I copy," said Li. "Where are you? Over." She let go of the key.

"Is that Graham?" asked Davis.

"I think so," said Li. "I don't know who else it could be."

"I'm in the compound," the man on the radio answered. *"What's the situation out there? Are they close? Are we holding? We're blind in here. Over."*

Li pressed the key again. "We're holding," she said. "How many do you have with you? Is everyone there? Over."

One of the Marines outside the compound signaled to Davis, awaiting the go-ahead. Davis signaled to wait.

The radio crackled again. *"Everyone is here. The last defense. We're good to go. How many do they have? How many TMF? I'm not hearing gunfire. Over."*

Li looked to Davis before answering. "Should I tell him to come out, that we need his help out here? Or should I tell him everything is good? Keep them pinned in there?"

Davis rubbed his chin, considering the best option. It was quiet now, a giveaway that the battle was in hand. Even Brina's sharp wailing laughter had stopped. Davis signaled to his men to breach the compound.

"Don't tell him anything," he said. "We're going in."

Li moved to put the radio back on her hip when the radio crackled with static and the voice returned. It was definitely Graham.

"Disregard last transmission. It doesn't matter. You keep fighting. We'll be ready if they try to get down here. What's left of them anyhow. Ov–"

An explosion knocked Li from her feet, blowing her back against the wall. Her head slapped on the hard surface and stars filled her vision. The world fell silent as Davis's weight landed on her injured hip. She cried out when the spark of pain shot through her body, but she couldn't hear her own voice.

Dazed, but conscious, she gathered her wits and rolled onto her side. She touched the back of her head, felt a swelling knot there, and pushed herself to her feet. Relying on the wall for balance, she blinked into focus the carnage a block away. What had been the entrance to the compound was a smoldering pile of burning debris, and so were the three TMF Marines who'd tried to breach it.

CHAPTER TWENTY-FOUR

The explosion shook the ground under Zeke's boots. He stopped running. "You feel that?" he asked Uriel. "What was that? It felt like an earthquake."

"It wasn't an earthquake," said Uriel, gazing skyward. "It was an explosion."

Beyond the buildings closest to them, only two blocks away, a fist of black smoke punched its way into the air and spread outward in a gray cloud caught in the breeze.

It had taken them only a few minutes to reach this point once they'd heard the beginnings of a firefight. It was loud, the staccato of automatic fire endless. Then it stopped. Zeke thought they'd been too late to help, or intervene, or attack—whatever was needed of them.

The explosion changed that. He led Uriel around a series of turns until they reached the dead-end street at the far corner of Tic territory. He entered south of what had been the entrance to the Tic compound where he believed Li might be. It was his last hope of finding her, and what he found instead was smoke, singed body parts, and flames.

Zeke's throat tightened. Uriel stopped next to him, her chest heaving, her breathing heavy but under control.

They stood at the corner of a building south of ground zero. Its facade was crumbling. Debris was everywhere. Ash filtered through the air above them, landing on their clothes, heads, and Zeke's hat. Uriel wiped flakes from her cheeks with the back of a hand.

"What is that?" she asked, motioning toward the epicenter with her chin.

Zeke's vision blurred.

Uriel put a hand on his back and leaned into him. Her now familiar floral scent mixed with the acrid odor of burning wood, metal, plastic, flesh, bone, and hair. The combination was nauseating, and his stomach lurched.

"Zeke," said Uriel, in a sympathetic tone that sounded alien, "what is that?"

"That was the compound," he whispered, fending off tears. "If Li was there, she's not anymore."

"What if she wasn't there?" A lilt of hope pricked Uriel's voice. "Maybe she wasn't there."

"Then I have no idea where she is," said Zeke, squeezing his fists. "Either way, she's gone. I've failed."

Uriel pulled her hand from his back, balled it into a tight fist, and punched his arm. He shot her a confused look, and she frowned at him with disappointment.

"Sheesh," she said, "you sure give up easily. That's a huge letdown."

She marched toward the debris, her weapon ready. Zeke followed with his revolver drawn.

"What are you doing?" he called after her.

"Not giving up."

Zeke caught up to her. His focus was on the afterglow of the explosion and on avoiding body parts. Uriel didn't seem to notice, stomping on a chunk of something that squished and snapped under the weight of her boot.

"Hey," he said, noticing a particularly large piece of some-one's body. It was part of a torso and wore familiar black fabric that resembled a uniform. "This is one of the Marines."

Other remnants also wore the same fabric. More than one was a Marine, though it was impossible to tell how many of them there had been. Two? Five?

Zeke looked east along the length of the street. The smoke was thick enough at eye level, he couldn't make out much of anything. He marched closer to the blast site, noticing burned sections of wire.

"This was rigged to explode," he said. "Looks like whatever detonated was inside the compound, not outside. Too hard to know for sure."

"Why would they blow up their own compound?" asked Uriel. "That doesn't make any sense."

"It's a last line of defense," said Zeke. "They didn't want those Marines getting into the compound. If they got this far, rigging the entrance with explosives would stop them."

"These Tics are sick dudes," she said. "You ran in some bad company, Zeke."

"Yeah," he said, head drooping. "I did."

They reached the detonation point, weapons aimed at the gaping hole in the ground. Despite the haphazard lattice of wood and metal that covered much of it, the steps that descended into the underground compound were intact and visible.

"We should go down," said Uriel.

Zeke scratched his forehead. "You think?"

Before Uriel could answer, another voice called out from behind them. It was forceful and commanding.

"We have you in our sights," he warned. "Do not make any quick movements or we will shoot."

TOM ABRAHAMS

The man sounded like a Marine. Zeke had heard the tone before. More than once Marines had tried, and failed, to stop him from making a delivery. He'd always managed to talk his way out of any predicaments before, but he imagined now was not a good time to say or do anything other than what the Marine ordered them to do.

"Slowly," said the Marine, "and I mean slowly, lower your weapons and place them on the ground. Kick them to the side and out of reach."

"Where we stand?" asked Uriel with more than a hint of mockery.

"Do it now!" ordered the Marine. "Lower your weapons and place them on the ground. Then kick them to the side."

Their backs were to the man and Zeke stole a glance over this shoulder. The man was dressed in the black-clad uniform of a Marine and had a rifle leveled at them. Several others were crowded around him, but Zeke couldn't make out how many there were. They were armed. That much was obvious.

"Zeke?"

A chill ran along Zeke's spine. His heart fluttered and his pulse accelerated. It wasn't the Marine who spoke.

He started to turn when the Marine snapped at him to comply. Zeke raised his hands but didn't lower the weapon.

Standing next to the Marine now, also dressed in black and thinner than he remembered her, was Li.

Li. Finally. She was alive. She looked okay. But for some reason, she was dressed like a Marine.

"It's you," she said, the color draining from her face. "How is that possible?"

Uriel had turned around too. She chuckled. "She looks like she's seen a ghost." She shrugged. "Then again…"

"You know them?" asked the Marine, shifting his weapon back and forth between Zeke and Uriel.

"I know *him*," she said, then shook her head. "I *knew* him. He's dead. Or he was dead. I don't know."

"What do you want to do?" asked the Marine. "We've got to get inside that compound. If these people aren't a threat—"

Li raised a hand, silencing the Marine. Tears streaked down her cheeks. Her chin quivered. "Give me a second, Davis."

The Marine said nothing, but he visibly relaxed his posture.

With a confused look on her face, Li marched toward Zeke, weapon in hand.

Zeke started to say something, even opened his arms to her, but her expression shifted from confused to angry. With a swift movement, and without Zeke knowing what hit him, she swung the butt of the rifle in an arc and caught him on the jaw, knocking him to the ground with a violent thud.

Uriel moved to pick up her weapon, but stopped when Li warned her against it. Zeke was conscious but dazed. Lying amidst the debris, he gingerly touched the side of his face where Li had smacked him so hard he thought she'd jostled loose his brain.

His vision swimming and a thick throbbing pain pulsing along his jawline and neck, Zeke squinted up at Li.

Li took another step toward him and aimed the rifle at him. Pulling the weapon tight to her shoulder, she stood there for a moment studying him. "I've thought about killing you," she said. "How are you here? I don't understand."

Zeke nodded at the blurry shape standing over him. He tried speaking again, but couldn't find the words.

"You've got ten seconds to explain why you left me," said Li, "and another ten to explain how the hell you're standing here after I saw your body."

"I can explain—" Zeke started, but Uriel cut him off.

"Beg your pardon," Uriel said with a hand raised, "but he's

not standing. You put him on the ground. So yeah, it's semantics, but if we're being honest here, thought I'd point it out."

Li's sour expression fell upon Uriel. She didn't look impressed. "Who are you?"

"Ma'am," Davis said, "we do not have time for this."

Li shot Davis a glare that had the Marine snapping his jaw shut. He scowled.

"Who are you?" Li repeated.

"I'm Uriel," she said. "We're together."

Li's expression flattened. "Why are you here?"

"To find you," said Uriel. "And let me say, Zeke oversold the goods."

"I came back for you," said Zeke. "I shouldn't have left. I came to help."

Li's face twitched, then hardened. "So now you have a conscience? You want to help?" she spat. "Help us clean the Tics out of the compound. Then I'll deal with you and you'll explain what's going on here."

Davis stepped forward. "What are you doing?"

"We lost three men in that explosion," she said. "We need all the help we can get."

"You trust them?" asked Davis. "What did you mean by saying he's dead?"

Li offered a hand to help Zeke from the ground. He took it and she pulled him up but backed away from him.

"It's a figure of speech," she said to Davis, her eyes locked with Zeke's. "Obviously he's not dead. And no. I don't trust him. He's a Tic. But we need them."

"You said it," said Davis. "He's a Tic. Why would you bring him along? If it were up to me, we'd have them in restraints."

Zeke watched Li consider the dilemma. He'd seen that look in her eyes before, when she weighed the balance of things, played out the string of possible outcomes.

"Li," he said, "you know me. I wouldn't have come back if I didn't want to make things right."

For an instant, Zeke thought he saw a flicker of recognition in her eyes, something that told him their connection still existed despite how frayed it may be. As quickly as it flashed, it was gone. She pulled back her shoulders, straightening herself like a soldier at attention. Without looking at Zeke, she nodded.

"Pick up your weapon," Li said to Uriel. "You'll need it down there."

Uriel saluted her with mock enthusiasm. "Yes, sir."

Zeke shot Uriel a frown. Uriel stuck out her tongue.

Li passed Zeke and shot him an icy glare so cold it burned. She was hurt. She was angry. She was confused. All of those things were obvious to him. And they were his fault.

This was not the reunion Zeke envisioned. And he wasn't sure how he'd explain what he'd done or what he'd become. In the moment, it didn't matter. Li was alive and needed his help. How she ended up with the Marines was a question for later. There were a lot of questions for later.

The squad began clearing the lattice of debris blocking the entrance to the compound, making quick work of it, and began their descent into the compound. One at a time they moved down the steps into the darkness and toward whatever resistance awaited them.

CHAPTER TWENTY-FIVE

G raham checked the magazine in his weapon for the fourth time through the reflective lenses of his glasses. With his index finger, he pushed the glasses up and wiped the sweat from his palms on his worn cargo pants. The explosion told him they were coming. He didn't know how many of them there were, but he was sure it was fewer than it had been before the trip-activated charge had rattled the compound and served as an alarm to the pending attack.

It was taking longer than he'd expected. His nine compatriots were restless, their nerves obvious as they held their positions and awaited the coming storm. They reminded him of children awaiting the revelation of a surprise, unable to contain or suppress their anxiety.

Graham sucked in a sharp breath, puffed his cheeks, and let it out. As anxious as he was, he was looking forward to this. It would send a clear signal to the Overseers not to trifle with the Tic. They were equals, not subjects. They were a parallel power structure that allowed the Overseers to manage the protectorates as they did.

Graham squatted in the corner of a long hallway that fed

into the corridor leading to the compound's stairwell and exit. His thoughts occupied him while he waited with his weapon at the ready.

He was long convinced, as had been Mogilevich, that the two organizations were symbiotic. It was fine to let the Overseers think they were in control. They weren't. Their hold on the protectorates was slipping. It was greasy and tenuous. The Overseers had let their power get to their collective heads. They'd grown fat and happy in their naivety. The protectorates' commanders and their lieutenants had the Tic to provide the black-market stability that kept the citizenry happy enough to prevent them from revolting. Without them, however, the protectorates would fall.

The damned Badlanders had already helped sow enough unrest from the wastelands that filled the empty spaces between disparate protectorates. They'd facilitated the near downfall of three protectorates so far and, if the Tic hadn't stepped in to provide triage for the wounded Overseer structures in those city-states, they'd be lost to the rebellion.

It was shocking to Graham and Mogilevich that the Overseers in their protectorate were so blind to this. He had intelligence that the hapless lieutenants Frederick and Archibald were the only ones who believed the rumors of revolt. The rest of the council refused to see it.

Now that Mogilevich was dead, the protectorate was Graham's to run, and he was damned if the clueless, navel-gazing proletariat would cost him this opportunity. That was why it was all the more important to beat back this ridiculous assault from the misguided Overseers. He wasn't the problem, he was the solution. And when he'd dispatched the Marines sent to deal with him, he'd march straight to the Fascio for a sit-down with Commander Guilfoyle himself.

They'd reach a renewed understanding about the importance of their partnership. He'd convince them of the threat the Badlanders beyond their borders truly posed. First things first, though. He had to kill everyone who entered the compound, one way or the other.

Graham touched the vest he wore beneath his synthetic leather jacket. It was cold in the compound. He ran his hand along the vest's rough fabric, and he took another deep breath in anticipation.

He'd positioned his men at strategic spots along the maze of hallways that connected rooms used for storage, production, torture, and other things best done underground. All the men, however, were between him and the stairwell. Graham was the last line of defense.

If he had to, and he didn't believe he would, he could detonate the explosives strapped to his body under his jacket. The vest, like something he was told fishermen used to wear when there were wild, naturally occurring fish to bait and hook, had a dozen pockets. He'd filled them with the rocks and pebbles that coated the edges of streets, nails he'd pried from cedar packing crates, and empty shell casings from target practice with his M27. The pockets also contained the unstable chemical explosive he'd made in the compound's lab. It was a powdery white substance cooked from concentrated hydrogen peroxide and acetone. Together they made up the highly volatile TATP, triacetone triperoxide. It had worked at the entrance to the compound as he'd planned.

While wearing a TATP-laced vest wasn't ideal—the explosives could be unstable—it was Graham's best option. He wanted to inflict maximum damage if needed, and the only way to insure it was to wear the vest and put himself as close to as many targets as he could. His own bones would add to the mixture of shrapnel inflicting wounds on anyone in close proximity.

A trigger at his chest would do the deed. Should he take a

gunshot center mass, that resulting impact would detonate the vest without him having to do anything.

All Graham knew was that he would not allow the facility to fall into the Overseers' control. It didn't matter if he had to die protecting it from the grubby council of thieves and gluttons, he would do it. It was what any man of principle would do in his shoes. Mogilevich would have done it, Graham was certain.

He listened for any hint of incursion inside the compound. Still nothing. Pulling his right hand from his rifle, he reached to his hip and unsnapped the sheath clipped there to withdraw the bone-handled knife Mogilevich had given him as a gift. Scraping the blade gently across the beard growth on his neck and under his chin, he purred at how good it felt to satisfy the fresh itch. The dull edge of the infrequently sharpened blade did the trick his fingers couldn't. Graham liked an unsharpened blade not just for this purpose, but because he believed it inflicted more pain than did one honed to a razor's edge.

Turning the knife over in his hand, he admired the bone handle into which the steel was affixed. He weighed it in his palm. The balance was perfect.

The first crack of gunfire shook Graham from his momentary daydream. He flipped the knife's handle over in his hand and slid it back into its sheath. He stood, removed his sunglasses, and tucked them into a pocket of the synthetic jacket. Then he braced himself for the assault.

A percussive staccato of automatic gunfire followed the solitary warning crack of that first gunshot and its echo along the solid corridor walls. Mixed with the rapid fire of the weapons and the deafening ricochet of sound that flooded the corridors, there were unintelligible shouts and screams.

From his position, Graham saw the back of one of his nine compatriots. He was stationed at the corner leading from Graham's hallway to the next. The man was on one knee, aiming. Graham couldn't see the man firing his weapon, but he saw the jerk of his shoulder and elbow from the recoil, and he swore he could make out its report amidst the crescendo of approaching hostiles.

Graham steadied himself the moment the man jerked awkwardly to one side and toppled over. His head landed beyond the pool of light nearest him, but his blood soon found its way there, spreading across the floor like crimson paint spilled from a bucket.

Adjusting his grip against the sweat greasing his palms, Graham worked to maintain his composure. He tried slowing his accelerating heartbeat with long, slow breaths. In through his nose and out through his mouth.

A pair of his men appeared at the corner near the body of the fallen comrade. One of them stumbled over the splay but caught himself and dropped to a knee to rattle off a burst of fire. The other stayed on his feet to return fire. Rounds zipped past the two, errant shots plastering the wall behind them.

The enforcer on his knee rolled over to one side and then retreated toward Graham. The other convulsed and dropped his weapon. It clattered to the floor and the enforcer went limp, a final shot to the head ending him.

The first hostile rounded the corner, a Marine in all black. Graham applied pressure to his trigger, unloading a stream of violence toward the man.

His first shots exploded into the wall near the Marine's head, but a slight recalibration helped Graham find his target. A spray across the man's thighs sank him to the floor. He was alive but incapacitated, his screams shrill above the thunder of the fight.

A flicker of a smile twitched at the corners of Graham's dry mouth. His compatriot joined him at his side.

Running his finger across his neck in a slicing motion, the

man shook his head. "We're it!" he shouted above the din. "The rest of them are gone!"

"What do you mean *gone*?" Graham asked.

"They're all dead," the enforcer repeated. "All of them. We're it, sir."

Then the man's expression flattened. His jaw dropped. He sank to his knees and fell face-first on the floor with a sickening thud. Graham glanced down and saw the pair of rounds that had found his back.

Without thinking, Graham retreated. Pedaling backward, he returned fire indiscriminately. More Marines emerged from around the corner. There were a half dozen of them now, perhaps more. They moved swiftly in formation. Too fast, Graham tossed his weapon to the side and waited for them to close in. Two more seconds and they'd be close enough for him to press the detonator.

Two. One.

Graham touched his chest to find the trigger. He put his hand to it and glanced up to see a dead man charging toward him. *Ezekiel Watson? How is he alive? And working with the TMF?* Behind him was the slender but delectable barmaid Adaliah Bancroft.

Graham processed all of this within a split second. It was disconcerting and confusing, but it was all the better he take Zeke too, however it was that he remained alive. All the better.

In that infinitesimal moment that stopped him from pressing the button and doing his duty as he'd planned, a pair of rounds drilled into his brain, severing any chance he had of signaling his finger to do the job.

Ezekial Watson, he thought. *A dead man killed me.* Graham's world went dark. The shooting stopped. The world fell silent.

CHAPTER TWENTY-SIX

Zeke stepped over Graham's body, noticing the wired contraption underneath the dead man's jacket. He bent over to get a closer look. "I think he's wearing a bomb vest."

Li took the bone-handled knife from the sheath at Graham's waist. At Zeke's pronouncement, she took several large steps back.

"If it is," said Li, "your shots saved us all."

Zeke motioned to Uriel with the M27 in his right hand. "Told you I needed another weapon."

Uriel moved next to Zeke, ignoring his comment and partially shoving him out of the way. She squatted over Graham's body and cursed aloud.

"Yep." She spat another curse. "That's an explosive vest. Give him a wide berth."

Li eyed Zeke. "Nice language. This is the company you keep now?"

Uriel looked up at Li, then shifted her gaze to Zeke. "Maybe we should have let her rot here. She doesn't seem too grateful."

"Grateful?" asked Li. "Grateful for what?"

Uriel stood up and stepped clear of Graham's corpse. "We came back here to save your ass."

"I didn't need saving," said Li. "And your boy here, I don't know if he told you or not, but he abandoned me. He left me to *rot*."

A smirk crept at the corners of Uriel's mouth. Zeke started to interject. Uriel beat him to it.

"He tells me everything," she said. "*Everything*. So yeah, I know. And if it'd been me, now knowing you, I'd have left you too."

"I told you this was a bad idea," Davis interjected.

Li bristled. "You don't know me."

"C'mon," said Zeke. "Enough of this. Uriel, I can talk for myself."

"She should get that tattooed on her ass," said Li. "It would complement the rest of her ink."

Uriel started toward Li, but Zeke stopped her with a hand to her shoulder. "Enough."

"Who is this guy?" Davis asked Li. "Why are we listening to him?"

Zeke offered his hand to the Marine. "I'm Zeke. I was a Tic. A bootlegger. Li and I—"

"Were nothing," said Li. "We were nothing. It wasn't real. You made that abundantly clear. Remember?"

Uriel rolled her eyes. "Holy mother of the good lord," she said. "This is a freaking soap opera. If I weren't already technically dead, I'd shoot myself."

The remaining six Marines who were alive, including Davis, gathered around the unfolding drama. Davis held up a hand, seemingly not catching the oddity of Uriel's admission. Who would believe that, after all?

"We need to clear this place," he said. "We don't know what other traps they've set. And we've only got so much time to gather the intelligence we came to get and report back."

"Fine," said Li. "I'll deal with this later."

Davis motioned to three of his men. "Take that corridor. Get what you can get and report back here in fifteen."

The men took off in the direction Davis had instructed. That left Davis, two Marines, Uriel, Li, and Zeke next to Graham's dead body.

Davis met the other two Marines and Uriel with a firm gaze. "How about the three of you take the opposite corridor," he ordered more than suggested. "I'll go with these two. We can cover the most ground and get out of here."

Zeke motioned for Uriel to go along. She mimicked him with a childish mocking of his request. Zeke silently asked for her to comply. Rolling her eyes, she relented and marched off with a pair of Marines. Once they'd disappeared around a corner, Zeke was left alone with Li and Marine Davis.

"All right," said Davis. "I think we need to cuff them. Now that we've secured the tunnel and Graham is dead, we should take this guy and his friend into custody. He clearly—"

Zeke stepped toward Davis. "I just stopped an explosion from killing all of us. Now you want to cuff us?"

Davis moved to Zeke. He was taller than Zeke and looked down at him, their faces inches apart. Zeke could smell his sweat, the stale odor of the Marine's hot breath.

"You're a Tic," said Davis. "Once a Tic, always a Tic. You're scum. I should off you right here, right now. Nobody would do anything about it. Nobody would care."

"I care," said Li.

Both men turned to face her. Zeke figured Davis was as surprised as he was to hear her say that, to hear her admit she still had feelings for him.

"Then I should cuff you too," said Davis. "You *were* in charge of the mission. The mission is over. I'll take command now."

"C'mon, Davis," Li said. "That's absurd. He saved your life as much as he saved mine."

Davis turned and raised his M27. He stood between Li and Zeke.

Zeke felt the push of the rifle's barrel at his gut. Davis's stare was cold, almost blank.

"You can't kill me," said Zeke.

"Is that so?" said Davis. "How about I test that theory."

"It's not a theory."

Davis took a step back, the rifle still leveled at Zeke. His finger slid onto the trigger. He lifted the weapon to his shoulder. Then his eyes went wide and he dropped the M27. It hit the tunnel floor and rattled as Davis grunted. A confused look spread across his face and he spun away from Zeke as he reached for the knife blade buried to its hilt in his back. He lost his balance and dropped to a knee. Davis tried speaking but only managed a squeak before he dropped face-first onto the floor next to his rifle.

Zeke stepped back from Li, his hands raised above his head. His voice trembled when he spoke. "What was that! Li, what's going on? You were with me, then with them. I-I—"

"He was going to kill you."

"Maybe," he said, "but not really. Now you're a killer. That's not who you are, who you were. You're with the TMF. You can't kill Marines."

"I'm still with you," she said.

She looked down at her feet for a moment. When she lifted her chin again, her eyes glistened. Her chin trembled.

Zeke wasn't sure what to make of this. Was she lying again? Was this a trap. Some part of him wanted to believe her. But so much had happened, how could he trust her again? Especially after watching her kill a man. He was suddenly cold. What had all of this done to Li? What had his failings forced her to become?

She grabbed Davis's wrists and motioned toward his feet. "Yes. Are you going to help me?"

Zeke reached down to grab the Marine's ankles and lifted the dead weight. The strain pulled at his back, but he managed, and the two of them carried the body into a spot along the corridor where the pools of light didn't reach. They put the body where the others wouldn't find him, at least not without searching.

They dropped the body, and Li stepped toward him, staying in the darkness near the wall. Still holding the knife, she pressed her body close to Zeke's. He backed up until he felt the cool texture of the wall on his fingertips.

A wave of fear washed through him. His purpose for coming here was to save her. He wasn't sure he had.

Yes, he'd helped her. He'd stopped Graham and the suicide bomb. She inched back from him, but was close enough for him to smell her, to remember when being this close wasn't close enough.

"We don't have long," she said, some semblance of the Li he remembered returning to her tone. "They'll come back. They'll find him."

Li looked different to him. Whatever had happened in the time between his disappearance and this moment had changed her. Sure, her appearance was altered; she was thinner, slighter in some way. But it was her demeanor, the way she carried that thin frame with a confidence that bordered on defiance. Never mind his sweet Adaliah had just stabbed a man in cold blood after leading a deadly charge on a compound that killed another dozen people.

"We don't have time for me to ask all the questions I have about you, about how you're even here after what I saw," Li said. "I don't understand any of it…" She paused to gather her breath. "Why did you leave me?"

Zeke didn't hesitate this time. "I had to come back. When I

left you, as much as it hurt to do it, I hoped that if I ran, they might let you live."

"They tortured me," she said, holding up her fingers to reveal missing nails.

Tears welled in Zeke's eyes. "I'm so sorry. I did what I thought was best."

"Running? Leaving a note like that?"

"I did that because I hoped whoever found it would believe it and let you be free. I hoped they would see I acted alone and out of anger rather than love."

"That makes no sense," she said. "That's naïve. You know these people."

"It is what it is," Zeke said. "I knew as soon as I left, it was wrong to leave you. We should have taken our chances together. I panicked. Thinking if they caught me and saw I was using you, or whatever, then—"

"You already said that," Li interrupted. "My bosses thought it meant you'd figured me out, that you knew who I was."

Zeke's gaze flitted toward the body of the man she'd killed. He swallowed hard. "It's clear I don't know who you are at all."

Li took a step back. She gripped the knife. "I'm a spy."

Zeke shook his head in disbelief. "A spy for what?"

"It's complicated," Li said. "The short version is I work for the Overseers. They recruited me when I was young."

"They put you with the Tic at the bar?" asked Zeke. He knew he should be shocked, but it all came together. A woman like her working at a Tic bar? It had to be too good to be true; he was only too lovestruck to see it.

Li nodded. "Yes."

"Why there? I don't get it. It was just a bar."

"I took you as smarter than that, Zeke. I guess you really

are a simple bootlegger who runs from place to place without ever stopping to look at the ground underneath his feet."

Zeke lowered his chin and stared at his feet. It wasn't fun being judged, alive or dead.

"It was to get to you," she said, "or someone like you. Someone I could play, someone who would give me information without even knowing he was doing it."

Zeke looked up. His lips trembled. "So my note to you was true even if I didn't mean it to be. Everything *was* a lie. Nothing about us was real."

Li steeled herself, pulling her shoulders back and clearing her throat. Zeke was certain her eyes glistened again.

"Are you going to help me or not?" she asked. "I think they're coming back."

"What's your plan now? You've got no friends on either side of this now. You've killed Tics." He nodded toward the body. "You killed a Marine."

"I want out," she said. "I'm sick of playing the games, playing both sides. I want away from here, this hellhole. I want something better. I-I-I want you."

Zeke felt his face grow hot. A tingle of adrenaline shot through his body. Despite everything, the lies, the betrayals, she still wanted him. And he knew in that moment, even after seeing what awful things he was capable of, he still wanted her.

"Fine, I'll help you," he said. "We'll get you out of here."

The echoes of the returning trio preceded them. From the sounds, Zeke knew this was the group Uriel was helping.

"Let me run ahead," he said to Li. "I'll delay her. Then you can...do what you have to do. That way she won't get in the way."

"Fine," agreed Li. "Go ahead."

Zeke started toward the approaching Marines and found them in a pool of light fifty yards down the hallway. He called ahead to let them know it was him.

"Don't shoot," he said. "It's me, Zeke."

The trio stopped. The Marines were carrying with them what looked like hard drives. Wires hung from them. Each of the men was carrying three or four in each hand, their weapons strapped over their shoulders. They couldn't have opened fire if they'd wanted to.

Uriel also cradled a collection of electronics.

"Hey," Zeke said to the group, slowing his approach. "Davis and Li are waiting for you. I've got to speak to Uriel for a second. You guys go ahead. We've cleared this corridor. Davis suggested you head that way."

Burdened with their trophies, the Marines acknowledged him. They started their march down a new corridor, away from Davis's body. Uriel stood still, a puzzled look on her face, and waited until the men had disappeared into the darkness beyond the scope of the pools of light to speak.

"What's going on?" she asked.

"Li isn't who she was when I left," said Zeke. "She's changed."

Uriel laughed. "I've spent a minute with that lanky crank and I could have told you she's three layers of nothing."

"I have no idea what any of that means, but I'm guessing you already know my relationship with her was phony," he said.

"No offense, Zeke, but that's the smartest thing you've said since you stumbled into Pedro's. Can't believe it took you this long to figure it out."

"You knew?"

"You walk into a bar," she said, handing him a couple of the hard drives to lighten her load, "and you spot a new girl. Woman, excuse me. Whatever. Anyhow, she takes a shine to you instantly and the two of you are inseparable. She moves in. She likes books. Banned books. You don't. She keeps a gun by the bed for protection. You don't like them. Then she shows up with your enemy, the same people who hung you from a building and let you die? Too much. Sorry. I don't buy love at first sight. I've seen too much in too many places to believe in it. This story, the two of you, was unbelievable from the get-go."

"Why didn't you say anything?" Zeke asked.

"Not my place. Part of the Watcher's journey is finding out what's real and what isn't."

They started walking along the corridor toward the others.

"So if my mission wasn't to save her," asked Zeke, "what was it?"

"Sheesh. I thought for sure you'd have figured this out, Zeke. I so much as told you that."

"Redemption, I get that. But how do I redeem myself if the reason I came back doesn't exist?"

"You'll see," said Uriel. "Or you won't. What's the play here?"

"She needs our help," he said. "I said yes."

She scowled. "Why?"

"I don't know," he said. "I still care about her. She said she does for me. She wants out of here, out of the protectorate. She wants to start over."

"It'll never work," she said.

He led her along the corridor, moving quickly. "There's something else," he said. "She killed a guy. Davis."

Uriel arched one eyebrow. "Really? How?"

"With a knife," said Zeke. "He was going to kill me. She stopped him."

"She knows you can't die, right?"

They reached Li. She was standing near the body. Blood leached across Davis's uniform, glistening against the black.

"You weren't all wrong about her," said Uriel. "She's no shrinking wallflower. I gotta hand it to her. She's all in."

"What now?" he asked Li, staring at the body.

"This is impressive," said Uriel. "Good stuff. If you're to be a double agent, be all you can be. And the knife? That's a personal touch you don't see too often anymore."

Li ignored Uriel and answered Zeke. "We figure a way out of here. I get a fresh start, a new life."

"You are not going anywhere," came a voice from behind the three. "Stay right where you are."

They all swung around to see a fat man dressed in purple flanked by a sextet of armed men. The men weren't Tic and they weren't TMF.

Zeke reached for the revolver at his waist, but stopped when the purple grape of an intruder cautioned him, wagging a scolding finger.

"Ah, ah, ah," said the man. "Don't touch the weapon."

The man's eyes flitted to the women and their weapons. He raised his eyebrows and then lowered them.

"What are you doing here, Lieutenant Louis Donne?" asked Li. "What do you want?"

The purple man moved forward, his stubby legs carrying his heft from one circle of light to the next. Armed guards kept pace with him, and their weapons remained at the ready, targeting Zeke, Li, and Uriel in sweeping motions.

"Adaliah Bancroft," said Louis, "I never trusted you. I knew you were too malleable. I tried to warn my uncle about threats from within. He wouldn't listen."

Li's eyes widened. "Frederick and Archibald know nothing about this," she said. "This is all me. I want out. Just let me go and nobody else gets hurt."

He shook his head. "Right," he said. "I let you leave. No punishment for what you've done. No justice. You should be hanging from the—"

He stopped abruptly and stared at Zeke. His mouth agape, he took another two steps forward to study him closer, eyes moving from the Stetson hat atop his head to the strange, large revolver at his waist.

"Wait," he said, his face shifting. "I recognize you. You're that bootlegger. You're the one strung up above the Fascio right now. Except, that's not possible. You can't be here if you're there."

His eyes shifted to Li and back to Zeke. Then he stared at Uriel and frowned. "But I don't know you. Not a Tic, not a Marine. Are you a Badlander?"

"I'm a rebel with a cause," said Uriel, wearing a wry grin.

Nobody reacted.

Uriel slumped her shoulders. "Come on," she said in disbelief. "Nobody? Nobody knows that one? I know it's an arcane reference, but, Zeke, as much as you love hot rods, I would have thought for sure you—"

"Enough!" Louis barked. "It doesn't matter who you are or how you're possibly here. No more tricks. All of you are coming with me."

Louis turned to motion to the half dozen Marines who flanked him. He said something to them about restraints. He seemingly wasn't aware that Uriel's body tensed, that her eyes glared at him with ill intent, and he surely didn't see the faintest hint of a blue glow throbbing at the ink on her skin.

"All right now," said Louis. "This is—"

The knife hit him in his throat. He never saw it coming. His mouth opened and closed like a fish gasping for air as he dropped the weapon and sank to his knees. His girth rippled with the movement. Simultaneously, Li sprayed the M27 to the dying lieutenant's left and Uriel disarmed the men to his right.

The trio to Louis's left were down within a second. They'd not had time to take aim before they were on the ground. The ones to the right likely would have preferred the quick dignified death of a cluster of high-powered projectiles. Instead, they took a brutal beating from Uriel, whose body was a constant blue. She finished the last of them with a solid heel jab to the center of a Marine's face.

Louis grabbed at the knife, at the handle. Eyes wide with fear, with the shock and recognition of what was happening, he tried to free the blade.

Instead, Zeke wrapped his own hand around Louis's. He took a deep breath, exhaled, and tugged. The knife slid from Louis's throat with a slurp and the man was done. His body hit the ground with a sickening thud. Blood pooled around him as if poured from a full glass.

Li stared at Uriel. "What the hell was that?"

Uriel's body was dimly blue now. Still, she stood there, fists clenched, body tensed and ready to strike. She shook her head.

"Hell hath nothing to do with it," she said.

Li looked to Zeke. "What was that?"

"We can explain later," said Zeke. "Now we definitely need to get out of here. Can we get back to my car?"

"The Superbird?" asked Li.

"How many cars does he have?" snarked Uriel.

Zeke sighed at her then shifted to Li. "Yes," he said. "The Superbird."

"Where is it?" asked Li.

"The tunnel," he said. "Near the Tic's underground entrance to the city."

"We can't get to it," she said. "We'll need to take a transport."

Zeke checked over his shoulder. "You sure?"

Uriel interjected, "I hate to say it, pretty boy, but skinny mini has a point. More of these soldier dudes are going to be here in minutes. Then they'll be swarming the city looking for us."

"But the car is in the smuggling tunnel," said Zeke.

"They'll have the tunnels blocked," said Li. "Remember, they knew you were coming."

"Then how do we get out?" asked Uriel. "Assuming we're still helping you."

Uriel shot Zeke a pleading glance. She raised her eyebrows. The blue glow was gone now.

"We're still helping," said Zeke. "I told you I was coming back to right my wrong. It's not right until Li's safe."

Li's face flushed pink. Zeke's chest tightened. Uriel groaned.

"We bust through the gate," said Uriel.

"Then where do we go?" asked Li.

Uriel shrugged. "I think we worry about that once we bust through the gate and get clear of this place. What's it called?"

Li and Zeke answered in unison. "A protectorate."

The two locked eyes and smiled. Zeke missed her. Despite everything, he missed her. He still loved her. And he was sure that she loved him too. *A true relationship isn't measured by the effortless times,* he thought. *It's measured by the struggles overcome.* If that was true, then what they had was real. It had to be.

"Sheesh," said Uriel. "Get a room."

Zeke's smile flattened. In that instant, he was reminded of the room in which he'd awaken not that long ago. He was reminded of sitting at the bar with Pedro, of the mission, of his own redemption. He was reminded that he was dead.

That was a struggle over which they couldn't climb. But he said nothing about it. Instead, he nodded.

"We need to go," he said. "Let's find the closest gate."

CHAPTER TWENTY-SEVEN

Guilfoyle put his hand on his stomach and belched. He could taste the steak he'd had for breakfast half a day ago. It felt like a week. He wanted to throw up. He spoke through his teeth, seething and fighting back the nausea.

"What do you mean there's more?" he asked. "Isn't it enough that your trusted spy is gone, in the wind, doing who knows what to undermine us?"

Frederick and Archibald stood opposite their commander, at attention. They were stone-faced, aside from the twitching at the corner of Archibald's mouth.

Guilfoyle's eyebrows arched. "Well?" he demanded. "What is it?"

The lieutenants exchanged glances. They swallowed hard at the same time. Finally, Frederick fell on the sword.

"Your nephew, Commander," he said in a tremulous voice Guilfoyle almost didn't recognize as belonging to the man who led the protectorate's surveillance and spy networks. "He's dead."

Guilfoyle flinched, but said nothing. The nausea in his gut swelled. Images of his sister flashed in his mind. He remembered his promises to her. A knot thickened in his throat and the emotion surprised him. He considered that it wasn't for his nephew, but rather for his own failure to protect his nephew.

"He and his entire protective detail were killed," Frederick continued.

"We found additional casualties at the Tic bunker as well," added Archibald. The TMF was his purview. "There are Tic casualties too. Graham is among them, we believe."

"How?" Guilfoyle asked.

Neither of them answered. Archibald ran his swollen knuckles across the top of his cropped, silver hair. He sniffed. His warped nose twitched.

Guilfoyle's face and neck reddened as his muscles tensed. A thick vein strained against the side of his forehead.

"How. Did. He. Die?" he spat venomously.

Frederick's shoulders slumped and he lowered his head. He took a step back from his commander.

"A knife wound," he said softly. "Maybe also M27 high-velocity rounds. There's so much blood and too many bodies. It's hard to know at the moment."

Guilfoyle sucked in another weary breath and held it. His jaw flexed. He turned from the men and stared out the window of his suite toward the city-state he commanded. Beyond the glass stretched the brown, dusty collection of run-down buildings.

He regretted popularizing the M27 now as his body shifted and bounced. It was a holdover from the end days of the United States military. The M27 Infantry Automatic Rifle had been in large supply. They were reliable. And there were unmanned warehouses full of the weapons and their ammunition.

Had it not been for that ten-pound weapon, his nephew, who'd masterfully handled their water supply, would be alive. His promise to his sister would be unbroken.

Yes, the fat man was a pest. He was a glutton. He salivated at both fresh meat and the taste of power. But Louis was family and he was, above all else, loyal to the protectorate and to his commander.

Guilfoyle's distant gaze focused and he turned from the glass to face his lieutenants Archibald and Frederick. Could he say the same for them? Were they loyal? Or were they what Louis had claimed they were?

His eyes shifted between the two of them. Both men held his stare for a moment and lost the contest, instead looking to the floor. There was a way, Guilfoyle decided, they could prove their loyalty.

"Go find them," he said flatly.

Archibald was the first to lift his head. "Go find who, sir?"

A wry smile spread across the commander's face. "The spy," he said, "and anyone who is with her. Find them. Bring them to me alive or bring me their heads. I want something to hang from the front of the Fascio."

"Yes, Commander," both men said in unison. They saluted and spun to begin their task. But before they reached the door, the commander called to them.

"Wait there," he said. "You're not going alone."

The men shot him confused looks. Neither said anything. Neither questioned him. They stood silently while awaiting, the commander assumed, an explanation.

As if on cue, Theo emerged from the kitchen. He strode confidently across the floor. His polished black shoes gleamed against the overhead light. His cufflinks sparkled at his wrists. The man walked with his chin up, his eyes fixed on the commander.

"I'm ready, sir," said Theo. "We can depart immediately."

The commander nodded at Theo and addressed the befuddled-looking lieutenants at the entry to his suite. He noticed the color was drained from their faces.

"Theo will accompany you," he said. "He is a skilled man and very loyal. He'll be certain to report back to me exactly what—"

"But, sir," interrupted Frederick. "I don't think we need—"

"Do not interrupt me," said Guilfoyle through clenched teeth. "I will tell you what you need. Is that understood?"

Both men quieted. They were at attention now, but there was something weak about their stature. A hint of defeat in their shoulders, of chastisement in their chests.

Guilfoyle cleared his throat. "Now," he said, the anger gone from his voice, "you will take Theo with you. He will do as he sees fit. He has my blessing."

The room filled with a heavy silence. Nobody spoke for several seconds. Then Archibald raised his hand.

Guilfoyle jutted his chin at his TMF lieutenant. "Yes?"

"What about our men?" he asked.

"What about them?" asked Guilfoyle.

"Does Theo have a say in how—"

Guilfoyle shook his head emphatically and waved a hand at Archibald as if to tell him how ridiculous he sounded. He stepped forward and motioned toward Theo.

"Theo is his own man," he said. "His job is to…"

"Bring balance to the operation?" interjected the servant.

Guilfoyle nodded. "Yes," said the commander. "He'll operate independently. You'll command your men as you've always done."

He waved them away and the trio left him alone. Guilfoyle then returned to his window. He moved close to the glass. Each breath produced a puff of condensation and evaporated.

A haze lingered on the horizon. Dust hung in the air like a thin veil. It was thick today and made it difficult to see the people on the streets below. He knew that somewhere down there, his loyal nephew was dead. Many of his men were dead. And a traitorous spy was on the loose.

Guilfoyle's chest tightened as he considered his nephew's murder. He could almost hear his sister chastising him for not having done a better job of keeping Louis safe. He tried pushing the thought from his mind, tried to reason with himself.

Louis was his own man. He was responsible for his own choices. He was arrogant and stubborn.

Guilfoyle's guilt dissolved into anger. He was angry at Frederick and Archibald, angry at the turncoat, angry at the Tic, at the Badlanders, at everyone who'd either failed him or who couldn't appreciate what he'd done for his people. They threatened the balance of things. They didn't understand the weight of his responsibilities.

Difficult times called for decisive leaders. And he was decisive, as his ancestors had been. Because of their actions, because of his actions, his people had food and water. There was relative peace. He'd found a balance, he thought, between wielding an iron fist and providing an open bosom.

Through the haze below him, a convoy of TMF transports emerged onto the streets closest to the Fascio. He told himself he could feel the rumble of their engines, the push of their tires against the gritty earth.

They would find this spy, he assured himself. They would find her, and they would hurt her, and he would hang her from the Fascio for all to see.

CHAPTER TWENTY-EIGHT

Zeke imagined himself behind the wheel of his beloved Superbird. He cursed that it was stuck underground in a Tic tunnel on the other side of the protectorate, and he hoped it would be there when he returned. Would he return?

His sweaty hands gripped the large wheel of the TMF transport they'd stolen. His body bounced gently in the straight-back seat as he navigated the streets. Li was in the back seat next to Uriel.

Zeke wasn't sure what was more dangerous, the prospect of getting caught or Li and Uriel within strangling reach of one another.

They'd behaved themselves so far, and Zeke focused on the challenging path in front of him. There were small miracles that didn't involve reincarnation and glowing blue weapons of mass destruction.

"The gate is up here," said Li, pointing to ten o'clock, "on the other side of this checkpoint."

Zeke was familiar with the gate, and the checkpoint, which he'd successfully avoided by the use of the tunnels plenty of times. He'd have preferred using tunnels now, but Li was probably right. It would have trapped them inside the walls.

Two guards manned the gate. One of them leveled his M27. The other raised a hand to slow them to a stop.

"Don't stop," said Uriel. "Just go."

Zeke took his eyes off the gate and the threat ahead, glancing in the mirror at Uriel with concern. His expression spoke for him.

"If you hit 'em, you hit 'em." She shrugged.

Zeke pressed forward, barreling toward the guards, who both now unleashed volleys of gunfire at them. The rounds smacked the windshield but didn't break through.

And, as Zeke hoped they would, the guards jumped out of the way at the last second. The transport roared through the gate and out into the open expanse of the Badlands. The truck bounded on a rut, its suspension responding with a dip and recoil as they sped into the desert.

"Which way?" he asked.

"Left," said Li. "Turn left."

Zeke took his foot off the pedal and swung the wheel to the left. The back end of the transport slid across the sand covering the packed earth, and the harness strained against him. It dug into his ribs and hips until he'd straightened the behemoth and found his new path.

He glanced in the side-view mirror and did a double take. His muscles tensed and he tightened his grip on the wheel. He pressed down on the accelerator, expecting the heavy transport to respond like his muscle car. It lurched, hesitating, and then surged.

"What?" asked Uriel, apparently sensing something.

"They're already onto us," he said.

Uriel twisted in her seat and leaned against her side window. Zeke couldn't tell if she could see what he did.

In the distance, maybe a couple of hundred yards back,

was a transport clearly giving chase. Dust billowed from its sides in heavy brown wakes as it followed them. Zeke wasn't sure yet, but he thought he saw at least one more transport. They were coming for them.

"No doubt," said Zeke. "They're chasing us."

"Their top speed is our top speed, right?" asked Uriel.

"Maybe," said Zeke. "I guess. I don't know."

Li leaned forward in her seat. She pointed through the windshield.

"Head to the far western protectorate," she said. "Maybe we disappear into the mountains. If we keep enough distance, we could lose them on the winding roads."

This was good and bad. From memory, Zeke knew the trip was long, and it wasn't easy.

"All right," said Zeke. "I've got a plan. Hang on."

Zeke jerked the wheel right and headed north. The digital compass on the display in front of him made it easy to know his direction. That was an advantage he didn't have in his Superbird. When driving his car, he relied on the occasional landmark, the position of the sun, or the stars, to navigate his way from origin to destination and back.

"What are you doing?" asked Li. "Why are you—"

"I know what I'm doing," he said. "I think this will work. If I can keep them at bay for a little bit, we'll be good."

The truth was, he wasn't positive. There was always the chance that landslides might block them, that dead nonengineered wild animals could slow them. It wasn't a sure thing. Zeke wasn't about to admit that.

Rather, Zeke Watson did what he did best. He drove. Increasingly comfortable behind the wheel, he cut corners. He drove at speeds at the top end of the transport's ability. While his pursuers might drive fast, they wouldn't push the vehicles' limits. Driving with more caution saved fuel and wear on the engine. He'd seen the transports before. Their drivers, even when giving chase, didn't take chances.

Zeke checked the digital readout on the dash in front of him. He had three-quarters of a tank. It was more than enough to get him all the way to the mountains and likely through them. It wasn't enough to get all the way to the next protectorate. But they weren't headed that far. If all went as planned, they'd disappear into the woods, and Li would be free to roam, to reinvent herself, to start a new life. If she could find water, she'd be golden.

He couldn't tell her that it was virtually impossible for them to be together. At least, he thought so, being dead and all. He still wasn't quite sure how it all worked.

Could I disappear with her? Could we start over?

———

They drove like this for more than an hour. Zeke headed north, and he'd put more distance between himself and the transports. They were content, he decided, to keep him in sight. That was good. It fit into his plan.

He checked over his shoulder and saw Li had passed out from exhaustion. Her head was leaning against the doorframe, bouncing with the suspension. Zeke missed watching her sleep. Yeah, maybe it was creepy, but he'd always enjoyed lying next to her, listening to her breathe while she dreamed.

Zeke realized he hadn't slept since waking up in the room above the cantina. How long had it been? A couple of days? Weeks? Time slipped for the dead. Of that, he was sure.

"We don't sleep, do we?" he asked Uriel. His voice was low enough so as not to disturb Li, but loud enough for her to hear him over the drone of the transport's large engine.

"We *can* sleep," she said. "It's just not needed. Neither is food, drink, whatever. I don't even think we need air to breathe, though I've seen a Watcher strangled before, so maybe we do."

"What about time? Is it the same for us as it was when we were alive?"

"It's been so long since I was alive, I can't tell. Others tell me it's different. There's slippage here and there. And of course, there's our travel to and from the cantina. That's completely outside the dimension of time."

"What do you mean?"

"I mean I've never been to the same place at the same time more than once," Uriel explained.

Zeke swerved on the road, having nearly hit a gaping pothole in the middle of the highway. Li jostled in her seat, her harnesses pressing against her. She didn't wake.

Though traveled, the highways weren't maintained. They were only moderately smoother on which to drive than the path they were about to take.

"Like time travel?" asked Zeke.

"Not exactly," said Uriel. "More like time jumping."

"What's the difference?"

"Well, we can't go from one point in time to another directly. We always have to go back to Pedro's. Then he sends us to our next destination. Wherever we need to be, we go. Whatever the mission is, we do it. If we don't succeed or get 'killed', we reappear at the cantina and wait for the next job."

"Balancing good and evil."

"Yep," said Uriel. "And sometimes something we do in one time messes up the balance in another. So we jump forward or back, depending on what's at stake."

"We're here," said Zeke, cutting the conversation short.

"Where's here?" asked Uriel. "I don't see anything."

"Hold on. It's about to get bumpy."

Uriel chuckled. "About to?"

Zeke drifted from the road, taking his foot off the accelerator, and guided the transport onto the hard-packed soil at its shoulder. Heading west, he sped up and then jerked the wheel to the right.

The transport bounced violently and sank on its suspension. It awoke the sleeping passenger, and a constant vibration that bordered on brain-shaking rumbled through the vehicle.

"What just happened?" asked Li, snorting herself awake. "Are we—"

"Yes," answered Zeke, "we're on a railroad track."

The tracks, some of which were in disrepair, were a great shortcut through the plains leading to the eastern edge of the mountains. Once in the tunnels, they connected with other various lines that sliced through the base of peaks and across valleys.

"The fastest distance between two points is a straight line," said Zeke, adjusting his grip on the wheel.

His hold wasn't as tight as it might be on a highway or salt flat. He wanted to give the transport room to react to the unsteady path of the tracks. Still in firm control of the heavy vehicle, he didn't want tension to force and overcorrect at a high speed, flipping the transport from the tracks.

He checked the mirrors. There was no sign of the transports chasing them. He'd lost them.

"The tracks aren't a straight line," he told the others, "but they're close enough to approximate it. And they're sure enough a straighter shot west than the highways. The old United States used to use them to transport goods. Food, water, fuel, I guess. So much of them is gone that they've got to make turn after turn to get to where they're going."

"So will they catch us?" asked Li. "If they don't take the tracks?"

"I don't think so," said Zeke. "There's no direct path to the western protectorate. Like I said, the roads are spotty. They exist, they're drivable, but there are a lot of detours that force you to turn, which adds time."

"What about avoiding the roads altogether?" asked Uriel. "Why not drive on the dirt like we did when we showed up at the protectorate? You know, when we were in your car and the transports were trying to stop us from hitting the tunnel?"

"It's safe to do that near the cities," Zeke said. "Not out here. Too many variables. Buried land mines, Badlander booby traps, petrified stumps that'll break an axle. You've gotta stay as close to the roads as you can, no matter how much of a pain they are. That's why these tracks are so good."

"Other than knocking my skull loose from my spine?" Uriel asked rhetorically, her voice warbling from the rumble over the track's prestressed concrete sleepers. Ballast kicked up under the tires, clanging and knocking against the undercarriage of the armored transport.

Zeke shrugged and checked his digital dash. He was cruising at the top-end speed of the transport's ability. The RPMs were under the red semicircle line reflected on the glass display. The tire pressure was good. The engine temperature was warm but within range.

The sun had dipped below the horizon now. The deep blue of the post-dusk sky was hardening into black. Zeke found the switch for the headlamps and flipped it up. Bright white lights cast a wide arc in front of the transport that stretched twice the width of the tracks and their right of way. Another switch illuminated bars of roof-mounted LED lights atop the transport. They shone in all four directions, creating a bubble of light that traveled with the truck like a glowing cocoon.

"How soon before we're in the woods where they won't find us?" asked Li. She'd been quiet until now. "Any guesses?"

Zeke checked the digital gauges again. "I'm guessing, but maybe we'll hit the mountains in an hour or so? Then we can jump the tracks and take old logging roads. They'll never find us."

"One question," said Uriel, "and just because I want to play the other side of this thing. Not because I want to piss on anyone's cornflakes."

"What does that even mean?" asked Li.

"It's an ancient saying," she said. "I'm older than I look."

Li smirked. "That's what you think."

Uriel frowned but didn't offer a retort. Instead, she finished her original thought. "What if they're not only chasing us from behind?" she asked. "What if they've got someone headed straight for us too? You know, they try to sandwich us."

Li shook her head. "It's really unlikely. The protectorates don't really communicate all that often. They operate autonomously."

Uriel raised an eyebrow. "It's unlikely," she said, "but not impossible."

She turned to look at Zeke in the mirror. He saw the concern on her face. And she was right. He exhaled and stared into the fan of light ahead of him, illuminating the tracks.

"No," he said. "It's not impossible."

CHAPTER TWENTY-NINE

Theo sat in the front passenger's seat of a TMF transport and tugged at his cuffs. He was board straight, with the harness pressed against his chest.

The tracks and loose ballast were unforgiving underneath the carriage of their vehicle. The ride was loud and uncomfortable. They were headed west. The spray of bright headlights revealed little else but the tracks ahead of them, the dried foliage on either side of the right of way, and the relentless, unending darkness that lay ahead.

But it wasn't the motion of the transport that made the ride unenjoyable. It was the constant sniping from the lieutenants in the back seat. They were like spoiled children sent to their rooms without supper. Theo, as calm as he'd remained, was at his wit's end. They couldn't push him much farther without suffering the repercussions.

"We've lost them," said Frederick. "They're gone. The commander is going to kill all of us."

"Ye have little faith," said Theo. "They will not escape. We will surround them and stop them. You'll have your spy. She'll hang from the Fascio next to the others."

"How's that?" asked Archibald.

"The western protectorate sent a transport at the same time we left," said Theo. "I saw to it. We will ensnare them at the foot of the mountains before they can disappear."

"What if they turn off the tracks before then?" asked Archibald. "Then what?"

"They won't," said Theo. "There's nowhere for them to go. The brush and woodlands are too dense. Especially with the deadfall on the ground and underneath the canopy, there's no path for them to navigate. The track is it."

They rode in silence for several minutes. The loud rumble of the transport's engines and the occasional thwack of a stray ballast rock bouncing off the underside of the truck were the only sounds.

"Who are you?" asked Archibald.

"I'm Theodore Pannopolis," Theo said without turning around.

"That's not what I mean," said the lieutenant. "You know that. Don't be coy with me. Who are you, really?"

Theo flattened his plucked eyebrows with his pinkie fingers. He narrowed his pinched eyes to slits.

"I'm not sure I understand the question," said Theo. "Are you asking for my job description? My family lineage? It's such a broad question."

He didn't turn around. Instead, he touched the sides of his head with his palm, checking the perfection of his expertly coiffed hair. He was unfazed by the line of attack. Theo had seen and heard much worse over the years. Archibald was nothing.

"Why is it," asked Archibald, "the commander holds you in such high regard? You're a manservant. You're a butler. You have no expertise in governance or the subtlety of management."

"That's what you think?" asked Theo.

"It's what I think," echoed Frederick. "I'm with Archibald. I don't understand why you're here at all, except to keep an eye on us. For some reason, beyond my understanding, the commander doesn't trust us to do the job. You're a babysitter."

"You said it," answered Theo, "not me."

Frederick reached across the back of the transport and shoved Theo in the shoulder. That drew the servant's attention and he checked back on the angry lieutenant.

Theo's eyes fell to the man's jabbing fingers. He spoke softly. "Don't touch me again," he said. "Please."

Frederick scoffed. "Or what?"

The child lieutenant then jabbed his fingers again, attempting to push Theo a second time. They didn't get there.

Before he could touch the servant, Theo had undone his harness, spun in his seat, taken Frederick by the wrist, and twisted his hand violently to one side. Bone snapped. Frederick cried out in pain. Theo wasn't done.

He released the broken arm and slammed the heel of his fist into Frederick's restrained chest. That silenced the lieutenant's wail as the man struggled to breathe. Theo then slapped one side of Frederick's face with the back of his hand and returned with a harder, open-handed swat to the other side.

That knocked the lieutenant unconscious. His body slumped against the restraint. His head dropped and his chin bounced against his chest.

Without ever saying a word, Theo swung back into his seat and buckled the harness. He fixed his hair and adjusted his jacket.

"So, you want to know who I am now?" he asked Archibald. "Or do you think you know enough?"

Archibald said nothing at first. Then, after a lengthy silence, he asked sheepishly, "Is he dead?"

Theo exhaled loudly. "Does it matter?"

The lieutenant was about to answer when up ahead, the dim vision of oncoming lights twinkled in the distance. Then they disappeared.

"We're here," said Theo. "Put on your big-boy pants."

CHAPTER THIRTY

The oncoming transports were heading directly at them. Coming from the western protectorate, Zeke saw them as the track neared the highway around a sharp curve on an initial ascent into the mountains. They stopped to avoid a collision, and he couldn't jump the tracks quickly enough to avoid them.

With only seconds of preparation for the skirmish awaiting them, Li and Uriel surprised him with how quickly they moved into action. They impressed him too.

Li was the first out of the transport. She didn't wait for Zeke to come to a complete stop. She swung open the wide armor-plated door and leveled her rifle at the vehicle in front, unleashing several volleys that shattered and extinguished its headlamps.

Zeke saw her move swiftly and confidently toward the driver's side of the first transport and then pivot to the trucks behind them. The instant the driver opened his door in front of them, she'd sprayed him with a burst of 5.56x45mm bullets.

Uriel worked opposite her, as if they were in some sort of telepathic tandem. She balled her fists as she approached, and when the Marine in the passenger's seat opened his door to exit, she bolted forward and punched it closed on his torso.

The Marine's wail matched the animalistic grunt Uriel unleashed with the blow. Her body was glowing already, and she used her Watcher powers to tear the Marine from the transport and toss him like a stuffed doll to the other side of the highway. His body crunched against the petrified trunk of a dead ponderosa.

Zeke slid across the front of the cab to exit on the passenger's side. Jumping to the highway, he locked the door and slammed it shut with a heave. He couldn't see where Uriel or Li had gone, but could hear the cracks of gunfire up ahead. The flashes of bright light told him where some of the armed Marines might be.

With his hands holding his revolver, Zeke moved carefully along the shoulder of the highway. They were stuck between a collection of transports. There was the one in front from the west. And now, because they'd stopped, the two chasing them from the city had caught up to them. All of them were engaged. In the dark, it was hard for Zeke to know exactly where everyone was and what was happening.

He decided, with the front transport handled by the women, he'd move to the rear. When he passed the first transport, he saw the second vehicle and a Marine with his back turned. The man was yelling something at someone inside the transport.

Zeke didn't see Li.

He glanced at a dead Marine on the shoulder. Zeke crouched near the body, sitting on his heels and tucking the revolver in the back of his waistband. As quietly as he could, which wasn't difficult given the now sporadic sound of gunfire, he picked up the dead Marine's M27. Once on his feet, he took one step forward toward the Marine at the second transport. In a single series of movements, Zeke drew the rifle to his shoulder, found the trigger, and applied pressure.

The weapon kicked repeatedly against his body, but he held it steady and found his aim. The shouting Marine spasmed when a series of bullets bored into him. Arms flailing, his legs gave way, and he fell forward into the open door before the side of his head slapped and bounced on the highway.

Zeke moved to the spot where the Marine fell and found the dark shape of a man in the back seat. He appeared to be alone.

"Get out," Zeke said. He didn't know who the man was, but he could tell the passenger wasn't armed. He motioned toward the open door with his newly acquired weapon. The man reached for something. In the darkness, Zeke didn't know what it was. He applied pressure to the trigger of the M27. A burst of gunfire thumped into the back seat. The man's body jerked. His head slumped.

As he moved to the door, with his weapon leveled at the man he now recognized was wearing an Overseer's lieutenant's uniform, a bright blue glow on the opposite side of the vehicle caught his attention. It was brighter than he remembered seeing it when Uriel attacked the transport. And it pulsed oddly: two heartbeats.

It throbbed in his peripheral vision. As he rounded the open door, he saw something else that stopped him in his tracks. On the opposite side of the transport, standing in the middle of the tracks, were two people.

One was a protectorate lieutenant. The other was Li. He had a pistol to her head. Its silver coating reflected the green glow from the digital display in the idling transport. It matched his short crew cut.

"Drop the rifle," spat the lieutenant. "Do it, or I'll put a bullet in her."

The pistol shook with his anger. Li was unarmed and

strapped in a harness. The lieutenant had her hands behind her and was pressed against her.

"This traitor deserves more than a single shot," he spat. "But I'll do it. If you don't drop that weapon, I'll do it."

It was the promise of a desperate man. Zeke had no doubt the lieutenant would pull the trigger. He was the same man who'd stood on the steps and watched dispassionately as Commander Guilfoyle had strung up Zeke in front of the Fascio. There was no heart inside that man's chest. If there was, the blood that pumped through it was ice cold.

Zeke raised his arms but didn't let go of the rifle. He was so focused on the lieutenant, he hadn't noticed the gunfire had stopped and the blue, pulsing lights had moved out of his range of vision.

Zeke locked eyes with Li. "Are you okay?"

"She's fine," said the lieutenant, "unless you don't drop that rifle."

The man lifted the weapon, his thick knuckles wrapped around its grip, and pressed it hard into Li's temple. She clenched her jaw. From his position, Zeke saw the bottom of the weapon in the green light. He lowered the weapon, aiming it at the lieutenant.

The lieutenant's brow furrowed with a combination of confusion and anger. "That's it," he said. "Three. Two."

The lieutenant pulled the trigger without counting to one. Instead of the crack and kick of the pistol against Li's head, the weapon clicked.

Confused, the lieutenant pulled the trigger again. Nothing.

"Drop it. Let go of her," said Zeke, unfazed. "Unbuckle the harness."

The lieutenant cursed but complied. Li hustled from the cab and moved to Zeke's side at the shoulder. He handed her the rifle.

322

"Take care of this," he said to her. "I've got to see where Uriel went."

"How did you know?" she asked.

"I saw the bottom of the grip," he said. "The idiot didn't have a mag loaded."

"There could have been a round in the chamber," she said, leveling the M27 at the lieutenant as the man struggled to exit the transport. "Then I'd be dead."

"I didn't think of that," admitted Zeke. "Didn't know that was a thing."

She bit her lip, then sighed. "Go find Uriel," she said. "I got this."

Zeke took two steps around the front of the vehicle, dodging bodies on the ground, and feeling good about the mission. Then he found Uriel, and his heart, had it been able to, would have stopped.

Twenty yards from him, on the opposite side of the highway among the rock-hard trunks of aspens and dead pines, Uriel was engaged in hand-to-hand combat with a man who, from underneath the fabric of his tailored white shirt, glowed every bit as blue as she did.

CHAPTER THIRTY-ONE

The roundhouse struck Uriel with force. The glossy black shoe left polish streaked across her jawline along with the wound she knew would bruise.

She maintained her balance and stepped back, putting some distance between herself and the rogue Watcher she hadn't seen in so many years she'd forgotten how long it had been. While Uriel steadied herself, he unclipped the cufflinks at his wrists, slid them into his pants pocket, and rolled his sleeves to the elbows.

The tattoos that adorned his arms from above his wrist to past his elbows throbbed electric blue. Theo bounced on his toes in a semicircle, gauging her, studying her.

"It's been some time, Ariel," he said. "I would have thought you'd be more skilled by now. I mean, Pedro did see fit to give you the same gift as me."

Uriel didn't correct him. They both knew he was screwing with her. She leapt at him, flipping forward and landing a heel at his neck where it met his shoulders. Landing on one foot, she held her leg straight and whipped the top of her foot along the side of his face, slapping him to one side.

As quickly as she'd pounced, she retreated. Theo was stronger than her, and he was right—his gifts were the same as hers. He had the inherent advantage of size, muscle, and speed, but he was rusty. Uriel sensed it. And she was faster than he was. Her twitchy muscles were on a wire.

"Okay," he said, the pain oozing through the strain in his voice, "that was impressive. Surprisingly effective for a Watcher who likes to play by the rules."

"The rules are there for a reason," spat Uriel. "They're a balance to things. You know this."

Theo laughed mirthlessly. "The *balance,* as you put it, is for the betterment of Pedro and those to whom he answers. It's not for the good of the world."

"You're right, it's for the good and the evil. Without darkness, there can—"

"Be no light," Theo cut in, mocking her.

"It's true."

"Is it? Can humans achieve balance? Can they thrive with it? No, they can't. They always tilt to extremes. You know this. Better to pick the extreme that works and help it along. That's what I've been doing here, helping along what works."

There was no reasoning with a Watcher who'd gone rogue. Pedro had warned them all about this. Should they ever come into contact with one, they should act quickly and decisively.

Running straight at him, she dropped on her knees, sliding at him across the hard soil on the shoulder of the highway. Uriel rolled to one side and jabbed her balled fists upward. One shot hit him squarely in the groin, the other in his sculpted gut, eliciting double groans. The blue aura intensified with the contact and launched Theo several feet into the air, upending him and slamming him into the trunk of a petrified tree.

The solid thud of his body's momentum stopping against the tree was sickening and almost made Uriel wince, but not quite. She flipped to her feet and advanced while he was slumped to the ground, trying to regain his strength.

Incredibly, he was up before she reached him. He leapt into the air, twisting his body into a spin, and caught Uriel in the jaw with the whip of his foot. It knocked her back, dimming her glow as his brightened. He landed on his feet and flexed his arms.

Theo charged at Uriel now. He unleashed a violent flurry of quick jabs to her gut and an uppercut under her chin that launched her off the ground. She landed on her back, grunting with the push of air forced from her lungs.

"The extremes are what keep the balance, Uriel," said Theo. "Moderation is overrated."

He stalked her now. His fists balled at his sides, he marched toward her, his body glowing and pulsing a blinding blue light. It was as if every strike made him stronger.

Uriel struggled to her feet. Her power waned. She bent over at her waist. Her hands were on her knees. She spat onto the ground and did nothing as Theo grabbed the mane of hair atop her head and yanked it back, forcing her to face him.

"You are about to experience an extreme," he said through his teeth. "And—"

Uriel used his hubris against him, the distraction of his didactic speech giving her the split second it took to spin and drive an elbow into his chest. As he let go of her hair, stumbling back, she caught his throat with the palm of her other hand, driving it up and knocking him down.

Stunned, his light dimmed, he put a hand on his chest and then touched his jaw. Uriel moved forward, closing the distance in the blink of an eye. She was a blur as she reached him with purpose.

Still on one knee, his head down, he didn't see her knee when it connected with his forehead, snapping him back and flattening him on his back. He lay splayed on the ground, his head resting against the base of the trunk. Theo appeared unconscious. He was breathing, but not moving. Uriel jumped to her feet and took two steps back. She wiped the sweat from her face with the back of her arm, watching her adversary in the pulsing blue glow emanating from her skin. The tattoos on his arms, and now visible on his torso from his torn shirt, were blue, but they were fading back to their normal colors.

"Uriel?"

Her fists tightened and she whirled around to strike whoever was behind her. Her tension eased when she saw Zeke standing on the road, the revolver in his hand at his side.

"What?" Her tone was snippier than she'd intended, but she didn't apologize.

"Who is that?" he asked.

"Theodore Pannopolis," she said. "Rogue Watcher."

"He's one of you? He has the same gift?"

"He has the same gift, but he hasn't been one of us for a while. He gave that up when he decided to go stick around for the benefit of one side."

"One side?"

"Good or evil," she said.

They looked at the unconscious man on the ground. He was awake now and rising to his knees.

Theo tore off the rest of his tattered shirt, revealing a chiseled physique painted with a menagerie of tattoos from below his neckline to beneath his navel. His chest, shoulders, and arms were covered with so many full-color designs, it was impossible to distinguish one from the other.

"Let me help," said Zeke.

Theo was on his feet now. For effect, he cracked his knuckles before balling his hands into tight fists. His tattoos flickered and pulsed. Instantly, the blue intensified. It was brighter electricity than Uriel had ever managed.

"This is my fight," she said. "I'm the Watcher."

As soon as she turned back to Theo, a blue blur bolted past her, knocking her to the ground with a forearm shove, and tackled Zeke. The collision knocked the Stetson into the air, sent the revolver skittering across the highway, and put Zeke on his back. Straddling Zeke, Theo wrapped a hand around his neck, squeezing the afterlife out of him.

CHAPTER THIRTY-TWO

His neck constricted; his chest burned. Zeke knew he was already dead. There was no way Theo could kill him. But what would happen to the balance of things if this rogue succeeded in sending him and Uriel back to Pedro's? Would the scales tip too far to one side?

Zeke's head was turned somewhat to the side, and through his darkening vision, he saw Uriel on the ground, dazed and clutching her chest. Then darkness shrouded his sight and the world went black.

As he felt the life slipping from him, the fight in his body leaving it for the second time in such a short period, and he was ready to give in to this monster of a man, the hands were gone, and the intense, crushing pressure on his throat stopped. The weight on his torso lifted.

Coughing and gasping, he rolled onto his side, grabbing at his throat. Jaw aching and head pounding, Zeke rose onto his elbows. He was surprised by how the air returned to his lungs and his breathing steadied.

He blinked and focused in time to see Theo shake himself free of Li. Then he turned and, with a single swipe of his hand, knocked her into the air and onto the ground yards away.

Then Uriel was on him, her legs wrapped around his upper body. She had the advantage only a moment.

Theo freed himself with a twist of his body and slip of his arms, reversing the position and putting Uriel on the ground with a flip. Her head smacked against the crumbling edge of the asphalt. Zeke scrambled to his knees, and then to his feet, before Theo stalked him and landed a solid punch to his chest.

Zeke was knocked backward, staggering until he fell. As he went down, he spotted his revolver two feet away.

Li was up again, dazed. She had her hands on the sides of her head and was uneasy on her feet.

Uriel was on the ground, her hand on her head. Theo was back on top of her. He picked her up and lifted her above his head, launching her into the air and against the same tree he'd struck minutes earlier.

Her limp body crashed to the ground, and Theo reached down to grab her ankle. Uriel's body had all but stopped glowing. Theo was pulsing neon. As he picked up the wounded Uriel, Theo threw his head back and howled.

"I'm sending you back to Pedro!" he bellowed and swung her body from side to side.

Before he could gain the momentum to whip Uriel back into the trunk, Zeke reached his revolver. Though off balance, in a fluid motion he drew it level and found his aim. He pulled the trigger.

The blast was more violent than all those preceding it. His proximity to the target made for a condensed pulse of energy that not only ended the threat, but ripped it and everything around it into unrecognizable pieces of matter.

The collection of petrified trees was torn from the roots and shattered into shrapnel that exploded outward in a percussive tear that sounded like a thousand sails ripping in the wind.

The earth itself was blasted backward, stripping clean anything above the hard-packed soil.

There was no sign of either Theo or Uriel left behind. Their bodies were gone, vaporized amidst the explosion of debris.

The revolver in his hand glowing as blue as it ever had, Zeke cried out for Uriel. He called her name, not expecting her to answer. It was compulsive. A swell of guilt washed over him and he choked back tears. Zeke steeled himself. The guilt gave way to resignation, to understanding.

He stood there, his wounded throat sore and tightening. Even without thinking about it, he'd known as he pulled the trigger this outcome was likely.

But to save the balance of things, even if it wasn't his job just yet, he had to do what was right. He had to pull the trigger and destroy the rogue Watcher. He knew now that was why he was meant to be here, at this exact time, with Li. To face Theo and right the balance of things.

Uriel would have told him to do it. The greater good, and bad, depended on painting that balance. Even if it meant blowing her to bits, it was what he had to do. He could only hope he'd see her again, that how he'd sent her from this world wasn't such that she couldn't return to Pedro's.

But he didn't know all the rules. They'd been hasty in explaining them. Maybe "dying" from a gifted weapon differed from other kinds of "deaths".

More than that, without Uriel, how in the world was he going to find his own way back to Pedro's?

Am I stuck here?

He was, for the first time in what felt like an eternity, alone. He stood in the middle of the road, the carnage around him. It was getting colder. The air chilled. The scent of smoke stung his nostrils.

A cough stirred him from his thoughts. He rushed back to

Li, who lay on the street, lucky to be alive. She offered him a frail smile. It was a smile he remembered from the first time he'd met her. It was a smile from when they were both different people, or at least, believed the other was a different person.

"Too bad about your friend," she said.

Zeke didn't acknowledge her. What could he say? His redemption had come at such a cost. Others sacrificed themselves for his benefit. He wasn't worthy of it. No matter what he did now to compensate, he wasn't worthy of what they'd selflessly given.

His vision blurred with tears. He opened his mouth to say something but couldn't find the words. They remained silent for what felt like an eternity as the world of ash and smoke and dirt dissolved around them.

"Take me with you," Li said, finally.

Zeke focused on her eyes. The connection between the two of them was unmistakable. It was every bit as electric as the energy that pulsed from Pedro's magical weapons. But when Zeke spoke, he could think of only one thing to say.

"You can't go with me."

Li's eyes searched his with a desperation he'd never seen in her before. Her chin quivered and she handed him her weapon. She licked her lips and looked away.

"Please," she said softly. "Don't abandon me again. I've got nowhere else to go."

"You seem strangely okay with all of this," Zeke said, and motioned toward the newly created debris-littered wasteland beyond the highway.

"You get used to it, after what they put you through…" Her gaze shifted to aim blankly over his shoulder, like she was looking upon horrors far beyond them.

"I wish I could have helped with that. I wish I could have done it all differently."

"Well, now you have a second chance."

"No, Li...I...I'm dead." He realized how foolish it sounded out loud. Her soft chuckle didn't help to ease that feeling.

"You're not dead, Zeke. I don't know who they hung from the Fascio, but it's not you."

She put her hand on his chest and held it there. Her gaze held his.

"Someone made to look like you, sure. But it's not you. You're flesh and blood and you're here. I don't care how. You're back."

"Li, it's not—"

"Could I do this if you weren't?"

Li eased against him. She brought her lips to his and kissed him passionately. In that moment, he didn't want to let her go. His arms slid around her and ran down the small of her back.

It was true that he didn't know her, at least not like he thought he did. But that kiss, what she conveyed through the warmth of her body, made him feel every bit as alive as he ever had.

Li lingered for another moment, the skin on her lips sticking to his when she pulled away. Zeke smiled at her and she returned it with flush cheeks that were red enough he saw them in the ambient light of the headlamps on the other side of the highway.

"You saved me," she said. "I don't care about the rest. Just stay with me."

He inhaled, hints of her scent on him. Even emaciated and after what he'd seen her do, she was stunning to him. His chest tightened.

Zeke stepped back. "I don't think I can."

He backed away and motioned toward the transports. "There should be plenty of fuel among those trucks to get you to wherever it is you want to go. You'll—"

And that was when he noticed the blood. He hadn't seen it

before. Her black uniform hid it until she'd pressed against him. She was bleeding. It was a lot of blood.

"You're hurt," he said. "You're bleeding."

Confusion washed across her face and she looked down at herself. She put her hands to her stomach and pulled them away bloodied. Her fingers trembled and tears pooled in her eyes.

Then, as if the realization made the wound real, she sank back into him. Even in the darkness, he saw the color draining from her face. Her body was cold against his.

Did I do all of this for nothing? He came to save her, only to have her die in his arms.

"I want to be with you," she said. "Always."

Zeke took another deep breath. He exhaled. Maybe there was a way. Maybe this was his final test, the last measure of his redemption. If he could deliver salvation to a woman he loved despite her betrayal and her sins, to a woman who loved him despite his, then he would pass. He would succeed in this task.

"There is only one way we can stay together," he said. "And I don't know if it'll work."

He didn't know. As much as this might be his final test, it might not. It could upend the balance of everything. His chest tightened. A knot formed in his throat and made it hard to swallow.

There was still so much he didn't understand.

"Just tell me," she said. "I'll do anything."

"Do you trust me?"

Her voice was weaker now, above a whisper. "More than I did a day ago."

"Li."

"Yes." She took his hand. "I do. I know I shouldn't, but I do."

Her expression brightened. She smiled. Tears welled in her eyes.

Zeke closed his eyes and whispered to himself, "God, I hope you were right, Uriel."

Li opened her mouth to speak.

Before she could say anything, Zeke lifted her weapon, pressed it to her chest, and pulled the trigger. With the echo of the blast still in his ears, with Li's dead eyes staring back at him, he aimed the weapon at himself and fired one last shot.

CHAPTER THIRTY-THREE

Zeke was on the porch, the swinging doors creaking lazily. It was hot. The sun was at its apex in the cloudless sky. Standing there at the entrance to the cantina, he had no idea how he'd gotten there, no memory of what had happened between the time he'd walked alone along a mountain highway and this moment.

The Stetson was on his head, the cushion of his boots felt good against his heels, his buckle was front and center, and tucked behind it was his revolver.

Before entering the cantina, he stared down the long highway. Across the road, beyond the haze of dust that danced in swirls and waves across the black asphalt, was an unflinching Horde. They stood there as they had before, watching him.

What a difference death makes, he thought. Sucking in the warm, dry air, Zeke spun on his bootheel to enter the cantina. Inside, he heard the strains of the jukebox mixed with the buzz of conversation, laughter, and the clink of glasses.

Before he stepped inside, something caught his attention. To his right in the parking lot was a familiar-looking car. His car. The Superbird was there, no worse for wear, shiny as ever and awaiting its next adventure. Zeke tipped his hat at his ride and stepped into the cantina.

Pedro's dog was the first to greet him. It was lying with his large head resting on its paws inside the entrance near the stairs. It lifted its head when Zeke whistled at it and said hello. It clumsily got to its feet, wagging its tail, and sauntered the short distance to him. It sat and offered a paw. Zeke took it, shook it, and rubbed the animal behind its ears. Then he turned his attention to the large open space of the cantina.

It was as he remembered. The tables were filled with men and women busy at cards or heated discussions. Some of them nursed sweating glasses; others took healthy swigs of whatever Pedro had seen fit to serve them.

Zeke didn't recognize any of the patrons. Some wore hats or bandanas and well-worn cotton garb. Others were in bespoke suits or donned head to toe in leather. It was as motley a collection of customers as it had been before.

He searched for any sign of Uriel. His eyes skipped across the room, hoping to spot her, to find her playing with her auburn hair or giving someone a hard time. She wasn't there. An unease filtered through Zeke, that indescribable discomfort that comes with knowing something is out of place, something isn't as it should be.

Then guilt flooded his senses. Why had he searched for Uriel first? Why hadn't his initial thought been to look for Li? Li was here, wasn't she?

Gabe and Phil weren't around either. Raf and Barach, both of whom he imagined would be playing cards or throwing darts, weren't anywhere to be seen. Zeke felt a tightness in his chest. Had Uriel told him the Watchers could reemerge to assuage his concerns, his guilt? Were they gone for good?

"Ezekiel," came the resonant call of the cantina's name-sake and barkeep. Pedro wore a wide grin on his face, evident even behind his thick beard.

His brown leather vest was unbuttoned at the top, his linen shirt rolled to the elbows. The large brass buckle that sat at his trim waist was barely visible above the bar.

Pedro's aged hands, replete with the off-color spots of a man who'd spent a lot of time outdoors, were planted on the bar, and he called Zeke over for a drink. The proprietor and grand-schemer-of-things didn't reach for a glass or a bottle. Zeke did eye the Book of Enoch on the shelf behind the bar as he bellied up and took a seat.

Pedro stared with the wide grin, studying Zeke. He looked him up and down, paying attention to his hands.

The music of the jukebox swung from one unrecognizable song to another. A blossom of laughter erupted at the table behind Zeke. He didn't bother to look over. Neither did Pedro. Uncomfortable with the silence between them, Zeke spoke up.

"How's it going?" It wasn't the best icebreaker.

Pedro responded by pounding a fist on the bar. It startled Zeke, who nearly fell from his barstool.

"It's going wonderfully," Pedro said. "Wonderfully."

The barkeep reached under the varnished bar top and pulled out a heavy leaded highball glass. With his other hand, he fingered a pair of large chunks of ice and dropped them into the glass.

Zeke steeled himself, not wanting an answer. "Where is everybody?"

"Whiskey?" asked Pedro. "Rye? Rum? Tequila?"

Zeke eyed the glass, considering his options. He wasn't thirsty, but he didn't want to refuse the offer. Before he decided, Pedro raised a finger.

"Oh, I know!" he said, his voice swimming with excitement. "I received a wonderful malted scotch. It's a sinus-cleaner, I assure you, but it's delightful."

Pedro clapped his hands together and spun to search for

the bottle of scotch. His enthusiasm was disorienting. Zeke didn't remember Pedro being so jovial. What had changed?

Pedro found the bottle, grabbed it by the neck, and brought it back to the bar, setting it down before uncapping it. The pour was generous, and the chunks of ice shifted, melting within the room-temperature scotch.

When he'd recapped the bottle, Pedro slid the glass over to Zeke, careful not to slosh the amber liquid.

"Drink up," said Pedro. "We have much to discuss."

Zeke picked up the glass, relishing its cold in his hand. Toasting Pedro, Zeke lifted the drink and then took a healthy sip. It was like fire at first, burning his throat and stinging his nostrils. He coughed and set the drink on the bar.

"Whoa, that's strong," he said.

"Perhaps," said Pedro, "but not as strong as you, I hear."

Zeke spun on the stool and searched the bar. His scotch-blurred vision drifted to the balcony that ran along the edges of the second floor. Still no Uriel. No pink ribbon at the end of a knotted ponytail.

"What have you heard?" asked Zeke. "Did Uriel tell you?"

"Plenty," said Pedro, not answering the question, but giving him hope she really was back. "I want to hear it from you though. Start from the beginning."

Zeke thumped his chest with the side of his fist. Checking over one shoulder and then the other, he leaned into the bar and lowered his voice. "The beginning of what?"

Pedro folded his arms across his broad chest, considering the question. "That's a good question," he said, stroking the beard now. "The beginning of what. So many beginnings. So many endings. So much in between the two. It's hard to keep track of it all."

Having become accustomed to the vague nonanswers that greeted his questions in the afterlife, Zeke tried formulating something more specific. He thought another sip of the drink might help, so through clenched teeth, he filtered more of the scotch into his gullet. It was as scorching the second time. But the tension in his muscles relaxed a bit. It was odd to him that while he didn't require food or drink, or even air, as a dead man, alcohol could intoxicate him. He'd heard someone once refer to something alcoholic as the nectar of the gods. Was that the meaning?

Zeke refocused. "How about I start with the moment we left this bar the last time?"

"Cantina," Pedro corrected. "It's more descriptive than *bar*. It connotes a certain desperation, a homespun earthiness to it."

Again, with a nonanswer. Zeke sighed.

Pedro eyed the glass, seemingly willing Zeke to take another sip. Zeke obliged and then began to tell Pedro everything that had happened, from his recollection, between the time he'd settled into his Superbird with Uriel to the start of his march through the mountains.

Admitting he didn't remember how he'd ended up back at the cantina, Zeke spent more than an hour telling his version of events. Perhaps it was less than an hour. Or it might have been three. Time slipped in the cantina.

After he was finished, Pedro spent several minutes cleaning the bar with a rag. When he was finished, he stepped back over to Zeke. The glass in front of Zeke was empty, the ice melted. There was a faded amber sheen at the bottom of the highball. Pedro didn't offer to refill it.

"What made you come back?" he asked. "And what made you bring Adaliah?"

Zeke's chest tightened. "Li's here?" He glanced over one shoulder and then the other. His eyes swept the open balcony on the second floor, moving from door to door.

"She's here," said Pedro. "Don't worry. That woman is a strong one. She'll give Uriel a run for her money."

"Where is she?"

Pedro smiled. "Resting. Being tough doesn't mean she's infallible. Remember, she was wounded before arriving here. It takes some time. Remember?"

"I remember. What will happen to her?" asked Zeke. "Will she get the same opportunity I did?"

Pedro shrugged. "That's up to her," he said. Then he hesitated, his mouth held open while he appeared to reconsider. "And up to me."

"Thank you," said Zeke.

"For what?"

"Letting her stay here, giving her the possibility of a second chance."

Pedro smiled broadly. He leaned on the bar and wagged a finger at Zeke. "You're a good man, Ezekiel," he said. "Not too good, mind you."

Zeke chuckled. It was a nervous response. He understood what Pedro meant but not why he'd said it.

"Who was it she worked for?" asked Pedro.

"Li?"

Pedro nodded. "Yes, Adaliah."

Zeke had a sense that Pedro knew the name of the protectorate's governing body. He answered the question anyway.

"The Overseers."

Pedro swung the damp bar rag over the shoulder of his vest. "Ahhh yes," he said, "the Overseers. I thought it a pompous-sounding name, didn't you? Overseers? It has a grandiosity to it that's best reserved for those who truly oversee. But what's done is done."

"I never liked the name," said Zeke.

Pedro raised an eyebrow. "But you liked Tic?"

"We were parasitic bloodsuckers." Zeke chuckled. "So I guess it fit."

Zeke searched the bar for any sign of his friends. They were his friends. They'd become his friends.

"So," said Pedro, "have you figured out yet what this was all about? What it is still all about?"

"My redemption," Zeke said. "This was about redeeming myself. I've done that. I went back to right some of my wrongs, help the woman I betrayed, and apparently rid the world of a rogue Watcher. It turns out she wasn't who I thought she was, who anybody thought she was, but I helped anyway. I wanted redemption."

Pedro's wizened stare locked onto Zeke, his ice-blue eyes penetrating, mesmerizing, and a little bit frightening. The old man shook his head. "Oh, Zeke. My dear Ezekiel Watson, who told you this was about your redemption?"

A flutter of unease sprinkled across Zeke's body. He shrugged. "Everyone?"

"No," said Pedro. "Nobody told you it was about *your* redemption. This was not about you at all. You were a mechanism, a cog, a part in a much larger contraption."

"I don't understand," said Zeke. The flutter was swelling into panic. A cold sweat bloomed at his temples and he adjusted the Stetson atop his head. "Whose redemption was it?"

The intensity of Pedro's gaze didn't wane. If anything, it sharpened. The ice blue seemed to glow, to pulse as the barkeep spoke.

"To seek redemption," said Pedro, "one must be doing it for others. It must be a selfless act. Everything you did, while noble and in some cases heroic, was ultimately self-serving. You sought redemption for yourself, which is, in so many ways, the opposite of how it works."

Zeke didn't know what to say to that.

"Redemption," continued Pedro, now leaning against the bar, "is not something born from a single act or series of actions aimed at a single outcome. It comes from a change in your heart forged during the course of a multitude of unrelated acts. Those unrelated acts benefit others, things from which you gain nothing but the cleansing of your soul."

Zeke's head was swimming. Whose redemption had this been about if not his? And how would he ever earn his own? He was about to explode with a thousand questions he knew Pedro would never answer when he felt a familiar touch on his leg and he inhaled an intoxicating floral scent that almost made him fall from his stool.

"Hey, big boy," said Uriel, sliding around him and onto the stool next to him. "Long time no see."

Zeke blinked to make sure she was real. His eyes darted between Uriel and Pedro, looking for an explanation.

"This was about her redemption, Zeke," said Pedro. "The others too."

Zeke felt a presence behind him. He spun around in the stool to find Phil and Gabe standing behind him. Behind them were Barach and Raf.

"I don't understand," said Zeke.

"Of course you don't," Uriel said brightly. "You can't be that good-looking and smart too."

Heat flushed Zeke's face, but he was quick with a retort. "So which one are you?"

That drew laughter from the others. Phil slapped Zeke on his back.

"Being a Watcher is about redemption," Uriel said. "That's why our job is to maintain the balance of things. We were bad enough in life to understand how the darkness works. We're good enough in death to find the light in things."

Zeke searched Pedro's face for confirmation of what Uriel had just told him. Her revelation made sense in a place where nothing made sense.

"Watchers are chosen because, despite how dark their lives were, there was something redemptive in them," said Pedro. "That's not an easy thing to find in someone. Sure, most humans live a life filled with a spectrum of color. Nobody is all good or all bad. But to be a Watcher, to be someone who can keep the balance, one must have the right mixture of both. Maintaining that balance between good and evil can require you to get your hands dirty."

"Hands dirty?" asked Zeke.

"Like we said before," explained Phil, moseying closer to the bar, "sometimes we have to fight for the dark side of things. If you were too good a person in life, that's too much of a leap in death. If you mixed it up, but had a soul, then you're Goldilocks."

"He means to say, you're just right," said Gabe.

"So what does this have to do with me?" Zeke asked, likely knowing the answer to his question for the first time in a long while.

"Being a Watcher is difficult," said Pedro. "You're stuck here in purgatory for an indefinite period. Until you've done enough to redeem yourself, you stay a Watcher. You go where I ask you to go. You do what I ask you to do. In between, you sit here at the bar awaiting the next mission, the next act toward redemption."

"Are you asking me if I want to be a Watcher?" asked Zeke.

Pedro winked. "If you're interested, there's an opening."

"How long does redemption take? And what if I say no?"

Uriel laughed and squeezed his thigh. He'd forgotten her hand was there. "You don't want to say no," she said.

"Saying no isn't an option," said Raf.

"Don't do it," said Barach.

"Nobody says no," added Phil.

Chuckling, Pedro took the rag from his shoulder and wiped the bar. It didn't need the scrub. "There's no telling how long it will take," he said. "But I can promise you, however long it takes, it'll seem a lot shorter than it is."

"Or longer," said Gabe.

"Or longer," conceded Pedro.

Zeke drew a long, measured breath. He looked to Uriel, who smirked and nodded him along. Then the others, all in eager anticipation of his answer.

The truth was, he'd made the choice, without even knowing it. The moment he sent himself back to the bar at the end of the world. He touched the handle of the revolver at his waist, making sure it was still there. It was.

"So," he said, "I guess the next round's on me?"

EPILOGUE

Without knowing how he'd arrived there, or where it was he was heading, Graham found himself in the middle of the Badlands. The last thing he remembered was shooting.

Was I shot? By a dead man?

Impossible.

A single two-lane highway stretched in front of him. He was driving a 1985 Buick Regal T-Type. The two-hundred-horsepower V-6 wasn't the fastest of the muscle cars in the Tic's stable, but it was fuel-efficient and fast enough to outpace the TMF.

Disoriented, Graham gripped the wheel and applied even pressure to the accelerator. He checked the rearview mirror and saw a Horde of bikers and truckers following close behind.

Gone was the sensation of confusion. Instead, he focused on the new task at hand: getting away from the men chasing him.

Why were they chasing him? They weren't TMF. They didn't look like Tic. They were Badlanders. They had to be

Badlanders, didn't they? But he had no idea how he'd gotten here. Maybe he'd hit his head too hard in the fighting.

He pushed the gas pedal to the floor and the car responded. Its Garrett turbocharger surged, and Graham put distance between himself and the pursuing Horde.

The gain was short-lived, however, and a pair of the bikers closed the distance. They moved to opposite edges of the road and held steady at his rear fender.

Up ahead, all Graham saw was dirt and rocks and the low rise of distant hills. The sun was high in the sky, straight overhead. How long had he been driving? How long had these men been chasing him?

The barren no-man's-land that surrounded him in all directions offered no clues. He couldn't tell in which direction he was driving. It felt to him as if he were on an endless treadmill of asphalt, surrounded on all sides by the brown and gray of petrification.

Graham tightened his grip on the wheel with one hand and wiped the sweat on his forehead and under his eyes with the back of the other. When he returned it to the wheel, it was darkened by red liquid.

Blood?

His pulse quickened. In that instant, his head pounded with the memory of a wound. What wound? How had he been hurt?

A pop interrupted his thoughts, and he checked the rearview mirror to see the back window was gone. Shards of glass littered the back deck of the Regal behind its rear seats.

Blood trickled from his forehead to the edge of his lips. He licked them and tasted the warm, coppery fluid. This was bad. Very bad.

One of the cyclists revved his engine and pulled alongside the passenger side of the sky-blue coupe. The bike appeared miniature beneath his girth. The weapon in his hand appeared even larger. A grin spread across the beast's face, and with one hand on the handlebars of his chopper, he leaned forward in the saddle seat and took aim.

Staring alternately at the endless road ahead and down the barrel of the gun, Graham instinctively did the only thing he knew to do—he slammed on the brakes. The biker zoomed past him, his shot grazing the front end of the Buick, snapping off the trophy emblem like a target at a shooting gallery.

A grinding crash overwhelmed his senses, and his body was hurled forward, over the steering wheel, through the glass windshield, off the hood of the sky-blue Buick, and onto the pavement not far from the emblem.

His head pounding, but his body functioning, Graham struggled to his feet. He was facing the car now. It was mangled, and what was left of it was perpendicular to the road. One of the large trucks had slapped into it.

There were a dozen men from the Horde standing in place, weapons in hand. Watching him intently, they didn't move.

"What do you want?" he cried out, stumbling backward to give himself distance from the Horde. Their silence was more intimidating than anything they could have said. The darkness of their eyes, the lack of sympathy in their blank, emotionless expressions, and their stoic patience all served to unnerve Graham.

Was he losing his mind?

Rather than ask the question again, he turned to run. As fast as his feet could carry him, the inner soles of his boots pounding against his heels, he ran away from them.

His chest throbbed and the heat of the sun bore down on him. Blood, trickling from the wounds on his face, found its way into his eyes and, mixed with his sweat, stung. His vision blurred, he kept moving. Glancing over his shoulder, he saw the Horde remaining motionless. None of them gave chase.

Graham kept running anyway. Ahead, and to the right, he

thought he saw something. It was a house, or bigger than a house. Fingers of smoke drifted skyward from it. Somebody was there. Though it was a half mile, maybe more, Graham kept moving. Head pounding, heels thumping, chest heaving, he ran.

The Horde started to follow now. The building grew larger. A stiff wind caught his face. Graham's legs began to feel heavy. His muscles thickened with exhaustion. His breathing was ragged now. The headache that had been a nuisance now blinded him.

His boots felt heavier now. Each step was harder to take. He pumped his fists and lifted his knees. The house was bigger. The Horde was smaller. Then it wasn't.

Graham heard the thrumming rev of engines growing into a roar. He could feel the vibration in the soles of those heavy boots. They were coming for him. It was a tease, a faster predator giving slower prey a head start just for the sport of it.

Graham lost his footing and tripped. He tried to scramble to his feet, but was too exhausted. He rolled over and looked around, crawling away from the Horde, but half resigned to his fate.

His surroundings were familiar yet foreign. Something told him he'd been here before, but he knew that wasn't true. This was unlike anywhere he'd ever visited. It wasn't the Badlands. It might *look* like the Badlands, but there was something more otherworldly about where he stood. It was like he'd created it in a dream. If only he could wake himself from it.

The earthshaking rumble of the Horde descended upon him. It was then, when the engines quieted to an idle, Graham turned his back to the house and drifts of smoke.

He wiped his forehead one last time with the back of his arm and faced the Horde. One of them, a tall man with skeletal features and sunken black eyes, stepped forward. The chain looped at his hip chimed as he approached.

The man marched deliberately to within a few inches of him before he stopped. He leaned in and sniffed twice, his nostrils flaring wide. He grunted, running a gray tongue across yellow teeth that looked like they'd been filed into daggers. When he spoke, his voice was like gravel, like the man had spent a lifetime gargling his surroundings to grind his vocal cords into something rough and jagged.

"Do you know who we are?" The man's skin stretched across the framework of his jaw and skull. "George Remus Graham?"

How do they know my name? Nobody knew his first name.

He hated his name. George was bad enough. But Remus? His mother had surely hated him. That had to be the only explanation. Yet this corpse of a man in front of him said it with authority. There was no doubt they knew him even if he didn't know them. A shiver ran along his spine as he considered where it was he might be. If he was right, the answer as to who these men were would come soon enough.

"No," he said. He fought every aching joint to stand before the stranger. "I don't know who you are."

The man turned his head to one side and then the other to crack his neck, resulting in a sickening sound. Graham was certain a bone would pop through the thin sheaths of skin that covered his frame.

The man raised his arms up and out to demonstrate his command of the Horde. "We are your reckoning."

Reckoning?

The man lowered the wings of his arms and raised a finger to point at Graham. The finger extended like a mechanical claw, the knuckles straining at the joints. "We are here to take you home."

Thirst unlike any Graham ever experienced filtered through his weakened body. More than anything, he wanted a drink of water. Motioning over his shoulder at the house a quarter mile away, he asked for clarification.

"Is that home?" he asked, hope lilting in his voice.

The thin man laughed heartily. He checked with his men and they too laughed. Graham swallowed against the dry knot in his throat. The ache in his head was close to debilitating now, and his knees were jittery, about to give out.

The laughter dried up and the thin man's expression flattened again, his black eyes widening into mesmerizing onyx pools. "No, it's not," he said, the gravel raking across the words. "Not for you, George Remus Graham."

The consonants hung in the air between them, the thin man appearing to relish the devilish way in which he spoke Graham's name. He'd never hated the sound of his own name as much as he did right now. Afraid to ask the next question, Graham slid his bootheels off the asphalt and onto the rocky dirt on the highway's shoulder.

"Who are you?" he asked, steadying himself.

"We are the Harbingers of the Real Death. Some like to call us the Horde."

"Real death?"

"The death from which you cannot return."

"What the hell does that mean?"

The thin man exhaled, impatience fuming from his nostrils. "It means there is no redemption for you, George Remus Graham. Now we are upon you, your lot is determined. There is no bargaining, no pleading, no begging, and no promise of doing better. What's done is done. You belong to us now."

"I belong to nobody," he said, defiant.

There was no answer. Not verbally. The thin man took two steps forward, reached out a bony hand toward Graham, and touched the side of his face. The fingers were cold on Graham's skin, and then they weren't. The world around him dissolved from the arid high desert to emptiness. Graham was alone and in the dark. The Horde was gone.

"Hello?" he called out into the void. His call echoed softer with each return into and from the endless space beyond. "Is anyone there?"

Graham was weightless, yet there was pressure on his body. It was difficult to move despite the sensation of floating free of anything earthbound.

"Hello?" he called again. There was no response.

He reached out, the heft of his own mass making the task harder than he'd have thought. It felt like an eternity before he'd fully extended his arm and spread his fingers wide, grasping for something just beyond his reach. He swept his outstretched arm in a wide arc, reaching, grasping, hoping. Nothing.

He closed his hand into a fist, tightening it.

Then, somehow, Graham knew where the Horde had sent him. He knew his home.

It was eternal. It was isolated. It was unbearable.

It was hell, and he was already dead.

FROM THE PUBLISHER

Thank you for reading *The Bar at the End of the World*, book one of *The Watchers*.

We hope you enjoyed it as much as we enjoyed bringing it to you. We just wanted to take a moment to encourage you to review the book on Amazon and Goodreads. Every review helps further the author's reach and, ultimately, helps them continue writing fantastic books for us all to enjoy.

If you liked this book, check out the rest of our catalogue at www.aethonbooks.com. To sign up to receive a FREE collection from some of our best authors as well as updates regarding all new releases, visit www.aethonbooks.com/sign-up.

JOIN THE STREET TEAM! Get advanced copies of all our books, plus other free stuff and help us put out hit after hit.

SEARCH ON FACEBOOK:
AETHON STREET TEAM

ALSO IN SERIES

You Just Read: **The Bar at the End of the World**
Up Next: **The Bar at the Edge of the Sea**
Then: **The Bar in the Middle of Nowhere**

ACKNOWLEDGMENTS

Thanks to you, the readers, who choose to join me on these adventures. Your support, reviews, social media posts, and emails make the many hours alone at the keyboard so worthwhile.

I couldn't do any of this without the constant and unwavering love of my wife Courtney and our children, Samantha and Luke. They are a collective muse and cheering section wrapped into one beautiful package.

The team at Aethon is incredible. They made this manuscript better when it was when it found their capable hands. Steve and Rhett are wonderful partners and advocates in this journey. Their confidence is my work is uplifting and motivating.

Steven Konkoly and Nicholas Sansbury Smith both read very early drafts of this and offered excellent narrative advice as did wordsmith Felicia Sullivan.

Thanks also to my parents Sanders and Jeannie, my siblings Penny and Steven, and my mother-in-law Linda for their viral marketing efforts.

Now back to the keyboard. More stories need telling...

ABOUT THE AUTHOR

Tom Abrahams is an Emmy and Edward R. Murrow award-winning television journalist and member of International Thriller Writers. He is also a Kindle Unlimited All-Star, an Audible 5 Star Favorite, and author of more than two dozen novels. He writes in several genres including dystopian, sci-fi techno-thriller, post-apocalyptic, and political thrillers. His stories combine the realistic with the fantastic and have sold copies all over the world. The dramatic rights for his "A Dark World" trilogy are optioned for television and film. He's married with two children and lives in Southeast Texas.

http://tomabrahamsbooks.com

CPSIA information can be obtained
at www.ICGtesting.com
Printed in the USA
FSHW022035180520
70370FS